A HEART SO SAVAGE

THE SAVAGE DUET BOOK 2

APRIL MORAN

A HEART SO SAVAGE

A Heart So Savage
The Savage Duet

Book Two

Crush~Conquer~Protect

A dark romance novel by April Moran

For everyone who believes the villain should give his girl as many hand necklaces as she needs with a happily ever after for them both.

And for James, I love you.
Always.

PLAYLIST

https://open.spotify.com/playlist/19fetAfxrTou4gMGpc6QWT?
si=9933547f4c794f35

"Sleeping With Lions" – The Cold Stares

"The Flood's The Fault Of The Rain" – L.A. Guns

"All My Life" – Foo Fighters

"Little Monster" – Royal Blood

"R U Mine?" – Artic Monkeys

"That Dress" – The Pale White

"Sex Type Thing" – Stone Temple Pilots

"Smoke Gets In Your Eyes" – The Platters

"The Difference Between Us" – The Dead Weather

"Sorry" – Buckcherry

"You Should See Me In A Crown" – Billie Eilish

"Love It Or Leave It" – Kickstand Jenny

"Devil" – Shinedown

"Do You Still Love Me?" – Ryan Adams

"Angel Dream (No 2) – Tom Petty and the Heartbreakers

PREFACE

He saw me.
He took me.
He ruined me.
Now, I'm his.

I belong here with this monster, yet I still long for freedom.

I say that I hate him, but my heart pounds faster when he kisses me.

He breaks me. Spoils me. Taunts me when I'm on my knees before him. His punishments are exquisite pleasures I willingly endure.

Because I crave how he puts me back together again and again.

I'm nothing more than payment for a debt, but Kingston treats me as though I am his most precious treasure. He swears that I'm safe, but the treachery of our enemies is subtle and cruel. They will not stop until I am at their mercy and Kingston is dead from a bullet in the back.

But I can ruin those seeking our destruction. I can save us

before all is lost. Will love weaken or strengthen us when it matters most?

I'm Ava Bella Blue. A prisoner trapped in a gilded cell of lust and secrets.

Kingston Vaughn Winter is the beast I have fallen in love with.

Crush~Conquer~Protect.

It's his personal motto, but I've adopted it as my own now.

His obsession will become our salvation. And I will win this king's savage heart before this is over.

CHAPTER

ONE

*F*reedom and captivity
    are one and the same
      when you kiss me.

FOR THE NEXT FIVE DAYS, Kingston only returned at night when Ava was already asleep. His careful movements as he slid into bed always woke her. She would lie perfectly still, barely breathing, waiting for her captor to roll over on top of her. Waiting for the moment he shoved himself between her thighs and took what he wanted with cruel, hurtful hands.

But he did not touch her. Not even inadvertently during his sleep. It was as though an invisible barrier existed between them, one that Kingston himself erected. Curled into a tight ball, Ava would drowsily listen to Kingston's steady breathing until she fell back into the dark oblivion of sleep.

It was all so very confusing. Especially after the intensity of their interactions before and his calm assertion she belonged

1

to him. That Kingston now practically ignored her was unexpected.

But Ava was thankful for the tiny reprieves while lying beside him in the darkness. Her head no longer ached from Malcolm's cuffing and the bruises were fading, but doing battle with Kingston now was unthinkable. Better to regain her strength and her wits before tackling this impossible situation head-on.

Ava wondered what Kingston did during his absences as she roamed the castle-like halls of The Den. She sat for hours on the terrace overlooking the deep woods surrounding the mansion and explored the grounds, always with Paulie or Jack trailing in her wake. In the mornings when she woke, Kingston would already be up and dressed. While she picked at breakfast from a tray delivered to the suite, he silently drank coffee, patiently waiting until she pushed away from the table. Other than that, she spent the rest of her days alone until the following morning when the routine repeated itself.

Kingston's silences were frightening. No way would she ask him where he went, especially since he barely managed a gruff admonishment that she be a good girl each time he left her.

This morning was different.

Once she showered and dressed, Kingston escorted her to the game room and issued a stern directive. It was the first time he'd spoken more than a few words to her since Malcolm's assault.

"You will stay in this room until I return. I have a meeting with Oliver and others, so it isn't wise that you roam the estate today." Tucking a stray curl behind her ear, Kingston smiled crookedly. "You'll find this a better alternative than confinement to my suite."

Kingston's command was infinite. There was no arguing or

defying him, but Ava's mind raced with scenarios as he left her without another word.

Why was he meeting with Oliver again? What were the two men doing? Were they disposing of bodies? Plotting the murder of her awful brother?

And the others Kingston mentioned. Who could they be?

Maybe they were potential buyers. Maybe placing her in the game room provided some kind of sick display. After all, cameras recorded everything in this mansion. Like a bird in a pretty cage, she could flit around the room while being assessed.

Ava's hands clenched into fists.

Be sensible. He has no intention of letting me go.

Kingston already said she would not be sold, but expecting a murdering kidnapper to keep his word was unrealistic.

Releasing a frustrated sigh, Ava leaned a shoulder against one of the window casements, tracing the intricate carving with her fingertips. Just outside the deep, tall windows, the mountains loomed. Awash in color from the late afternoon sun, scarlet and burnt orange hues blazed in vivid contrast with the dull green of the lawn. As if one entity, a flock of small birds darted and swooped against the brilliant blue sky before disappearing into the thick trees.

Considering everything she'd been through since arriving at The Den, the quiet of the game room and the autumn-hued beauty outside this lavish prison was a sanctuary. She should be grateful.

"Stay here," Ava muttered aloud, repeating Kingston's command. His dominion over her new life meant obeying him in all things.

The five rules laid out following Malcom's attack were clear enough. The terms of her imprisonment might as well be literal chains binding her body. Disobey and she would be punished.

She moved away from the window, restless in captivity as the hours passed. Maybe Kingston had changed his mind about keeping her.

Realizing she was chewing a fingernail, Ava quickly distracted herself by selecting a pool stick from the wall rack.

Absently, she considered the usefulness of the room's items as weapons. So many things could serve in that capacity... from pool sticks and cue balls to chess pieces. Even the numerous decanters of scotch and whiskey lined up neatly on the built-in bar would make excellent missiles.

How hard would it be to take one of the animal trophy heads off the walls? There was one she eyed with more than a passing curiosity. It was an antelope of some sort, with wickedly sharp horns jutting out like twin daggers. The whole thing could be utilized as both shield and weapon.

Ava's gaze drifted to the cavernous stone fireplace. The iron stand beside it contained all the usual instruments for tending a fire. A miniature shovel and brush. Tongs. A poker with a curved hook on its end. All potential weapons but not practical if she intended on hiding the fact she was armed.

But there...mounted on the wall over the rough, wooden beam mantle was a pair of daggers that looked real enough. They flanked an exotic ceremonial mask which might have been used during some sort of ancient ceremony. An enormous, hairy boar's head hung beside the daggers, leaving one to conjecture the ugly beast was slain using those sharp instruments.

If those daggers were real, she could slice a man's neck open with barely a flick of her wrist. Stab him through the heart until the ivory handle was flush against flesh and the blade buried deep. It would be easy. Killing a man with those daggers.

Can I do it?

Shuddering at the bloody path her thoughts careened down, Ava turned to the heavily carved pool table. Like everything else in this house, it appeared antique. An exquisite game piece which likely cost more than her entire college education.

Ava rolled the white cue ball across the length of the pool table. What was taking so long for Kingston to return? Why did she even care? His absence allowed her to think clearly for the first time in days.

Why did I agree to be his?

Her fingers tightened around the pool stick. Matters were much simpler when she'd been held in the dungeon cell. When she was an untouchable prisoner. A valuable prize to be protected with her choices snatched away.

And now? Now, Ava wasn't sure what she was other than *his*.

And being the property of Kingston Vaughn Winter was a dangerous, confusing thing to be.

The click of the double doors swung Ava's attention around. Gripped with mounting apprehension, she watched Oliver enter the game room. A scowl twisted his lips.

He was alone. Fear twisted Ava's stomach, but she remained silent.

Where is Kingston?

"Don't worry. He's coming." Oliver answered the unspoken question. Leaning against the bar, he poured a finger of bourbon into a cut crystal tumbler. "My brother wouldn't dare dream of leaving us alone for too long."

Ava gripped the pool stick tighter, unable to keep her gaze from drifting to the daggers over the fireplace.

Oliver raised his glass in mock salute. "You are quite the

surprise, Miss Blue. Don't know how you managed it, but you've completely captured my brother's attention."

"I don't want his attention."

"He can't seem to help himself." Oliver grinned. "I think you marking him, scarring him just that little bit, brought out a previously unknown side of my brother. He's suddenly very possessive. I've never seen him act this way before. He's become even more of a psychotic asshole than I ever thought possible."

Psychotic? Ha! Oliver had no room to judge on that score.

Oliver stalked closer, but Ava refused to cower. She stood her ground while he circled her.

"I saw the video feed of Malcolm attacking you." His breath skated over her shoulder. Aware of the camera system inside this house of secrets and betrayals, his words were low enough that they would not be picked up on audio. "Gotta admit, it pisses me off that dumb motherfucker got a taste of you."

"He was as repulsive as you are."

Oliver trailed a finger down her arm. "Yeah, well, he died for it, but at least he went out happy with your flavor in his mouth. I'm fucking jealous as hell about that. But who knows? Maybe I'll get my own chance with you one day."

Ava's chin lifted higher with shaky bravado. "Try it. Kingston might slice you up, too."

Oliver's laughter was genuinely amused. His blue eyes gleamed. "Your dear brother underestimated your worth, Ava. He gave you up too quickly. Carson could have paid the debt and recovered his losses plus more if he'd just sold you to begin with. His stupidity is Kingston's gain. And I know King will come up with all sorts of creative ways you can pay off two million. That's a hell of a lot of blowjobs. Maybe he'll show me the tapes when he's done with you. I deserve a little bonus— since I can't get my hands on the real thing."

"Is your offer to help me escape no longer an option?" Ava asked with a sarcastic lilt to her voice. Any assistance from this man could not be trusted. She knew that now. The plans she once entertained of playing Kingston and Oliver against one another must be abandoned. She would *never* ask him for anything. He was a sadistic, evil snake who would bite the hand of anyone who ventured too close.

The man was possibly more damaged than Kingston himself. Kingston wanted to possess her. To own her innocence. Drag her down into wickedness and pleasure. But Oliver —his desires ran to deeper waters. He would hurt her simply because she was a woman who now belonged to his brother.

Oliver's covetous gaze turned heated as it raked her form. "Oh, I'll still help you, Miss Blue. If you pay the price for my assistance. My tastes are a bit more primitive than King's, but you look like a quick learner. I'd love to teach you everything I like. Everything I need from a woman. There won't be much of you left afterward, but at least you would be free of my brother."

Ava's eyes flashed green fire. "You are disgusting. Stay away from me, or I'll kill you myself."

Oliver chuckled. "Become quite the spitfire, haven't you? It's all King's doing, damn him. I liked it better when you were cowering at a man's feet. He's ruining you. Turning you into something fierce and wild. I bet my dear brother has no idea what you're capable of."

"How precisely am I ruining her?" Kingston asked, his countenance grim as he entered the game room. In one hand he carried a dark blue folder, much like the one containing the ledger sheets documenting Carson's debts.

Oliver stepped away from Ava, taking a nonchalant sip of his bourbon. "Seems your pretty prisoner is finding her backbone. But we both know how flashes of rebellion end for women involved with the Winter men. They just don't have a great track record of surviving us, do they?"

In customary fashion, Kingston ignored Oliver's taunts. He stalked toward the pair of them, head tilted quizzically upon seeing the pool stick Ava gripped so tightly. A twinkle of understanding lit his eyes upon realizing she held it like a weapon. The smirk on his face only deepened at seeing her unspoken relief at his return.

Tsking softly, he easily disarmed her, plucking the pool stick from her cold hands and flinging it onto the table where it clattered noisily against the dark grey worsted wool. The blue folder was casually tossed down beside it.

"Did you miss me, lamb?" Kingston murmured. He circled her in a predatory manner, brushing Oliver aside in an overtly masculine show of ownership.

Ava's gaze zeroed in on the folder.

What does it contain?

Kingston pressed closer, filling her senses. Demanding her attention until Ava's eyes raised to meet his dark blue ones. He lifted a lock of her hair, rubbing the strands between his thumb and forefinger. "Well? Did you?"

It was a mocking question. He knew Ava would not, and could not, give the answer he expected. Such an admission was an indicator of affection. And she certainly did not harbor that emotion.

"No." She would not show fear, but she also could not conceal the relief that he stood beside her. A necessary barrier between herself and Oliver.

"Liar. I suppose I'll add that to the growing list of your transgressions." Kingston cupped Ava's elbow, carefully avoiding the bruising Malcolm left behind. His fingers caressed her skin through the fluttering, long sleeves of the green silk blouse. When he touched her so gently, so possessively, it was as though fire licked along her limbs.

Ava's gaze flickered to Oliver. He had returned to stand beside the bar, a little smirk stretching his cruel mouth as he watched them. Those light blue eyes of his glittered like ice.

Kingston spun Ava so she faced away from him. Her hands automatically gripped the edge of the pool table, but even as Kingston's body pressed harder against her own, she did not bend. Standing straight, she resisted the subtle insistence that she submit to his wishes.

"Shall I punish you now? With my brother as witness?" Kingston murmured in her ear.

"You won't," Ava gasped out, fear mingling with red-hot desire. It was horrible. This dizzying, irrational need for this man's touch. His mouth. His cock. She could not understand why the degradation he subjected her to always turned her into a trembling mess.

Kingston's hands skated down to her hips. He gripped her harder, fingers digging in through her blue jeans. "It would prove my ownership. Show everyone you are truly mine now that Carson has abandoned you. And Oliver, well, he likes to watch these things." Kingston nuzzled her ear. Skimming his lips along the side of Ava's neck, he directed his words to the other man. "Don't you, brother?"

"You know me too well, King," Oliver confirmed with a quick draining of his scotch. His gaze contained hot glints of resentment, but he remained on the opposite side of the room, the glass held loosely in his hand.

Ava's breath ratcheted higher. Would Kingston really punish her while Oliver watched?

"You are toying with me. Playing with my head. You won't let him near me like that. I know you won't." She sucked in a quick breath when Kingston nipped her earlobe.

"You don't know what I will and won't allow, Ava." He chuckled, a dark sound that spiked Ava's heart rate. "I can do anything I wish with you. Anything. And you *will* obey."

Ava's mouth clamped shut, her grip on the pool table tightening with the truth of Kingston's statement.

"Isn't that right, lamb?" The words were a low purr. "If I tell you to drop to your knees for another man's pleasure, you will obey. If I let him fuck you, use you however he desires, you will obey. Because I own you now. And my word is law while I own you."

"Are you fucking with me right now, King?" Oliver grunted. "Don't flash her at me like a shiny toy if you have no intention of letting me play. It's a shitty thing to do, and you know it."

A tidal wave of fear washed over Ava. Would Kingston give her to Oliver? Let him touch her? Abuse her? Would he let other men do unspeakable things? He couldn't... he wouldn't. She had to believe his lust demanded she served only his own depraved needs.

"What do you wish me to do, sir?"

Ava's bold question surprised Kingston. He hesitated, fingers loosening on her hips as he absorbed it. She sensed the struggle within him. The need to control and dominate her fighting against his possessive nature.

"Bend your ass over this table." His reply was silky smooth. "Now."

Ava complied, heart pounding with trepidation. She could not say why she obeyed his husky command. Why she bent at the waist and remained perfectly still as Kingston encircled her wrists within his much larger hands.

When he anchored them in the small of her back, Ava moaned. There was a terrible darkness inside her that relished the way he handled her. It was wicked and twisted, silently begging for more. That darkness encompassed her rational nature, leaving Ava horribly off-balance and adrift with confusion.

How can I like this? How can I want his roughness? His domination. I must be going insane.

Kingston simply waited until Ava's panicked breathing slowly leveled out. A strange calmness seeped into her bones. Hadn't he taken care of her so far during this ordeal? Admittedly, her situation could be so much worse. She could be drugged into submission. Beaten. Raped repeatedly by multiple men.

Tortured.

She would have been shattered into a million pieces by now in the hands of someone else. Someone like Oliver. Instead, she'd been kept relatively safe.

Now, she must trust Kingston to keep his word that no one else would hurt her.

No one other than Kingston himself.

"Turn your head, Ava. Place your cheek flush against the table."

Ava obeyed, the wool of the table's surface surprisingly cool against her flushed skin. The folder containing God only knew what sat within her line of eyesight.

He won't hurt me. He won't.

"Impressive," Oliver drawled. Ava could not see him from this angle, but she heard ice tinkle and the sound of liquid as he poured another drink. "Does she sit up and beg for treats, too? More importantly, will she be so obedient when we take her at the same time? Will she snap at me when I fuck her? I hope so. God, I hope she bites me. I can't wait to sink my teeth into her. To taste her. Have her blood on my tongue. Her pussy caught between my teeth."

Ava jerked in response to the filthy ugliness of Oliver's words, but Kingston's grip tightened on her wrists. Moving closer, his body pinned her hips to the table until she was immobile. The carved wood railing pressed painfully into her belly.

She focused on the warmth of Kingston's hips against her bottom. The implied violence of his strength was all that kept her from falling into a heap of hysterics.

She focused on *him*.

"Shhh," Kingston soothed. "Steady, lamb."

Ava experienced a swirling moment of déjà vu. He'd said those same words once before. The day she arrived in this house of madness. The day her life turned upside down in a jumble of lust and fear.

Steady, lamb.

"Make no mistake, Oliver," Kingston said in a deadly soft tone. When Ava shifted slightly on her feet, she was held in place with an even heavier hand. "I'll not share her. I'll not allow anyone to touch her. And I'll be damned if I let anyone else fuck her. I'm telling you this, and proving her obedience, so you do not make the mistake of thinking otherwise. This one is not available for your enjoyment."

Kingston ran his hand down the length of Ava's spine. The soft threat of his fingertips told her to remain still or suffer the consequences. But she could not help her response. Squirming against him, panic rose once more in her chest. The depths of Kingston's possessiveness spoken aloud was eye-opening.

"She isn't here for your pleasure or for you to torment," Kingston continued calmly. "She's here because she's mine. Until I decide otherwise, she's *mine*. You will treat her with respect and deference for her position as mine. Otherwise, I'll have no choice but to dismiss you in the same manner I dismissed Malcolm. All of my men understand this. Do you, brother?"

There was a long stretch of silence. With her face smashed

against the table, Ava could not see either man, but violence swirled in the air between them. Like electrical jolts of energy, animosity and hate shimmered and snapped. She was caught in the middle of that bad blood now. A target for Oliver. And an outlet for the younger man to hurt the half-brother he despised.

The danger of her new status was glaringly obvious. She was not safe as Kingston's property. As his personal toy. If anything, she was at a greater risk than ever before because of it. His enemies would use her to get to him.

Did Kingston realize what he had done in claiming her with such ferocity?

A little sob escaped Ava's throat before she could swallow it back down. Terror bubbled inside her. She kicked out a leg in mindless reaction.

Kingston's hand around her wrists tightened imperceptibly. It was a subtle reminder that he ruled her and everyone else in his orbit.

Oliver laughed softly. "Of course, King. I get what you're saying. I should treat your new pet as if she were a dear, treasured sister." His tone was slightly sarcastic. "Right?"

"Something like that," Kingston replied in a mildly amused tone. "Now, get the fuck out and close the door when you go. It seems this *pet* requires firmer instruction when it comes to her new status."

CHAPTER

TWO

hese chains hold me tight.
Your arms, even tighter.

KINGSTON KEPT Ava's hands imprisoned in the dip of her lower back even after Oliver's departure. How he wanted to wrap his hands around her throat. To squeeze until the flutter of her heartbeat tickled his fingers. He craved the motion of her swallow reflex. Wanted to experience the futile struggle as she tried breathing without his permission. Because that's what she was doing to him. Strangling him within the depths of an irrational possessiveness.

It left him feeling unbalanced. Unhinged. He did not like it at all. Damn Oliver for reminding him just how shaky his hold on Ava Bella Blue really was. And damn her for making him care so much about protecting her.

Claiming her so forcefully opened him up to enemies who

14

would use Ava against him. Enemies like Oliver, who constantly prowled for evidence of Kingston's weaknesses.

Ava squirmed again, shifting her feet in restless response to the tightening of Kingston's grip. She feared Oliver, and that was good. But she should be far more terrified of the man currently holding her down over a pool table. After all, her life was in his hands. He could squeeze it into non-existence in a matter of seconds.

"Be still, Ava."

"What are you going to do to me? I obeyed you..."

His fingers dug into her hip, biting through the jeans she wore. "But you haven't. Not really. Now, do as I say and be still."

She huffed in frustration, but Kingston waited until her strained muscles relaxed, and she finally slumped against the table in reluctant defeat.

A wry grin twisted Kingston's lips. "Good girl."

Her fingers curled into the palms of her own hands with the unexpected praise. A tiny shiver, almost unnoticeable, passed through her body. It was proof of how much she needed those words.

"I think I should make a rule. No jeans. Ever," he said in a deep voice. "They make it too damned difficult to touch what I want most." Backing away a few inches, he inserted a knee between her thighs and nudged. "Spread your legs for me, Ava."

For a brief second, she hesitated before shifting her feet into a wider stance. Obediently, she waited for his next command while sprawled over the priceless antique pool table as though it were a patrol car, and he was an officer patting her down.

Kingston debated ripping the garments from her body. He

could strip her bare, shred every article of clothing she wore, and she would not dare fight him. But that might be too much.

He would still punish her, but it would be tamer than what he genuinely wanted. What he needed. What *she* needed.

Smoothing his palm over the swell of her ass, he squeezed each rounded cheek in turn, gratified when a low moan slipped from Ava's lips.

"I want to spank your ass red for that fucking stunt you pulled the other morning," Kingston murmured. "But I'm afraid if I start, I won't stop until I've broken you. And I don't want that—not yet."

Ava was silent, but she did jerk away from the abrupt sting of his hand striking her bottom. He did it again, harder this time, and she cried out in feeble protest.

"I wonder if you realize the danger of your actions. How close you were to being raped by Malcom. Let this be a warning, Ava. *Always* obey me. Always. Even when it twists your guts with hate to do as I command."

He spanked her hard three more times. Ava panted, fighting to be still rather than wiggling away from his hand. Tears trickled down her cheeks, marring the table's fabric with dark splotches.

"Do you understand, lamb?" Kingston ran a palm over her ass, well aware of how much it stung. "Don't roam this house or anywhere alone. Ever. It isn't safe."

"Maybe... maybe you should employ better men worthy of your trust," she whispered defiantly in a voice broken with gulps for air. "If I'm not safe here, of all places, in this dark castle where you rule..."

"Watch your mouth." Kingston gritted his teeth and spanked Ava again. This time she did squirm about, unsuccessfully attempting to escape his heavy hand. "Let me clarify things for you in simpler terms. You are not safe unless I am with you. And even that is debatable."

Ava's legs trembled, closing on their own accord when his hand drifted lower. It swept her body in a fleeting caress before slipping between her legs. Pushing hard while rotating his palm against her clit, Kingston soothed both the pain he inflicted and ratcheted up her desire.

Ava moaned, melting into his touch, legs buckling beneath the onslaught of Kingston's talented fingers as they traced and molded every fold and curve of her sex through the jeans.

And Kingston prayed for the strength to keep himself from ripping the denim off her body and claiming what was his.

"Stand up."

When Ava did not immediately obey the harsh command, Kingston used the grip on her wrists to haul her upright. Keeping her wrists anchored in the small of her back, he spun her so quickly that she careened into him with a tiny yelp of surprise.

Their faces were now mere inches apart. Kingston's free hand came up, lightly encircling Ava's throat but stopping short of tightening. She whimpered, staring up at him in dazed awareness with dark green eyes, the pupils blown wide with confused arousal.

Kingston breathed deep, inhaling her soft perfume. Her sweet breath brushed his lips, and the tears rolling down her flawless cheeks called out to the most sadistic part of his soul. The part he usually kept tamped down. The part he fought against daily and struggled to keep contained when he was near her.

Goddamn, how he wanted to unravel her. Ruin her. Save her. Keep her.

It was madness, of course. This bewildering, possessive desire. This raging need to own Ava's body. Her heart.

Without warning, Kingston's mouth crashed down on hers, and he groaned with the perfection of their kiss. It was brutal and yet, it was a culmination of every emotion experienced since the day he met her while standing in her mother's perfect, suburban kitchen.

Lust. Possession. Anger. Fear. Wonder. Helplessness.

Ava kissed him back, surrender vibrating low in her throat. Their mouths ravaged together. Explored each other. Discovered shared desire. Incinerated obstacles and sanity.

Somehow, their souls entwined through that kiss. Swirling branches of thorny vines and blood-soaked honeysuckles twisted and tangled until there was no beginning and no end, and Kingston realized a sad truth.

He would break his word. Shatter his reputation as a man who delivered on both promises and deadly threats.

Thank God Ava's father was no longer alive to see the depths into which Kingston had sunk. His disappointment would have stung like an open wound.

I won't let her go once the debt is paid. Ava is mine.

Kingston tore his mouth from hers.

"Fuck. I could kiss you for a thousand years and it wouldn't be long enough."

Ava's eyes were volcanoes of desire. Bubbling, molten rivers that Kingston was drowning in. Hell, he was happy to drown. To never come up for air. To never escape.

And all that just from a simple kiss of ownership.

"Where do you go at night?" Ava countered softly, testing the strength of the hands encircling her wrists. A million questions shimmered in her eyes, a frown creasing her brow at the tightness of his grip.

A tingle of shame rippled through Kingston. He had held her prisoner like this for so long that her hands were likely numb. Abruptly releasing her, he watched as she carefully rubbed each wrist as though encouraging the nerve endings to work again.

"I'm a very busy man," was his cryptic response.

He would not tell Ava how they disposed of Malcolm's body. Nor that he and Oliver fought over the absolute necessity of the man's death. There'd also been the issue of Carson's debt and the paperwork absolving him for the payback. The final bit of business was the placement of Ava Blue in her brother's place as the payor of the debt.

Oliver had shaken his head in bewilderment as Kingston notified the security teams of his latest acquisition.

"You are forfeiting two point six million for a bit of pussy?" Oliver asked in his customary, sardonic way.

To which Kingston growled, "Refer to Ava like that again and Malcolm won't be the only one passing through the incinerator."

It did not sit well with Kingston that Carson skated away without paying *something*. His former friend must forfeit at least one thing, even if his debt was being transferred. Something he would hate losing. Of course, the price paid would be insignificant in comparison to Ava's virgin blood, but still, Kingston would take it.

He planned on handling the matter in a very personal fashion, but first, he had a new pet to tame.

"Is Oliver angry about Malcolm?" Ava asked.

"If he is, it doesn't matter. It needed to be done."

Ava's eyes swept downward. "I—I'm sorry, Kingston. If I could go back and do things differently, I would."

"You aren't to blame for that man's actions. Your only culpability lies in disobeying my instructions."

She shot him a glance from beneath lowered lashes. "And you've punished me for that mistake."

Kingston said nothing. It would frighten her to know how

much he ached to do even more. The things he wanted, all the wicked, immoral things he ached for, made his head swim.

His little lamb had no idea how much he had changed since the day of her parents' funeral. How mired in violence and danger he'd become. It was a deep hole he couldn't emerge from.

Ava's gaze darted to the folder still laying on the billiard table. "What is that?"

Kingston picked it up, his gaze tracing her features as he considered his next move.

Ava's eyebrow rose high at his silence. "Is it a list of souls you own or something? An accounting of people you've killed?"

A muscle twitched in Kingston's jaw. "It's the contract detailing your debt. I want you to sign it."

She retreated a few inches, her eyes flaring with alarm. "I'm not signing that."

"Oh, but you are."

"I won't. How could such a thing be binding in a court of law anyway? That's insane." Ava's chin lifted in stubborn resistance, and a pang of guilt stabbed Kingston's gut at his methods of keeping her.

He brushed it aside.

"You'd be surprised how binding this document truly is. I'm giving you two choices, Ava. Sign it and spend your time paying the debt in relative freedom. In luxury. Your every whim granted... within reason, of course. Or don't and spend your days in the cell. I'll visit often to fuck you and punish you."

"Pretty much the same thing, aren't they? The fucking..." Her eyes narrowed as she spat out the epitaph. "And the punishments."

"You've no idea how unpleasant I can make both," he growled in annoyance. "Make your choice."

Kingston could see the mutinous bend of Ava's thoughts so clearly in her translucent features as she reasoned things out. She wasn't very adept at hiding her emotions from him, and he relished these little peeks into her soul. She desperately wanted to defy him... recklessly wanted to choose the cell as a means of avoiding the contract's finality. Her sweet, sensible, practical nature demanded otherwise.

"I *will* fuck you whenever I please, Ava." His voice remained calm. "Might as well enjoy some freedom along with that reality and in between punishments. Who knows? You may even enjoy the things I do to you."

"You won't allow another man to touch me, but you will take whatever you want from me." Ava's words were strangled with outrage. "And I must allow it because a piece of paper gives you that right."

"It's how things must be. I told you before. I don't forgive debts. Someone must pay. Someone *always* pays."

Ava glared at him. "You made me think I would be safe with you."

Kingston could not help his smirk. "Safe *with* me, lamb. Not safe from me."

CHAPTER

THREE

The needles and pins
You pushed in
So deep you scarred my heart.

"I trusted you."

"Come on. Did you really? Why?" Kingston appeared genuinely puzzled by Ava's statement. "Look at me. There is nothing that could be considered even remotely trustworthy."

Ava's gaze fluttered down. "I trusted you anyway. After what happened with Malcolm..."

"That's a terrible mistake, lamb. Trusting me." His eyes were so dark. So dark they were almost black. "And your bad luck if you ever did."

"You were never this cruel before," Ava whispered, searching his features. There must be a sliver that remained of the serious but decent man her father admired. "What happened to you, Kingston? Were you hiding behind that façade to fool my parents into helping you? To trick them?" She bit her lip, backing away from him. "To trick me?"

He stiffened. "I became what was necessary to survive. You're fortunate I did since I'm the one keeping you safe right now."

"But I'm not safe, am I?"

Kingston followed her retreat until she was pinned against one of the richly paneled walls. Above their heads, a massive water buffalo glared at them with dead eyes.

"Here is what is going to happen, Ava." His voice was smooth. Low. Deadly. And threatening. Always threatening. "You will sign this contract. And when you do, I'm gonna fuck you. Maybe tonight. Maybe tomorrow. But at some point, I'm gonna fuck you and fuck you hard. I won't stop until you agree that you are mine. Not until you say the goddamn words and quit fighting me at every turn."

From his suit's breast coat pocket, Kingston withdrew a gorgeously crafted fountain pen of burled wood and gleaming gold.

"Sign it, Ava." He trailed the ornate pen from the point of her chin down to the valley between her breasts. "Sign it so we can begin. Or..." He smiled, his dark eyes flashing with anticipation. "Don't and I'll have your things moved back down to the cell within the next fifteen minutes."

Ava shoved his hand away. She snatched the contract up from the billiard table, but in her fury, she could not read it. The words jumbled together in a blur of lines and symbols, the rules he'd verbally given her spelled out in stark black and white.

Sections of the contract assaulted her like whiplashes. Single words jumped off the pages.

Words like *whenever*.

Owner.

Master.

Want.

Knees.

Ava's eyes watered. What she would give up for the sake of this man's greedy lust was almost more than she could bear. But she had no choice.

Kingston was terrifyingly confident that she would sign this contract with the Devil. His ability to manipulate and control her was a force she could not withstand.

"Give me the pen." Ava snatched the instrument from his hand. Slapping the contract on the pool table, she quickly scrawled her name across the bottom of the last page. "Happy now? I've signed my life over to you." When she hurled the expensive fountain pen at him, it bounced off his chest and landed on the thick rug at his feet. "Now you've permission to do whatever you want, you monster."

Very slowly, Kingston bent at the waist and retrieved the pen. It was tucked back into the pocket on the inside of his coat with careful movements, as though he was considering her defiant attitude and how best to proceed.

When he straightened to his full height, Kingston's blue-black eyes glowed with retribution. "That contract is a blueprint for everything I intend to do with you."

Ava skittered to the opposite side of the billiard table, her movements quick and cat-like. So quick, in fact, that Kingston's eyes widened in surprise when she was suddenly out of his reach.

His upper lip quirked with amusement. A predatory air stole over his features. It was dark and dangerous and frightening. "Must I hunt you again? You know how much I enjoyed it the last time."

Ava's gaze flickered to the pool stick, still laying where

Kingston tossed it earlier. What would he do if she dared strike him with it?

"Careful, Ava," he warned, eyes narrowed. "Unless you want those punishments to begin immediately, I would advise against following through on that particular thought."

He moved closer while Ava inched away. Her hand rested on the smooth edge of the table, fingers twitching with the urge to snatch up the weapon. "You promised you wouldn't hurt me."

His grin was genuine. "No. I said I wouldn't allow anyone else to harm you. Pay attention, little lamb."

Before she knew it, Kingston was suddenly beside her, an arm snaking around her waist. There was barely time to blink before she found herself imprisoned against his chest. Her hands balled up into fists, digging into the muscled planes of his body.

"Fight me, Ava."

Reeling from his swift attack, Ava's head reared back at the husky command. "What?"

"You heard me. Fight me. I want you to."

"Why?"

"Because I like it. And so do you. You need it more than you realize."

Ava's blood raced. The suggestion she might enjoy a physical altercation made her sick. It was even worse when she realized Kingston was right.

Before he said another word, she leaned back, opening a tiny bit of space between their bodies.

Her palm cracked against his cheek, louder than a gunshot. The sound hung in the air, reverberating like thunder.

"That's not true," Ava snapped, anger boiling until it was on the verge of spilling over into everything messed up in her world. "You don't know anything about me. You never did."

Kingston laughed. "Yes, I do. The sooner you admit this, the better for both of us." His arms tightened around her, strangling her anger and somehow ratcheting the hopeless attraction she had for this man. It was dizzying how quickly her mood swung from hate to desperate hunger. It must be some sort of bipolar reaction she couldn't help.

"Fight me, Ava," he murmured again. "Or give in and let me have you the way I need you. And in the way I think you need me."

She obeyed, fighting him with frantic desperation, kicking his shins, her fists pummeling his chest. She even tried biting him, her teeth snapping as he effortlessly controlled her. It felt *good* to struggle, fear and anger leaching into her actions until it was almost a cathartic experience.

"Little monster," Kingston murmured, his pleased amusement stinging her pride. "So very fierce. So determined. And yet, still so helpless."

Ava cried out, a furious sound that made Kingston laugh out loud. He restrained her easily, controlling the reckless attack as if she were nothing more than a spitting mad kitten delivering a few scratches.

As if suddenly weary of the resistance he had encouraged, Kingston's mouth swooped down on hers, abruptly crushing Ava's fragile resistance.

She should battle back until he was bloody and tattered, but how could she when she craved him with all the madness roiling inside her? He touched her, kissed her, laid claim to her, and she capitulated like a spineless fool.

It was impossible fighting this when she was exhausted from strategizing. She simply wanted to feel and fall into everything this man promised. The pleasure and the pain.

With a tortured moan, Ava kissed him back. Fiercely. Without hesitation or thinking.

Kingston's reaction was instant. The kiss changed from punishing to voracious. He attacked her mouth. Ate at her lips. Devoured as much as he could get now that she wasn't resisting.

Ava clutched at Kingston's suit lapels, gasping softly when his lips left hers. She was completely off-balance. Ravenous for him despite her hatred for the situation.

"Fuck, Ava." Kingston moved until she was again pressed against the pool table. The wood edge bit into the small of her back while his rough hands held her in place. In a move Ava now anticipated, one hand came up and palmed around her neck, his fingers curling at her nape.

"You don't know what you do to me, do you?" Kingston's words grated over her lips as he took and took until she was drowning. "I want to punish you and cherish you all at once. I want to fuck you until you see only me. Until you don't want *anyone* but me. Damnit, you are driving me crazy, Ava. I don't know what to do about it. I don't know what to do about *you*."

Clutching her tighter, his gaze crashed into hers in a firestorm of heated fury.

Flames of desire to incinerated Ava. She wanted Kingston as much as he wanted her. The knowledge was a sharp betrayal of her self-preservation. Allowing him to do whatever he desired was suicidal. It was beyond depraved. She could not forgive herself for giving in so easily.

The man was a sociopath, and her life was in increasing danger every second she was with him. But she would not leave. Not now. Not when there were others who would hurt her in terrible ways she couldn't begin to fathom.

It was far easier submitting to this man. This lesser of all evils looming over her. This monster who promised protection while completely destroying her.

"Then do it," she recklessly, *stupidly* challenged. "There's nothing stopping you, Kingston Winter. Nothing. Not even my hate."

Kingston's eyes flashed with something primal.

Something... *vulnerable.*

The spark vanished as quickly as it appeared. Left in its place was a rueful smirk of cruelty and ownership.

"You don't hate me, Ava. But you do fear me and that's entirely different." He brushed her lips with his while a tiny smile curled at the corners of his beautiful mouth. "I'll use that fear until you crave me as much as I crave you. Should I take you right here? Right now?"

"You won't." Ava's voice quavered, betraying her conviction.

Kingston laughed. "Try me."

She pushed at his chest again with balled-up fists. "Empty threats."

What are you doing, Ava? You are deliberately taunting him. Do you want this man to tear you apart?

"You think so?" Kingston's fingers tightened around the column of her throat. His eyes narrowed.

"Yes," she squeaked out. "And... if you want the truth, it's losing the desired effect."

CHAPTER

FOUR

I watched you change
Into something wild and untamed.

THAT'S IT. She'd officially gone insane in this house of madness.

She was poking the beast. But she was insanely desperate for an end to this limbo of agonizing waiting. Desperate for his teeth to rip her apart so it would all be over that much sooner. Like ripping off a band-aid, the pain would hopefully be fleeting.

"Hmmm."

That's all Kingston said. *"Hmmm."* As though she were nothing more than a science project revealing unexpected results following a tragic experiment.

"You continuously threaten me with it." Annoyance crept into Ava's tone even as she shifted closer like a timid mouse desperate for shelter.

Oh, God. I'm pathetic.

29

"Then by all means, Miss Blue. I'll happily oblige your need for a good fuck."

Ava swallowed hard. "Here? But someone might come…"

With one hand still wrapped around her throat, Kingston nonchalantly pulled his phone from his suit pocket. He pressed a button and opened the call in speaker mode. A familiar voice answered from the other end of the line.

"Yes, Mister Winter?"

"Jack, no matter what you hear or how loudly Miss Blue might scream," Those fingers tightened around Ava's throat until she could barely swallow, "nor how prettily she begs for God or someone to come to her aid, no one enters this room. Is that understood?"

There was a second of silence before Jack responded—crisp and matter-of-fact. "Very much so."

There would be no assistance coming from Kingston's righthand man. No rescue from this self-inflicted danger she had thrown herself into. That much was clear.

"No one, Jack. I've no need for an audience while Miss Blue is initiated into her new reality."

Another pause, this one far more pregnant with understanding before Jack responded. "Understood, sir."

Ava's skin flamed hot with embarrassment. Anyone lingering outside the game room's doors would hear every response to Kingston's *initiation*. She would not have the strength to contain her moans. Nor her cries. It wouldn't take a stretch of the imagination to guess the activities underway inside the locked room.

Kingston ended the call and pressed a few more buttons, all while his dark blue eyes traced Ava's features. He slid the phone back into his trouser pocket. "The cameras in this room have been disabled. Now, will you voluntarily remove your clothes? Or would you rather I tear them off?" His fingers loosened from around her throat.

Ava remained quiet, fear abruptly seizing her tongue and rendering her incapable of speech.

"There's my answer," Kingston murmured, reaching for the top of her blouse with the intent of ripping the delicate fabric.

Ava quickly slid her fingers up to his wrist. "Wait."

Head tilting at her soft order, Kingston's hands went motionless. A questioning light sparked his gaze. The dark blue depths were an ocean Ava had no idea how to navigate.

"I'll do it." Her voice was resolute as she tugged his hands away from the edges of the blouse. Would he let her control this encounter? Allow her the right to orchestrate her own destruction?

Kingston's hands lowered, even while his brow slightly furrowed in puzzlement.

Ava's fingers were clumsy as she unfastened the row of pearl buttons. When she finally reached the last one, the emerald green silk hung in two fluttering pieces, framing her breasts like pieces of art for Kingston's appreciative gaze.

"What a surprise you continue to be, Ava." The husky timbre of his voice sent a shiver down her spine. Their breaths met and swirled together in the quiet of the room. Ava swayed toward him.

"Do you want me to keep going?" She tugged her bottom lip between her teeth as Kingston's fingertips drifted over her exposed chest. Large, slightly calloused hands gently explored the dips and curves of flesh not contained within the boundaries of the lacy black bra. Memorizing her in the most primal way, his determined touch incinerated her efforts to control the situation.

A shocked gasp escaped her when Kingston lightly pinched one nipple through the fabric.

"Not yet. Let me look at you first." His gaze was hot. Dark, burning, and filled with promises of pleasure for her unexpected obedience. He stroked her nipples through the fabric, palming the fullness of each breast. Staring into her eyes, he gently squeezed.

Warmth flooded Ava's panties. He was deliberately making her wet for him. God, how she hated that about her body. Hated how easily he could excite her and extort these unwilling responses.

You are doing what is necessary to survive. Give in. Be submissive. Let him have what he wants. And this will all be over that much sooner.

It was the smartest thing she could do. The most sensible course of action. Only... a dark and twisted portion of Ava's soul writhed in full rebellion. Reminding her how much she wanted this. She craved the danger along with the semblance of controlling her own path deep into this treacherous labyrinth of lust and possession.

Kingston deftly unsnapped the bra's front closure. Like her blouse, the fabric separated into two halves.

Ava sucked in a breath. Kingston's fingers coasted over her flesh, down along her stomach, then traced the button of her jeans. His knuckles brushed across her bellybutton in a rhythmic motion that made the muscles there clench.

"You're so soft." His fingers dragged over her skin in a leisurely motion. "Like velvet. Fuck, I cannot wait to have you wrapped around me."

Hearing the triumph in his words, Ava swallowed hard past the lump in her throat. Her bravery was short-lived. She was falling apart at the thought of Kingston claiming her. "Here?" The words came out in an almost comical squeak. If the situation wasn't so horrific, she might have even giggled.

"Yes, here. Were you expecting a bed of roses and romantic candlelight?"

Ava shook her head at that ridiculous notion.

Kingston dipped his fingers below the waistband of her jeans, tugging at them and pulling her closer. "It's as good a place as any to claim what's mine."

"There will be... you know... um...blood." The words came out in an agonized whisper. She'd not thought this through at all.

"I know. I'm counting on it." His hand slid even further into her jeans.

"This beautiful table... it will be ruined."

Kingston huffed out a laugh. "I'll buy a dozen more and fuck you on all of them just to prove a point. Wherever and whenever I want you, I'll have you."

Ava's eyes closed. "Oh, God."

His grin flashed white. "At least let me get inside you before you start praying to me."

Ava's lips clamped tight, her hands splaying across his wide chest as if that little bit of resistance would hold him back. The warmth of his skin burned her palms through his elegant dark suit.

"Take your blouse off." He cocked his head, removing his hand from the low waist of her jeans.

He was waiting for her obedience to die a quick death. Expecting her to halt this madness. The flare of brutal excitement in his eyes clearly said he anticipated taking what he wanted. And how much he would enjoy it.

Ava's chin lifted. The slightly red imprint of her hand on his cheek, and the curved scar she'd given him that first day in his office, swelled her heart with a burst of shocking pride.

Kingston might own her for the moment, but she'd left her mark on him. She had physically wounded this violent, heartless man. Was it possible to inflict even more damage by taking away the element of his domination?

Could she defeat him with something so simple?

Realization left Ava breathless.

Her greatest weapon lay in her submission. An instrument twisted and forged in the form of surrender. A sword she would use to stab him in the heart.

A sword that might save them both.

"What's going round inside that pretty head of yours, lamb? Something cunning, I suspect."

His husky murmur shook Ava from her thoughts. Dismayed that he could see through her so clearly, she frowned. "I'm wondering how it is you are so rich when you are so eager to waste your money."

Kingston *tsked-tsked*, then in a completely unexpected move, his hands gripped her waist. With disgusting ease, he lifted Ava and resettled her so that she sat perched on the edge of the billiard table. Now they were closer in height and nearly nose to nose. If she tilted her head back just a little, she could stare into those cold, indigo blue eyes.

"Do *you* think you are a waste of money?" His mouth was a rigid line of disapproval.

Ava shrugged at the question. Hunching her shoulders made the shirt drape over her breasts. The bra, however, hung in halves, the molded cups awkward and uncomfortable. Would he let her refasten the undergarment? Or would he knock her hands away and finish mauling her?

"Answer me, lamb. Where did you get the notion that you aren't worth two point six million?"

Ava turned her head from his searching gaze. "I thought we were talking about antique pieces of furniture. Not my questionable value as your prisoner."

"Sit up straight, Ava." Kingston scowled, curving his hands

around her shoulders until they bracketed her shoulder blades. After forcing her upright, her breasts now jutted forward. It was a position indicative of pride, but Ava only wanted to fold into herself and hide from the heat of his blue eyes.

"Prisoner or not, I won't tolerate your shame." His eyes flickered with something fierce as he admired her bared flesh.

"Don't you want me subservient, sir?" Ava asked quietly. "A woman to be commanded and used at your leisure. You've made it quite clear what my position is. I am to be your whore until you grow tired of playing with me. It doesn't matter that my parents loved you and helped you. It doesn't matter that without my dad, you would have lost everything. All that matters is your power. Your money. Your name. You would have lost all of it without my parents' support. So, go ahead. I know nothing will keep you from doing your worst."

I revel in your beautiful surrender
Even while I hate it.

KINGSTON DID NOT UNDERSTAND what the fuck was wrong with him. With her. With this... situation.

Her accusations pounded in his head.

It *was* what he wanted, right? Ava's submission. Her obedience. Her body bowing to his. He had wanted that for a long time. Part of the reason for taking her in the first place was this long-held fantasy of possessing her.

No matter the existence of her damn brother's debt. That was laughably second to his true motivations.

So, why did victory taste so sour in his mouth? Why did the thought of Ava meekly obeying his demands send faint stirrings of guilt and nausea tumbling around in the pit of his stomach?

The reminder of her parents' affection was infuriating. He

barely managed to keep his roiling anger expertly hidden behind a façade of cool aloofness.

Why wasn't this working out the way he'd envisioned?

He could not follow his own rules when it came to this girl. This obsession—sharp and double-edged—pricked like a constant thorn in his side. And the vulnerability in Ava's green eyes when she looked up at him somehow restricted the blood flow to his heart. A heart he was certain no longer existed. It was something he'd lost long ago.

It wasn't wise to keep Ava, but damn if he would release her before he was good and ready. She had foolishly signed the contract binding her to him for as long as he wanted her. For as long as it took to ensure her safety from Carson and the men he owed blood money, he would keep her.

Maybe that's forever. If I never find the video of that awful night, maybe forever isn't such a bad thing.

Kingston grunted at the thought, pushing it away as quickly as it formed. That weak sort of sentiment wasn't realistic for men like himself. Hard, cruel, bloodthirsty men did not deserve love or kindness.

And they certainly did not deserve forever.

No. Men like himself, men like Oliver and Carson, were hell-bent on crushing weakness. Determined to use whatever means necessary when it came to destroying innocence.

Kingston was especially skilled at that last part.

His jaw tightened, and before he could stop himself, he was kissing Ava. Deep, hard punishing kisses that spoke eloquently of his intentions. His tongue stroked hers, jabbed into the recesses of her mouth, taking what he wanted and proving to both of them that he was not a gentle man.

When he finally tore his mouth from hers, leaving her lips bruised and dark pink, Ava was panting from the roughness.

"Let's get these jeans off you." His words came out in a growl.

Removing her taupe-colored ankle boots was quickly done. With hard hands, he stripped away her jeans next, but Ava did not fight him on their removal. She merely stared up at him as if shocked by the turn of events. Motionless and silent.

Kingston almost wished she would fight him. He wasn't sure he liked this pliant, pale creature before him. For some godless reason, he liked her better when she was spitting and snarling like a little hellcat.

His eyes roamed over her body—from the silk shirt covering her shoulders to the dainty socks she still wore.

For fuck's sake, she looked like a teenager in those innocent little socks. Trembling with anticipation for a stolen kiss at a frat party. Hopeful the cute football quarterback would put his arm around her and ask her out on a date.

Goddamn it. Don't think about her like that. Don't think about how she was before me. Before Carson and his fucking friends traumatized her. Before I stole her away from the world.

With a grunt of frustration, Kingston ripped the socks off her feet. And after a moment's consideration, he yanked and tugged until the shirt and bra were gone as well.

There. Now Ava looked like the sweet temptress he had always imagined her to be. Her hair streamed in soft, golden waves over her shoulders, only partly concealing the rounded globes of her breasts and pretty budding nipples. Her long legs dangled off the edge of the table, tempting him to lift and wrap them around his waist. The only part of her body still covered was her pussy, and even that was debatable considering the skimpiness of the underwear he provided her. The tiny scrap of black lace barely covered her.

Kingston's mouth watered, thinking what delights lay

hidden beneath the fragile material. How wonderfully sweet she tasted the last time he feasted on her.

He was starving for a bite of what now belonged to him. She wasn't immune to him. To this. He smelled her arousal as it drifted in the air like exotic perfume. It made his cock hard as stone. Made him throb with unrelenting hunger.

It was frightening how much he wanted her.

Ava simply watched as he manhandled her, allowing her body to be twisted and turned as her clothing was removed. Meek, compliant, and malleable. That submission should please him—being hardwired as he was when it came to dominating his women.

Instead, it was infuriating.

His hand curled over the nape of her neck, meshing into the softness of her hair.

The small knot there was something Ava would never notice unless she knew to look for it. He personally implanted the tracking device the first night she spent in the dungeon cell. Smaller than a grain of rice, no one knew of its existence other than himself. Even Neil had no idea what he had done.

Brushing a gentle finger over it now, Kingston was pleased when she did not react with any sign of pain. That he would always know her location eased a tiny bit of the turmoil raging inside him.

But not enough to keep him from taking what he wanted.

Squeezing hard, Kingston forced Ava's head back as he pushed her legs apart, holding them open with the force of his body.

Ava's mouth curved with a tiny smirk. "Am I not obedient enough, sir?"

Kingston's hand tightened. He gave the fistful of hair a little jerk, gratified when a spark of pain lit the depths of her eyes.

Her smug expression wavered before calmness stole back over her.

Is she fucking playing with me right now? When I'm a heartbeat from ramming myself into her sweet, tight cunt?

"I don't know what game you are playing, Ava, but you won't win. I can promise you that."

"No games, sir. Just doing as I'm told," Ava replied a little too serenely. It was as if she'd figured out some kind of hidden trigger and now gleefully used it against him. Something about her submission didn't ring true, and secretly, Kingston was glad.

"I'm this close to fucking that smirk off your face, lamb." He deliberately rocked against her, pressing his cock against the heat of her pussy. A strangled sound rolled from her throat, and her eyes fluttered shut only to snap back open when he accused, "Maybe you want that. Maybe you've done this before. Maybe Carson's friends did more than I already know. Did they, Ava? Did they fuck you until you screamed? Did you take them all at the same time? Every man there filling your holes until you were overflowing and hurting?"

Her eyes flashed fire at the mention of Carson while Kingston smiled at how easily her anger was roused. That's what he wanted to see... Ava not just accepting what he was doing to her but surrendering and hating him for it.

"Guess you'll have to fuck me to find out if I'm really a virgin and worth all that money," she breathed out.

"Guess so."

Kingston's smirk rivaled hers as he released the grip on her neck. Her sigh of relief ended in a strangled cry when he abruptly ripped her panties from her body. The tiny straps gave way with relative ease, torn to shreds in his large hands and leaving a slight fabric burn scrape on her inner thigh.

Instead of being tossed aside like the other articles of

clothing, the ruined garment was forced into her mouth. Her clenched teeth were no deterrent. He simply pinched one of her nipples until she let out a soundless cry then shoved the panties in.

The sight of her with that scrap of black lace serving as a makeshift gag was the hottest goddamn thing Kingston had witnessed in a long time.

"Spit that out and I'll spank your ass so hard you'll not sit properly for a week."

Ava's eyes blazed at him, her hands instinctively coming up to jerk the offending bit of cloth away from her mouth. But Kingston encircled her wrists in one fist, trapping them between their bodies. He shook his head in mock disappointment.

"What did I just say? That stays while I'm fucking you. It will give you something to bite down on when it gets too intense."

Ava moaned.

Kingston grinned. "That excites you, doesn't it? The thought of my cock hurting you. That I might actually fuck you so hard it's painful. Is that what you need, Ava? That little bite of pain tempered with pleasure? Maybe deep down inside, you really are a monster just like me."

Ava's increased breathing revealed volumes about her body and her secret desires. She might not understand why she wanted to be taken rough and hard, but Kingston did. And he would damn sure do his best to fulfill her needs while satisfying his own.

"Lie back. I want your hands stretched high above your head when I let go of your wrists. Don't move from that position, and above all else, do *not* remove that gag, Ava."

He ruthlessly pushed her shoulders down until she lay prone across the billiard table. He'd spent five years locating the mid-nineteenth-century antique and it was only one of three in existence. The massive piece of gleaming mahogany and gilt trimming cost a small fortune. Now, it served as a makeshift altar for the ruination of one Ava Bella Blue.

Ava did as she was told. Even while making a low sound of protest deep in her throat, she stretched her arms above her head, fingers automatically linking together in a gesture of self-imprisonment.

Smirking at her display of obedience, Kingston shrugged out of his suit coat and tossed it toward a chair. His gaze fell on the folder containing the contract. It lay beside Ava's right elbow, the blue-colored stock ugly and businesslike in a room of such decadence and death.

Seeing it there against the lush grey wool of the table was disturbing. All the mounted animals in the room appeared to be staring at that innocuous folder as well, their dead eyes holding judgment on what was happening below.

He didn't need a visual reminder that Ava only allowed this because she'd foolishly inked her name into a worthless piece of paper. Snatching up the offending folder, he threw it aside, sending papers fluttering into a disorganized heap.

Ava's eyebrows rose high in question, but she didn't shift away when he settled back between her legs.

The position of her body put her lower body on display in the most salacious manner. Her legs still dangled from the billiard table, but now her hips were in the right spot for him to grip when he entered her. But first, he wanted a taste. Fuck, he *needed* a taste.

He spread the folds of her pussy with his fingers, exposing everything to his gaze. Stroking the pale pink flesh, he carefully watched her expression while he played with her. Ava's breasts rose and fell with strangled breaths as she struggled to remain still under his hand. Her nipples hardened into tight little jewels he would soon be rolling between his teeth.

"You are so pretty and perfect here, Ava. Plump and ripe like summer peaches and fresh cream. And so smooth. I'm going to fuck you with my fingers first until you are desperate to come. I want to see your tears before you do. Do you understand? Because you're so goddamn gorgeous when you cry for me."

The whimper of lust that escaped around the makeshift gag in Ava's mouth was a bolt of lightning zinging straight to Kingston's balls. They tightened in a familiar, delicious way, sending ripples of pleasure throughout his body. His cock strained behind the fabric of his trousers, desperate to be free. Desperate to feel Ava. Desperate to plunge deep inside her. He had waited so long for this moment, but he would wait a few minutes more. He wanted to please her first before his own satisfaction was fulfilled.

She was already so wet. Wet from the descriptions of what he planned on doing with her. Wet because she craved him with the same bewildering intensity. Knowing she feared him but still wanted him left Kingston lightheaded. The things he would do to her were mind-boggling. The many ways he could play with her. Torture her. Pleasure her.

Love her.

Fuck. Not that. Never *that*. Loving someone was like signing a death warrant in his ugly, sinful world. He couldn't condemn Ava to that fate.

He wouldn't.

But that reluctance did not mean he wouldn't use her for his own enjoyment.

"You're dripping for me, Ava. Dripping all over my expensive billiard table. Bad, bad girl," he *tsked* under his breath. "I think you should be punished for that. What do you think?"

Ava squirmed at the mention of punishment, but Kingston shoved his middle finger inside her pussy, curving the digit until he found her g-spot.

She let out a muffled squeal as he flattened his palm against the heat of her mound.

"Be still," he warned, reaching up and lightly pinching one of her nipples. Her body responded with a flood of warmth, melting into his touch. She was like an inferno. Bemused, Kingston wondered if the heat of her body could incinerate the finger impaling her. "And be quiet. Unless you want Jack to know just what's going on in here. He might think about rushing in here to save you. Ill-advised but possible."

Ava's hips lifted at the murmured threat. Kingston's grin disappeared. Jealousy, sharp and nauseating, permeated his blood. Seeped into his bones. Turned his voice hard and cruel.

"You like that idea, do you? That another man might watch as I ruin you? Too bad. Because no one gets to see you like this except me. No one will hear those sweet sounds you make when you come except me. And no one is going to fuck you except me."

He drove his finger harder into her, rubbing the inside of her walls with quick, jabbing motions, slapping her clit with the palm of his hand until she shook in his hold and detonated in a shocking burst around his finger.

He could become addicted to this. To her. He was supposed to be making her beg. Supposed to be keeping her on the edge of lust, but seeing how sweetly she came undone was danger-ously addictive. The tears rolling down her cheeks at her own body's betrayal were little atom bombs to his restraint. He wanted more of the part of herself she kept wrapped up so tight. And if making her climax over and over was how that was accomplished, then he would delight in orchestrating her destruction.

"Again," he muttered. "Again, Ava. You need reminding who you belong to." He swiftly drove her to a second climax. Then a third. A fourth. All in quick succession, with no reprieve from the onslaught of sensations and pleasure that rolled into what probably felt like one long orgasm.

Ava screamed helplessly around the gag, desire flooding his fingers with moisture as she gasped and choked on sobs of panicked ecstasy. She shifted weakly against the weight of his hands. Her face flushed a lovely pink from both exertion and confused embarrassment at what his expert manipulation wrung from her body.

"Good girl," Kingston crooned. He leaned over, licking the salty moisture from her cheeks, pressing his lips to hers although she tried turning her head away in shame. "That's what I wanted first, Ava. You gushing over my hand with tears streaming down your face."

SIX

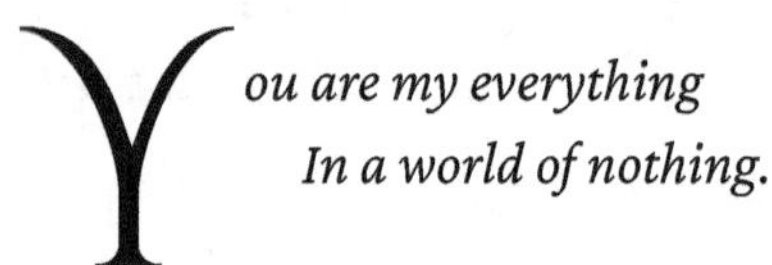

SLIDING his finger out of her body, Kingston leaned back just enough to unbuckle his belt and unbutton his pants. Before freeing his aching erection, he bent over her, licking the sweet essence of her release from her thighs. Pulling her legs over his shoulders, his tongue explored the crease of her pussy. Every bite and little nip made her body flinch, but she also melted into his mouth like gourmet chocolate. Warm and liquid. Sweet and sharp.

Fucking delicious.

"Mine," he growled, devouring her as though he were a starving man. She was likely sensitive after what he'd just done to her, but he didn't care. He wanted her taste in his mouth and her blood on his cock.

Sucking her clit into his mouth, he ruthlessly worried it

between his teeth, sending another climax, the fifth, rippling through her body. Ava screamed again through the gag, her hands flying down to grip his head, pressing him even harder against her flesh. Fingers meshed into his hair, demanding and frantic, and Kingston was so enraptured by her helpless, mindless response that he didn't even care she'd disobeyed him.

He needed her touching him. Needed her wrapped around him, wrapped so tight he'd never be able to breathe without her again. Maybe she could erase the demons that chased him. The nightmares haunting him. He didn't care how wrong it was to keep her. All that mattered were these rare moments when he didn't have to think about being Boss or getting a bullet in his back. He could enjoy the pleasure Ava gave him and savor the memories for a future without her.

It was fucking stupid, but he wanted the impossible. He wanted so badly to have this *mean* something even if she hated his guts.

Kingston stood up to his full height, towering over her. One hand slipped down again between her trembling legs, cupping her bare mound. The way her flesh quivered when she came was addicting. Her clit thumped in time to her heartbeat, leaping against his palm.

Ava watched him with drowsy, heavy-lidded eyes, tears clinging to thick sable eyelashes and tracking down her flushed cheeks. She was gorgeous in her languorous stupor, her body soft and willing, the delicate scent of feminine arousal and honeysuckle body wash perfuming the air.

Kingston smiled, pushing her knees up so her legs bent with her heels on the edge of the table. Spread wide for his enjoyment, the lewd position put her arousal on full display.

"That's it, Ava. Show me who this pussy belongs to." His free hand pulled his dick free of his trousers. Gripping the base of his erection, he dragged the head of his cock through the slick wetness of her center. He pushed himself in just enough that her body clamped around him in a blind, reactive panic.

His knees nearly buckled. His eyes flickered shut for half a second. She was so warm. So soft. *So fucking soft.*

"Christ," he choked out, gazing at her in wonder. "You feel amazing wrapped around my dick."

Ava gripped his wrist, holding his hand still. Her eyes locked with his. Deep green melting into dark blue. The warm, tranquil sea crashing into a cold, violent ocean.

He was ready to take her. To fuck her. To claim her. But for some reason, Kingston hesitated.

"Do you want this, Ava?" His voice was hoarse and low and goddammit, why was he even asking the question? "Do you want me?"

Ava's eyes never left his. Her fingers dug harder into his wrist. Her hips rose upward in welcome, her legs wrapping around his waist just like in his fantasies. Jerking her head in a quick nod, a tear leaked from the corner of her eye.

It was her sigh of resolute defeat that nearly ripped his heart in two.

Kingston couldn't help himself. He leaned over, licking that tear up, savoring its saltiness as he carefully eased his way into her body.

She stiffened at the feel of him, although she was so wet that at first, he glided smoothly.

But he was so big and she was so small. He was not far enough inside her. God, less than half of his cock's length was in, and he was having doubts this would even work.

Sweat broke out on his brow as Kingston fought his urges. The ones demanding that he thrust through the fragile resistance. His cock would stretch her wide. Tear her, more than likely. Like an ugly battering ram destroying a tiny, rose-covered cottage.

Beneath him, Ava sucked in a deep breath. A whimper escaped her throat, strangled by the gag. She was biting down on it as he predicted she would. Her enormous eyes were hazy with pain, but she did not push him away. Instead, his little lamb tightened shaky legs around his waist and gripped his forearms when he braced above her.

His hips flexed. His cock moved a little deeper inside her. Ava moaned.

He did it again and slid further into nirvana. Jaw clenched, Kingston waited until her body accepted that new invasion, and then... he held still.

"Am I hurting you too badly, lamb?"

Ava stared up at him, apparently surprised by his concern. Her eyes were so wide and so impossibly green. After a few seconds, she shook her head, shifting against him until he had no choice but to sink further into her softness.

"*Fuck.*" The curse came out in a hiss. Her pussy was strangling him, and the sudden excruciating tightness meant he'd reached the barrier of her virginity. A fact reinforced when a distressed groan rippled through Ava's body.

It was a good thing she'd already bitten her fingernails down to the quick. She would have ripped his forearms to bloody shreds by now.

Jaw clenched, teeth clamped down on her own panties, she seemed determined to bear the pain in relative silence, and Kingston suddenly couldn't look away. From her beautiful face. From the juncture of their bodies. From the sight of his cock sliding into her warmth.

This was wrong, but goddamn, he couldn't stop it. *Wouldn't* stop it.

Before he could reconsider, he reached up, ripping the cloth away from her mouth. Ava stared at him in astonishment.

"I want to hear you scream my name when I make you

mine." The growl was primitive. Feral. Completely unreasonable and an awful truth he could not deny.

"Okay," Ava hiccupped, her voice broken and weak from crying. "Please, sir. Tell me what to do…"

"Say my fucking name when I'm making you bleed, Ava. Say it now."

Her pink, bruised lips trembled, confusion lighting her gaze even as a strange, swirling excitement filled the minuscule space between their bodies. It was something wondrous and terrifying. Something neither one could control despite the tight rein Kingston kept on his emotions.

"*Kingston.*"

Her sigh was a breathy surrender, and it stabbed Kingston straight through the heart he swore no longer existed. Pierced the armor he'd worn his entire life and laid him open, bare and vulnerable.

He would do anything for her. Anything to keep her right where she was. Pinned beneath him and taking what he gave her. Even if such twisted devotion meant his eventual downfall.

"It hurts," she accused softly. "Is it supposed to hurt so much?"

"Fuck, lamb. I'm not even all the way inside you yet."

"How can there possibly be any more of you?"

Kingston groaned at her words. His cock swelled as her virgin cunt stretched to accommodate him. The realization only made him more feral. Harder. Ruthless. Then he was surging past the thin membrane with a grunt of satisfaction. "Goddamn you, Ava. You truly were pure and untouched before I got my hands on you. But not now. Now, you are as dirty as I am…"

Kingston thought she would recoil in disgust. Cry from the

weight of her helpless situation. Fight back against his cruelty. Struggle to free herself.

But Ava surprised him again, locking her heels at the small of his back, urging him deeper. "Don't stop, Kingston. Go ahead. Make me as filthy as you. Ruin me like you've been ruined. Drag me down to your level."

He let out an angry growl at her scathing words, driving into her body with feral intensity.

Ava's eyes glittered like fierce, dark stars. She bit her own hand to keep from sobbing aloud as he seated himself deep within her.

"I'm sorry." The words escaped Kingston with no conscious intent. He wasn't sure how they even formed in his mouth. He was never sorry for his actions. For his words or deeds. But this woman made him feel something suspiciously close to shame. Ducking his head to escape the censure in her eyes, he drew the tip of one breast into his mouth. He sucked the bud gently, rolling it along the edge of his teeth and tracing its puckered surface with the tip of his tongue before lavishing attention to the other side.

"Finish what you started or let me go," Ava whispered defiantly, the words catching on a sob. Tears tracked down her cheeks like a sprinkle of tiny diamonds.

Kingston reared back, his features hardening. "I'm not letting you go, Ava. Not now. And maybe not ever."

He palmed her bottom, lifting her slightly from the table so he could move deeper inside her until Ava abruptly sat up. For a moment, he thought she was intent on escaping him, but she simply looped her arms around his neck. It was an oddly poignant action. Almost as if she sought comfort from him, of all people. The feelings it provoked were so puzzling that he allowed it.

She huddled against him, burying her face into the crook of

his shoulder. Sweet tears seared his skin while inside his steel-encased fortress of emotionless cruelty, Kingston splintered a little more. His wicked little lamb was so very brave. Braver than anyone he knew. Braver than himself.

She's worth a hundred of me. More valuable than anything I own. I have no right taking anything from her, but damned if I won't take it all.

"I'm going to ruin you for any other man." His gut twisted at the thought of someone else having her like this. He'd kill the bastard first. "Whenever someone fucks you in the future, you will think of me and this moment. I'll make damn sure you *never* forget it."

In response, Ava hesitantly pressed a kiss to his hard mouth, searching for a hint of softness. Their mouths fused, her tongue sliding along his as Kingston began fucking her with measured desperation. With every brutal thrust, she tightened around him as he unraveled her. He wanted her to come at the same time he did, but he wouldn't last much longer—not with the heat and wetness of her channel clenching around his cock. She was now rocking against him and the friction of their bodies was enough to make Kingston's eyes roll back with pleasure.

"That's it, baby. Fuck me back. Take your pleasure and come with me," he hissed before taking her mouth again in a brutal, vicious kiss that left her bottom lip bleeding. He nipped her neck, enjoying her frantic breaths and sounds of distress. She was hurtling toward a climax, and God, he wanted to be right there with her when it happened.

Why that was suddenly so important, Kingston couldn't say or explain. He shouldn't care if she came. He shouldn't care if she found even a tiny bit of pleasure in his arms. But he did. God help him, or save him, but he did.

"Don't you dare stop rocking on my dick." With his palms

cupping her bare ass, he helped her keep the pace, his fingers digging into the soft flesh. The position of his pelvis hitting her clit with such brutal precision sent visible goosebumps skittering across her skin. Her fingers dug into his shoulders as she arched against him.

She was close. And so was he.

He thrust particularly hard, jamming himself as deep as he could go inside her. She whimpered against his mouth.

"Fucking come for me, Ava."

The hoarse command sent ripples of ecstasy cascading through their entwined bodies as he slammed into her again and again.

Maybe he was too rough, the blood staining the length of his cock every time he glided out of her channel evidence of that but fuck if he could stop now. Not when she was just as hungry for him and demanding her pleasure.

"God, Kingston," she gasped, clutching him so tight she was likely leaving her own bruises on his body. "Don't stop. Please... Oh, right there... God..."

"That's right, little lamb. I am your god. Now, come for me. Scream my name. Let me see you cry."

Kingston's hand wrapped around her throat, holding her hostage. His fingers squeezed just enough to send her hurtling toward the stratosphere.

Ava came with a strangled scream, her orgasm so strong that Kingston felt it pouring into the depths of his black soul as she went limp in his arms. He lowered her until she was again sprawled across the billiards table, one hand remaining loosely wrapped around her throat, the other now gripping her hip and holding her in place. His movements became erratic, all control dissipating like an elusive mist. He was as ravenous as a wild beast, fueled by her sweet, unexpected response and the mix of blood and desire.

"Fuck, Ava. *Fuck...*" he groaned, holding so deep inside her that he could have sworn his cock battered the very entrance of her womb. "Take it like a good fucking girl... *my* good girl. Take all of it. Take all of me. I want my cum dripping out of your sweet little cunt."

He kissed her hard, swallowing whatever response she might have had to the exquisite filth of his words. Then he was detonating inside her, shooting every bit of his pent-up, frustrated desire deep into her tight, lithe body.

Shudders of delight cascaded through his bloodstream. Euphoria left him lightheaded. He was dizzy with lust and resolute with unapologetic possessiveness.

Ava was truly his now. There was no going back.

Not now.

Not ever.

CHAPTER

SEVEN

T*ake my heart prisoner.*
Never let it go.

AVA CONCENTRATED on steadying her breathing. The room spun out of control as she turned her head as far as the hand around her throat would allow. Tears slid down her cheeks, staining the table's surface. She did not have the energy to wipe them away.

I'll move in a second. I just can't right now...

Regret was already sinking in, the rational portion of her brain screaming for foolishly surrendering herself to this man.

Kingston was still deep inside her. His fingertips were digging into her hip, leaving nothing to cushion her buttocks from the hard wood railing of the billiard table.

Ava belatedly realized how much that stung. Or maybe the space between her thighs hurt badly enough that it radiated in all directions. Kingston's head hung low, his breath warm where it skittered across her chest. He seemed to be having a hard time regaining his composure as well.

But he's not the one who just lost his virginity, is he?

She felt battered. Bruised. Her body must be covered in bite marks and scrapes from Kingston's beard-scruffed chin. She frowned when she saw the wounds on her fingers.

She'd caused those with her own teeth during a moment of intense, bewildering madness.

My God. What the hell is wrong with me?

"Let me go."

Her voice didn't sound like her own. It was hoarse and rough. Broken but strong. She sounded so strange, even to her own ears.

"Over my dead body," Kingston replied lazily, letting go of her throat. A second later, he wrapped his arms around her waist and helped her sit up. Her arms automatically encircled his neck, holding onto him for support.

Still buried inside her, his cock already twitched impatiently for another round. Fighting back a sniffle, Ava's vision swam, the room swirling as she gathered her bearings. The dead animals within her line of sight watched her, their stares cold and impassive.

Like those stuffed creatures, she was a trophy now. Maybe Kingston would mount her head on the wall, too. Give him something to admire and brag about while playing games on his bloodied, ruined billiard table.

"Let me go, Kingston." Her tone was stronger this time. Sliding her hands down from around his neck, they now curled into fists, pressed into his chest.

Minus the coat he'd tossed aside earlier, he still wore all his clothes. He'd destroyed her without even removing his expensive Italian leather dress shoes.

Leaning back, he smirked. "But I want you again, Ava. This

time, I'll bend you over this table. Or maybe over the balcony railing just outside the terrace doors."

Ava hit his chest with a balled-up fist. "No!" The refusal exploded from her before she could bite it back.

Kingston's eyebrows soared. "No?" He repeated softly. His jaw hardened. "That's a word no longer available to you."

Ava glared at him. Maybe the loss of blood was making her reckless. Maybe that's what happened when a girl's virginity was torn apart. Maybe losing that tiny bit of membrane meant the emergence of a backbone.

But it also meant ignoring the warmth seeping through her bones. It was a lassitude that drained her of any semblance of true resistance. She wanted to curl up beside this man in a bed heaped high with cool, silk sheets and fall into a slumber so deep she would never need to face her body's betrayal.

Slowly, Kingston pulled out of Ava while she winced. Tucking himself back into his pants, he did not bother fastening them as he picked up his coat from where it lay in a heap on the floor. Silently, he rummaged through the coat's inner pocket, withdrawing an expensive silk handkerchief etched with his initials.

Ava slid off the billiard table, excruciatingly conscious of her nudity. When her attention helplessly navigated to the vee of his open trousers, her legs wobbled.

Even satiated, Kingston was huge. His cock was barely constrained, the bulge of it twitching the longer she stared.

Dragging her gaze away, tremors shook her while she stood there, an arm crossed over her breasts. Silly of her, actually. This man had seen every inch of her and used his mouth as an exploration tool. She was probably suffering something like aftershocks, but a bigger concern was making itself known. Specifically, between her thighs where his cum dripped from her body and slowly dried on her skin.

Ava steeled herself as he carefully folded the handkerchief into a neat square. Would he shove the bit of silk into her mouth and start again as he'd already threatened?

Why did that possibility make her knees buckle with anticipation?

She trembled, blushing furiously when Kingston nudged her knees apart. With excruciating care, he cleaned her flesh. A hiss escaped her at the sting, but she allowed it. What choice did she have in the matter, anyway?

"I'm trying to be gentle." Cobalt blue eyes, the Devil's eyes, bored into Ava's. "I've never fucked a virgin before so my experience with the aftermath is nonexistent."

"Well, I've never been fucked before," she snapped without thinking. "Now we truly have something in common."

The corners of Kingston's eyes crinkled slightly, apparently amused by her impetuous response.

"We are more alike than you think, Ava."

"No, we're not."

Kingston's mouth tipped in a smile. He continued wiping her so tenderly that Ava's eyes almost fluttered shut. It really did seem that he was trying not to hurt her. She wasn't sure how she felt about that, now that she was becoming accustomed to his brutality.

"We're both addicted to this. The way we make each other feel. This fire between us. You may hate me, but we both know that doesn't matter. You want this. What I do to you. You need it." He kissed her softly, his lips moving over hers but barely making contact as he spoke. "And I crave you with every goddamn breath I take."

Ava stiffened at his confession. She wanted to cover herself up and hide from him, but Kingston would not grant her even a sliver of dignity. The heat of his body, so close but not touching hers, made her nipples contract into tight buds.

Again.

Aching for him.

Again.

Wanting him.

Again.

Her body's betrayal was horrifying. And God help her, she loved every excruciating moment of being his.

"Now, this is what we're going to do." His voice was raspy with satisfaction and lust. "We're going up to our room, and we're going to take a bath. We'll order in an early dinner, and afterward, I'm going to fuck you a second time. And likely a third and fourth."

"You should realize that I'm sore." Ava's gaze fixated on a mounted elk head on the opposite wall. The stuffed specimen stared back at her in apathetic sympathy. "It will hurt too much and—"

"What part of being mine do you not understand?"

His dispassionate tone made Ava's skin prickle with dread.

Kingston stepped back from her, carefully folding the blood-tinged linen handkerchief so that the stain was not visible. With deliberate slowness, he slid it into his trouser pocket while she watched.

"What are you going to do with that?" Ava choked out, dreading his answer.

Kingston grinned. "Send it to your brother, of course. Proof I've taken the one thing he counted on to repay his various debts. Don't worry, lamb. I intend on collecting his blood as well. He'll pay a stiff price as tribute for your unwilling sacrifice."

"You can't do that." Ava's eyes narrowed as her shirt was handed to her.

Kingston's brow rose high. "Can't I?"

"*Please* don't do that," Ava hastily amended, her tone softening. "Please, Kingston. Do not humiliate me like that. Not now. Not after you've taken everything you wanted."

His brow furrowed. "It's not meant to shame you—but rather drive the point home. You're mine now."

"You've made that very clear." Her acknowledgment carried a tinge of bitterness she could not conceal.

Kingston bent down, retrieving her ruined panties. Those were tucked into his pocket as well. With no inflection to his voice, he said, "Get dressed now."

Wincing, Ava silently did as she was told. Before pulling her jeans on, she slanted a glance at Kingston.

"I—I still need to clean myself up."

"You'll do no such thing." Kingston smirked, pulling the vibrating cell phone from his pocket while addressing her request. "I like knowing your pussy is drenched with my cum. You'll stay as you are until I decide otherwise." His attention turned to his phone.

"Psycho," Ava muttered under her breath as Kingston answered his phone.

"Yeah?" Jaw tightening, his eyes flashed with dark anger as he spoke to the caller. "When?"

Whatever was being said by the person on the other end of line was not welcome news. Ava listened as she tugged on her jeans, hissing as the rough denim slid along tender flesh. She was sore and swollen *there,* her inner thighs abraded by the scruff on his chin, her clit throbbing from being sucked into his cruel mouth.

"Where's Oliver?" Kingston inquired, his gaze drifting over Ava. A possessive gleam lit the blackish-blue depths of his eyes. "I'll be there in a moment. No. Keep them in the foyer and let Paulie know what's going on. Yeah. Fully armed and ready for whatever happens."

He ended the call and fastened his pants, smoothing the

belt flat and adjusting his shirt collar. By the time he shrugged into his suit coat, Kingston appeared so coolly polished it seemed impossible that he'd just destroyed her only minutes before. Had feasted on her body and claimed every inch of her soul.

Ava ducked her head, peeking at him from behind a curtain of wild, tangled curls as she dressed. Her scalp still tingled from his fingers raking through the loose waves of her hair while he took effortless control of her body.

A painful lump rose in her throat. She wanted him manhandling her like that again. Wielding that control and using it against her. That she *liked* it was baffling.

"Stay here."

"Why?" she dared question, yanking her bra on under his heated gaze.

"Because I said so, brat."

Her hands were shaking from the earthquake of the climaxes he'd given her, making it hard to fasten the bra. She didn't understand what was wrong with her. Kingston's gruff response made her want to lie back and spread herself wide for him again, even though her brain recoiled in disgusted shame. Biting her lip helped control that urge.

A little.

"Stop biting your lip," Kingston growled. "I can't fucking handle my business when you do that."

Ava immediately stopped chewing her lip and worked on fastening the buttons of her shirt. Anger curled around her bones as reality sunk in. What did he have to be so irritated about? She wasn't to blame for his lack of control around her. She'd done exactly what he wanted. Participated in the taking of her virginity with hardly a single tear shed for its loss.

Kingston let out a frustrated grunt at her silence.

"We have unexpected... *uninvited* guests," he abruptly

explained. "Since they are not the sort I welcome with open arms, you will stay here until I've dealt with the nuisance. It's safer."

Ava meekly nodded, but her mind whirled with questions and ways she might escape this room before Kingston had the opportunity to haul her off to his bed.

*I pulled off your wings
Watched you flutter in front of me.*

KINGSTON CLOSED the door behind him and motioned Jack over.

"She doesn't come out and no one goes in. Seems her brother sent associates here in an ill-advised attempt at recovering her. Whoever he has running cover for him when it comes to law enforcement in Bitter Springs won't help him here, but he insists on acting foolish."

Jack pulled a handgun from a holster, checking the clip. "Should we anticipate trouble?"

Kingston shook his head, smoothing the fabric of his coat with a brush of his hand. "We'll be ready, but these guys aren't stupid enough to insist on searching the house. They don't have a search warrant, but I wouldn't put it past them to get one for LIST just to prove they can."

His biggest concern was not the possibility of a raid on his exclusive club, but how to secure Ava's safety. Carson's actions would likely turn more desperate, which meant he would become more dangerous.

"Does she, um, need anything?" Jack nodded toward the billiards room.

Giving the bodyguard a chilling stare, Kingston cocked his head. "I don't know, Jack. Do *you* think she's in need of something?"

Jack flushed. "Not if you don't think so."

Kingston's jaw clenched. "Don't go turning into another Paulie, for Christ's sake. If it were left to him and Neil, she'd have full run of the mansion and everyone in it. Just make sure her little ass stays inside that room."

With a quick nod of his head, Jack positioned himself beside the door.

"Don't let her fool you. She's got a devious streak I never knew existed." Kingston strode toward the end of the hallway, throwing over his shoulder, "And she's learning how to use it."

Upon reaching the mansion's foyer, Kingston paused, raking his hands through his hair and restoring the waves to order. It gave him a moment to consider his approach before confronting the two men standing in the center of the wide, marble-lined space.

Examining his hands, a rueful smile flickered across his lips. His fingers... they smelled of sex. Like honeysuckles drenched in lust and possession.

Ava.

It was a sweet, intoxicating perfume. A reminder of his obsession and the unexpected, deep-seated need to keep her safe. It was a development he was becoming increasingly accustomed to. Now that he'd taken her innocence, there wasn't a bastard alive who could steal her from him. She was his for as long as he wanted her, whether she liked it or not.

"Gentlemen."

Kingston's greeting drew the attention of the men as he descended the marble stairs.

The older of the two was Aaron Redding, son of Bitter Spring's senior district attorney, which explained the man's swift rise to the rank of detective. Aaron was a distant friend of Carson's during college, but their partnership now bridged the gap between criminality and getting caught.

The other man simply provided the illusion of local law enforcement endorsing this impromptu visit. The young officer was the muscle, so to speak, since Aaron was out of Bitter Springs' jurisdiction.

"Kingston." Aaron adjusted his tie. "Been a long time."

"It has." Kingston continued descending the stairs, waving off his men when they imperceptibly moved closer. Paulie stood posted near the front door, effectively blocking the exit. The kindly twinkle usually present in his eyes was replaced by a hard, sinister gleam.

"Mister Winter, sorry to bother you like this, but we're here concerning the whereabouts of a missing woman." The young officer's eyes traveled around the foyer, obviously impressed by the grandeur of the space, and mildly concerned to see the half-dozen men now silently surrounding them.

Aaron grinned, throwing his hands up in the air in mock exasperation. "So fucking eager when they first graduate the academy, aren't they? Officer Holt, if you don't mind, I'll ask Mister Winter all the questions."

Kingston's eyebrow lifted, his entire demeanor one of acute boredom.

The younger man flushed. "Sorry, Detective."

Aaron turned back to Kingston with a knowing smirk. "Do you have information regarding the whereabouts of Ava Bella Blue?"

Kingston understood that this was a game of sorts. Who would blink first and show their hand.

Aaron Redding had no idea he was playing against a master.

"Who wants to know?"

"Her family." Aaron's voice was relaxed, but beneath the calm was the first real quiver of frustration.

"Her family is dead."

"Her parents, yes, but you are aware that her brother is very much alive. Of course, he's worried sick that she's met up with some unsavory characters." The detective smirked. "You know, bad people."

Kingston's lips twitched. "What makes you think she's in danger?"

"Just a hunch." Aaron's head cocked. "We've received some disturbing tips from an anonymous source. Possibly being held somewhere against her will. Perhaps in a basement. Maybe even in a cell or something similar. Mind if we look around?"

Fucking Oliver. He's behind this. He's given them just enough detail to incite action but still vague enough to avoid closer inspection and leave him in the clear.

"I do mind," Kingston drawled, crossing his arms and staring Aaron down. "You see, the maid hasn't been around for a couple of days. Place is a wreck. I'd rather no one see it in such a state."

Officer Holt's head tilted in confusion, his gaze quickly darting around the immaculate foyer. "Detective Redding? You need a warrant if Mister Winter declines a voluntary search of the property."

"No shit," Aaron muttered, his attention distracted by a disruption at the top of the staircase. "I'm well aware, Officer Holt."

Kingston half turned toward the sound of pounding footsteps. His blood pressure soared as Ava made her way toward him, stilted but still graceful. Only Kingston recognized the pain in her movements. His cock twitched as though she tugged it with an invisible string.

He was responsible for her discomfort.

Jack was the culprit for the heavy footsteps. Sprinting behind Ava, he skidded on the marble before slowing to a swift walk. His jaw set with grim determination as he watched her descend the stairs. There was nothing he could do but let Ava go, his hand hovering over the hidden holster containing a nine-millimeter. He was ready for whatever Kingston decided.

Even if it meant keeping their prize by force.

Ava practically floated down the stairs, and while Kingston considered how he might handle the situation without bloodshed, his prisoner surprised him. Rather than dashing toward the safety of law enforcement, she gravitated to Kingston like an errant kitten. Snuggling beside him, her arm slipped around his waist.

With her mussed hair, smeared mascara, and clothes obviously thrown on in a hurry, she looked as though she'd just rolled from their bed after an afternoon of lovemaking. Her pink lips were swollen from both hard kisses and the gag that had been forced into her mouth.

Even her feet were bare, adding to the impression that she'd recently been thoroughly fucked. And for God's sake, her scent was driving Kingston crazy. As though he'd marked her for his own like some sort of animal, he could *smell* himself on her.

Aaron's eyes lit up with satisfaction while Officer Holt frowned in almost comical confusion.

"I hope I'm not interrupting," Ava said with a languorous pout, her gaze sweeping over the strangers gawking at her and the security detail ringing the foyer. Paulie gave her a wink, and she returned it with a smile before gazing up at Kingston in an admirable imitation of sultry adoration. "Kingston, you said you'd be right back. I got tired of waiting."

Kingston squeezed her hard against his side, ignoring her inaudible squeak of alarm. Turning his head, he brushed a mockingly affectionate kiss against her temple and whispered, "I'm going to blister your ass for this, Ava."

Ava plastered a serene mask on her face, ignoring the threat. "Is there some sort of problem?"

"This is Officer Holt with the Langston County Sheriff's office." Kingston introduced the man with a wry smile.

Officer Holt nodded. "We're actually checking on your welfare, ma'am. That is, if you are Ava Bella Blue."

Ava's eyebrow lifted. "My welfare?"

Aaron pushed past Officer Holt. "Your brother is very concerned, Miss Blue. You've been missing for more than a month with sporadic and deliberately vague texts to explain your absence. We suspect you aren't the author of those texts. Your boyfriend, Drake Cornerstone, is convinced that the one he received was not sent by you."

Kingston stiffened at the mention of Drake.

"Mister Cornerstone is not my boyfriend." Ava bristled. "Anyway, is it illegal to get away from everything? People do it all the time." Her grip tightened around Kingston's waist. "As you can see, Detective Redding, I'm alive and well."

Aaron's smile was cruel. "So, you remember me. Carson and I were never that close in college, but we recently reconnected our friendship along with your boyfriend. Drake's a fine attorney. DA's office is pretty impressed by him. He is as worried for you as your brother."

"Perhaps you didn't hear me the first time. Drake and I dated briefly. It went no further than that." Ava's tone turned icier. "I'm sure my brother needs many allies within the justice system. People who can be bought for a price and bribed."

Aaron's face hardened at the insult. "All pleasantries aside, Miss Blue, if you'll come with me back to the Bitter Springs police station, I'm sure we can straighten all of this out."

Kingston's men, lounging along the foyer's periphery, all shifted into a stance of readiness. A hint of violence and impending bloodshed permeated the air. Each man was ready for the cue to defend their boss's property.

Paulie's gaze shot to Jack where he stood at the top of the staircase. The two men communicated in silence, and Kingston's shoulders relaxed, knowing the situation was well under control.

Ava shook her head. "I'm not going anywhere with you. I'm here because I want to be here. There's no need to explain myself, but Kingston and I reconnected during a chance encounter in Savannah. He invited me here as his guest and, as you can see, I'm in no danger."

"The *fuck* you are, lamb," Kingston muttered under his breath, adjusting her body so they now faced one another. To anyone watching, it appeared as though they could not stop touching one another. He rubbed his nose alongside hers in an affectionate gesture while whispering, "I can smell myself on you, Ava. The mix of our cum and your blood. Once these men are gone, you'll bleed for me again in a different way." His hand traveled down until it rested on the curve of one ass cheek. He pressed her against his hardening cock.

Ava shuddered but still, the little brat rose up on tiptoes, brushing her mouth across his in a teasing manner. "Better that you hurt me rather than whoever pays my brother the highest bid."

"Should I give them evidence of how I've already ruined

you?" Kingston murmured. "We'll settle this bullshit right now."

He was talking about both the handkerchief smeared with evidence of their previous encounter, as well as her ruined panties shredded by his hands and her own teeth.

"Please don't." Her eyes shimmered with sudden tears, understanding the motive behind his threat. "I'm trying to make them leave."

"Work harder at making them believe you're here willingly, lamb. Before I kill them both." There was little doubt he would commit murder to keep his prize. If provoked, he'd slaughter anyone her brother sent to collect her.

Aaron cleared his throat in an obvious attempt at getting Ava's attention.

Ava gave the detective a distracted look as Kingston tightened his arms around her waist. Fuck, both men were practically salivating at the sight of her disheveled perfection. Possessive rage vibrated through Kingston's veins when he witnessed Aaron's gaze fixate on Ava's ass. The man was actually licking his lips.

Ava's laugh sounded only a little forced. "Mister Redding, I've no intention of going anywhere. Please pass that along to my brother. He's never worried about me in the past. No need to start now."

Aaron's gaze dragged up Ava's body. "He wants to see you in person. Make sure you are okay. I mean, some damage has been done, that much is clear, but it's nothing that can't be worked out."

Kingston tensed, a low growl escaping him, but Ava's head tilted at Aaron's assessment.

"Being Carson's friend, you probably have a good idea of just how *damaged* I am," she replied softly. "Regardless, would you arrest me for taking a vacation?"

"Of course not, Miss Blue," Officer Holt interjected, glancing at Aaron in confusion. "She's here of her own choice, Detective. We can't force her to come with us. And obviously, Mister Winter is not restraining her in any way."

"Not yet, anyway," Kingston hissed in dire warning, his breath stirring the hair on Ava's temple.

She trembled but did not pull away from his embrace. Instead, with a steadying breath, she laid her head against his broad chest as if she wouldn't dream of ever leaving him. Smiling at Officer Holt and Aaron, her fingers found the open vee of Kingston's shirt and curled against his skin. "You'd have to force me to go. Which would certainly violate my rights, don't you think, Officer Holt?"

Kingston fought the urge to lay this woman out on the cold marble floor of his foyer, spread her legs wide, and fuck her until everyone understood she was his.

"Yes, ma'am. If you are here freely and willingly, we can't force you to leave with us. There's been no crime committed, none that I can see anyway."

Aaron fumed in frustration, but he could do nothing.

"Thank you for understanding, Officer." Tilting her head back, Ava stared into Kingston's eyes and moved closer until her sweet warmth permeated his clothes. "Will you see yourselves out, Detective Redding? And be sure you tell Carson I'm right where I need to be. Drake, too."

NINE

Whatever you want, little lamb.
Whatever you fucking want...

THE MOMENT the mansion's ornate doors closed, Ava's knees buckled with relief. Just as quickly, Kingston's hand was around her throat, his thumb forcing her chin up until she had no choice but to meet his artic blue gaze.

"How did you get past Jack?" he asked softly.

Ava swallowed. "I said I had to use the bathroom." Her own hand came up, gripping his fingers so they wouldn't tighten any more. "It's not his fault —"

"What did I tell you, Jack?" Kingston cut her off in a dispassionate voice. "Devious." His hand remained locked around the slender column of Ava's neck, but it did not frighten her as it once had. The way he held her hostage was almost... tender.

"Sorry, boss. She got a head start on me," Jack apologized,

raking a hand through his hair. "I wasn't expecting her to be so fast. Or that she would be armed."

Kingston huffed out a disbelieving laugh. "Armed? With what, for fuck's sake?"

"One of the ornamental daggers from the display over the fireplace."

"Is that true?" Kingston inquired, tilting Ava's chin higher.

"I thought I might need to defend myself." Ava refused to be sorry for her actions. Kingston's own words left no doubt as to the danger posed by their visitors. "I wouldn't have used it on Jack. Or you."

"Where are you hiding it?"

"My back pocket," she confessed in a sullen whisper. It wasn't fair, nor was it right how he manhandled her, but the truth was it made her shamefully wet, her body humming with anticipation.

Still holding her by the throat, Kingston's free hand slid over her ass again until it closed over the dagger's ivory handle which was hidden by her shirt's flowy hem. He pulled it from her pocket. "Devious and bloodthirsty. You are a fucking treasure, Ava."

He trailed the dagger's sharp edge along the side of her throat, tracing her collarbone and further down to the softness between her breasts. "What did you plan on doing with this?"

Ava's mouth hardened, her attention snapping from the dagger's path. "If they had taken me, I would have killed them."

"How, precisely?" He sounded amused by her ferocity. "You aren't exactly trained for combat."

"I would have cut their throats," Ava choked out. Kingston's mockery stung her more than she thought possible. He thought her weak and ineffective. Unable to defend herself. How she burned to prove otherwise!

"And if you failed, my wicked little lamb?"

"I would slit my own," Ava's grimly stated. "I won't ever be Carson's pawn again."

In a fluid movement, Kingston tossed the weapon to Jack, who skillfully caught it one-handed.

"It would be a tragedy to destroy such a pretty little neck. I'm sure I'll never find another that looks as gorgeous with my hand wrapped around it. Guess I'll need to be more careful when it comes to you and sharp objects." Kingston laughed softly. Glancing at Jack, he casually added, "Return that to its rightful place."

"Sure thing, boss. Apologies again for letting Miss Blue get past me."

"Don't worry." Kingston stroked the underside of Ava's chin with the pad of his thumb. "She'll pay for her impulsive decision. Obviously, I must reconsider the parameters of her confinement here at The Den since she has trouble obeying orders."

Ava squirmed. "You're being unreasonable."

"I'm never unreasonable, brat, but I am occasionally surprised. It's barely been an hour since you signed yourself over to me, and already, you've shattered certain rules of our contract. A disappointing development but not entirely unwelcome." Jerking Ava forward, Kingston nipped at her bottom lip. A tiny droplet of blood welled up as some of his men chuckled.

Ava had the impression Kingston *wanted* them to see her conquered and defeated. Her gaze darted around the foyer, seeking allies and finding none. Even Paulie averted his eyes, refusing to look at her.

"I cannot allow insubordination, lamb. Not even from you. Do you understand?" He licked the blood from her lip with a languid swipe of his tongue, his dark eyes shuttered.

Ava nodded her head the best she could, and Kingston growled, his fingers tightening with the threat of violence.

"Try that again."

"Yes, *sir*," Ava bit out from between clenched teeth. She couldn't quell the shiver of fear his stern demeanor sent coursing through her. But even worse was how her body instantly clenched with helpless lust, her blood pounding in recognition of his ownership. She *must* remember his craving for obedience and continue using it as a weapon.

Because the more she submitted, the more confused he seemed by her.

Kingston grinned, a wickedly handsome grin with the power to make a girl forget her own name. "Better but far from ideal. You're much too defiant. Too willful and far too stubborn. Oh, Ava." His voice dropped into a husky promise, and her resolve to obey like a good girl faltered with his words. "It's going to be a pleasure breaking you."

FOR SOME REASON, Kingston allowed Ava time alone after escorting her to their room.

Their room.

Funny how she considered it a mutually shared space when everything in The Den and on the grounds belonged solely to Kingston Winter.

Including herself.

Ava did not dare voice a complaint. Cleansing herself in the huge marble walk-in shower, wincing at the tenderness between her thighs, she reminded herself to be thankful for small mercies.

While in the shower, she shed more than a few tears. Scrubbing away all evidence of Kingston Winter on her stained skin, she cried for her lost innocence. Wept for the loss of her independence and any possibility of escape.

She would be here until Kingston tired of her, or until Carson's debt was paid in full. Whichever came first.

I was so confident that morning in Savannah. Right before Oliver snatched me from the hotel elevator. So certain of my ability to stand completely on my own. To be happy with my decisions knowing they were mine. I was ready to live without regrets or fear. Too bad it was just an illusion. I couldn't control my own destiny and how pathetic is that?

Emerging from the shower's steamy heat, Ava wrapped a towel around her body. Studying the mirror's reflection, she touched her fingertips to the dark smudges under her eyes. She looked worried. Tired. And worse still, resigned.

When the bathroom door opened quietly, her gaze remained on the mirror. There was no need to turn around. Only one person held reign over this house and everyone under its roof. Only one man came and went as he pleased. One man. A king. A monster. Her tormentor.

Her savior.

Kingston met Ava's stare. His eyes were burning lumps of sky-sparked coals locking with hers.

She didn't speak, but neither did he as he approached. Keeping eye contact in the mirror, he now stood close enough that she could slap him. Her breath caught in a gasp when his fingers drifted down her spine to the edge of the towel.

"Why didn't you run from me when you had the chance, Ava?"

Ava's eyes closed. "You know why. Must I say it aloud?"

She sensed the smile in his voice when he replied, "I want to hear you admit it."

Ava met his dark gaze, her heart clenching with dread. She'd never felt so trapped before. Kingston no longer used chains or dungeon cells to imprison her. He utilized words and her own incessant need to belong somewhere. The need to belong to someone. Someone like him. "I'm safer here. With you."

Kingston's head tilted. He looped wet strands of her hair around his hand and used it to tug her back against his hard body. "It's much more than that, Ava. What else?"

"The contract you forced me to sign."

He *tsked* in disappointment. "Oh, lamb. You've much to learn about yourself."

"I don't understand what that means," Ava mumbled, but deep down inside, she knew exactly what he meant. A spark had ignited within her soul. One that found a sense of belonging in this man's ruthless possession. And he was cruel enough to use it while exploiting her reluctant submission.

"I'll make things clearer for you, Ava. We'll start with reinforcing the rules."

Untangling his hand from her hair, Kingston stepped back and removed two cell phones from his pocket. He set them on the marble countertop.

Ava's heart jumped. One of the phones was her own. She stared at it in disbelief as Kingston began undressing.

As his body was slowly revealed, Ava's gaze helplessly drifted away from the cell phone. She greedily devoured every inch of his hard, muscled, spectacular form while clutching the front of the towel. She trembled with something far worse than fear.

Excitement.

The snarling lion's head tattoo inked across Kingston's chest looked especially fierce in the unforgiving light of the bathroom. Ava could see every line and swirl, the artist's expertise apparent in the intricate design. It incorporated the thin scar etched into his skin with such precision that one barely recognized it for what it was, a lion's fang constructed of pale, damaged flesh.

Her gaze fell lower, reading the words inked along his flank. The motto that Kingston fiercely believed in.

Crush~Conquer~Protect

Ava shuddered. So far, he'd done just that when it came to her.

Pivoting away from the sink, she faced Kingston as he stepped out of his trousers and boxers. He stood before her naked. Unabashedly savage in his nudity, his body truly was a work of art with its muscled expanse and taut lines.

And his cock... it jutted toward her. Straining to reach her. Angry and throbbing that it wasn't buried deep inside her.

The pang of lust twisting Ava's stomach became a physical ache. Her nipples tightened at the sight of Kingston's obvious desire, her skin tingling. Even her thoughts were suddenly fuzzy, her common sense popping and fizzling like champagne bubbles. How could he affect her this way? *Why?*

She gripped the towel tighter. *You know why. Stop fighting this and go to him.*

Kingston's eyes darkened, evidence that he knew the thoughts racing through her mind.

"Ava."

His voice was low. Husky. Beguiling. Ava shivered, choking back a whimper when he continued.

"Face the mirror, place your hands on the sink, and arch your back. Ass toward me."

"I don't think— "

He cut her off. "Did I ask you to think? Do it now."

She spun around, thankful for the cloth still covering her nakedness. Their eyes met and clashed again in the mirror's reflection. The same confusing, heart-pounding excitement she experienced following Kingston's commands earlier that day flooded her now.

She hated it. Hated the need that made her body clench with longing. Hated the breathless anticipation for his touch and how easily he sent her tumbling into an ecstatic abyss of sensations. She hated herself for wanting it more than she needed her dignity. Kingston reduced her to a quivering, desperate creature every time he touched her, and Ava now craved that high like a heroin addict seeking a fix.

"Good girl."

His voice rumbled through her, and Ava dropped her head against a wave of lust so powerful it made her weak.

"No, Ava. I want you to see your eyes in that mirror. I want you to see yourself as I see you. Do you understand?" Kingston slid her phone across the countertop as he moved closer, a sinister glint in his blue eyes.

He left the phone beside her hand where she clutched the sink's edge for dear life, her fingers pale and bloodless. Sidling into place behind her, he lifted the edge of the towel up and over her buttocks. "I asked you a question. Do you understand?"

"Yes, but—"

"Wrong answer." His hand, huge and rough and so warm, slapped one ass cheek like a lightning strike.

Ava gasped in shock, lurching forward until Kingston gripped her hips and yanked her back into position he wanted.

"Let's try that again." His whisper was silky, hands gliding over the skin of her hips and buttocks. "Do you *understand* me?"

With a quick tug, the towel fell away and Ava bit back a cry. She'd never felt so exposed. So helpless with desire. She was already wet for him. Her flesh, sore and sensitive before, now throbbed with renewed longing.

Kingston abruptly buried a hand in her damp hair, jerking her head back until Ava had no choice but to meet his expectant gaze in the mirror's reflection. His eyes were completely dark now—the pupils blown wide with hunger.

"I'm waiting, lamb."

"Yes, *sir*. I understand!" The words tumbled out in such a needy cry that Ava bit her bottom lip in anguish.

Kingston's smile was one of delight. It was the Devil's smile. It came out whenever he played with her. Another distressing trickle of moisture dampened the folds of her pussy.

Loosening the grip on her hair, Kingston smoothed greedy, rough hands over the rounded globes of her bottom. "Pick up that phone, Ava."

A sense of doom unfurled along her nerves. "Why?"

"Because you are going to call your *boyfriend*," he growled, "and personally assure him of your safety."

CHAPTER
TEN

T*he stars align*
And the world tilts on its atlas.

AVA GAVE him a look that was nothing short of panic-stricken. Her eyes were already that bright emerald green he recognized when she was aroused, but now apprehension danced in her gaze.

"Call him?" she repeated.

"Yes. Call him, and no matter what I do, you will continue the conversation until I say otherwise."

Her hand shook as she picked up the phone. For a long moment, she simply stared at it then closed her eyes.

"I can't. Please don't make me, Kingston. I don't know what I would even say to him. Drake was never someone I was serious about. Regardless of what you think."

Kingston ran a firm hand down the middle of her back, tracing the line of her delicate spine. "What I think is that you will do what I tell you. If you don't, I'll call him myself so he can hear every filthy thing I'm doing to you. And how much you enjoy it."

Ava made a little noise in the back of her throat, her mouth tight with that humiliating possibility. But she obeyed, scrolling through the few contacts with shaky hands until she found Drake Cornerstone's name. Taking a deep breath, she pushed the button.

"Put him on speaker, Ava. Place the phone on the counter and get your ass back into position."

The sound of the phone ringing filled the room as Ava arched her back. Using his feet, Kingston kicked hers apart as she sucked in a shocked gasp.

On the third ring, a man's voice boomed through the phone's speaker. "Ava? Ava, is that you, sweetheart?"

"Yes, Drake. It's me."

Kingston went down to his knees behind Ava, gripping her hips with both hands, and pulling until her delectable ass was in front of his face. He palmed those perfect globes, squeezing and admiring the imprint of his fingertips while she whimpered in distressed arousal.

"Are you okay? Where are you? Good God, I've been worried sick," Drake spoke in rapid-fire fashion. "We've been trying like hell to get you back home."

"I'm okay," Ava responded in a high, wobbly voice. "Really, I am—*Oh!*"

Her words stuttered into a breathless squeal when Kingston pressed an open-mouth kiss to her pussy, his tongue darting into the sweet wetness. The instant she tried jolting away from him, he growled and jerked her back into place. He began devouring her in earnest, his mouth a pervasive entity that would not cease until he succeeded in wringing an orgasm from her.

And he wanted Drake *Fucking* Cornerstone to hear every second of it.

"Tell me where you are, Ava. I'll come get you," Drake swore vehemently. "I'll bring the FBI. Every state and local policeman I can get hold of. Just let me come get you."

"I'm fine, Drake. Stop pretending you don't already know where I am. And who I'm with." Ava panted softly, gripping the edge of the sink with such force, Kingston thought she might snap her own fingers in half. "*Oh, God.* I am safe, and y-you can stop worrying about me. Stop sending people to bring me back." Her back arched into a perfect half-moon as she rocked back against Kingston's mouth. "I, uh, don't need you to come get me."

"Your brother won't stand for that. Besides, you can't possibly be thinking of staying with Kingston Winter. Fuck, Ava. The man is a certifiable psychopath. A criminal, even if no one's ever managed pinning a charge to him. Come home and we'll forget all about this. Carson says we can work things out between us. Goddamn, I miss you. I was an idiot for letting you get away from me."

Kingston paused in his pleasurable task and nipped the inside of Ava's thigh. A reminder she should continue talking until he decided conversation was no longer necessary.

She yelped, then moaned when Kingston resumed slowly teasing her clit with the tip of his tongue. He groaned, too. Because she smelled like honeysuckles and tasted like peaches. And this obsession with Ava Bella Blue would be his downfall.

"Drake, I'm not coming back. Ever. You need to understand that." She sounded almost normal until Kingston ruthlessly buried his face deeper between her legs. "As for Carson... *God...* my brother has nothing to do with my future. He doesn't control me."

Her legs were shaking, goosebumps visible on the smooth

skin of her ass. With a wicked smile, Kingston mercilessly sucked her clit into his mouth then leaned back just enough to shove a thick finger into her pussy. He didn't care if she was still tender from being fucked earlier. He needed her climax and her cum dripping from his chin.

Ava cried out in soft, helpless surrender, "*Please... please.*"

"Ava? Are you hurt? Is he hurting you right now?" Drake was furiously desperate. "Goddamn it, I'll kill him myself if your brother can't manage it."

Kingston knew Drake heard the sounds Ava made. Fuck, she was sexy trying to keep those moans contained so he wouldn't hear her coming apart. Slowly, he withdrew his finger before plunging it again, harder this time, and hooking it until it made contact with Ava's g-spot.

She let out a low wail, no longer caring that the man she once dated was listening.

Her body contracted around the digit, succumbing to the erotic intensity forced upon her. Speech was impossible for several seconds as an intense orgasm overtook her.

Kingston let out a growl and pushed back between her legs. Her release flooded his mouth, and he relished every moment of it. He lapped at her, sucking her luscious flesh between his teeth, feasting on her juices until she sagged against the countertop.

She was so delirious with satisfaction she ceased responding to Drake's threats.

Kingston finally leaned back, his mouth drifting to the curve of her buttocks. He pressed kisses there, leaving tiny bitemarks in the soft flesh before rising fully to his feet. He was hard as a rock, his dick straining to enter the paradise of Ava's sweet cunt.

"Ava? *Ava?!*" Drake barked in alarm. "Answer me, goddamn it!"

"Mmmm," Ava mumbled in reply. "Can't talk anymore." She deliberately met Kingston's gaze in the mirror with dreamy eyes, her features glowing with pleasure.

She was gorgeous like this. So gorgeous and so sweet that Kingston couldn't resist taking what was his. He slid into her body in one smooth thrust, the sensation taking his breath away for a moment. A moan stuttered in Ava's throat as he clutched her hips in a brutal grip.

"Fuck, Ava. You feel like heaven on my cock," Kingston murmured, and she responded by pitching back against him, her hips rotating to take him even deeper. A muffled hiss escaped her when he slapped one ass cheek, the sound bouncing off the bathroom walls. He did it again to the other, and she let out a strangled cry of pained pleasure. "Don't stop moving your ass. Yeah, keep going, baby. Just like that."

"Ava?" Drake grunted in absolute panic, demanding the obvious. "Is that bastard there with you now?"

Time to end this and get down to enjoying his sweet little prisoner. With one hand, Kingston pushed Ava's head down until their eyes were no longer locked in the mirror and her cheek pressed against the cold granite.

Kingston picked up her phone, continuing to glide in and out of Ava's slick pussy. Switching the call to FaceTime, he strategically angled the camera and waited for Drake to join.

Yes, it was wrong. It was fucking awful, especially without Ava's consent. But so necessary when he was drowning in the murky depths of obsession.

And goddamn, he loved watching his dick plunging into her channel, her firm ass shaking from the violence of his movements.

"Sorry, Cornerstone. Ava can't talk right now." Kingston chuckled, holding the phone high for the perfect bird's eye of the action. All that was visible was the heart-shaped curve of

Ava's ass, her slender waist, and his cock plunging inside her body, but it was enough. Hearing Drake's strangled curse made the moment even more satisfying. "You see, I just ate her sweet, tight pussy like it was my fucking mission in life. While she explained why she isn't going back to Bitter Springs, I feasted until she came all over my face. Now, I'm obviously very busy fucking her senseless. You heard what she said. She's right where she wants to be. Accept that and move on, counselor. Because if you ever try taking her from me, with or without her brother's help, it won't end well. Ava's mine now. And I never share my toys."

Kingston ended the call as Drake sputtered vile threats against his life.

Turning the cell phone completely off, he tossed it back onto the counter and gripped a handful of Ava's hair. He tugged her head back up so he could see her eyes, holding her still so he could fuck her harder, thrilled to know she was witnessing her own destruction.

"Very well done, lamb," he whispered as she accepted every brutal thrust. "I think I'll let you come again as a reward. Would you like that?"

"You didn't tell him I am safe," she accused with a whimper when he forced himself deeper. Her eyes flared with rebellion. "You didn't tell him that you won't hurt me."

She was already coiling around him, her body delighting in the sensations of being filled and used. Hating how he made her feel but still so fucking desperate for it.

Experimentally, he brushed his thumb over the tiny star of her asshole, hauling her back into place when she jolted forward in alarm. His little lamb wasn't ready for that kind of play.

Not yet, anyway.

"Because that would be a lie." Kingston's hand moved to

the middle of her back. Bracing himself, he plunged harder until he was sure he must be hurting her. "You are never safe from me. I *will* hurt you, and in all the ways you desperately need."

A glint of crushed defeat flickered in Ava's gaze as she stared at Kingston. He didn't know why, but that annoying pang of regret once again stabbed the pit of his stomach. Then she dutifully nodded as best she could with the tight grip he had on her hair.

This was exactly what he wanted. Ava's submission. Her obedience. Proving his ownership of this elegant creature had become more important than any sum of money.

But even as he fucked his prisoner to another shuddering climax, and he came so deep and hard inside her that it left him lightheaded, the victory rang hollow.

CHAPTER

ELEVEN

Trading lies for secrets
She'll never keep.
Something in her eyes
Makes me want to believe.

DESPITE HER SILENT fury at the way he treated her early, Ava did not protest when Kingston tumbled her onto the bed and gathered her close. Now, she lay sprawled across his body, her head cushioned by his broad chest while he wound a lock of her hair around his forefinger.

The same finger he used to violate her while she writhed in pleasure.

She was so tired. Her body and mind were fractured and exhausted from the whirlwind of being Kingston's prisoner. Confusion seeped through her veins. How could she enjoy the degradation he lavished upon her? Was she that messed up from her experience with Carson and his friends?

Without conscious thought, Ava chewed a thumbnail, lost in contemplation of her situation.

Kingston reached across with his free hand, capturing her chin and forcing his thumb into her mouth. Tugging her bottom lip down, he rubbed the pad of his thumb across it. "I told you to stop doing that, lamb."

Ava fought the urge to bite him, which of course, he recognized. His mouth curved upward.

"Do it and see what happens," he taunted softly, stroking her lip before dipping his thumb into her mouth. "Go on, wicked little lamb. Bite me, if you dare."

Ava turned her head, dislodging his hold "I don't know what you're talking about. And I'll chew my nails down to the quick if I feel like it. You're not my lord and master."

"Ahhh, but I am. I control every aspect of your life now."

Ava struggled to sit up, but Kingston's muscled arm lay looped around her waist. There was no moving that heavy manacle although she pushed and pulled with furious intent.

"Settle down," he finally grumbled in a low voice. "Unless you enjoy getting me riled up and dealing with what happens when I am."

Ava huffed, the threat of Kingston taking his agitation out on her an effective deterrent. Lying beside him, her body was stiff.

"You're always fighting me, Ava." Disgruntled amusement laced his words.

"You're always giving me a reason," she snapped in response.

A chuckle escaped him. "I suppose that's true enough. It's hard to believe you turned into such a prickly little thing."

"Being kidnapped and assaulted changes a person." Ava's voice shook with unvoiced resentment.

With a sigh, Kingston tugged her closer, his free arm

cradling his head. "It's fascinating to watch the good girl struggle with her darker side. Especially when I know the dark will win out. It's inevitable."

"If that's true, you should be very frightened. I might give you another scar to match the ones you already have," Ava flung at him, her eyes drawn to his chest. It was a reckless threat, but this man had crawled beneath her skin. She could no longer think rationally. Or even carefully.

Kingston's lips twisted. "I'll likely deserve it, too. More so than this one."

Ava eyed the scar in question. It blended perfectly into the tattoo's design, the lion roaring in pain. Or maybe it was triumph. Hard to tell.

"How did you get it?" Anger and self-loathing did not dampen her curiosity. She was even capable of feeling pity for him, depending on the origins of the old wound.

Kingston hesitated, cursing under his breath. "I was sixteen and stupidly defied my father when he gave me a direct order. He decided I would be taught a lesson."

"A lesson?" Ava shifted when his arm loosened from around her waist, but she did not attempt to get away again.

"Yes. He hung me in chains and sliced my chest open with a filet knife. Said if I was going to be a bleeding heart pussy, I should look the part."

Kingston's voice was soft, but Ava felt the tension coiled inside him. Like a snake ready to strike at a threat. Or a lion stalking prey.

"Why would he do that?" Horrified by the confession, Ava wondered how a father could do something so horrible to his own child. "What did he want you to do?"

Kingston's gaze clashed with hers. "Kill the man he believed was screwing my stepmother. I told him I wouldn't do his dirty work, which he didn't take very well."

Ava's stomach lurched as she pictured Kingston hanging in chains. Helpless and wounded so viciously by someone who should have loved him.

Kingston's eyes were hollow. "When he was done, he had Neil stitch me up. And after... I followed his orders."

Ava pushed herself up and peered down at him. "Did you hate yourself for it?"

Kingston shrugged. "Mostly, I was angry that my father succeeded in getting his way. He got what he wanted, and a man innocent of that particular charge died as the result. But he knew that."

A shiver passed over Ava. "Your stepmother wasn't cheating after all?"

"Oh, she was." A thin smile creased Kingston's lips. "But not with the man assigned to guard her."

"How did you know that?"

"Because the man she was fucking was me."

Ava wasn't sure she heard him right. Her heart thumped in her chest so hard she wondered if it was bruising her insides.

He can't mean that. I misunderstood him. I must have...

"I don't understand," she murmured in confusion.

Kingston's eyes were hard as obsidian stone and just as dark. "You heard me, Ava."

Ava said nothing. She couldn't. Not when her mind was whirling from Kingston's revelation.

"My father knew I was in love with Rebecca. He also knew she had seduced me, although she didn't need to try very hard on that account. Ordering me to kill that man was a test. A twisted way of determining if I was worthy of his empire. He wanted proof I could disassociate from my emotions. It was all part of the punishment. The goddamn mind games. I didn't find out until later that he knew all about Rebecca and me. Things only got worse after that." Kingston's voice lowered as old memories were rekindled. The softness of his tone did not make the tale any less repulsive.

"Why are you telling me this?" Anguish and faint disgust colored Ava's voice. She wanted to clamp her hands over her ears and not hear another word. "Why?"

Kingston and his stepmother... they'd had sex. And an innocent man was murdered because of the affair.

Well, probably not so innocent considering the family employing him. But innocent of the false accusations leveled by Alan Winter on a whim.

Kingston gripped Ava by the arms, hauling her body up and over his own. Her naked breasts were smashed against his chest; their faces practically nose to nose. A contemplative expression mixed with relief crossed his face.

"I can't explain why. Especially when I shouldn't trust you. But I know your secrets. Maybe it's only fair you learn a few of my own." His hands slid from her shoulders, capturing her wrists and keeping her imprisoned. "Other than Neil, no one else knows what I just told you, Ava."

"You shouldn't have told me. I don't want to know what you did with your stepmother. Or how many people you killed," Ava replied in a tight voice. "You're up to two now, counting Malcolm."

Kingston's lips curved in a rueful smirk. "Sure. Two."

"Did you murder them?" Horror trickled down Ava's spine. Maybe Kingston was more of a psychopath than anyone realized. Beneath that handsome face and tight muscular body lurked a monster too terrifying to contemplate. A spiderweb of fear etched across her heart. "Your father and stepmother. Did you kill them?"

A flash of disappointment lit Kingston's stormy blue eyes. His jaw clenched, and for a moment, Ava thought he might shake her like a rag doll. Frustration rolled off him in waves and maybe even a little bit of hurt that she would even entertain the thought.

"Other than that unfortunate guard, I've never killed anyone who didn't deserve it, Ava. And while my father's death was a goddamn blessing, I'm not the one who put a bullet between his eyes." Brow slightly furrowed, he carefully considered his next words. "My infatuation paved the way for Rebecca to get what she wanted. A permanent way out of the nightmare my father had created of her life. For months, she begged me for a gun. Said when my father's enemies stormed the house, she would need it. She could defend herself. Protect Oliver. She wouldn't listen when I promised I'd protect them both."

Kingston took a deep breath while Ava held hers. Despite herself, she was held spellbound by the dark story he wove. Sick with realization at the horrors Kingston endured.

"I did what she asked. I got her a gun and I believed her lies right up until the moment she shot him in front of us at the dinner table. She then turned the gun on herself while we sat there in complete shock with my dad's brains splattered over the Waterford crystal. It was worse for Oliver. He was only twelve and already so ruined. We both were. We'd seen women whipped and abused. Fucked and choked until they begged for mercy. And I can't count the number of men tortured by my father and his men. I was one of his monsters in training. Someone he could twist and mold into a reflection of himself. Had Allan Winter lived, Oliver would have been treated the same."

His hands loosened the grip on Ava's arms, and she slumped against him, eyes prickling with hot tears. Not for herself but for *him*. Her heart thumped against his as if in sympathetic commiseration. She tried imagining what it must have been like growing up in that house of horrors. And for the first time ever, Ava understood why Kingston looked up to her father and why he was always around their house. He'd been searching for something... normal.

Suddenly, without her consent or even an understanding of *why*, Kingston's pain was her pain. His torment, hers as well. And Kingston Vaughn Winter *was* tormented, although he concealed it behind an icy façade of dominance and control. Realizing she felt empathy for his upbringing was sobering. During the years her father helped him, she never would have guessed the depraved and violent truth of Kingston's upbringing. The things endured simply because he had the misfortune of being born to a sadistic parent.

"I knew many of those women he brought down to the basement were not there voluntarily. My father dabbled in sex trafficking, and in his opinion, women were objects he could exchange for various favors or sold for profit." Releasing one of Ava's wrists, Kingston smoothed a hand over her hair, brushing wayward strands out of her eyes. A sad smile twisted his lips, his eyes dark with remembered nightmares. "He demanded that I do horrible things to them, always with the threat of harming Rebecca or Oliver if I defied him. Sometimes, I did those things to Rebecca while he watched and directed my actions. It was punishment—for falling in love with something he owned. But in my own fucked up way, I was protecting her. After all, better that the abuse came from my hand rather than my father's."

"I'm sorry, Kingston," Ava's said sadly.

Kingston's hand closed around her throat. He did not squeeze, though. In fact, almost curiously, his grip remained light, almost caressing. As if he simply wished to remind her who was in control. But his eyes blazed, the blue depths so dark and cold that Ava shuddered with foreboding.

"Don't feel sorry for me. I don't want your fucking pity," he snarled softly. "I did some of those things unwillingly, but the darkest, twisted part of my soul also found pleasure in it. I like having a woman gasp and moan my name when I make her come. I love striping sweet little asses like yours with a flogger or even better, my belt. I relish the submission of a beautiful woman, and nothing is more enjoyable than putting her on her knees while I command her. I'm a monster who *needs* those things. They're woven into my very being. Don't even think about romanticizing my past and making me into some goddamn tortured hero who needs a good girl to save him from himself. I'm the bad guy, Ava, with a cruel streak a mile long. Don't *ever* forget that. Do you understand?"

Ava's strangled sob came from deep within her, but she nodded. She could not comprehend how Kingston's confession —his revelation—made her feel. On one hand, her soul ached for her captor. Hurt terribly for the unimaginable horror of his childhood and the way he'd grown up. But her heart also faltered in its beat, consumed with real fear of this man. He was unapologetic in his savage wickedness, his intent plainly stated. He wanted to hurt her. He would enjoy it. He would do what he wanted, regardless of her wishes and the lack of even the most basic consent.

And Ava felt a thrill with the realization of how much she craved it. Her body reacted in the most primal way to his outrageous dominance, her blood roaring like an out-of-control river until it pooled between her thighs and left her damp and aching. Kingston would protect her from other monsters waiting to snatch her in the dark even as he made her suffer for the privilege of security. As long as he wanted her, she was safe. He'd already proven his willingness to kill a man for her sake.

His possessiveness made her insides clench with something that felt an awful lot like satisfaction. Belonging to him meant safety. The unfortunate encounter with the law enforcement sent by her brother highlighted the danger of her situation.

I need Kingston Winter. And like the saying goes, it's better to sit at the right hand of the Devil than to be in his path.

She shifted her legs, remembering what this man had done to her after Detective Redding and Officer Holt departed the estate. How could she forget the way he buried his face between her thighs while her ex listened on the phone? How could she forget how hard she came when he let her fall over the edge?

The tiny frown creasing Kingston's brow melted as a knowing smirk played across his firmly molded lips. He knew what she was feeling. Knew that she wanted him to take and take even while she fought the inevitability of it. Between their bodies, his cock hardened and swelled until it stabbed at Ava's stomach with ruthless lust.

"This is a fucking problem, isn't it?" he inquired with a soft growl.

"What do you mean?" She sounded drunk. Or high, even to her own ears. Felt it, too. Desire sapped away all resistance, and she reveled in the control he exerted over her. She was woozy with the things Kingston made her feel. Addicted to the floaty dreamlike state she tumbled into every time he kissed her.

"This thing between us. This... fucking *need*. It's a goddamn problem. Now that I've had you, I can't get enough. That makes me weak." Kingston's eyes glowed in the room's dim light, desperation lacing the steel of his voice. "*You* make me weak, Ava."

Ava nodded, leaning forward until his rough hand closed more firmly around her throat. Sharp hunger lanced her nerve endings.

It wasn't difficult remembering the plan of remaining submissive to his every demand. She couldn't help herself, anyway. This man touched her, and she melted into a puddle of stupid obedience. "And you make me feel reckless. Wanted. Desired..." She met his gaze with unblinking honesty. "Safe. You make me feel safe, Kingston."

"Safe?" he grunted in surprise, eyes narrowing. "Fuck. That's the last thing you should feel with me. Oh, whatever will I do with you, lamb?" His thumb stroked the underside of her chin

"Anything you want," she whispered. "I don't understand what is between us anymore than you do, but I must pay your price in exchange for your protection."

"You already have that." The admission was gruff as the air thickened and swirled around them, but Kingston released her, gently pushing her away. "I've got business to attend this afternoon, but I'm taking you into the city tomorrow night. Wear something appropriate for dinner at a five-star restaurant."

Ava stared at him as he rolled from the bed. She caught a quick view of his exquisitely carved buttocks and wide, muscular back before he disappeared into the huge walk-in closet. Her nipples contracted into hard buds of desire, throbbing for his touch even though he obviously had no intent on fucking her at that moment.

"And Ava?" Kingston's voice, hard and stern, floated from the closet's depths as she hugged the sheets to her bare chest, willing her body to calm itself. "No underwear. No bra. So, choose your clothing wisely."

CHAPTER

TWELVE

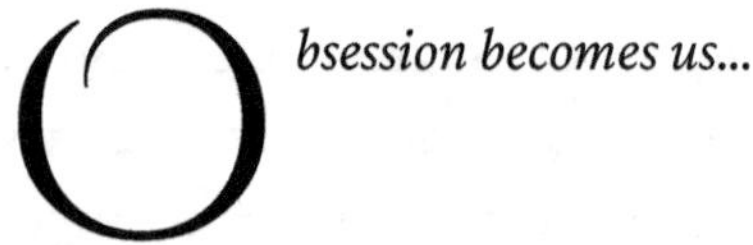

bsession becomes us...

KINGSTON SWALLOWED the bourbon left in the tumbler.

It was his fourth since arriving home almost two hours before. Now, he waited in the spacious, formal living room. Decorated in pristine white and grey tones, it shouted sophistication.

He'd sent word that his little prisoner be ready within the hour, and it was nearing that deadline now.

Maybe she called for help during my absence. Maybe she's doing it right now as I pace back and forth like a nervous asshole going out on a high school date. Will the goddamn Navy Seals break down my doors any minute now, executing an extraction of a live hostage?

Fuck. How much longer would Ava be? And why the fuck had he returned her cell phone to her possession in the first place?

Yesterday, she'd stared at him in mistrust when he tossed it onto the bed.

"You were very convincing when informing Detective Redding of your intention to stay. I especially like the part where you said how much you enjoy my company. And later, when you told Cornerstone that you were never coming back to him, I truly believe you meant it."

Ava had remained quiet while he continued dressing in a dark suit with a smokey grey button-down shirt.

"No harm in letting you have it back now," he had added nonchalantly as she frowned at him, still ignoring the phone.

Which was a lie. He was a complete idiot for giving her that cell phone. He might as well have handed over a loaded gun and watched while she blazed her way out of The Den.

Lifting the decanter, he was pouring another when the sharp click of high heels on the marble floor outside the double doors signaled Ava's arrival. He heard her soft murmur as she thanked Paulie for his escort. A second later, she slipped into the room.

Every nerve in Kingston's body popped off like fireworks at the sight of her.

Framed by the intricately carved doors imported from Turkey, she was an absolute vision in a silvery blue slip dress with a small silver purse clutched in her hands. The garment's shimmery strands were subtle but eye-catching, turning her eyes a darker shade of green. To balance the dramatic dress, she'd swiped her lips with a sheer pink color that made Kingston desperate to bite them until they turned blood red from the pressure of his teeth.

He set the decanter down on the bar, leaving the glass of bourbon beside it. Sauntering toward her, he came to a halt in the room's center.

His gaze slid over her body and the dress she wore. The

garment ended around mid-thigh, accentuating the length of her legs, as did the delicate silver heels she wore. A wrap constructed of sheer, gauzy material dangled from the crook of one arm. She looked ethereal. Elegant. Confident yet scared.

Scared of him.

And Kingston suddenly, inexplicably, didn't want that. At least, not at that moment.

"You didn't say if we were dining at a five-star burger joint or something more refined." Ava's jaw tilted as she walked toward him. Then she was gliding past, her shoulder brushing his. The soft scent of honeysuckles drifted in her wake, and Kingston watched in faint amusement as she continued until she reached the bar.

With her back to him, she lifted his abandoned glass of bourbon. "Do you mind?"

Kingston smiled. "Not at all." He could not tear his gaze away from the expanse of skin exposed by the dress's design. Her entire back was bare from the draping cowl and the way she'd twisted her hair into an intricate bun at the nape of her neck. As he demanded, she wore no bra.

With one quick swallow, Ava downed the glass's contents before turning to face him. Her eyes were bright with challenge, her cheeks flushed pink from the bourbon's heat.

"I'm ready to go, sir," she ground out.

"In a second. Let me look at you first." Taking her hand, Kingston pulled her forward. "You are stunning." It'd only been a day since he'd seen her but it felt like a century.

"Thank you. I assume I'm dressed appropriately?"

"Very." Kingston's gaze touched the small silver purse clutched in her hand. "Where's your cell?"

Ava's mouth tightened. "It wouldn't fit. I've been without it this long, what's one more night? Besides, in my current situation, it's an unnecessary piece of technology."

"I gave you permission to use it."

"I don't require your permission to use my own phone," she bristled, eyes flashing fire.

"You're right." Kingston chuckled. "At the moment, you don't. But remember, privileges may always be revoked at my discretion." Releasing her hand, he curled an arm about her waist. As her sweet scent drifted into his nostrils, his eyes closed in delight.

"You always smell so delicious, Ava," he hummed. "Like a forbidden treat waiting to be devoured."

Ava's responsive shiver was a tempting invitation, but Kingston resisted with an apologetic sigh. A second later, his cell phone buzzed with the notification that their car was ready for the short journey to the private airstrip.

"Come along, Ava. Time to show the world that you are mine."

Kingston sat on one side of the limo, arms stretched along the back of the cushion, legs sprawled in the open floor space before him.

Ava was perched on the opposite seat, hands clasped primly in her lap, the silvery wrap shielding her bare back from the cold leather. She kept her gaze trained on the tinted window although it was too dark to see the landscape flashing by.

"Are you cold?"

His question caused her to noticeably jump. She adjusted her position with a shake of her head.

"You look cold," Kingston continued. "Shall I have Jack turn the heat up? That wrap doesn't offer much protection from the chill."

Ava's eyes darted to the smoky black opaque glass separating the limo's interior from the front cab. "It's fine." She pulled the material closer around her chest and finally met his gaze.

"Stubborn little lamb," Kingston sighed in recognition of her strange mood. "Are you sore? In pain?"

The pointed questions had Ava squirming on the seat, her lips a tight line of censure. "No more than should be expected."

Kingston patted the seat beside him. "Come here, Ava."

She shot him an exasperated look. "Why?"

"Because I command it."

A flash of disappointment lit the forest-green depths of her eyes. "That's not a good enough reason, Kingston."

"Forgetting your place already, lamb?" The slow drawl of his voice was a warning, but Ava was too agitated to pay it any heed.

"How can I?" she scoffed. "You remind me of my imprisonment every chance you get."

Kingston smiled. "Have you found no pleasure in it, Ava? Even when I made you bleed, you still came on my cock and cried out my name."

"Stop!" She clapped her hands over her ears before gaining control of herself. Her hands lowered to her lap, fingers twisting together. "No matter how safe I might be with you, it's not right that you are deliberately cruel."

"Cruelty is the way of the world, sweetheart." Kingston shrugged. "With Carson for a brother, you should know that."

Her gaze was accusing. "My parents shielded me as best they could. You know that. But they loved Carson. They could never see him for what he was, the awful things he did. And I never wanted them to know. Especially the worst of it."

"Carson wouldn't have been able to hide his true nature forever. It would have come to a head, eventually."

Ava's features transformed into an expression of cunning watchfulness. "I've given you everything. Everything you demanded. Everything you are owed by my brother is being paid with *my* body. My tears. My blood. When will you tell me what you know about my parents' deaths? When will you honor *your* promise?"

Kingston regarded her silently, weighing her words. The information he'd gathered was still in the process of being verified although deep down inside, he already knew the truth. But could he shatter this girl even further without ironclad proof?

"I will. When the time is right," he conceded after an extended pause. "Now's not the right time."

"When?" Ava snapped in frustration. "When I've reached the end of my usefulness? When you no longer want me, and I'm left broken and battered? I guess it never occurred to you that I might want my own form of retribution if your accusations are truthful."

Her temper amused him, but Ava was right. She deserved the chance to seek her own revenge. Even if placing her in that kind of danger would never be allowed.

"Tell me, Ava. What becomes of your inheritance if something happens to you?" Kingston asked quietly.

Ava's brow furrowed at the conversation's unexpected shift. "I suppose Carson would naturally receive my half of the funds provided in my parents' will."

Kingston smiled. "Selling his little sister into slavery, having her declared dead at some point, with or without a body, gives him not only a small fortune from that misdeed, but her inheritance as well. An inheritance that was most likely murderously obtained to begin with."

Ava bit her bottom lip, glaring at Kingston even as she

leaned toward him. "You truly believe Carson murdered my mom and dad?"

Kingston's gaze remained steady and fixed on Ava. The last thing he wanted was for her to fall apart in hysterics. "I believe it's a strong possibility, and it's likely he paid someone to handle the messy details. You are in more danger than you can comprehend, Ava, if that is true. Because he needs your death to get what he wants. Money. All of it. And you out of his way."

"Why hasn't he acted before now? Why not kill me when he had the chance in Bitter Springs?" Ava asked. "Why wait years to put this nefarious plan into action?"

"Because I suspect he needs distance between the two of you for that plan to work. It would be too suspicious if he lost both parents and a sister close together and so close to home. Once he sold you to the highest bidder, I think he would have you declared dead as soon as it was legally possible. I fucked up those plans by taking you first. Now that you've lost value as a virgin, he'll look for a man willing to pay for your beauty and the privilege of destroying that beauty."

The limo slowed as they approached the small airport where Kingston's private jet was kept.

Ava turned her head, focusing on the runway lamps glowing in the darkness. The jet's lights outlined its sleek shape as they drove directly onto a section of the tarmac and up alongside the aircraft.

"Where are you taking me?" She could not hide the shaky timbre of her voice.

Did she think he was sending her to her doom? Maybe to a mystery buyer residing out of the country? Or transported to a place where no one would ever find her or even think to look for her?

Ava glanced down at her form, dressed so alluringly at his instruction. Kingston saw her fear as it boiled and grew. He abandoned their discussion of Carson and his greed for the moment.

"I told you. To dinner." He wanted to draw her into his lap and reassure her that she was safe but she was too fragile for that right now. "My restaurant, CRUSH, occupies the only floor in the building open to the public other than the club downstairs."

"We're flying to New York City?" Ava breathed. "Just for dinner and nothing more?"

"We may stay the night in the penthouse, depending on how our evening goes." Kingston smiled as the car came to a halt. The husky promise in his voice had Ava squeezing her thighs together, a look of aroused panic flashing across her features.

"But I've packed nothing," she frowned, turning the tiny silver purse over and over in her hands. "This barely holds a tube of lipstick."

Kingston's lips twitched. "I'll provide everything you need, Ava."

In the distance, car doors slammed shut just before the ones to the limo's interior flung open. Kingston climbed out first, dismissing Jack's assistance before turning back to the vehicle. His large hand extended, waiting to take possession of Ava's smaller one.

Drawing her from the limo's depths, he tucked her hand into his arm and nodded up at the jet's black-carpeted steps. "I hope you tolerate flying. The last time you flew on this jet, well, let's just say you were incapacitated."

"Drugged, you mean," Ava shot back while admiring the shiny white jet. "And at your brother's mercy." A tiny shiver ran through her body as Kingston urged her up the steps. He stayed close behind her, protectively shielding her from the chilly breeze with his own body.

Her words gave him pause though. He didn't want to think of those hours when Oliver held control over his little prisoner. How easy it would have been for his half-brother to touch her however he pleased. The possibility left Kingston's skin feeling extra tight and hot. As if tiny volcanoes were waiting to erupt just below the surface.

"Good evening, Mister Winter." The pilot greeted them both as they ducked through the jet's threshold.

"Hello, Granger." Kingston shook the older man's hand. "You remember Miss Blue?"

The man had the decency to flush, but otherwise, his demeanor remained so warmly professional no one would have guessed he was part of Ava's abduction.

"I hope you enjoy the flight this evening, Miss Blue. The weather is perfect, and we should have no issues on the ninety-minute flight into the city."

Ava's cheeks suffused with pink as she nodded at the pilot, but storm clouds darkened her brow. "I'm sure being conscious this time will result in a whole different experience, Mister Granger."

Kingston bit the inside of his cheek, containing his grin as Granger looked appropriately chastised. Ava's feisty outrage made him want to kiss her until she was breathless.

"Yes, miss," Granger said. "My deepest apologies."

Kingston gripped Ava's elbow in amused warning. "Captain Granger simply follows orders, Ava. *My* orders, to be exact. He provides the services I require." Giving the pilot a small nod, he said, "Thank you, Granger. Our plans are dinner and some time spent at LIST. We may not fly back tonight. Jack will let you know for certain, but for now, you may take off as soon as possible with clearance."

"Very good, sir." Granger tipped his pilot's cap to Ava. "Miss."

"Let's get you settled, Ava," Kingston murmured as he maneuvered her through the galley and the crew's area. "Jack? Stay here."

"Sure thing, boss." Jack grinned, giving a flirty wink to the attractive stewardess waiting there.

At the doorway leading to the jet's main cabin area, Ava abruptly halted. "This can't be real," she muttered, taking in the sleek and stylized design of the interior.

The living room-like space contained curved leather couches crafted of expensive white leather and individual chairs surrounding a futuristic coffee table. A line of tiny rope lights traveled around the ceiling, which had its own illumination and highlighted a swirling masterpiece of blues, greys, pink, and soft yellow. It looked like a dramatic, artistic impression of the sky at sunset.

A built-in desk occupied one corner, constructed of the same material as the coffee table and mimicking the curved lines. A large flat screen hung on the wall, and below it was a wet bar. Beyond that was a wall with a single door leading to yet another section of the jet.

The opulence was staggering, and Ava looked a little weak as Kingston settled her in one of the high-backed chairs and fastened her seatbelt.

Flopping onto the seat beside her, he buckled in as well. "You seem surprised by our transportation."

Ava shot him a glance. "This jet must have cost a fortune."

Kingston grimaced. "It did. And does. My crew is on standby twenty-four hours a day. That sort of readiness does not come cheap."

"I don't like flying." Ava gripped the cushioned armrests. "In fact, I hate it. The idea of being this tiny speck in a vast openness where anything could happen. Like, a black hole opens up and we're sucked into it. An emergency landing in a field of dairy cows. A wing falls off during a storm and the pilot is incapacitated with fear. The unknown makes my anxiety run rampant. It's terrifying."

Kingston reached over and threaded his fingers with hers. "It'll be okay, lamb." He squeezed until she looked at him. "No one dares disappoint me and this situation is no different. You're safe, or I'll have the head of whoever jeopardizes that."

A sad smile curved Ava's lips. "Why should you even care?"

"Because you're mine and I protect what's mine. No matter the threat." When her eyes widened at his fierce response, Kingston realized how much he liked the idea of Ava being his forever.

"Ready for take-off, Mister Winter," Captain Granger announced via the speaker system.

Using his forefinger, Kingston tipped Ava's face toward his. "I'm right here, lamb. When you are frightened, just squeeze my hand as hard as you like. Dig in your nails if you must. The alternative is giving you a reason to forget you are even on a plane."

"How would you accomplish that?"

"By fucking you senseless."

Ava's chin trembled the slightest bit as the jet began its taxi down the runway. Closing her eyes, she tightened her hand around his and said in a soft murmur, "I'll be fine. But if I begin hyperventilating, I'm sure you'll do whatever you think is best."

CHAPTER

THIRTEEN

*F*ollow me into the fire,
    Burn with me until we are but cinders.

AVA TOOK a deep breath as the jet leveled off. When a melodic ding indicated their seatbelts could be removed, she reluctantly untangled her hand from Kingston's and released the latch.

Now that they were in the air, classical music played over the cabin's speakers. It was soothing, with no lyrics to decipher or hidden meanings to figure out. Just the soft, lilting sounds of violins and pianos.

Ava nervously shifted on the leather seat and glanced about the cabin. It was luxurious in a way that was suited for royalty.

"Was this your father's?" she asked suddenly.

Kingston shook his head. "I sold his when I took over the business. This is mine."

"The business," Ava slowly repeated. "What precisely does "the business" consist of? Other than your philanthropic effort of rescuing abused women and running a sex club."

Kingston flashed a smile. "I explained before how LIST operates. Mutual experiences for like-minded adults in a consensual setting. There's nothing lurid about it or its members. Just an exchange of pleasure."

Ava clutched her wrap closer to her body. "Do you... ah... do you visit it often?"

"Only when I'm in the city. I stay apprised of any issues that occur. Of course, I also personally approve membership requests."

"I suppose women from there visit you at The Den?" She didn't know why it mattered, but it suddenly did. Her chest was tight as she questioned Kingston, but to his credit, he *was* answering her.

"Sometimes," he drawled. "Although I've not had another woman since the day Oliver dropped you in my lap."

Why does that please me? Why does the thought of his self-restraint make my insides tremble? It shouldn't, especially when I've no idea if it is the truth. He tells me what I wish to hear. Whether it is intended to make me more obedient, or simply for his own amusement, I have no idea.

"What else do you do?" she questioned bravely as he slowly swiveled his chair back and forth in a languid manner. With an elbow on the armrest and his chin cupped within his hand, he watched her with dark eyes and a wicked curve to his mouth.

"You know what I do, lamb. I loan money to foolish men and collect double what they owe. If man doesn't pay his debt, I take everything he has."

She should stifle her curiosity, but Ava couldn't help

herself. He was patiently answering her questions, treating her with gentle concern. And gentle was not a word normally used when describing a man such as Kingston.

Amicable.

He was being amicable, but it was much more than that.

It was the way he looked at her. How he held her hand during take-off, as though he could somehow erase her irrational fear. There was an implied intimacy when it came to holding hands. It was a declaration of belonging. Of comforting one another. Holding hands existed on a different level. It spoke of affection and caring. It meant more than kissing. More than sex.

People in relationships held hands all the time. It was just something that couples naturally did.

She didn't want him holding her hand. The simple act was a lie. One she wanted no part of.

"But what else?" Ava's voice wavered with awareness of the subtle shift in their situation. Did he feel it, too? This sense of belonging. Of fate. Of lives entangled until the end of eternity with no end to this captivity.

Leaping to her feet, she began pacing, suddenly terrified at what she was feeling.

Kingston reclined in his chair, watching her nervous burst of energy. "I've business ventures and investments all over the world, Ava. Some are legitimate, others, not so much. If you want to know whether I traffic women or children, I don't. I don't deal drugs, although the nature of this business makes it a factor in certain dealings with associates. My father was heavily involved in such criminal behavior. My way of doing business is very different."

If she wasn't so scared of plummeting to her death, Ava would have considered flinging open an emergency door and leaping from the plane. Everything felt as though it were crowding around her. Suffocating her until she could hardly breathe. "You would have sold me to the highest bidder, Kingston. *You* were willing to auction off my virginity to pay Carson's debt. How do you explain that?"

"I never said I was different in *everything*, lamb. Although, if it makes you feel better, I probably wouldn't have gone through with the auction."

"Don't tell me you've developed a conscience," Ava mocked. "Don't tell me you grew a heart after you planned on selling me and profiting off your crime. You would have handed me over to anyone with the right amount of cash."

"Oh, I haven't a heart, lamb." Kingston's smile was dark. "Lucky for you I changed my mind about the auction. And as you can see by your current position, I *couldn't* let you go once I fucked you. I told you before, Miss Blue, I'm not a good man. Thinking that I'll suddenly sprout wings and a fucking halo while professing undying love simply because I enjoy your sweet cunt squeezing my cock would be very foolish."

Ava's mouth tightened into a hard line, dismayed by his crudeness. "I'm not stupid, Kingston. Monsters don't fall in love with their victims. They devour until there's nothing left and move on to the next unfortunate person."

A gleam sparked in Kingston's dark gaze. "When the offering is as goddamn delicious as you, it is rather hard to resist."

A discreet knock on the privacy panel door interrupted whatever Ava might have said in response. The door slid open, and the attractive brunette stewardess popped her head into the opening.

"Would you care for refreshments, Mister Winter? The Dom Perignon is perfectly chilled."

The brunette's faintly accented voice was sweet as honey

and cloyingly solicitous. Ava's gaze narrowed on the young woman who gave her a simpering smile. The claustrophobia from just moments before eased away with this new distraction. But how sick was it that the implied threat of another woman was enough to change her headspace? The dizzying ups and downs was making her think she was schizophrenic.

"That would be wonderful, Monique." Kingston smiled the young woman. "Two glasses, please."

"Of course." Monique ducked into the crew's galley. A few minutes later came the dull thump of a cork being popped. When the stewardess reappeared, she carried a silver tray with two exquisite crystal flutes balanced upon it. "Here you go, sir."

The seductive way Monique uttered the word *'sir'* had Ava clenching her teeth. The stewardess offered one flute to Kingston with a sweet smile and a lingering brush of her hand.

Ava wondered if she could get away with dumping a glass over the woman's head.

Monique handed Ava the second flute with a smile not nearly as friendly as the one she gave Kingston. "Miss."

Kingston motioned toward the back of the jet. "There's quite a bit more to see, Ava."

Ava sipped the champagne, wrinkling her nose at the bubbles when they tickled. The only area left was probably a sleeping area of some sort and a private bath. She definitely did not need to see that. "I'm good here. Thanks."

His brow lifted slightly as if he could not believe her refusal. "Come with me, Ava." Grabbing her free hand, he tugged her toward the sliding door.

"Let me go," Ava demanded, the champagne sloshing over the rim of the flute as she tried twisting out of his grip. She wanted to dash the beverage in his handsome, smug face but lacked the courage.

"Must I remind you of our contract, lamb?" Annoyance

darkened Kingston's features as his hand tightened around her fingers. The next moment, the jet hit a pocket of turbulence, sending Ava jostling against him. Champagne soaked the front of his suit.

"Now look what you've done!" Monique scolded Ava, her tone one of scandalized shock. Taking their flutes, she set them down in a secure area and *tsked* at Kingston. "Sir, let's get you out of that coat."

Unscathed by the spill, Ava retreated while the stewardess bustled between them, dabbing at the wet spots on Kingston's coat with a white cloth. Rubbing the broad expanse of his chest, Monique stared up at him with an inviting smile stretching her pouty lips.

Ava rolled her eyes at the woman's painfully obvious tactics even as a perplexing mixture of hatred and jealousy suffused her veins. She watched the stewardess fuss over her captor. Oh, how she wanted to dive onto the girl and pummel that perfect face with her fists. Yank all the shiny, brunette hair out from Monique's scalp and scratch the smooth planes of those alabaster cheeks until they bled.

The depth of such emotions, the overwhelming sense that Monique touched something that was *hers*, made Ava dizzy. She shouldn't feel this way, much less harbor an intense desire to act upon her urges. It was beyond sick. It was twisted and wrong. Kingston did not belong to her, and she didn't belong to him, and yet...

And yet... she *was* his. He vowed he had no use for other women during this damnable arrangement. Was it unreasonable to expect him to stand by his word?

Kingston's gaze clashed with Ava's, a glint of smugness lurking in the dark blue depths. He was fully aware of the disturbing turmoil surging through her body and her confusion on how to handle it.

"Thank you, Monique."

"Of course, sir," the stewardess purred.

Monique sashayed into the dark area beyond the sliding doors. A second later, soft light illuminated the space. The edge of a platform bed was visible through the doorway, and Ava could see the ceiling with its curving lines illuminated by ambient lights in a soft, pleasing blue. The room glowed with luxury. It screamed of sensual nights and languid days spent flying around a world where Kingston Winter ruled everything and accepted adulation from dozens of stewardesses just like Monique.

Kingston followed Monique into the room while Ava stayed behind and listened. She heard the whisk of another door opening and closing, fabric rustling and soft murmurs. Then... Kingston's low chuckle and Monique's breathy giggle. Ava's hands clenched tight.

I don't care.

She really didn't. Why should she? Did it matter if the man slept with a hundred women like Monique? Did it matter the stewardess was probably smoothing her hands over his bare chest at that very moment? She did not care if Kingston's perfect lips explored that woman's mouth. Her neck. Her breasts.

Ava did not care that her own heart thumped so rapidly inside her chest that it burned.

No. She did *not* care. But she also would not accept this intentional humiliation. She wouldn't be his plaything, tossed aside whenever he was displeased with her. She, Ava Bella Blue, was worth two point six million to Kingston Winter, and that was a damn sight more than Perfect Stewardess Monique and her alluring French accent.

Ava stalked toward the room, slinging the door open wide and just in time, too.

Monique was sliding her hands over the fabric of a new suit coat Kingston now wore. Glancing back at Ava, the other woman's eyebrow lifted at the intrusion. A haughty smile spread across her pretty features.

Kingston's face morphed from boredom into amused satisfaction. Eyes twinkling with devilish delight, he simply watched the two women as Ava focused on Monique. An unfamiliar emotion suffused her, a bewildering cocktail of rage and envy. It made her almost feral with possessiveness, and that was probably the most surprising thing about it. That she would experience intense jealousy at the thought of another woman touching Kingston.

"Remove your hands from Mister Winter right now," Ava said in a tone laced with violence. "Or I'll remove them myself."

The corner of Kingston's mouth twitched. "Miss Blue, you forget your place. I give the orders on this jet, and I will not tolerate animosity toward my employees. Approach the bed, if you please. I want you on your knees, back straight, head lowered, and hands resting on your thighs, palms up."

The casualness of Kingston's command shocked Ava. His tone was the same as though he were simply placing an order for his favorite coffee. He couldn't mean it... especially not in front of Monique.

The stewardess's smugness evaporated, her dark brown eyes flashing with envy as she glared at Ava.

The snap of Kingston's fingers woke Ava from her state of shock. "Now, Miss Blue."

Angry frustration swelled within her until she feared it would explode in streams of scarlet-hued ribbons. "Fuck you," she snarled. "I'll do no such thing. I'm not a dog you can command to obey."

Monique's perfect red lips rounded in an "oh" of shock.

Apparently, no one dared speak with such blunt animosity to Kingston Vaughn Winter.

But Kingston merely sighed—the long-suffering sound reminding Ava how dangerous this man could be when faced with disappointment. The last person who'd done so ended up in a body bag, disposed of without a shred of remorse.

"Monique, please see to it that my coat is dry-cleaned by tomorrow morning." Kingston calmly ignored Ava's heated outburst.

"Of course, Mister Winter." Monique's gaze slid away from Ava while she continued leaning into Kingston. With unnecessary care, she straightened his tie, smoothing a hand down its length until her red-tipped fingernails ghosted over his belt buckle. "May I do anything else for you, sir? I'm here to attend to your every need, after all."

Ava's stomach twisted with abrupt nausea. Kingston must have slept with Monique in the past. After all, he certainly appeared comfortable with her flirtatious attention. So comfortable, in fact, he failed responding to Ava's foolishly bold words.

Instead, his head dipped until he and Monique shared an exchange of breath. The stewardess swayed, clearly enthralled by Kingston's close proximity.

Would he kiss this woman... right in front of her and with no regard for her rioting emotions? Ava swallowed past the sour taste in her mouth as Kingston's lips hovered over Monique's full red ones.

Then he pulled away while Ava's ridiculous, infuriating sob of relief hung in her throat.

"That will be all, Monique. Miss Blue and I are not to be disturbed for the remainder of the flight."

Monique's lips thinned with disappointment at the curt

dismissal, but she nodded. Snatching up the soiled suit coat, she hurried out of the cabin.

Once the door slid shut, Kingston reached for Ava's arm, hauling her against his hard form. The gauzy wrap was flung aside, leaving her arms bare.

"Is this jealousy I detect, lamb?"

She glared up at him. "If you want to sleep with her—"

"I'm not interested in fucking anyone other than you, Ava," he grumbled, crushing her closer. "And while this little display warms my heart, I expect you to obey my commands."

Ava's eyes filled with helpless, angry tears. "I *won't*! Not like that. Not in front of a woman who wants you so very badly. I won't let you humiliate me like that."

"Humiliate you?" Kingston's head tilted. "Oh, sweet little lamb. You've got it all wrong." His voice softened, the air growing heavy and thick as he tucked a stray tendril of hair behind her ear. Cupping her chin in the palm of his hand, he forced her to meet his gaze. "My ownership is something you should covet. Monique, and others like her, would gladly trade places with you. I need only to snap my fingers to make it happen. However, it is not her obedience I crave. It is yours. And I *will* have it."

Ava steeled herself, hating his arrogance, remembering submission meant a quick exit from this nightmare. Compliance would bore him. Her resistance only excited him more.

"I'm sorry, sir," she murmured, carefully interjecting the right amount of remorse in her tone.

Kingston's gaze darkened. "I realize this is an unfamiliar situation for you, Ava. You are inexperienced, but my intention is to exercise patience as I teach you. Well, as much patience as I can manage, anyway." His hand slid from her chin until it cupped the back of her neck. "But my leniency has been sorely tested tonight. You must be punished for your willfulness."

Ava's heart skipped a beat, thudding with apprehension and regret for her hasty, thoughtless behavior.

"Punished?" she repeated with a slow blink. "You will spank me again?"

Kingston shook his head. "I'm afraid you've earned more than that."

CHAPTER

FOURTEEN

So completely you take me.
So fiercely.
Like a fire consuming all in its path.

KINGSTON WATCHED as the subtle threat sunk in. Ava's breathing increased, her eyes dilating with alarm. But a spark of reluctant arousal also lurked in the green depths of her gaze. His words were beginning to intrigue her more than they frightened her.

"What do you have in mind?" His defiant girl huffed out a derisive laugh. "Will you send me to bed with no supper?"

"Oh, you'll end up in a bed. Eventually," Kingston drawled.

Ava shrugged. "I said I was sorry. It's just that... that *woman*..."

"Is none of your concern," he sternly interrupted. "Your greatest worry right now should be focused on how I will deal with this transgression."

Ava regarded him warily. "What do you mean to do?"

"I want to see how well you obey me. You do want to obey me, don't you, Ava? Remember, my protection comes with a price."

Her chin lifted higher at his taunting. "You said you wouldn't hurt me."

The way she trembled reminded Kingston how much he wanted to wrap her up in his arms and hold her tight. There was no understanding the conflicting emotions warring inside him. This dual urge to both protect Ava and fuck her until she cried out his name in helpless abandonment was maddening.

"I won't hurt you in the manner you are imagining right now." Kingston trailed his finger over her collarbone.

"What do you want me to do?" Ava's words were drenched in surrender.

Releasing her, Kingston moved to sit on the platform bed. The small distance between their bodies made it easier to think more clearly. "Get on your knees, lamb."

Ava bit her bottom lip at the softly spoken command, but she gracefully sank to the floor. Whether subconsciously or because she sincerely wished to appease him, she arranged herself in the manner he'd previously demanded. But she failed in lowering her head in obedience. Instead, she glared at Kingston with such heated ferocity he could not help the chuckle rising in his chest.

"Your atrocious attitude needs work, lamb, but for the moment you've pleased me."

Cheeks flushed pink from the unexpected praise, she shifted her body in a futile attempt to keep the short dress from riding any higher on her bare thighs.

"Be still, Ava."

The sharpness of the correction snapped her into something resembling a statute of golden marble. She still refused to bow her head. After several seconds passed and she remained completely motionless, Kingston snapped his fingers. The sound echoed like cannon fire over the low hum of the jet's engines and the soft music.

"Down on all fours, little lamb. Crawl to me."

If it were possible, Ava stiffened even more. Her eyes narrowed, glittering with resentment and confusion as to why he would request such a thing of her. Just when he thought she would refuse, Ava surprised him once again. Locking her gaze with his, she bent over and placed her hands on the soft carpet.

Fuck, she's beautiful.

Like a feral lioness, Ava slowly moved toward him, green eyes glowing with something indefinable. She was a gorgeous creature hunting her prey, and Kingston wondered if she had any idea just how much power she held in that moment. She was crushing him in the palm of her tiny hand and didn't even know it.

From the slightly elevated position of the bed, he could see the roundness of her perfect ass as she crawled. It swayed back and forth with her movements, and Kingston nearly groaned out loud. He couldn't stop thinking of when he'd fucked her that second time in his bathroom. How he bent her over the vanity and watched those round, firm globes quiver with every thrust of his hips.

His dick swelled to impossible proportions, remembering the desperate way she moaned while he took what he wanted. How she cried during the orgasms he gave her. Goddamn if he didn't want to shove himself between her thighs and make her come again.

But he wouldn't. After all, a punishment was a punishment.

Upon reaching the tip of his black Ferragamos, Ava hesitated, a flash of uncertainty darkening her features. But like a good little lamb, she remained on all fours and waited for his instructions.

His gorgeous little pet. So desperate for attention. So needy for the dominance and control only he could give her.

"Stand up."

With the same gracefulness exhibited while crawling like a slave, Ava rose to her feet. She swayed with the motion of the aircraft, balancing precariously on those fuck-me stilettos until she was once again steady.

"Drape yourself over my lap."

Her lips parted, no doubt intent on refusing the direct order, but Kingston's eyebrow rose high, daring her to defy him.

Letting out a brazen huff of irritation, Ava did as commanded. Her hands automatically gripped his leg, fingers digging into the fabric of his trousers.

"Both hands flat on the floor, lamb."

Once she was arranged to his liking, Kingston lifted the hem of her dress. Ignoring her muffled gasp, he bunched the material at her narrow waist. The draping cowl of the dress's back exposed her shoulder blades. Her spine. The sweet hollow of her lower back.

His gaze drifted down, tracing her bare thighs and the curve of her perfect ass and the thong she wore. While the sight of black silk against the smooth paleness of her buttocks was erotically gorgeous, she had deliberately disobeyed his specific order.

Kingston ran a finger under the thin band hugging the dip of her back, pulled it tight, then released it so the material snapped back into place. A strangled moan escaped Ava's throat as the undergarment agitated the tender flesh of her pussy.

"What's this?" His question was softly dangerous.

Ava shifted, the heat of her body searing his thighs through his trousers. "Underwear. Obviously."

The abrupt smack of his hand on her bare bottom jolted her forward. Biting back a strangled cry, she quickly readjusted herself until she was back in position.

"I see that." Kingston smoothed a palm over the red mark left behind on her creamy skin. "Why are you wearing it?"

"Because that's what *normal* people do."

Kingston's lips tilted in a grin at the sarcastic rebellion of her tone. Good thing she couldn't see how much she amused him, otherwise her power might swell to unmanageable proportions. He slapped her ass again over the same spot and much harder than before.

Ava sucked in a breath, clenching her buttocks against the radiating pain. She reached back a hand in anticipation of the next strike, but Kingston caught it.

"Give me the other," he said calmly, pinning her wrist tight in the small of her back. When she refused, he lifted her arm higher toward the middle of her spine. She cried out, a little sob that made his dick hard, but he simply waited until she finally obeyed.

Now, he had her effectively restrained, her lithe body quivering across his lap and both wrists captured in his large hand. "Stop defying me, Ava. You won't win."

"I can't help it." She adjusted her weight, pressing her thighs together as if that would dissuade him. "You-you just can't do whatever you want."

"Watch me, lamb." Kingston's amusement melted into something darker. "Don't close yourself off to me. Spread your legs."

"Go fuck yourself."

Goddamn, she was fucking adorable. Her defiant snarl dissolved into a squeal when Kingston rapidly delivered three consecutive strikes to her bottom. Then his fingers were between her legs, shoving past the flimsy barrier of the thong while she squirmed and panted.

"Be still. Let me touch you." His admonishment whispered against her ear as he skimmed the soft skin of her pussy with a callused index finger. "I know you don't hate this as much as you let on. You're soaking wet for me, baby." With deliberate intent, he teased her opening, dipping in shallow exploration while gliding the pad of his forefinger over the tiny bud of her clit.

"Kingston…"

His name passed Ava's lips in a breathy sigh. The tension in her body eased as he continued softly petting her.

"Do you know what edging is, Ava?" He eased a single finger inside her, waiting for her response. When it did not come, he added a second digit. She was so goddamn tight. Again, he wondered if she was sore from how ruthlessly he'd fucked her the day before.

"Answer me. Do you know what edging is?" Pumping his fingers in a shallow motion, his thumb insistently rubbed the tiny button of nerves.

"N-no," she stuttered, her breath coming in gasps. Her legs helplessly fell further apart, granting him easier access. When her head dropped lower, it was not in submission but something that reeked of defeat.

Kingston hated it.

He would have her fear. Her submission. But damned if he could accept abject surrender.

Pressing deeper, his fingers twisted until they found that perfect spot. The one that made her breath catch and her hips twitch in agonized delight.

"Please…" Ava breathed in despair. "I need you."

"There's my bad girl," Kingston crooned, giving her what

she wanted, what she begged for. "You might be sore from my cock, but you still want this. Want me to make you come. As much as you hate me, you still want *this,* don't you?"

"Yes. Yes." Ava writhed on his lap, her fingers clenching and unclenching in unison with his own as they moved inside her.

"Beg me."

She let out a little sob of disbelief, her hips rocking with the motion of his fingers. "Please, Kingston. Damn you. Please...let me come."

"I'm going to explain some things to you, Ava. I want you to listen very carefully since you are so very innocent when it comes to these matters. Edging is when I take you to the very cliff and leave you there. You won't fall over unless I let you fall over," Kingston hissed because although that was his intention, he wasn't positive he could follow through with the threat. Especially when her warm pussy constricted so delightfully around his fingers and the sweet sounds of her reluctant arousal echoed in the room. He wanted to shove himself inside her perfect, wet cunt and feel her come all over his cock.

But he wouldn't. This was meant to be a punishment. Not a reward for bad behavior.

The three-tone alarm signaling the jet's imminent landing made Kingston's decision easier. Withdrawing his fingers from her pussy, he ripped the thong off her body with relative ease. The scrap of silk was tucked into the interior pocket of his coat while she desperately gulped in air.

"I expect full access to your body, Ava, as detailed in our contract. Don't disobey me again." Sitting her upright, he maneuvered her until she sat in his lap like a dazed marionette doll. Her face was flushed from the blood rushing to her head while hanging upside down, those full, gorgeous lips parted in surprise. Green eyes simmered with lust, and her body trembled with the sensations he'd deliberately provoked and now abandoned.

When he allowed her to stand, he saw evidence of her arousal had stained his thigh. The small circular patch of dampness made his cock thicken with impatient need and her cheeks turn even brighter pink with shame. It only made him more desperate to be inside her wet heat. Any resolve to remain distant and aloof evaporated every time the bewitching scent of honeysuckle hit his nose.

Still gripping her wrists, his hold tightened in warning when Ava tried jerking free. "You won't come until I allow it," he explained again, his gaze boring into hers. "*If* I allow it. Now, let's get you back in your seat. We'll be landing shortly."

"Wait." With her bottom lip tugged between her teeth, Ava looked adorably confused and flustered. "You mean you aren't going to...you know..."

"Fuck you until you're screaming for me?" Kingston grinned. "No, but I will drive you to that point several times tonight. Until you are mindless with the need to come. Begging for it. And you'll be left unsatisfied unless I decide otherwise."

"Edging." Anger flashed across her delicate features as the meaning of the word finally sunk in.

"Your punishment." Brushing a soft kiss across her mouth, he laughed. "You're a quick learner, Ava. And I'm the lucky man who will teach you a much-needed lesson."

CHAPTER
FIFTEEN

*H*eaven and Hell
Crashing together.
Unavoidable.
Stars colliding.

Kingston watched as Ava slumped against the limo's cool leather seat. No doubt her ass was sore from that well-deserved spanking on the jet. But he ached, too, so who truly suffered the aftermath of the imposed punishment?

Crossing his legs took the pressure off his dick, but it did not eliminate the powerful compulsion to flip Ava onto her stomach and slide between her thighs.

"Ava."

Her attention ricocheted to him.

"Sit here beside me," he commanded.

An almost imperceptible shudder racked her body. "Must I?"

Kingston's head cocked. "I won't ask twice."

Grumbling beneath her breath, Ava moved to the space he tapped with his hand. She sat stiffly as though expecting an attack at any moment.

"Would you like something to drink?" he asked, pouring himself a Macallan 30 from the limo's bar.

Ava nodded. "The same as you."

Kingston smiled. "You don't drink scotch, Ava."

She shrugged. "You don't know everything about me. Maybe I've tried it before and liked it."

"At eleven thousand a bottle, I hope you have a greater reaction than just liking it." Kingston handed her a tumbler while her eyes widened at the mention of the extravagant cost. "Let it rest for a minute... give it time to develop and ripen with the ice."

"Maybe you shouldn't waste it on me." Ava rolled the glass as she'd seen him do and sniffed the liquor.

Kingston slid his free arm around her waist, tugging her closer. She frowned but allowed it.

"I don't consider it a waste. More like an experiment." Witnessing Ava's plump, pink lips delicately touch the crystal rim was enough to drive a man crazy with desire. She sipped the liquor, letting out an appreciative hum when she slowly swallowed.

Kingston's pulse leaped as the muscles of her throat contracted and relaxed.

"It's... good, I think." Taking another drink, she examined the scotch's color reflecting through the cut crystal and chunk of ice. "It's very pretty."

Kingston stretched his legs out. "One glass is more than enough, lamb. I don't want you inebriated at dinner."

The stubborn tilt of Ava's chin wavered, her voice laced with soft resentment. "You're always telling me what I can and cannot do."

"Someone must keep you safe, lamb, and it might as well be me for now. You can go back to being reckless when you are no longer mine."

"A day I look forward to with great anticipation," she responded tartly.

Kingston laughed. "You'll be surprised to know that I'll be just as happy when this damned obsession has run its course. You'll be free and so will I."

A flash of something that may have been pain crossed Ava's features, but Kingston did not pursue it. He was too busy wondering why the ache in his chest bloomed at the thought of losing her. Draining his own glass, he set it down and took Ava's.

His cell phone chimed at that moment, Oliver's name flashing on the screen. No doubt his brother was curious about Kingston's decision to take their prisoner on a pleasure outing.

He answered it. "Yeah."

Oliver sighed through the receiver. "What the fuck are you doing, King?"

"Since when must I answer to you, little brother?" Kingston calmly replied. Ava tensed beside him, her lips flattening into a thin line.

Kingston understood her fear and was glad for it. It meant she wouldn't dare seek out Oliver's assistance for any reason. He lightly caressed her arm with the pad of his thumb, the motion soothing and tender, but she didn't relax under his touch.

"You don't. But taking her away from The Den opens the door for... complications."

"Dinner is hardly a complication. Besides, she's had a life-altering experience this week. She deserves a reward."

Ava shot Kingston a heated glare at the glib referral to

losing her virginity, but her lips remained pressed tightly together.

Oliver chuckled, cruel cynicism bleeding into his words. Kingston was suddenly glad Ava could not hear him. "Is she that fucking good? To the point you throw common sense to the wind? You're giving every enemy we possess, including Carson, an opportunity to snatch her back from us. Instead of trotting out our little prize for fucking date night, you should have her chained up in the cell, waiting to be sold for two million."

A muscle ticked in Kingston's jaw. "She's mine now, Oliver. I'll deal with her as I see fit. Don't expect us back tonight. I've decided we'll spend a few days in the city." He ended the call and slid the phone back into his suit coat's inner pocket.

"We aren't flying back?" Ava asked in a pitiful attempt at sounding nonchalant.

"Don't get any ideas about running, lamb. I'll shackle you to my own wrist to keep you from attempting an escape during this little vacation. Or maybe I'll just fuck you into a state of satisfied submission."

Ava slumped against the seat again, her chin back to that mutinous tilt he adored. "One sounds as unpleasant as the other."

Kingston could not contain the bark of laughter that exploded from him. "Sounds like a challenge. Shall I prove how easily those two ideas can be combined for our mutual pleasure?"

Ignoring the taunting suggestion, Ava stubbornly focused her attention on the bright lights beyond the limo's window as they eased into heavier traffic. Soon, they would arrive at the elegant building Kingston owned containing the restaurant on the ground floor and the exclusive club below it. High above those entities was the private penthouse used as a base whenever he visited the city. In between were offices where several of his business ventures were conducted behind a shield of legitimacy.

Kingston sighed, regret needling his usually absent conscience. "Apologies, lamb. That was crude of me."

Ava's gaze slanted his way, her eyes dark and unreadable. "So, you're saying you won't handcuff me?"

"Not without reason."

She mulled that over, nibbling her index fingernail before catching herself and slowly lowering her hand to her lap.

"I must play this part you've forced on me in public. The role of willing girlfriend... lover...companion." Her voice vibrated with defiance. "But if I did run, begged for help, found someone my brother is not indebted to, or even someone you don't already own, you couldn't stop me. This is a public place. Lots of people around. I think I could find someone who would help me."

Kingston's gaze softened. "No one would be so foolish, little lamb. Not only would I eliminate the random person you involved in our private business, you would still find yourself in grave danger. Don't you understand, Ava? I'm the only one standing between you and a life of abuse and torment. Possibly even death." Lifting her hand from her lap, he entangled his fingers with hers and brought them to his lips. Brushing his mouth over her pale knuckles, he murmured, "But I almost hope you try getting away. I'd enjoy punishing you just for daring to think you could accomplish it. I want you to experience my wrath and my mercy. I want to hear you scream my name when you finally surrender and realize I am your salvation." His other hand snaked around the back of her neck, pulling her to him until their lips nearly touched.

"Salvation?" Ava breathed unsteadily. "You are my destruction, Kingston."

His mouth curved slightly. "As you are mine, Ava."

He claimed her mouth but not in the savage manner she surely expected. No, this was gentle and searching. An assault brimming with persuasive desire and longing. Exploring her lips, the sweetness of her mouth, was an exercise in the kind of patience Kingston never knew he possessed. His instinct was to take and take and take until he ravaged all Ava's attempts at resistance. Until there was nothing left but complete surrender.

He wanted *everything* that was *her*. He wanted her off balance and unsure. He wanted her pain and her joy. Dependent upon him and the pleasure only he could give her. And he would utilize all methods in his arsenal in achieving what he wanted.

Whether Ava recognized it or not, she *needed* him.

Maybe as much as he needed her.

And that was a surprising revelation as she reluctantly relaxed against him and opened further for his kiss. As twisted and depraved as his reasons were for keeping her, he suddenly understood it wasn't only for her benefit. He would gain something, too.

Maybe it was the promise of his own redemption that lurked within the depths of Ava's prickly submission. Deep inside her tender body, maybe he could find it. By exploring her quick mind and wit, her innate goodness and purity, he might absorb just enough to save his soul. But it was her elusive wickedness, an element he'd only received glimpses of, that was a temptation he couldn't resist.

When he finally pulled away, Kingston gave her delectable bottom lip a sharp nibble as a reminder he was in charge. She moaned but did not jerk away. That little exhibition of her trust turned something inside him all warm and melty.

"You're unhinged." Ava's eyes flashed with aroused betrayal at the way he ended the sweetly tender kiss.

"You make me that way, lamb." Kingston moved her until she was once again sitting upright. "Now, be good and don't attempt an escape tonight. I've neither the patience nor the restraint required for hunting you down."

"You just said you hoped I tried. These mixed signals you throw out are terribly confusing."

He grinned at her disgruntlement. "It's a perplexing situation." Settling the silvery wrap around her shoulders, he tucked a wayward curl back behind her ear. "Seeing how I'm constantly torn between wanting to kiss you and spank you, it's understandable."

"If I did get away and you caught me," Ava boldly met his gaze. "What would you do to me?"

Kingston did not say anything for a full minute while Ava's chin tilted higher.

It was a bratty challenge. And so foolishly naïve.

When Kingston finally spoke, it was his obsession on full display. There were no pretty words or sentiments. No gentle hearts and flowers. Just an honest brutality and proof of his unreasonable depravity when it came to her.

"Make no mistake, lamb. Just like that night in the woods, I would chase you. And I *would* catch you. Only this time, I'd make sure you completely understood what imprisonment meant. I'd start by clearing a table in the middle of my restaurant and anchoring you to it with the thickest ropes I could find. Then I would fuck you until you screamed while God and everyone else there watched."

CHAPTER

SIXTEEN

ake me.
  Break me.
    Save me.
I'm only yours.

"I don't believe you," Ava said, chewing her bottom lip. He couldn't mean it. He wouldn't dare do something so depraved. So outrageous.

He's just trying to scare me.

Kingston laughed. "Want to find out? We'll be arriving there any minute. I'll escort you inside, turn you loose for five minutes and hunt you down."

"You would hurt anyone who helps me?"

"If it's a man, yes. His life would be over the moment he touched you. A woman? Depends." Kingston shrugged. "Shall we play this game and find out?" His hand snaked between her thighs, blunt fingers finding the exposed folds of her pussy and tracing the flesh.

Ava gasped, unsure if she squirmed to avoid his searching touch or if she was desperately seeking it. "Don't!"

"Answer me, lamb. Do you want to play a game?" He ignored her protest, his thumb strumming her clit until she moaned. "There are certain rules you must follow." His free hand curled around her throat. High up under her chin, just below her jaw, his index finger and thumb pushed on opposite sides against the pulse there.

His eyes were darkly intent, watching her response as he deliberately slid one finger inside her and crooked it against the inner wall of her pussy. Ava quivered. She could not deny how good it felt. For a long moment, an eternity maybe or perhaps only a matter of seconds, his thumb swirled in her wetness and, damn him—*damn him*—his thick finger tapped along the inside her depths.

"Kingston," she breathed unsteadily, the need to climax rushing through her body like a rogue summer thunderstorm. With a mind of their own, her hips shifted, giving him better access to her body. She couldn't help it. She wanted to lie back against the sleek leather seats of his luxurious car and let him do whatever he wanted just as long as she was given permission to come.

"Does that feel good, Ava?"

"Mmmm," she moaned. Kingston pressed more firmly until she saw stars.

"Lie back, baby. Spread your legs for me. There's my good girl." His hand moved almost leisurely, bathing her flesh with her own juices until she was slippery with lust and heat. "Do you want to come?" It was the Devil's own whisper, husky and full of unfulfilled promises. The hand around her neck tightened until the ceiling of the limo swirled dizzily overhead.

God. Just a few more circles and I'll explode. If he just keeps doing... that... Please don't stop doing that...

Ava vaguely acknowledged the moment his hand eased its grip. Taking a deep breath, she realized he was shuffling through the inner pocket of his coat. Whatever he searched for, she didn't know, nor did she care. Because she was going to explode in the space of a heartbeat, and she would pull herself together after that.

"I asked you a question, Ava. Do you want to come?" His finger moved out of her body, and Ava nearly wailed in protest.

"Yes... *yes*. Please, Kingston." She was begging but she didn't care. He had cruelly primed her until the simplest touch was now enough to detonate her from the inside out.

"God, I love hearing you beg. I love seeing those pretty tears on your cheeks, knowing I am the reason for them." Kingston pressed a kiss to her mouth, gently running his tongue over the small cut he inflicted earlier to her bottom lip. "I love how you struggle to breathe with my hand around your throat. How your eyes fill with fear and excitement. And I especially love the way this tight little cunt squeezes whatever I shove into it."

Ava moaned, on the verge of climaxing from Kingston's filthy, crude words. Her back arched off the cold leather seat as something small and cylindrical in shape glided into her vagina with his tender insistence. Her body accepted the foreign object, clutching it in greedy desperation.

Kingston's soft chuckle washed over her. He leaned back as though admiring his handiwork while Ava shuddered, chilled but burning without his large body pressing down on her. With careful hands, he pulled the dress down over her hips, straightening the fabric and sitting her back up again.

Ava stared mutely at his granite-like features. Nerve endings fired off like bottle rockets inside her veins but fizzled frustratingly short of the orgasm her body so urgently craved.

She was lightheaded, hanging over an invisible cliff, empty and wanting, but somehow full.

There was *something* inside her. Something seductively wicked. An instrument of this man's terrible power.

Kingston's lips quirked as he studied her reaction. "You're wondering what I put inside you."

Ava's hand immediately flew to the space between her legs, but his low growl stopped her.

"Don't you fucking dare remove that. It stays until I decide it comes out."

"What is it?" Her terrified squeak amused him because the lines around his eyes crinkled.

"Something designed for our mutual enjoyment. An app on my phone controls it."

"Take it out," she demanded in a shrill voice threaded with panic.

Kingston pulled up the app, flashing the screen of his cell phone at her so she caught a quick glimpse of the vibrator's capabilities. "Where would be the fun in that? This will keep you on edge all night if that's what I want. Try running from me and I'll push this little control here to the max. You'll drop to your knees where you stand, Ava. You'll come so damn hard you won't be able to get up from the floor without my help."

"Why would you do something so awful?" Ava scrambled away the best she could within the limo's confines. She reached again between her legs, intent on yanking out the offending object but found her wrist captured in Kingston's large hand. He squeezed in warning but stopped short of hurting her. Which was surprising because if he truly wished to show off his power, he could easily grind her bones to dust.

"I'm dangerously close to handcuffing you and leading you into the restaurant like this, Ava. You belong to me. Your body belongs to me. Your cunt belongs to me. And that vibrator stays inside you so there is no doubt who controls you. Now, do you want to enter the building cuffed, on fire with the need to come and the inability to do anything about it? Or will you be a good girl and behave?"

Ava choked on a furious sob. "People will know... if you... if you... turn this thing on. They'll know what you are doing to me, you monster."

Kingston grinned, dark blue eyes flashing with the thrill of controlling her. "I certainly hope they do. I want everyone to know, sweet Ava. I want them to hear you beg me to let you come. But you didn't answer my question. Will you be a good girl?"

Even as her mind whirled with a hundred possible ways of outsmarting him, Ava deflated in defeat. There was no other choice. Kingston would activate the diabolical toy with the slightest provocation, either real or imagined. She knew her infuriating captor well enough by now, and he would not hesitate to truss her up in handcuffs and parade her around like the spoils of war.

"Yes. I'll behave," she muttered through clenched teeth.

"Excellent. Now, dry your tears and reapply your lipstick. We've arrived, and as I expected, the paparazzi and tabloid reporters are hanging around. Smile pretty, stay close to me, and for God's sake, don't answer any of their questions. Just follow my lead and ignore them." Kingston pressed a soft kiss to her forehead, his hand gripping the curve of her jaw to hold her in place. "Relax and breathe, Ava," he murmured. Tilting her chin with the slightest pressure of his thumb, he stared into her eyes. "You may actually enjoy yourself tonight."

～

THE INSTANT the car door swung wide, a blinding array of flashes popped. They invaded the limo's softly lit interior like a swarm of angry lightning bugs.

Jack was already on the sidewalk, busily pushing the more aggressive paparazzi out of the way. A steady stream of shouted questions accompanied the flashbulbs as Kingston exited the limo. He reached a hand back into the car to help Ava emerge.

She took it, although what she really wanted more than anything was to shrink back into the vehicle's luxurious safety.

"Mister Winter, what do you say to the accusations you've abducted a young woman?"

"Is this the person in question, Mister Winter? Do you have a statement?"

"Do you always bring your prisoners out on dates, Mister Winter? Or is this the first time?"

"Back the fuck up," Jack said calmly, planting an elbow into the ribs of the closest reporter.

Kingston merely smiled that wolfish grin of his before dragging Ava up alongside his hard, muscular body. For a moment, they stood motionless. Hip to hip. Molded to each other from the waist up as his arm slipped around her waist. It was a pose. An illusion. A photo his enemies could examine and admire. A display of Kingston's power and his newest possession. They could have a Hollywood super couple traipsing down the red carpet based on the dazzling pop of flashes and the clicking of camera shutters.

The urge to sink into his warmth, the sense of protection she *shouldn't* feel around him, swamped Ava. Instinctively huddling closer, she wished Kingston's arm was tighter around her waist as the moment ended. He gave a mocking wave to the photographers before propelling her toward the building's vaulted entrance.

"Miss, are you a member of LIST? Do you and Mister Kingston come here together often?" One man surged closer through the throng. He thrust a cellphone into Ava's face, somehow maneuvering around Jack's impressive wall of muscle. "Did you meet him in one of the dungeon rooms? Were you forced into having kinky sex with him? Is he forcing you now?"

Ava was stunned by the reporter's crudeness and the rapid-fire questions. When he grabbed her elbow as they pushed through the crowd, a tiny yelp of alarm escaped her. The reporter's hands were hard and cruel.

Kingston whirled on the man, his expression forged of cold fury.

"Get your goddamn hands off her." He shoved the guy back with one hand. Using his body as a shield, he whipped Ava behind him. The quickness of his actions made her dizzy, and she clutched his waist just to keep her balance in the silvery high heels. Her shimmery wrap had torn during the altercation, one end now hanging in a ripped tatter of material.

"Touch her again and I'll cut off every single one of your fingers. And then gift them to her like they're a fucking bouquet," Kingston snarled, his manner so ferociously protective that even Ava blinked in surprise. The way his eyes softened the tiniest bit when he turned to check her over was intoxicating. He looked at her as though he truly cared for her safety. As though he would burn the world down for her if she asked him.

The reporter was stunned, but with blatant disregard for his own safety, he again pushed forward.

"Isn't it true you snatched Miss Blue off the streets of Savannah just over a month ago? Have you held her hostage in upstate New York while bribing authorities to look the other way? Some say you're following in your father's footsteps but better at hiding your crimes and looking legitimate. What do you say to that? Do you have a statement for us?"

"Get her inside, boss. Unless you want a brawl out here on the sidewalk," Jack warned Kingston, pushing the reporter aside again. "I'll handle this."

Kingston quivered with rage, the muscles in his arms tight beneath the bespoke suit coat. "Not before I get the opportunity to knock this bastard's teeth out."

Ava was frozen with indecision. If Kingston accosted the reporter, he'd likely find himself in handcuffs. Maybe even arrested for assault. This could be a chance to escape. The police could save her, sort it all out. She would be free of Kingston and his threats and the easy way he commanded her body's responses.

But on the other hand, was she that certain of her safety if Kingston himself wasn't the one providing it?

As if he possessed magical powers and could hear her every thought, Kingston's gaze narrowed on Ava. His hand encircled her wrist, keeping her captive. "Whatever you're thinking, it won't work, Ava," he muttered beneath his breath. "The police force in this precinct is in my pocket and my debt."

"Are you a murderer like your father, Mister Kingston? Do you abduct women and sell them into the sex trade?" The same reporter was still shouting questions when Jack grabbed his arm. Forcing it high behind the man's back, the security guard increased the pressure until the cellphone fell to the ground. More flashbulbs clicked, cell phones recording every moment of the impromptu altercation as Jack ground the phone beneath his heel.

"I'd advise you to shut the fuck up, dumbass. Otherwise, you're looking at a defamation suit that'll bankrupt you and the next seven generations of your miserable bloodline," Jack muttered, flashing a grim smile in Kingston's direction

"Mister Winter has more money than the Devil himself, and you are in danger of finding out just how ruthless he really is."

"Can't the girl speak for herself?" The reporter grunted. "Or did he rip out her tongue like Alan Winter is rumored to have done to some of his victims?"

Kingston let out a feral growl, his fist closing convulsively around Ava's wrist even as she tried pulling away. She pinned the reporter with a steely glare. "Of course, he hasn't ripped out my tongue. What's wrong with you? And no, he didn't kidnap me off the street. I'm here of my own free will, you miscreant. Mister Winter has been a friend of my family for many years. Your accusations are outrageous and... and... unfounded!"

"Be quiet, Ava," Kingston muttered, snatching her back against him. "I ordered you not to engage with them. This reckless disobedience will not be tolerated."

"But he's spreading rumors with those ridiculous questions. I can't allow someone like him to tell such scandalous lies," she hissed. Attempts to jerk free of Kingston's grip proved futile so she directed her fury at the reporter. "For your information, this is the first time I've been invited to Mister Winter's restaurant, and even if I had visited the club's... dungeon... it would be none of your damn business. How dare you treat him like he's a criminal. Like a serial killer. Or a human trafficker. You obviously know nothing about him. Or me."

"Goddamnit. Shut up, Ava," Kingston hauled her toward the building's entrance as uniformed police and security guards swamped the plaza.

The four muscular and very physically fit guards were obviously in Kingston's employ. They immediately followed Jack's barked commands in dealing with the gaggle of reporters and photographers. Meanwhile, two uniformed policemen went about disbursing the crowd that had gathered on the sidewalk.

"No. Wait a minute, Kingston. I *won't* shut up. Someone must state the truth and I want to—" Ava was so angry and indignant that at first the annoying buzz tickling her insides did not register. It hit her again. A tingling sensation. Low. Insistent. Invasive. It felt like a hoard of lazy bees swarming around a honey hive that had somehow grown between her thighs. The orgasm Kingston denied her earlier roared into sudden life, demanding to be set free. It was awful and monstrous and yet so pleasurable Ava's eyes nearly rolled into the back of her head.

She stumbled but Kingston caught her around the waist and dragged inside the portico. Holding her flush against his body just outside the elegant glass doors of the foyer, his mouth brushed her ear.

"Shall I increase the level, lamb? Will you obey me now and shut your sweet mouth? Or should I push you to your knees right here and shove my cock down your throat while I use this toy to tease your wet pussy with the promise of an orgasm?"

CHAPTER

SEVENTEEN

A little bit of lamb
Served up for dinner.
And I'm a starving man.

AVA LOOKED as though she might pass out. Whether it was from the shock of his filthy threat or the toy's vibrations rattling her world wasn't quite clear.

Kingston slid his phone back into his pocket, satisfied she would listen to him now that he'd caught her full attention. The toy was set on the lowest level, and to his delight, she responded as though he'd turned it up full blast.

She was such a responsive little creature.

Leaving Jack to handle the shit show behind them, Kingston held Ava up by the arm and nudged her further into the grand foyer. She managed two steps before her knees buckled again. A small, helpless moan escaped her lips.

Kingston grinned. "I'll happily carry you inside, Ava, if that's what you want. But I suggest you pull yourself together."

Her eyes fluttered shut. "Turn this damn thing off." The words were hissed from between gritted teeth, her hands clenched into tiny fists. She would definitely take a swing at him if given the opportunity.

Kingston continued walking, forcing her to trip alongside him. He nodded at the tuxedo-clad doorman. "But we just started playing, Ava," he murmured. "And you must learn to obey me."

"It's too much." Ava's gaze found his, her green eyes wild and stormy. Coming to a stop in the middle of the cavernous space of the building's lobby, she resisted his efforts to keep moving forward. Instead, she wrapped her arms around her waist, glaring at him in a mix of arousal, fury, and desperation. "I don't want..."

The words trailed off. She looked like a shiny, expensive jewel nestled in the midst of the lobby's creamy marble and crystal accents. The silvery blue dress shimmered around her body, her full, pink lips parting in small gasps. Beneath the dress material, her nipples were plainly visible. Sweet, puckered rosebuds that made Kingston's mouth water when he thought of tasting her.

Everything about Ava was intoxicating. Alluring. The perfect counterpoint of innocent temptress to his ruthlessly dark persona. And to Kingston's mounting irritation, she drew the attention of every male with a beating pulse in the spacious lobby.

Possessive anger and the need to protect what was now *his* roiled inside his gut. Despite his calm exterior, he still wanted to smash his fists into the face of the reporter who dared touch Ava. Or any man who dared even glancing her way.

But it was his brother who deserved the lion's share of his wrath.

Damn you, Oliver. Without a doubt, Oliver was to blame for this fiasco. What else explained the probing questions? The vile reminders of their father's proclivities for abusing women?

Yeah. He'd bet his life as well as his fortune that it was Oliver who tipped off the more aggressive press members. Just like he had notified the local police to pay them a visit.

"Good evening, Mister Winter. It's wonderful to see you tonight. I hope the unfortunate incident you experienced outside the building has been dealt with to your satisfaction."

Kingston's gaze flickered away from Ava. His hand itched to snatch her up, throw her over his knee, and spank her until she cried. He would enjoy it. She would as well, especially with that toy buzzing around her insides and making her frantic with the need to come.

"Hello, Tipton," he addressed the executive concierge. The elderly man supervised the building like the captain of a tightly run ship. "Don't worry about that." He waved a dismissive hand, indicating the scene outside the building. "Jack has it under control."

"Very good, sir. I'm sure he does." The man straightened his jaunty tuxedo bowtie and gave Kingston an indulgent smile. "They're anticipating your arrival at CRUSH; however, I'll inquire as to your pleasure this evening, sir. Downstairs or up?"

"Dinner, I believe. Tipton, excuse me for a moment." Turning his back to the man, Kingston covered the few steps between himself and Ava. She trembled at his approach, fidgeting with that minuscule purse, and shifting from one foot to the other. Leaning into her personal space, he whispered in her ear, "Do you know what I'm considering right now, Ava?"

A breathy sigh escaped her when he trailed a knuckle down

the bare expanse of her back. "No." She swayed as though teetering on the verge of swooning.

"I'm thinking about skipping dinner. I'm thinking about taking you downstairs to one of the private rooms in my exclusive club and turning that toy up to its highest level. I'm thinking I want you screaming my name as I make you come again and again."

Ava's eyes lifted to meet his. Tears sparkled in the unfocused depths as the vibrator did its job of keeping her on the edge without allowing her to fall over. Her hands clenched and unclenched, her honeysuckle perfume mingling with the sweetly intoxicating scent of her arousal. *I hope no one else gets close enough to breathe her in. She really will start a brawl. A goddamn war.*

"Okay," she replied in a strained voice barely above a whisper.

A grunt of satisfaction escaped Kingston but it was tempered with a bit of regret. He wasn't playing fair with her. Why that bothered him proved mystifying. Why he suddenly wanted to shield her from everything bad in the world—including himself—was infuriating.

Reaching into his suit coat pocket, Kingston swiped the vibrator's app off.

Relief washed over Ava's features. She sagged against him, biting her bottom lip in confusion at the abrupt display of dubious mercy.

"Upstairs, Tipton, if you please," Kingston said over his shoulder to the concierge. "Miss Blue requires sustenance before we can even think of exploring the scandalous delights offered elsewhere inside this building." Smiling down at her, the hint of wickedness curving his lips provided just enough assurance that he certainly wasn't done punishing her. "So, dinner first, my needy little lamb." His promise was meant for her ears only. "My dessert will be served later."

~

AVA MURMURED A SOFT 'THANK YOU' when the maître d indicated they'd reached their table.

"Henri, a bottle of Cristal Rosé, please," Kingston murmured, following Ava as she slid across the booth's black leather. "Two flutes."

It was interesting to watch how Ava hid her uncomfortable expression both from Kingston and his employee. No one would ever guess that a pleasure toy rested snugly inside her tight little pussy. His finger itched to turn back on.

"At once, sir." Henri snapped his fingers at the head waiter, and turned back to Kingston. "David will be your server tonight. Will you have the usual for your evening meal, Mister Kingston? Or perhaps indulge in something out of the ordinary? Miss Blue, we can prepare anything your heart desires. Our chefs are among the finest in the world. I'm sure you'll agree once you've sampled the artistry of CRUSH's culinary masterpieces."

"The usual will be fine," Kingston paused. "For both of us."

Ava's frown was downright mutinous. "Maybe I don't want the usual. Maybe I want something else. Like a cheeseburger. Or ribs. Henri? Do you have barbecue spareribs?"

Henri froze, no doubt surprised by the resentful tone of Ava's response.

"Don't mind Miss Blue, Henri. She's simply frustrated by something I denied her earlier this evening. I've erred in spoiling her, and this sullen attitude is the result." Kingston chucked. "And yes, we will both have the usual."

"Of course, sir. I shall put in the order myself and instruct the chef to apply all his skill in creating a magnum opus." The elderly man bowed again and briskly walked away, his fingers snapping again at their waiter.

"Ava, you don't like cheeseburgers, and CRUSH doesn't offer southern barbecue. You'll have the blackened sea scallops tossed in a creamy wine sauce instead."

Ava's chin tilted. "I'm allergic to scallops."

"No, you're not."

"I'm allergic to blackened seasoning."

"Try again," Kingston smirked.

"Fine. I'm allergic to you," Ava snapped, her mouth pulling tight when she saw the obvious aggravation flash in Kingston's gaze.

"You should amend your tone, lamb."

Taking a deep breath, Ava folded her hands in her lap and lowered her head. After a few moments of silence, she finally muttered, "Forgive my rudeness, sir. My temper got the best of me just now. I can't...I can't seem to think straight at the moment."

Kingston nearly crowed in victory but stopped short of expressing delight. Because suddenly, her meekness, the way she caved, it all felt... hollow. The words were simply a way of appeasing him. What did it say about him that he liked it much better when she fought him?

But that wasn't realistic. When she struggled against his will, he was left with no choice but to punish her, and although her spirited behavior was enchanting, he couldn't let her lash out however she wanted.

How far would Ava take these displays of rebellion? Would she push and push until he snapped in anger and truly punished her? Would she make him hurt her?

Would she want him to? More importantly, would she allow it?

"Let's start again, Ava, shall we?" His voice remained even. Composed. He was positive he could get what he wanted out of her, and have her happy to give in, if he just applied himself to the task.

Ava gave him a startled look, clearly not expecting his calm demeanor. Especially since their interactions were usually rife with heat and lust and maybe even a thread of insanity. "Start again?"

"Let's pretend this is something other than what it is. Let's treat this evening as though we were on a real date."

"A date." Her emerald-colored eyes narrowed. "Are you being serious right now?"

Kingston captured her hand, rubbing a thumb over her knuckles. He wouldn't let her pull away, not even when the champagne arrived. Henri ceremoniously popped the cork, pouring the sparkling beverage into exquisitely cut crystal flutes before backing away from the table.

Kingston's smile was both deadly and infinitely charming once they were alone again. "Very serious. What do you like to do on dates?"

Ava sat quietly for a moment, a calculating gleam in her eyes catching the candlelight. "Drake Cornerstone took me bowling once. It was fun, in an eighth-grade kind of way. Do you like to go *bowling,* sir?"

His jaw tightened. He knew what she was up to, and it worked. The young lawyer had done nothing more than kiss Ava, but Kingston couldn't keep from thinking of the places the man's fingers might have invaded. Given more time to gain her trust, Cornerstone might have succeeded in fucking Ava first.

Jealousy nipped Kingston like an angry beast.

"I despise bowling. I'd rather sink my fingers into other holes." he raised Ava's hand, brushing his mouth over her soft knuckles. "Shall I demonstrate?"

Ava sucked in a breath, the pulse pounding in her neck with such force Kingston could see it in the dim light.

Ducking her head, she pulled her hand from his grip and grabbed the champagne flute. "You've already done that." She took a long drink before setting the glass down beside gleaming silver cutlery. Picking up the thick napkin, she gave her lips a delicate swipe before laying the cloth across her lap.

"Ahh, but you've not received the full treatment yet, lamb. There are so many ways I can use these fingers to your enjoyment. Ways you are still so innocent of." Kingston picked up his own glass and let out a sigh. "But we've veered off topic. Tell me your idea of a perfect date and I'll make it happen. Within reason, of course."

Ava's gaze flickered to his then returned to studying the champagne bubbles fizzing inside the glass. "What difference would it make? You are only using my body to erase a two-million-dollar debt. Talking about dates and what I like is just your way of messing with my head."

Were those tears in her eyes? It was hard to say for certain. She wouldn't look at him, her thick eyelashes concealing her distress. Her sadness tweaked something inside his chest. Made it tight and achy.

"You forget I'm keeping you safe as part of that agreement." Kingston took a sip of champagne. "Humor me, lamb. If it helps, you can pretend we're a real couple."

"You said once before you knew everything about me," Ava said softly. "Was that a lie?"

"You know the answer to that." Kingston smirked. "When it comes to you, nothing is a secret."

Ava's eyes were diamond bright with tears and flashing anger. There was not a submissive bone in her body at that moment, and Kingston was thrilled to see it.

"You tell me what I like to do on a date," she practically

snarled. "*You* pretend you want to impress me. Pretend you would do anything to make me happy. Give me a reason to give you a goodnight kiss at the end of the evening. Work for it, Kingston Winter. Because not everything you want should fall into your lap."

EIGHTEEN

Tighten your hands.
Around my neck.
Around my heart.
Hold me tighter.
Hold me closer.
Stop me from flying away.

"I've already had you in my lap," Kingston reminded her. "And across it."

"That's not an answer," Ava bit out. The man was deliberately provoking her.

"All right. First, we would visit the museum of your choosing because I know you love them. I'd give you a kiss every time you stopped to read the information plaques for each piece of artwork. Afterward, I would buy your favorite butter pecan gelato at that Italian café near the Met. I'd feed it to you, Ava. Watch you lick the spoon and imagine it was my cock sliding over the coolness of your tongue and deeper into your warm mouth until I hit the back of your throat. I'd hold it there. Waiting until you swallowed what I gave you." Kingston's head tilted as he raked her face and body with his blue-black eyes. "Then I'd take you to a quaint little bookstore that's nearby this building. Give you all the money you need to buy as many first-edition books as you could possibly want and build you a library to keep them. And on the first rainy day, I'd read your favorites aloud to you and serve your hot tea in antique China cups."

Ava's heartbeat slowed as his words sunk in. Like a roller-coaster speeding downhill, it began beating faster and faster until she feared she might hyperventilate. She'd asked Kingston this question for the sake of proving that he really didn't know her at all. But it was glaringly apparent that this man, this monster, knew her better than anyone else in the world.

That someone so perfect and beautiful could also be so terrifyingly dangerous was a true tragedy.

"Is that all?" Ava's mouth was tight with the desperate need to press against his lush mouth. Abruptly conscious of her nudity beneath her dress, her thighs helplessly clenched. She was throbbing with lust. Her body did not care how much she hated him.

Kingston gave her a sinfully slow smile, rubbing a thumb over his bottom lip. "No. That's not all, little monster. I'd make sure it was impossible for you to walk away from me when this is all over. You would never forget how I made you come over and over on my cock. On my fingers. On my tongue."

Ava fingered the salad fork beneath the napkin laying across her lap. Arousal and fear smeared the inside of her thighs. Her pussy throbbed around the motionless vibrator inside her, and with irrational anger, she wished he would turn it on. The booth's black leather seats and the dim lighting from the numerous crystal chandeliers probably hid the evidence of her condition, but still, she squirmed in a heady cocktail of resentful lust.

Kingston had not yet noticed the elegant place setting laid out before her was short an item. The brilliant white tablecloth was useful in concealing her actions. No one knew she'd swiped a salad fork when she dabbed her lips with the napkin. How often did one check for a missing utensil? A salad fork wouldn't be missed. If it was, a natural assumption would be its absence was simply an oversight by the waitstaff. It was why she'd not taken the butterknife. It was the obvious choice but more quickly missed.

What she intended on doing with the fork remained to be seen. She filched it on pure instinct and now, pricking her finger with the sharp tines, she wondered if she had the guts to use it on someone.

Would she use it against Kingston? Did she even dare?

Punishment would be swift, that much was certain. There was no telling what he might do if she injured him with such an insignificant weapon. But remembering Detective Redding's visit to The Den and his thwarted plans to snatch her away was incentive enough to arm herself.

So, maybe she wouldn't threaten Kingston, but it could be useful in other situations. Or maybe it was crazy to think a tiny salad fork would be of any help if she was caught in a desperate situation.

Pulling lipstick and a small compact from her purse, Ava shakily repaired the damage done from biting her own lips while Kingston's possessive gaze remained locked on her. She surreptitiously stashed the fork inside the handbag along with the makeup.

With a deep breath, she calmly regarded Kingston, her

heart pounding so hard it boomed like a drum in her ears. "I need to use the ladies' room."

Kingston's attention was caught by the sight of Jack entering the restaurant. The two men nodded at one another, and Ava wondered what silent message passed between them. Once Jack slid into the shadows, Kingston noticeably relaxed, his fingers unclenching from around the flute's stem. His gaze slid back to Ava. "On two conditions, lamb."

"And those are?" She dreaded hearing what he would demand of her.

"You don't make yourself come and you don't remove that toy."

She managed a tight nod at his audacity. As she went to slide out of the booth, Kingston caught her wrist. He gave it a warning squeeze, his fingers brutal and hard against the fragile bones.

"I'll know if you disobey. And Ava, you don't want to disappoint me."

Ava's nodded, smoothing her dress down once she was standing beside the booth. The sparkly purse was clutched almost desperately against her midriff as she looked around the spacious restaurant, unsure which way to go.

"Down that hall and to the left." Kingston waved a hand in the general direction of where Jack stood. His eyes were piercing as he stared at her, and for a heart-stopping moment, Ava wondered if he was aware she'd successfully stashed a weapon for future use.

"Excuse me," she murmured, walking away without a second glance back at their table. Doing so would raise his suspicions, something she wanted to avoid at all costs. That he let her go alone was shocking, but then again, there were multiple people inside the restaurant guarding her. Kingston could allow her the use of the restroom without his piercing gaze watching her every movement. After all, the men working for him served as his eyes and ears.

The restaurant was sleekly elegant, highlighted by dramatic lighting and old-world opulence. Slightly raised booths like the one she and Kingston occupied were lined up along black, wood-paneled walls. A gleaming white marble floor was filled with round tables situated with a view of a stage at one end. A live band was currently playing, and couples swayed to the music on a designated dance floor. Multiple chandeliers lit the space, catching the light and bouncing it off white tablecloths and silver accents.

Ava hurried past the dance floor, barely paying the band any attention although they were playing the type of music she loved. It was music like her mom and dad always danced around the house to when they were being silly. The kind of music that had Dad pulling her off the couch so he could swing her around while she laughed in delight.

It made her homesick. Both for her parents and for the home she'd grown up in. The same home Carson had taken over with his druggie friends and hungry prostitutes.

Ava brushed past a waiter and entered the hallway leading to the restroom. It was sumptuously decorated with pale gray, brocade-style wallpaper and sconces crafted into modern spheres of chrome and glass.

Ducking into one of the stalls, she rested her head against the coolness of the solid Lucite door. Taking deep breaths, she calmed her racing heart. What was in store for her the rest of this evening? How much more must she endure of Kingston's taunts and arrogance? In the privacy of those few moments alone, Ava realized just how exhausted she was. Mentally worn out and dazed from the events of the past five weeks.

He'd done so much to her in such a short span of time.

While finishing up, Ava seriously considered pulling the

toy out and flushing it down the toilet as though it were a tampon.

She should. Rid herself of the damn thing and to hell with Kingston's threat of punishment. Her fingers sought out the vibrator's tiny loop. Giving it an experimental tug, she was unprepared for the result. With a whimper, she snatched her hand away, the triangle between her legs flaring as if on fire.

This was a game she had agreed to play. A secret part of her was thrilled about it—wanted it. *Needed* it. She hoped Kingston was going mad knowing he'd placed this thing inside her. She hoped his fingers twitched with an unholy craving to turn it on. Because that meant he was thinking of her constantly. And she wanted that. More than anything, she wanted that.

God help her for wanting something so deranged.

Exiting the stall, she washed her hands while considering her reflection in the mirror. Could anyone tell by looking at her that she'd been stuffed with something so wicked? Probably not. She looked perfectly normal to the casual observer.

A young woman entered the restroom as Ava reached into a gilded basket holding thick, soft disposable towels. Drying her hands, she averted her gaze, but the woman only stepped closer. Ava's cheeks reddened when she sensed her critical gaze skimming her body.

"That's a gorgeous dress."

"Thank you." Ava tossed the used paper towel into the trash receptacle. Tucking her purse under her arm. Knowing the fork was in there made her clutch it even tighter.

"I imagine *he* bought it for you. The man does have excellent taste when it comes to dressing up his women," the light blonde woman said, blood-red lips pulling back in a faintly hostile smile. "It fits you well. Shows off your attributes. That's what he likes to do. Flaunt his newest toy for all the world to see."

"I beg your pardon?" Ava tugged at the hem of the dress, conscious of just how short it was without this stranger pointing it out.

The woman rolled her eyes. "Don't be embarrassed, sugar. Enjoy it while you can because his interest won't last forever. It never does. Take it from someone with firsthand experience." Bright blue eyes narrowed as they raked Ava up and down. "He hasn't shown you off around LIST yet, so you must be really new. Don't worry. Looking like you do, you'll experience it soon enough. You are simply too delicious to keep hidden for long. Good thing he's never shied away from sharing his toys with others."

"That's enough, Nadia."

Ava jumped, whirling around to see Kingston leaning a broad shoulder against the propped-open door to the ladies' room. He was scowling, his brow lowered as he glared at the other woman.

There was a spark of terror in Nadia's eyes, but she ran a blood-red fingernail down Ava's bare arm anyway. She stared at Kingston as though challenging him.

"Maybe we could all play together, King You'd like that, right? Both of us fucking you. You fucking her. Me fucking her. Me fucking you."

Ava jerked away in shock. This girl wanted to have sex with her? With Kingston, too? At the *same time?*

Kingston's response to that was like a whiplash. "Let's go, Ava."

Ava did not move. What if... what if this woman, who looked to only be a few years older than Ava herself, could help her? Nadia obviously wanted Kingston if the hungry, terrified gleam in her eyes was any indication. Maybe it could be used to Ava's advantage.

Kingston's sigh reverberated with frustration. "Goddamn it, Ava, enough already. Get your ass over here. Now."

"Oooh." Nadia giggled softly. "Going all caveman over this one? That's certainly new."

"You shouldn't be in here, Kingston." Ava checked her lipstick and made a show of running a finger over her bottom lip. Tracing the faint bite mark his teeth left behind when he taunted and teased her on the jet was a deliberate action.

Kingston's eyes darkened.

"I own every part of this building. Nothing here is off-limits to me." His lips pressed tight, but he remained in the doorway. "Must I prove it?"

Slipping his hand into his pocket, he withdrew his phone. When he tapped open the app, Ava's knees wobbled.

"N-No, sir." The words slipped from her mouth in a breathy exhale of defeated hate. She glided to him while Nadia's head tilted at her abrupt compliance.

"What an adorable pet she is."

"Keep your distance, Nadia, or I'll have you expelled from this building and all privileges revoked," Kingston drawled, returning the phone to his pocket. Ava breathed a sigh of relief as he stepped aside so an elegantly dressed older woman could enter the ladies' room.

"Good evening, Kingston," the woman said, the creases at the corners of her eyes deepening as she smiled. "Is everything all right?"

"Of course, Mrs. Ellerby. Just helping my date with a small wardrobe malfunction. This is Ava Blue, Mrs. Ellerby. Her father provided services as my attorney." Kingston flashed the elderly woman a warm grin. "But that was many years ago. Anyway, I do hope you are enjoying your evening."

"Oh, yes. The food is superb, as always," Mrs. Ellerby

exclaimed before shaking Ava's hand. "Lovely to meet you, my dear."

"Won't you excuse us, Mrs. Ellerby? I'm doing a fine job of creating a roadblock to the use of the facilities, and we should return to our table. It was wonderful seeing you. Please give your husband my regards." Kingston's arm snaked around Ava's waist in a blatant display of ownership. He nodded toward the young woman standing at the polished marble countertop, her forehead creased in agitation. "Remember what I said, Nadia. I won't repeat the warning."

Nadia's head bobbed in a quick, jerky motion, indicating her agreement.

Kingston dragged Ava down the darkened hallway. In the high heels, she barely kept up with his long strides, but it was more difficult curbing her tongue.

"Who was that woman?"

His pace slowed, allowing her to catch up. Pulling her against his lean form, his eyes sparked with something unde-fined. "Mrs. Ellerby. Her husband is Senator Patrick Ellerby. He's also one of the men I vetted for the auction."

"A senator?" Ava sucked in a breath. "A *married* senator?"

"A very powerful senator and a good friend to have when the situation calls for it. His loyalty is rewarded with certain perks. And married or not, he treats his women very well. Mrs. Ellerby looks the other way when it comes to such things."

"Oh, I'm a perk now."

"You are no longer available to anyone other than me, Ava, so what does it matter now?" Kingston's gaze narrowed as Nadia emerged from the restroom. The girl brushed past where they stood in the corridor, her mouth curving in a smirk for Ava before averting her eyes from Kingston's disapproving scowl.

"What about that one?" Ava's temper flared higher.

"Would she have been on the approved list of buyers? Or it that a privilege reserved for wealthy men like yourself and the senator?"

With a sigh, Kingston pulled Ava into a small, dark alcove. "Nadie is no one. Just a girl with a big mouth and an even bigger ego."

"You've slept with her?" Ava blurted out before tightening her lips in dismay. She had no impulse control around this man. It was disgusting.

He smiled. "There's that jealous streak again."

Ava tried jerking her hand from his steely grip but failed. "I'm not jealous! But you obviously have some sort of history. She's interested in you and..." Her words faltered. "And you could let me go. You could be with someone like her. Or even Monique, the stewardess."

"I've no desire to be with another woman."

"But you've been with her. With Nadia." Ava wanted to kick herself for this need to interrogate him. Her mouth was on autopilot. Spewing out questions she had no business asking.

"Everything okay, boss?" Jack interrupted, his large body blocking out the quiet bustle of the restaurant and the elegant strains of music. His hand rested at his hip, disturbing his suit coat and reminding Ava the bodyguard was armed when she caught a flash of metal.

"It's fine, Jack. Go back to your post." Kingston's gaze never strayed from Ava.

With a quick nod, Jack retreated as silently as he'd appeared.

"Now, back to your question, curious little lamb." His eyes crinkled at the corners. "Nadia's been a partner for Oliver on multiple occasions, and yes, I regrettably once fucked her along with him. Was hardly a memorable experience. At least not enough that I wanted a repeat performance."

Ava turned her head, embarrassment flooding her at his crude response. "I-I don't want details."

Kingston placed a forefinger beneath Ava's chin, forcing her to look at him. "Don't you?"

When she did not answer, he surprised her by stating softly, "Come dance with me, Ava."

She stared at Kingston, confused by his abrupt request. "I don't think that's a good idea…" she finally stammered.

"I wasn't asking. But promise you'll say yes, and I'll swallow my damned pride and ask nicely."

"People will get the wrong impression."

"Oh? And what impression might that be?" The corners of Kingston's mouth kicked upward.

"That I'm content to be here. That I *want* to be here." Ava sighed in exasperation. "They'll think we're a couple rather than what we really are.

"I don't care what anyone thinks. I want to dance with you."

"Why?"

He chuckled at her annoyance. "Because I want to feel your softness pressed against me. Have your sweet perfume tickle my nose. Are those good enough reasons? Besides, you've been a good girl since we entered the restaurant. I want to reward you."

CHAPTER

NINETEEN

*S*weet like sugar
    I gorge myself until I'm sick.
    Then come back for more.
Always more.

RELUCTANT INTEREST FLASHED across Ava's features as Kingston rubbed his thumb across her bottom lip. He thought about kissing her.

Hell, I'm always thinking about kissing her.

"One dance, Ava."

She shifted on her feet. "May I remove the toy? Sir?"

"What do you think?"

She sighed at that, seemingly resigned to his insistence that she endure the rest of the evening with the vibrator in place.

"One dance," she agreed as though she held any bargaining power at all.

Before she could change her mind, Kingston pulled her

from the alcove. Nodding at an almost invisible bodyguard—the building was filled with them, not withstanding Jack—he led Ava onto the dance floor as the band drifted into a new song, the arrangement sweetly stirring and infinitely classic.

Kingston reeled her fully into his arms, one large hand resting at the low curve of her spine just above her buttocks. As the band's singer, a young hipster guy around Ava's age, crooned the lyrics of an old song by The Platters, Kingston trapped Ava's free hand with his. He tucked it against his heart while her other hand rested lightly atop his shoulder.

Kingston's lips tightened. Even in her high heels, he towered over her. Big. Scary. Brutal.

He truly was the monster who had stolen the princess.

They swayed in silence for several moments before Ava tilted her head. "This was one of my parents' favorite songs." There was a glint of moisture in her eyes.

"Was it?" Kingston drew her closer until her arm draped loosely over his shoulder. Her fingers hovered close to the nape of his neck, softly brushing the skin exposed by his shirt collar.

"Yes," Ava said quietly. "They often danced to it."

"I did not know that. If it's too painful, I'll have the band play something else."

She shook her head. "No. I like hearing it. It reminds me of them and it's a happy memory."

"I'm sorry I wasn't there when they passed. It must have been difficult for you following the funeral."

Ava bit her lip, her gaze darting away from his. "It was a nightmare. Carson was worse than ever. He-he broke into my apartment. Stole things my mom and dad had given me. Anything he could sell. Jewelry and artwork. Stuff like that. And when he ran out of money, he began harassing me to give him the little bit I had saved up. When I refused, he trashed my car. I lost my job at the bookstore because he kept coming there and hounding me for funds. That's when I decided I should get out of Bitter Springs. Get away from him."

Any further mention of their brief encounter at her parents' funeral went unspoken, but Kingston felt a jab of remorse all the same. What kind of hell had she gone through when he moved away?

He remembered the harsh words he said to her the day of the funeral. Instead of berating her and instructing her on being strong, he should have enfolded her in his embrace and promised to shield her from the ugliness of the world. He should have done more to protect her from Carson. He failed her then, but he wouldn't repeat that mistake. "I'm sorry, Ava."

She shrugged. "It isn't your fault Carson is morally bankrupt. What could you have done in that situation? We barely knew one another, and you had your own troubles to overcome. You had no obligation to me."

As they swayed to the music, Kingston's shoulders tightened with unexpected tension. Something about Ava made him feel... *different.* It was frustrating and unsettling, but he realized he would gleefully slaughter anyone who dared hurt her like he had.

Lowering his head, he rested his temple against hers and inhaled her intoxicating scent. She smelled like honeysuckles and roses. Like innocence and lush decadence. He smelled himself on her as well, the faintness of scotch and his own cologne mingling with hers to create a heady blend. She felt so *right* in his arms. He couldn't imagine anything being more perfect than this precise moment in time.

When he tugged her closer, Ava allowed it, her body naturally conforming to his. She melted against him, his arms a steady ballast holding her aloft. He kissed the tips of her fingers softly, delighting in her quick intake of breath. Turning her hand palm up, he pressed his mouth to the center of it.

The song came to an end, the last notes fading away but Ava did not retreat from the circle of his arms. Leaning slightly back, she stared at him while his lips moved softly over her palm.

"The song's over," Ava whispered, her gaze like molten fire.

"Is it?" Kingston's words rumbled as he continued exploring her silken skin. He didn't want the song to end. Didn't want this moment to end.

"Yes," she affirmed, stealing a glance at the stage. "The band stopped playing. I think they're taking a break."

"I'll tell them to keep playing."

She looked disturbed by that prospect. "I don't want to dance anymore. Besides, you said it would be only one."

"I could demand that you dance for me all night, and you'd have no choice but to obey."

Ava took a step back as far as the muscle-clad arm around her waist would allow. Kingston cursed under his breath. He wasn't sure why he'd said it like that. So cold and aloof.

Brutal and uncaring.

It shattered the previous melancholy sweetness, reminding him she was his prisoner. But still. Being this close to Ava, breathing her in, holding her in his arms as though they were really a couple out on a date, was twisting something loose inside him that had been tethered to walls of stone for a long time.

"Like a stripper? That kind of dancing?" Her tone was horrified, her green eyes wide.

"Yes." It was so wrong giving that idea room to run, but the thought of Ava's lithe body undulating while she undressed before him had Kingston's cock hardening into a rod of steel.

She tried pulling free. "I might be your prisoner, but I won't be your whore, too."

"You're not my whore, Ava. You're just mine. Simple as that."

"Not forever, though. There is an expiration date to all of this." Ava clutched her purse closer to her body, something secretive flashing across her pale features.

"We'll see." Kingston shrugged. With the band no longer playing, the few couples also on the dance floor were now returning to their seats. The normal chatter of diners and the faint clinking of silverware were underscored by soft music playing over the restaurant's sound system. The fact the two of them still stood in the middle of the dance floor was drawing attention.

"Time to return to our table, Ava." Kingston gripped her arm a bit harder than necessary when he spied Nadia sulking back to her own table. Her companion was an older man, a distant business associate who enjoyed the company of younger women.

"Of course, *sir*," Ava replied darkly.

"Damn it. Don't give me that. Not right now," he growled, pulling her along with him with such finesse it appeared he was simply being attentive.

"Oh, I'm sorry." Ava's tone dripped with sarcasm. "Wrong venue, is that it?"

She practically threw herself into the curved structure of their booth, sliding across the leather until she reached the very back of it. Kingston followed her, his body pressing close against hers. She immediately tried scooting away but his hard hand on the inside of her thigh stopped her progress.

With a scowl, she grabbed the champagne flute and took a big swallow of its contents.

"I think we should forgo dinner and satisfy your curiosity at LIST," he purred. Two of his fingers anchored the underside of her chin, turning her face so he could smile into her eyes.

"I'd love hearing you try to say 'sir' while you are on your knees with my cock deep in your throat."

Ava sputtered, the descriptive threat catching her off-guard. He removed his fingers from her chin but maintained the grip on her thigh. While she dabbed her chin with a napkin, glaring at him, the waiter appeared with the first course of their meal.

"Behave now," Kingston admonished quietly. "Or suffer the consequences with an audience."

"You wouldn't dare." Gritting her teeth around the words, her panicked gaze flitted to David, their blissfully unaware waiter.

"Care to try me?" His brow rose high.

"My apologies, Miss Blue. You seem to be missing a salad fork." David's brow creased in confusion as he set the plates before them. "I'll bring you one immediately."

"It's fine," Ava said quickly. "I'll use my dinner fork in its place."

Seeing the pink flush creeping across his prisoner's cheeks, Kingston's head tilted.

Interesting.

"Oh, we can't have that, miss. Won't take but a second to bring you a new one," David said. "I can't imagine where the other went. I double-checked this table myself when notified of your arrival, Mister Winter. Accept my apologies for the inconvenience, sir." He hurried off when Kingston waved his hand in dismissal.

"You'll use mine, Ava."

Kingston picked up the fork, testing the tines as he regarded Ava. Shifting on the booth's seat, she flushed even more and nervously ran a hand over her purse.

"That's not necessary." She took another sip of the champagne in an obvious attempt at calming herself.

He laid the fork on her plate while watching her intently. Did she steal the missing utensil? Would she have even dared? His gaze flickered to the small purse she kept touching as if assuring herself it was still nearby.

Without a doubt, that fork was in her purse, but for the moment, he would let that transgression pass. More concerning was the subtle defiance of his authority.

Such a reckless little lamb.

"Pick up that fork and eat your salad, Ava."

"No," she replied. "I've lost my appetite."

Kingston sighed heavily. "You're testing my patience, lamb."

"I don't give a damn about your patience, Kingston." Her fingers trembled with defeat as she picked up the fork, stabbing at a few pieces of the spring mix lettuce. "You are a tyrant."

"Yes," he calmly agreed as she delicately nibbled at the greens. "And there's little hope of changing that."

She'd only eaten a few bites when David swooped back to their table with the missing utensil. Refilling their champagne flutes, he left once again with the explanation he would check on their main courses. By the time the band returned from break, the empty salad plates were removed and replaced with steaming dishes of seared scallops and spinach risotto.

"As much as I enjoy watching you swallow that champagne, I believe you've had enough for the evening," Kingston remarked, pushing his plate away when he finished the last bite.

"That's what you think," Ava smirked, tipping the flute toward Kingston in a mocking salute. She'd barely eaten a third of the meal, although she did remark how delicious it was. "Maybe you should order another bottle since I've got the last of this one."

Kingston smiled. "Don't you think champagne will have the same effect on you as white wine?"

Her brow furrowed in that delightful way. "I don't think it will. It hasn't in the past."

"I want all your facilities intact, lamb. For later."

"Later? What does that mean?" She smiled at David as he removed their used plates. Behind him, Henri approached with two servings of Crème Brûlée and set them down with a flourish.

"Thank you, Henri. David," Kingston addressed the two men, ignoring Ava's question. "The meal was superb. My compliments as always to the chefs."

"Yes, it was *sooo* good," Ava gushed, her face glowing from too much champagne. She wasn't drunk. Just good and tipsy.

"Miss Blue and I would enjoy a bit of privacy while we finish our dessert," Kingston said crisply. "As a matter of fact, there's no need to check on us for the rest of the evening."

"Of course, Mister Winter." Henri bowed at the waist, his face splitting into an indulgent grin. "Miss Blue, we are honored to have you dine with us tonight. We hope to see you again."

"Thank you. I hope so as well." Ava glanced at Kingston before granting the waiter a guileless smile. "And thank you, David, for such excellent service. I don't recall ever being attended to with such care during a meal."

The handsome young man grinned. "It was my pleasure to see to your every need, Miss Blue. I look forward to serving you at some point in the future."

Kingston's blood flared inside his veins. "That will be all, David."

David's gaze shot to Kingston upon hearing the unmistakable annoyance in his words. "Of course, sir. Good evening, Mister Winter. Miss Blue."

Kingston waited until the pair left the table before turning his attention to Ava. She watched him with a strange gleam in her eyes, perhaps recognizing the jealousy swirling inside his gut like a rogue typhoon.

"Flirting with the help, lamb? That isn't acceptable behavior. Not to worry, though. I've ways of breaking you of that."

CHAPTER

TWENTY

*T*wist and turn me about.
*I'm yours to torment.
Yours to keep.*

Ava's maintained her composure with masterful effort.

"Flirting? I don't know what you mean."

"Lying isn't acceptable either." Kingston picked up a spoon, dipping it into his Crème Brûlée. "I've already explained these rules." He held the spoon to her lips, waiting until she reluctantly accepted being fed by him.

She couldn't help the small sound of pleasure she made as the decadent dessert slid down her throat. "You keep changing the rules, Kingston. How am I expected to keep up with all of them?" He fed her another bite and she moaned again. "Oh my God. This is amazing."

"I thought you would enjoy it," he murmured, taking his own bite. "Now, to continue our discussion."

Ava grabbed her spoon and broke through the caramelized

sugar crust of the dessert. "I wasn't flirting. It's called being polite. You should try it sometimes."

"You must really enjoy being punished." A faint smile lifted the corners of Kingston's mouth at her insolence. "Or maybe you just like pushing my buttons."

The accusation startled Ava. She shook her head, concentrating on tapping the Crème Brûlée's crust and shattering it bit by bit. "That's not true. It's just that you can be so infuriating sometimes. And I can't always keep my reactions in check around you."

"You don't always have to, lamb."

Ava pensively admitted, "I don't like being so... angry about this situation. I don't like having my choices taken from me. And I especially don't like being at your mercy all the time."

"I don't expect you to like it, Ava. But you will obey me."

"Doesn't it get exhausting? Being a heavy-handed, irrational brute all hours of the day and night?"

Kingston laughed out loud. "It's my nature. Besides, I've told you repeatedly that this is for your own protection. My enemies would love to get their hands on you. You wouldn't last long if that occurred."

Ava licked her spoon before realizing Kingston's gaze was fixated on her mouth. She slowly lowered the utensil to the bowl. "Do you have any intention of telling me what you know of Carson and my parents' death?"

"Not much has changed." Kingston drained his champagne flute. "The details are murky, but outside individuals are covering the truth for their own benefit. I have a team on it, but even my best hackers haven't reached the bottom of this particular well. All I can say for certain is that Carson is involved somehow. And that means you are not safe."

It was hard to believe her own brother could be so cruel,

but Ava had discovered that power, money, and greed could turn ordinary men into monsters.

Pushing away the bowl of dessert, she slumped against the leather booth seat, feeling defeated and incredibly stupid. Tears pricked her eyes and she let out a huge sigh.

"You are tired, aren't you, lamb?" Kingston asked softly.

"Yes," Ava admitted, putting her pride aside as exhaustion seeped into her bones. She *was* tired. Bone tired. Soul tired.

"Too tired to come for me?"

The question was a silken web of temptation. It could also be a trap and back her into a corner.

"Yes... no. I don't know." She glanced at him from beneath the fringe of her eyelashes. "I'm afraid of what you will do. You always use my words against me. And you enjoy punishing me entirely too much."

Kingston moved closer. "Pain and pleasure straddle the same edge, Ava. Let me show you." Reaching into his coat pocket, he withdrew his phone.

Ava stiffened at the sight of it. But he simply sent a text before setting the device on the table between them.

Within seconds, the restaurant's lighting dimmed, leaving the space in shadows. Only the glow from wall sconces and tabletop candlelight illuminated the room along with the stage lights.

"Yes or no?" Kingston murmured. "Answer quickly."

"Here?" Ava fought down the wave of panic hammering inside her chest. How could he expect her to do something so private in such a public place? Even if no one could see precisely what was happening, the fact someone might figure it out was terrifying.

"Yes. Here. Give into me, and I'll remove the toy."

"You will?" Her voice trembled. Did she really want it removed?

Yes, you foolish, desperate girl! You do!

Kingston's hand drifted to the nape of Ava's neck. He squeezed with just enough pressure to ratchet her breathing even higher. The intoxicating scent of his cologne, crisp pine and fragrant Earl Grey tea, wove around her like a magical fog from a fairy tale.

"I will. But only if you do exactly as I say." He twirled a wisp of her hair around his pinky finger and tugged.

"Okay," Ava murmured before she could rethink her answer. She'd been in a state of simmering arousal since that spanking on the jet. Her body quickened with the promise of satisfaction. The blood in her veins practically hummed in anticipation of Kingston's hands roving over her flesh. The way he touched and kissed her was captivating.

Her quick capitulation made her stomach roil but the lust for this man could not be denied. She would do what he wanted. She would surrender, if only for the fleeting sense of belonging it provided.

Kingston was smiling. Even in the shadows, Ava recognized the corners of his mouth tilting upwards. Was he mocking her willingness to obey him?

Agitated by that thought, she tried shifting away, but his hand tightened on the back of her neck again. The bite of pain made her whimper.

"Put your hand between your legs, Ava. Touch yourself the way you imagine me touching you. Use your fingers and make yourself come. I want to watch you unravel."

Shock left her speechless, but every thread of Ava's soul fluttered in delight when his mouth skimmed her ear, his breath so warm on her skin it scorched like a lit flame. "Do it, Ava."

Tentatively, she did as he demanded, her lungs on fire as she fought the need to inhale huge gulps of air. Her fingers rested lightly on the smooth skin of her pussy. Not moving. Not stroking. Just barely touching, but still, obeying his wicked demand.

"Good girl," Kingston purred. "Now, rub your clit."

Ava nearly snatched her hand away from her body. Hearing both the praise and his dark edict sent her tumbling into a world crafted of decadent sin.

God. What is becoming of me? He is consuming me. Turning me into a creature I do not recognize. Why do I crave him when I should fight him for my freedom?

Kingston must have recognized her momentary flash of rebellion. Exhaling a soft *tsk* of disappointment, his free hand glided over the screen of his cell phone.

The toy inside her roared to life. And every cell in Ava's body violently responded.

A moan broke free of her lips as overwhelming pleasure ignited every nerve ending. Her head fell back against the high-back leather booth, her hips lifting of their own accord.

Kingston's hand tightened around the nape of her neck in a stark warning.

"Do as I tell you, Ava. Make yourself come. Stroke your tight little pussy and imagine my fingers there. My mouth tasting you. My tongue fucking you."

Ava whimpered as images of Kingston worshipping her assailed her. Regardless of other diners just feet away and the waiters hustling to and fro, the band playing softly in the background, she did as Kingston demanded. Her fingers slid over her clit until the need for an orgasm became a clawing, desperate thing.

But the vibrator held her hostage. Straddling an invisible line between oblivion and damnation, its insistent hum broke down every tiny sliver of humility and self-control she still possessed.

Kingston's pleased groan rumbled through Ava like a freight train. "That's it, my savage darling. Show me how much you want to come for me. Show me how much you fucking love this. That you love being controlled. Prove that you are mine, and that I can do whatever the fuck I want with you, and you will beg for more."

"Kingston?" She panted, an orgasm barreling toward her like a runaway train. "I'm going to come if you don't stop... God.... please don't stop."

With no warning, Kingston's free hand dove between her legs. Pushing Ava's hand aside, he secured the loop of the vibrator. It was yanked free just as she helplessly began to crest, driven to madness by his words and actions.

The toy was shoved into his pocket, Kingston's cruel laughter assaulting her ears as her body struggled to make sense of the abrupt deprivation. A low wail bubbled up from her throat. She was trembling on the edge of paradise. Dangling in the abyss. Empty. Wanting. Hungry.

"*Please,*" she gasped, writhing in a desperate search for relief.

"Did you seriously think I'd fucking let you come like that? Using your hand and a goddamn vibrator? I *own* this pussy, Ava," he hissed along the curve of her shoulder, his teeth raking the tender skin. "I own your mouth. Your hands. Your body. Every inch of you is mine. *I'm* the sole deciding factor when it comes to your pleasure and the orgasms I allow you. Ride my fucking fingers and come for me now. Here, in the middle of this restaurant with God and everyone else watching."

Kingston arranged his body until his large form loomed over Ava. Despite his threat to expose her to a public exhibition, he shielded her from view. To the casual observer, it would look as though they were having an intimate discussion. But there was no conversation necessary for what he did next.

His middle finger plunged inside her, the long, blunt-tipped digit roughly filling the aching emptiness. With ruthless intensity, he pumped once, twice, while his thumb circled and pressed her swollen clit. He knew exactly how to shatter her soul into a million, glittering pieces, the shards cutting her to ribbons. How could she defend herself against something that felt so good?

Ava cried out, biting her own hand in a pitiful attempt to contain the unmistakable sounds of bliss. The edges of her eyesight dimmed, Kingston's face and his velvety blue eyes fading into tiny pinpoints. Her body arched into his hand. Into his touch. Feverishly, she wished it was more. Wished it was all of him taking all of her.

Did everyone know Kingston was fucking her with his fingers? It didn't matter if they did. All that mattered was the overwhelming, humiliating pleasure. The awful, beautiful cascade of ecstasy washed all the ugly away, but it left her aching for that sense of belonging she felt only with him.

She could fight him. Hate him. Despise him. But she could not deny herself. This was who she was. A lost girl searching for a safe place to belong. A girl who needed this man to break her down and build her back up again and again. She hovered in a pitch-black world between Heaven and Hell, caught in the arms of the very Devil himself until Kingston's lust-roughened voice sank into her veins like the sweetest drug and pulled her back to him.

"Shh," he soothed, his fingers gliding through the wetness of her arousal in a gentle motion as she shuddered in his embrace. "Let it all out for me like a good girl. Let me have your tears... Fuck. You're goddamn perfection like this."

I'm crying? She was. Tears rolled down her cheeks in

sparkling silver streams. Exhaustion like she'd never known before crushed her bones. After being held prisoner on the cusp of completion for so long, her body shut down as it succumbed to an overload of sensations. Kingston had driven her to a cliff of madness. A place where she shook and trembled like a silly doll while he manipulated the strings.

Curling toward his leanly muscled form, she pressed closer. It was stupid to think he provided some sort of shelter from the storm inside her. Because this man *was* the storm. A hurricane flattening her resistance and sweeping away everything that came before him.

Kingston.

Her tormentor. Her captor. Her shameful, hated obsession.

"I don't want to be yours. I can't. I can't…" she choked, burying her face in the warm column of his neck.

She couldn't manage anything else. Couldn't move her arms or legs. She was drowning, the sea swallowing her up and destroying any desire to stay afloat. She wondered why it seemed he was very far away when he held her so close. She could hear his heart beating. It was louder than her own.

"Easy, Ava. Easy. I'm very aware of the fact you don't want to be here." Kingston's fingers slipped away from the junction of her thighs. "But I'm a heartless, selfish bastard, and you have no choice."

He sounded… sad. Maybe even remorseful. But Ava only nodded because, in this jumbled state of emotions, she liked how gently he spoke while efficiently tugging her dress back into place. His voice spilled over her like a warm summer rain, the tenderness in his hands repairing the damage of his onslaught.

Ava sank into his darkness, too tired to fight being his.

"Shhh. Let me take care of you now," Kingston murmured, gripping her throat with his large hand. Tipping her head back, he stared down at her before rubbing the pad of his thumb, still wet from her arousal, along her bottom lip. Ava watched in dazed contentment as he brought it to his mouth and licked her essence from it, his eyes glittering like stars in a sea of deep blue. "Like it or not, you are mine, Ava. And I always take care of what's mine."

TWENTY-ONE

S urrender is never easy.
Except when one wishes to be conquered.

KINGSTON CARRIED Ava out of the restaurant. She was crashing from the gauntlet of sensations, and he needed to get her someplace safe where he could counteract that.

Jack's accusatory stare as he cleared a pathway to the penthouse's private elevator only added to Kingston's mounting sense of guilt. He returned the bodyguard's censure with a raised eyebrow as the three of them entered the elevator. Silently, he pressed the elevator's security fingerprint pad and leaned back against the wall while Jack took up a stance at the doors.

Ava should not have been pushed to such extremes without a plan in place to take care of her. She wasn't accustomed to this type of play. She'd never been warned about what could happen, the dangers and the precautions one needed to take. And she sure as hell did not have a safe word. He'd not been thinking clearly, his mind reeling with the heady power he had over her. Remaining calm and unattached was impossible when the woman in his arms was a fucking temptation.

Ava blinked up at Kingston as the elevator silently carried them to the penthouse suite.

"Our evening is over, sir?" She seemed puzzled as she stared at Jack's broad back before turning her gaze back to Kingston.

"Yes, lamb." Kingston hugged her tighter.

Ava frowned but did not try to extract herself from his arms. "And now we're going to sleep?"

"We are."

"Okay," she acquiesced with a little yawn. "I'm really tired."

"It's been a very long day," Kingston replied as the elevator came to a stop. The sleek steel doors slid open, revealing an elegant antechamber decorated in soothing cream and gold tones. A double set of ebony black doors took up one entire wall of the space while the opposite ends offered floor-to-ceiling windows with impressive views of the city.

Jack stepped out first, his hand on the butt of his gun as he checked out the space. "Clear."

Kingston shifted Ava in his arms and touched his finger to a second entry pad on the wall beside the doors. Jack entered the penthouse first, quickly moving through the rooms then returning to the foyer.

"All clear, Boss."

"Thanks, Jack." Kingston carried Ava into the living room area. "I'll let you know our plans in the morning."

Ava's head raised from Kingston's shoulder as Jack exited the penthouse. Giving the large contemporary space a brief glance, she gave another yawn and dropped her head once more. Nuzzling her cheek against the lapel of his suit coat, she mumbled, "Very pretty."

Kingston's jaw clenched with concern. This lethargic drop of energy she was experiencing should be addressed quickly. He needed to both hydrate her and feed her something to combat the side effects that came from sensory overload.

Setting her down on the black leather sofa, he grabbed a sable throw blanket that lay draped over one end. After tucking it around her body, he also quickly unbuckled her shoes and tossed them to the floor.

With a sigh of contentment, Ava curled into the blanket's furry warmth. Her eyes drifted shut again, and a small smile curved her full lips. The silver purse was clutched to her chest as if it were a pillow.

Kingston passed a hand over the crown of her head in an oddly affectionate gesture before stalking into the kitchen. His phone beeped once, alerting him to a message. After reading the text from Paulie, he slid his phone back into his pocket with a distracted frown.

With the open floor plan, he could keep an eye on her while gathering necessary items. Ava never budged from the spot he placed her. Even when he set the tray containing gourmet chocolates, strawberries, and a glass of water on the sleek chrome coffee table, she did not move. Nor did she stir when he carefully positioned himself beside her on the oversized, plush sofa. The leather squeaked softly in protest as he settled in.

She'd fallen asleep, her body curved into a fetal position and her feet tucked beneath her. Her hands curled beneath her chin, the purse's strap entwined in her fingers. Although reluctant to wake her, Kingston knew it was necessary.

"Ava, I want you to sit up for me now." He gently wrapped

an arm around her shoulders, pulling her upright. Ignoring her grumble of displeasure, he tugged the purse from her grip and placed it on the table. He knew what it contained; the makeshift weapon she'd stolen from the restaurant.

That brazen act of foolishness would go unpunished for the moment but Kingston could help but wonder if she would try using it against him. Would he wake up later and find that fork embedded in one of his eyeballs?

Tucking her against his side, he pressed the glass of water to Ava's lips. "Drink this."

Ava drowsily pushed his hand away. "Too tired."

"I know, but just a little sip. There you go. Good girl. Look, there's chocolate. And strawberries. I know you love straw-berries."

"Why are you doing this?" she asked, taking another longer drink of water. Then, in a perfect display of obedience, she opened her mouth and allowed Kingston to pop in a slice of fruit. Once she'd chewed and swallowed, she obediently opened her mouth a second time for a piece of hazelnut-infused chocolate sprinkled with sea salt.

"Because it's necessary."

Ava shot him a bemused look. "But why is it necessary?"

"Because you require proper care after I play with you. You were dropping. This will counteract that," he explained patiently.

"You carried me here, right?" Her gaze flitted around the spacious room with its bright white marble floors and vaulted ceilings. Light from the kitchen provided dim illumination, accented by the darkness beyond the expanse of glass walls studded with the glow of other high rises and the restless city below. "You didn't drop me."

She clutched the blanket closer to her chin, opening her mouth as Kingston fed her another slice of strawberry followed by more chocolate. Her gaze was slowly clearing of the cobwebs.

"Dropping happens sometimes after experiencing extreme pleasure or a release of some sort. It's especially common following a prolonged period of orgasm denial." Kingston watched as Ava turned the explanation over in her mind. Despite the weariness rolling off her in waves, he felt her reaction once his words sunk in and made sense.

"In the restaurant. What you did to me..." Faint outrage laced her words but she was still too weak to do anything other than open her mouth for another sip of water.

Kingston laid a finger over her lips when she indicated she was done. "Thank me later, lamb. Now that you are feeling better, let's get you ready for bed."

Ava's gaze darted around the living room until she found what she wanted on the glass-topped coffee table. "I need my purse."

"You'll manage without it." Kingston rose from the couch, pulling her up along with him. He almost tossed the blanket back across the end of the couch before noticing how Ava shivered without its warmth. Tucking it around her shoulders, he assured her, "Everything you need is already here. It was all delivered while we were on the jet."

Ava glanced back at the purse while Kingston took her by the elbow. He guided her down a long, wide hall lit by sconces of sleek silver metal. The soft padding of her bare feet on the marble floor and the sharp click of his dress shoes echoed in the silence.

Passing though the master bedroom starkly decorated in shades of white and ebony black, they entered an expansive bathroom constructed entirely of marble and gleaming silver fixtures. Kingston withdrew new toothbrushes and toothpaste from one of the vanity drawers. He waved a hand at Ava, indicating she should begin brushing her teeth while he did the same.

There was a strange familiarity in the actions of readying for bed. As though the two of them were a normal couple rather than prisoner and captor. Surprisingly, Kingston found himself enjoying the illusion of domesticity when he'd once sworn against such situations.

But this was vastly different from time spent with other women. Those meaningless, faceless, forgettable women meant nothing to him.

Yes, this was different. What he and Ava shared felt incredibly *right*.

He wordlessly pulled Ava into the walk-in closet, opening a set of drawers containing a selection of lingerie. While she stood motionless, Kingston stripped the silvery blue dress from her body. For a few seconds, she stood bare before him, so perfect and beautiful that it left his mouth dry. Hands shaking, he settled a black chemise-type nightgown over Ava's head and tugged it until the silk flowed around her body.

"I prefer you wearing nothing at all when you are in my bed, Ava," he murmured, spinning her around so she faced away from him. The urge to press his mouth against the tenderness of her bare nape was ignored as he carefully extracted bobby pins from her hair. The dark blonde waves tumbled almost to the middle of her back. He wanted to rake his fingers through the mass, use the silken strands as a way of holding her still so he could ravage her mouth. "Tonight, however, I'm making certain concessions based on your fragile state."

Ava did not respond as he took care of her.

One bedside lamp was burning when Kingston tucked her beneath the thick comforter. Ava silently regarded him when he finally stepped away, his hands shoved into his trouser pockets.

"Go to sleep now. I must take care of some business before I join you."

"What kind of business?" Her voice was husky with exhaustion. She slid further into the cloud-like softness of the bed covers, prompting a little sigh of pleasure that shot like a lightning bolt straight to Kingston's cock.

"Just the usual world domination type stuff," he replied in an almost teasing manner.

Ava's mouth curved with the beginnings of a real smile. "No rest for the wicked, I suppose." She snuggled deeper into the pillows, hugging one to her chest. Her eyes were already closing. "I'm pretty sure you've cornered the market on domination."

"We've yet to fully explore that concept." Kingston turned the lamp down until it was a soft glow. "But we will. Go to sleep now, Ava." He nearly reached out to stroke her hair before clenching his fist against the urge. Instead, he quickly exited the room, pulling the door closed before making his way back to the living room.

After pouring himself a scotch, he flung himself onto the couch and withdrew his phone. Clicking on Paulie's number, he waited impatiently for the man to answer.

"What's the news?"

"Hackers finally got it," Paulie replied. "I've sent you the file under the secret account in an unlabeled file. I also took the liberty of having IT assign it an encrypted password."

"Give me a second to pull it up." Kingston made his way down the hall and entered his office using the fingerprint security pad. Firing up his laptop, he punched in the information Neil provided. Sure enough, there it was.

He hesitated to open it right away. The cursor arrow

hovered over the file icon, blinking like a cheap neon sign. "Has anyone seen what it contains?"

"Just me, boss," Paulie replied, his tone grim. "And only the first minute or so. I wanted to be sure they'd captured the right file." There was a long moment of silence before he angrily continued, "The bastards were laughing while they held her down."

"All the individuals we suspected are visible on the video?"

"Yeah. Even the brother. Son of a bitch recorded himself for about five seconds before the camera focused on her."

Kingston rubbed his forehead with the tumbler of scotch, attempting to dull the sudden pain blooming in his temples. Realizing there really was video evidence of Ava's assault at the hands of Carson and his friends knotted his stomach with overwhelming rage.

"What else?" He swallowed a gulp of scotch, his head pounding with dread. Clicking the file, he waited for it to load.

"Just what you expected, King. Collaborated by both text and email correspondence. Carson was with Judd Vanderhoff the night of the wreck." Paulie did not bother hiding the disgust in his voice. "They planned it together after Carson blackmailed him and the others with the video. And Judge Vanderhoff orchestrated the cover-up to conceal his son's involvement."

"Don't worry, Paulie," Kingston murmured as lightning from the storm on that fateful night lit up Carson's face in the video. "I'll take care of matters in the only way that makes sense to a man like me. The only way that permanently ensure Ava's safety."

CHAPTER
TWENTY-TWO

The truth can be brutal.
And betrayal illuminating.
Nothing remains in the darkness for long.

KINGSTON SLID BENEATH THE COVERS, one arm curving around Ava's silk-clad form. He was careful not to wake her as he hauled her closer against his naked body.

Bad idea.

Everything inside him roared to life, his cock swelling with the feel and smell of her. That honeysuckle perfume was a potent aphrodisiac. God, how he wanted her.

But fucking her was an even worse idea than holding her. He wouldn't do it. Not after what he'd already put her through. He'd spanked her, edged her with a vibrating toy, and finished her off with his fingers. No wonder she dropped.

Look at yourself, asshole. Feeding her chocolate and strawberries, for fuck's sake. She's my prisoner. My property. Not my goddamn girlfriend. I could fuck her right now if I wanted. A monster would. A monster like me would take whatever he wanted —however he wanted.

But then he would be no different than Carson. No different than Judd Vanderhoff. Or Brad and Jeff, the twins who held her down during the assault. It was of little comfort that those two would be found dead soon enough. One brother would die from a drug overdose, the other, suicide by hanging. The arrangements were already in place for what Kingston considered low-hanging fruit. Those two pieces of scum deserved to die for their callous treatment of Ava.

What makes me any different?

It was an unavoidable fact he had asserted his authority over Ava upon her arrival at The Den. Yes, he had restrained her on multiple occasions. He even trapped her into giving him a blowjob while his men listened as the encounter played out. But didn't he always counter those moments of degradation with great pleasure for Ava? Wasn't it true he had granted her too many orgasms to count?

What I've done to her is much worse. I used her responses to my touch, her need for approval, and the thrill of danger as justification for my own actions. I've used her craving for my own pleasure. And I'll do it again, no matter how much I hate myself for it.

It did no good to beat himself up about all that now. She was here in his bed and for the near future, he could do whatever he wanted with her. Testing that theory, Kingston experimentally rocked his dick against her backside. It felt good, the silk of her nightgown caressing his flesh. But it would feel even better if it was her bare pussy sliding against him.

Ava mumbled something in her sleep, her ass wiggling against the cradle of Kingston's crotch.

Stars flashed before his eyes, but somehow, Kingston strangled his reaction. His brain whirled with a million thoughts. How easily he could slide into Ava's pussy from behind. His hands cupping her breasts while his fingernails scraped her hard nipples until she begged him to taste them. God, he would devour her whole in a matter of moments if he obeyed his body's demands.

But he wouldn't. Even if he owned her to the tune of two point six million dollars and could do as he pleased, Kingston hesitated. Torn between ignoring what the Devil insisted was his for the taking or listening to that tiny sliver of decency still lurking deep inside his soul.

A scene from the video, Judd Vanderhoff caressing and licking Ava's naked breasts, flashed in his mind.

"Shh, Ava. Relax and enjoy it." Judd laved the tip of her exposed breast with his tongue. "Doesn't this feel good?"

Fucker. Kingston already planned on ripping the man's tongue out, stomping on it, and feeding it back to him.

Letting out a heavy sigh, he shifted until there was a healthy bit of space between his and Ava's bodies. He could just make out the elegant curve of her bare shoulder peeping over the edge of the blanket, his arm resting lightly in the hollow of her waist. It was the only part of himself touching her now.

Somehow, he lassoed a leash around his urges. There were so many things he must focus his attention on. Namely, Ava's brother and the weak men stupid enough to be blackmailed over a video. He would put aside his lust and do whatever was necessary in securing Ava's safety.

But Kingston knew this self-imposed restraint wouldn't last. The demons he harbored would eventually break free of their chains. He would use Ava until she cried for mercy, and then use her some more. It's what any monster would do with such an entrancing prize caught within his claws.

And if he was anything in this life, it was a monster.

THE SUN WAS CREEPING into the room when Kingston opened his eyes.

Stretching out his free arm, he half rolled toward Ava, intent on moving her off his bicep so he could stretch that one as well.

"Good morning," Ava whispered.

Kingston eased back against the pillows, twisting his body until they were face to face. "Good morning."

Silence fell between them. Ava chewed her bottom lip. She appeared reluctant to move from her current position so Kingston stayed where he was, waiting for her to dictate how the morning would begin.

"You, um, you took care of me last night." Ava's expression was serious. "Thank you for doing that."

"I'll always take care of you, Ava. Don't you realize that by now?"

A tiny frown creased her brow. Tucking her hands beneath her chin, her gaze drifted helplessly over Kingston's naked torso until it landed on the tattoo inked across his heart and the motto scrawled along his ribs. "I don't understand what happened to me. Why I felt so... so strange. Like I was, I don't know, floating maybe. Everything was fuzzy and yet, my body felt so alive. Then, it was gone, and I wanted to curl into a ball. Shut everything out."

Kingston took one of her hands and kissed the tips of her fingers. "I gave a very basic explanation last night but you probably didn't understand. You were on a sensory high, Ava. Every interaction between us, beginning with what occurred on the jet, pushed your body into a heightened sense of awareness."

He paused, acutely aware of her reaction to this information. Her pupils dilated when reminded of the spanking, the green of her irises swallowed up by black. The pulse in her neck fluttered wildly against creamy skin as her breathing increased. The memory of the toy inside her as he drove her to the very cusp of an orgasm stained her cheeks pinks with embarrassment.

"When I made you come, it was more pleasure than your body could handle after being denied for so long." Rubbing a thumb over Ava's mouth, Kingston tugged her bottom lip free of her teeth. "The crash you experienced is normal, but I should have been prepared for it. I wasn't. And for that, I am sorry, Ava. When you drop the next time we play, I'll catch you a lot quicker. I promise."

"Next time?" Ava breathed. Her tone was an odd compound of both trepidation and innocent curiosity.

Kingston cupped her chin in the palm of his hand. "I intend on giving you unimaginable pleasure on a regular basis. This will happen again. I'm asking that you trust me not to hurt you."

Ava's gaze hardened. "A prisoner doesn't have the luxury of trusting their jailer, Kingston."

Kingston's jaw clenched. Was it any wonder Ava did not believe him? After the horror her brother put her through, and all the things Kingston himself had done, could anyone blame her for doubting a man's sincerity?

He should tell her the video of her assault had been found. He should reveal the full extent of Carson's betrayal and his part in her parents' death. It would drive home the incredible danger she was in.

But selfishly, Kingston clammed up. He could not reveal that kind of horror and despair on a morning already flooded with sunshine.

He wanted to enjoy Ava's company today. Wanted to see

her smile. Hear her tinkling laughter. He wanted to witness her quiet, intelligent contemplation as they perused the artwork of the closest museum. He wanted Ava to voluntarily grab his hand and entwine her fingers with his.

Most of all, he wanted to steal quick, warm kisses from her cinnamon-infused mouth, courtesy of a cup of warm apple cider purchased from a little antique bookstore and café located less than a block away. He'd take her there and lead her to the back of the store. Push her against the dusty shelves filled with fragile, forgotten books and kiss her until they were both breathless.

Why he wanted all of that didn't make sense. It was infuriating those thoughts bounced around inside his brain. But when Ava looked at him, the innocence of her expression so pure and sweet, he forgot why he fought this obsession.

"Let's negotiate our time together, lamb," he slowly replied. "I escort you around the city today. You allow it and enjoy it."

Suspicion flitted across her delicate features. "What do I have to do?"

"Not a damn thing, other than stay close by my side the entire time and be a good girl. You can do that, can't you?" Kingston's lips twitched with amusement at the sudden fierceness of her glare. "Be a good girl, that is?"

Ava might be a natural submissive, but there was also a rogue streak of newfound strength that Kingston found fascinating. Maybe she would do as he requested and obey, but it was just as likely she wouldn't. This would open up an opportunity for her to escape but it would be easy enough to track her down.

"I won't try to run, if that's what you mean," Ava finally responded with a stubborn glint in her eyes. "It would be stupid to even try. I've no money. No ID. I don't even have my cell phone to call someone to come get me. Lucky for you, I never memorize phone numbers."

"9-1-1 is easy enough to remember," Kingston pointed out.

Ava's face smoothed into a blank canvas. She was becoming more adept at hiding her emotions when it suited her purposes. "The police would just return me to you, though. Wouldn't they, sir?"

A wide grin spread across Kingston's mouth. "I think you are finally beginning to understand your situation."

How he'd gone so quickly from captor to protector was mystifying, but Kingston would not shy away from the responsibility.

Yes, Ava was his, and seeing evidence of her abuse left him with an almost desperate need to keep her safe. Images from the video kept flashing in his mind. Like clips from a horror movie flickering across a dark screen in rapid succession, they played out until Kingston wanted to howl with rage.

"Carson," Ava sobbed. She twisted in vain against the attackers' hard, hurtful hands, eyes wild with panic as she sought out her brother's form where he stood in the darkened corner. Lightning lit up the space in a blinding burst of energy. Thunder immediately rumbled behind it. Paired with the distant thumping bass of the music downstairs, it nearly drowned out her cries. "Carson, help me! Make them stop."

"Don't fight them, sis," Carson advised. The men holding her down laughed like a deadly pack of hyenas, pulling her dress apart. After ripping away her bra, they went into a frenzy over her exposed breasts. Licking and squeezing every inch that was bare. Judd bit her nipple after sucking it into his mouth, the expression of ecstasy on his face hard to conceal. When she let out a muffled scream, he merely laughed and ravaged her other breast.

Jeff gripped both of her hands, forcibly rubbing them over the erection in his jeans while Judd shifted until he loomed over Ava's midsection. He licked her face, savoring her tears as Brad jerked her legs, forcing them to spread wide apart.

Kingston's insides clenched.

His poor little lamb.

He was going to thoroughly enjoy carving up the mother-fuckers who dared to hurt her. Hunting them down and hearing their screams for mercy as he sliced them into pieces was the only way to make this right. After all, he was the only one allowed to torment Ava Blue. The only one who deserved her tears, her sweet cries. Although Ava most certainly did not appreciate his obsession, she damn well better get used to it.

Because she was his.

Had been since the day he laid eyes on her in her mother's kitchen. And despite his vow that he would release her someday in the future, Kingston knew it wouldn't happen. He would break his word... something he never did... and he would do it for her. They were bound to each other. Caring for her was a vulnerability he couldn't afford, but he cared anyway with a wild, feverish abandonment that would probably end up getting him killed.

Ava was his. He was hers. It was always meant to be.

He accepted it and she would, too. Ava Bella Blue had wiggled her way into his cold, lifeless lump of a heart and was breathing life into it. Into *him.*

Sucking in a quiet breath of utter clarity, Kingston tucked a tendril of honey-gold hair behind her delicate ear. It meant everything when Ava did not flinch from his touch but continued staring at him, a look of worried confusion in her eyes at his suddenly somber mood.

"Come on," Kingston murmured. "It's going to be a beautiful day. Let's not waste a minute of it."

TWENTY-THREE

From behind the clouds
A ray of light
Bright and stabbing.

KINGSTON TUGGED on a pair of black sweatpants before throwing a robe on as well. Ava watched from the bed with the covers rumpled around her waist. She could not stop staring at his body. The man was so perfectly built that it hurt to look at him. All those muscles and ridges were like magnets—holding her gaze against her will. It wasn't fair that he was so damn effortlessly good-looking. Even with his dark hair mussed and the shadow of a beard gracing his chin, he was stunning.

"I'll have breakfast on the table by the time you are done getting ready. Everything you need for a shower is in the bathroom, and there's clothing and shoes for you in the closet there."

"You aren't going to...?" Ava bit back the words, embarrassed that the disappointment of bathing alone was so appar-ent. The fact she'd been granted this privacy was an unexpected gift. And here she was, stupidly questioning it.

"Join you in the shower?" Kingston grinned. "As tempting as that is, feeding you is more important. You hardly ate anything at dinner last night, not counting dessert. I don't want you fainting from hunger later."

"Wait. You're going to cook breakfast?"

"Don't get too excited. Pancakes and sausage are easy enough." Leaning over the bed, he tweaked her nose. "And don't dawdle. I need to make a quick stop by my office before we head out today. It's on the eleventh floor. We'll hit it on the way down."

"Are all of your offices in this same building?" Ava tilted her head. How convenient that his legitimate businesses were so readily accessible. Not for the first time, she thought of Kingston's wealth and power and the numerous ways he used it to his advantage.

"No. I have others scattered across the city. Other coun-tries, too, if you're curious."

Ava's couldn't help it as her thoughts turned dark. How many people had this man trafficked? How many helpless, abused women had been bought and sold like cattle while she enjoyed dessert in his façade of a restaurant?

"Whatever you're thinking, Ava, and I have a pretty good idea of what that might be, it's wrong." Kingston's tone went from teasing to whip-sharp in a matter of seconds. "Many aspects of my business are legitimate, and the ones that aren't do not involve trafficking. My father had no qualms about those things, but I do."

Ava drew her knees to her chest and wrapped her arms around them. There was no need to remind him again of his hypocrisy. How quickly he would have sold her to the highest bidder if not for a selfish desire to keep her for himself? "But you do kill people. At the very least, someone else does it for you."

Kingston sighed, the harshness in his eyes mellowing into vague annoyance. "When the situation warrants it, yes, I've killed men. Men like Malcolm. Men like your brother. It's best not to dwell on this, Ava. It will only upset you, and you'll never have answers for those questions racing through your mind. Now, go take your shower and get dressed. I expect you to see you at the dining room table in half an hour."

Inside the closet, Ava discovered an array of clothing in her size with the price tags still attached. Boxes revealed shoes of all kinds, and in the bathroom, an assortment of high-end makeup items sat lined up for her use. She quickly showered and dressed and now, twenty-nine minutes later, she slid into one of the chairs surrounding a glass and chrome dining table that could seat at least twelve people.

Kingston smiled, placing a plate heaped high with a stack of fluffy pancakes and a side of sausage in front of her. "Look at my good girl. So prompt and obedient."

"Did you make these from scratch?" Ava deliberately ignored his snide words of praise.

"I did," he said without a hint of sheepishness. "One of my more useless talents."

Ava remained silent as he returned to the kitchen and poured her a cup of coffee. After serving her, he grabbed his own plate and sat at the head of the table. Taking a position of power came naturally to him.

"My stepmother showed me once. And when I was a starving college student, this was a relatively cheap meal that went a long way." Kingston took a sip of coffee, then swirled his fork through the melting butter on top of his pancakes.

Ava cut her eyes at him, remembering she had never seen him in anything other than dress clothes back in those days. At the time, she'd simply thought it was a pretentious way of distinguishing himself from the frat boys and jocks. "You were always very well-dressed for a struggling student."

"Speaking of being well-dressed, you look gorgeous, lamb." Kingston changed the subject, his gaze raked over her form. "I like that color on you."

Ava tugged at the neck of the deep magenta sweater. It was paired with dark blue jeans, knee-high brown boots, and a Louis Vuitton purse in dark brown. It suddenly felt claustrophobic to wear the clothes he'd purchased for her.

"Thank you," she murmured, rolling the sausages on her plate back and forth with her fork. The utensil was of finer quality than the one stashed in her evening purse.

Her gaze drifted to the coffee table in the open-concept living room area. The pretty accessory still rested on the glass surface where Kingston tossed it the night before. A guilty flush stained her cheeks as she quickly looked away.

She couldn't say for certain why she'd stolen the item. In retrospect, the misguided idea of protecting herself seemed incredibly foolish. But how could she explain that to the man sitting beside her? Would he believe she had no intention of using a weapon against him? Or would he punish her for what she'd done?

Would it be so terrible if he did?

"Eat your pancakes now, Ava."

The sternness of his voice jerked her back to awareness. Robotically, she cut into the pancakes and ate a forkful. It melted in her mouth, sweet and buttery, but in all honesty, she barely tasted them. Dread that he would discover her rebellious act turned the food into a tasteless lump of cardboard.

"It's really good," she said in a small voice.

Kingston's mouth twitched with a smile. "Vanilla is the secret. And a bit of cinnamon."

She took a sip of coffee. "That's not much of a secret. My mom made them the same way."

His shoulders rose in a shrug. "I always thought it was a trick no one else knew about. Rebecca never let on, either. Doesn't make them any less delicious, though."

Ava continued eating as silence stretched between them. The sight of Kingston's chiseled jaw working silently as he chewed the pancakes did things to her heart rate. Emblazoned with that fierce lion tattoo, his bare chest revealed itself in little peeks each time his robe fell open. It made her mouth water, leaving her emotions in turmoil and her weakness something to be despised.

And the other tattoo etched across his ribs? How could she forget it?

Crush. Conquer. Protect.

He'd certainly done all that and more when it came to her.

"We'll stay another night or two in the city and return home in a couple of days," Kingston remarked, standing to remove both of their plates and carrying them into the kitchen. Scraping them clean into the garbage, he gave them a quick rinse before loading the dishwasher. "Would you like that, lamb?"

Home. When did that come to mean anywhere this man might be?

Anxious for something to occupy her hands, Ava carried the two coffee cups to the sink. "If that's what you want."

He took the mugs from her and stuck them in the dishwasher's top rack. "I thought you might like visiting an art gallery that's nearby. I know the owner."

There was a note in Kingston's voice that sounded cautiously hopeful. As if he really was trying to do something nice for her but thought his offer might be rejected.

"An art gallery?"

"Yes," he said with a smile. "Or we could go to a museum. Your choice."

Something quivered inside Ava's stomach. When Kingston turned his charm on full display, he was practically irresistible.

Retreating to the other side of the wide kitchen island, she watched as he continued cleaning up. Standing awkwardly beside a sleek barstool, she nibbled a fingernail until Kingston's pointed look of disappointment reminded her that the anxiety-soothing activity was no longer allowed.

"We'll start with the bookstore I mentioned before," Kingston said, coming around the island and taking both of her hands in his. "I also made you an appointment at a lovely spa I think you will enjoy."

Ava gave him a look full of suspicion. "A spa? What for?"

Kingston's features were deceptively neutral. "I want you pampered and prepared for me."

She sucked in a breath. "What does that even mean?"

"Waxed and whatever else those places do. I want you so smooth and bare that I can see your arousal glistening on your skin. I will lick you clean over and over until you are worn out and allow me to do anything else I want."

Ava clenched her thighs at the image his words conjured up. Sweet lord, that's all it took to set her aflame.

"Feel free to look around the penthouse while I take a quick shower. Apart from my office, there is nothing here that is off limits to you," Kingston casually remarked as he let her go. Heading down the hallway, he thew a vague warning over his shoulder. "Do not attempt using the elevator without my assistance, Ava. The alarm is always set as a precaution when I'm here."

Ava waited until the door to the bedroom snicked close before grabbing the purse she had selected earlier. Perched on the edge of the sofa, she quickly transferred the items from the elegant evening clutch to the much roomier designer purse. The fork settled nicely at the bottom of it.

Her gaze darted around the penthouse. It was so sleek. So modern. Completely different from the gothic, castle-like feel of The Den. With a shiver, Ava wrapped her arms around her body. Without Kingston's presence, it also felt cold and impersonal. It was a place used strictly for life and death decisions. Deals where money exchanged hands and contracts were signed in ink and blood.

Standing back up, she drifted around the living room. For a few moments, she stood before the huge windows and marveled at the bird's eye view of the bustling city below. The penthouse was so high up, it was dizzying to look down at the streets surrounding the building. Vehicles appeared to be minuscule toys and people scurried around like ants.

Tearing herself away from the view, Ava looked around the living room. It shared space with the large kitchen and was constructed much like the hub of a wheel with different hallways serving as spokes. Moving toward the kitchen, she lingered by a large knife block.

Touching the gleaming handle of an elegant paring knife, she decided against taking it. No doubt Kingston would notice its absence. He would search her and her purse. She would be caught with an actual weapon and that would be the end of that. With a sigh, Ava moved on, trailing her fingers over the expensive countertops.

Further exploration of the penthouse revealed one hallway

containing three additional bedrooms with attached baths, and a guest bathroom meant for general use. Another hallway led to an impressive gym with several workout machines and free weights and an entire wall of windows overlooking the city.

On the opposite side of the kitchen was a large window and a glass door with a keypad leading to a private rooftop pool. Lush landscaping and several canopy-covered seating areas surrounded the lovely space. Too bad she didn't know the code. It would have been nice to sit in the sunshine.

A third, shorter hallway led to a single room and a locked door with the same style keypads as the others she'd seen.

This must be Kingston's office. Ava traced the wood grain of the door, wondering what secrets were held within that necessitated it being locked up so tight.

"Are you ready to go?"

Ava let out a little yelp of alarm. Whirling to meet Kingston's gaze, her back pressed against the office door. "You scared me."

He smiled at the accusation, moving closer until there was nowhere she could go. His hands settled on her hips. For a long time, he simply held her there then murmured beneath his breath, "I forgot my own rule."

"What rule is that?" Ava hated that her voice sounded breathy. She didn't want Kingston to know how much he affected her, but it seemed impossible to keep it hidden. He wore his usual somber outfit. The custom-made suit and tie only made him appear more dangerous than she already knew him to be.

"No jeans for you, ever. It keeps me from being able to fully access every part of you." His thumbs rubbed the fabric covering her hips.

Ava turned her head, bracing her hands against his wide

chest. His cologne teased her nostrils, the scent spicy, sweet, and enveloping. "You had more than enough of me yesterday, don't you think?"

Kingston shook his head with a little grunt of annoyance. "It won't ever be enough, Ava, and that's the damnable thing about all this."

"You could still let me go. Even after everything you've done... I wouldn't tell anyone. I promise." Ava held her breath as Kingston gripped both her wrists in one hand, pulling them high above her head and pinning her against the solid door.

"Yeah, I could let you go." His lips skimmed across hers in a teasing motion. "But I won't. I told you before, Ava. You're mine, now. Mine to protect. To torment. To adore." His voice grew rougher. "To fuck."

He claimed her mouth, devouring her until Ava couldn't breathe. She could only kiss him back and hope her heart survived his possession.

"I didn't fuck you last night, Ava. Nor this morning when I easily could have taken what I wanted." Like a warm wind, his words fanned across her cheek as he nibbled the corner of her lips.

"Why didn't you?" She was genuinely curious about that. Why he had restrained himself after the incident in the restaurant.

He chuckled softly, his hand tightening around her wrists. "Because I thought I might try being a gentleman. An unfamiliar role, to be sure. But if I had taken you in that fragile state, being the bastard that I am, I would not have stopped until you were completely ruined. Oh, don't misunderstand me. You would have enjoyed every minute of it, but it was unwise to push you any further. After you dropped so hard and fast, I didn't want to risk triggering one of your night terrors."

Strangely enough, Kingston's explanation made sense. He

only wanted to claim her when she was fully aware and functional. Anything less than one hundred percent participation in her own destruction was unacceptable. Finding out that he voluntarily locked down his own desires for her sake sent a tingle through Ava. The idea that he had taken care of her sank a little deeper into the cracks around her heart.

It wasn't much, but it was something. A sliver of consideration he would never have extended before. Unexpected warmth spread tendrils around Ava's insides, but she was still torn between self-preservation and willing self-destruction.

He could have done anything he wanted, used me in ways that would have broken me—both in mind and spirit—but he didn't. Why? Why spare me that torment if he means to destroy me anyway?

Could it be that Kingston was beginning to care for her? Was it possible this callous man with a heart as cold as winter snow was falling for his captive?

Of course, it was possible. After all, wasn't she falling in love with her jailor?

"I wouldn't stop you now, sir," she whispered recklessly. The thought of Kingston thrusting himself inside her made her core ache in the most delicious way. Offering him any part of her soul was crazy, but Ava could not deny how badly she wanted him. It was stupid and dangerous and would be the end of her life as a sane person, but it couldn't be helped.

"I'll warn you not to play with fire, Ava. I was a fucking idiot last night, and I'm definitely not a gentleman. Don't offer me a single thing unless you want me to take it all."

"Take everything." Ava arched toward him, her breasts grazing his chest in a teasing manner. A harsh laugh escaped her. "I already know you aren't a gentleman. Show me how crazy you are for me because I swear to God, I'm beyond psychotic for wanting you after everything you've done."

One of Kingston's hands tangled in her hair while with the other, he kept her wrists imprisoned in a lose grip. A feral gleam sparkled in his eyes. Ava shivered at the madness she saw in those velvety blue depths. A madness that was surely mirrored in her own gaze.

"You want the monster to come out and play, little lamb?" His words were a growling reminder that he was an untamed creature with very little control when it came to her. "Be very sure of your answer. I won't let you change your mind once we start."

Ava leaned into him, her mouth brushing his clenched jaw. While he quivered with restraint, she softly kissed the column of his strong, corded neck. Licking the tender spot below his ear, she followed it with a teasing nip of her teeth to his earlobe. When he groaned in response, her lips immediately moved to the front of his throat. She bit him there as well, rewarded when she felt his muscles tighten. The air thickened around them, heavy and fraught with sexual tension.

"Tell me what to do, Kingston. Tell me how I can please you."

"You want to please me?" He hissed in disbelief.

Ava was so breathless with desire, she could not muster up the words to respond. She simply nodded until Kingston squeezed her wrists so hard she gasped at the sharp bite of pain.

"No, you don't get to fucking nod your head when I ask you a question. I want to hear the words from your own sweet lips, Ava. Tell me what you want and maybe I'll let you come afterward. It depends on my mood and how well you please me."

"I will do whatever you want." She damned herself with this show of submission, but ignoring how she felt every time she was in his arms was impossible.

Kingston's face split into a wide smile. It was the smile of a predator who had finally caught a fragile doe after a long, intense pursuit.

"Get on your fucking knees for me, lamb. And open wide."

TWENTY-FOUR

Madness is a shared affliction for those in love.

KINGSTON'S HEART nearly stopped when Ava nodded. Eyes locked on his, she slowly slid down the length of his body until her knees made contact with the cold, marble floor. With her wrists still caught in his large hand, her arms remained stretched high above her head.

Sick bastard that he was, he loved seeing her kneel before him. Keeping one hand tangled in her silky hair, his brow arched high. "What should you do next, lamb?"

Her chin jutted upward at the mocking tone in his voice. Obviously, she could not accomplish what was necessary when her hands were secured by his grip. "Your pants, sir."

"Get on with it," he chuckled, letting go of her wrists. He watched as she reached for his belt with trembling fingers. Unbuckling it seemed to take forever in Kingston's heated mind. When she clumsily tried unfastening the button of his dress pants, he abruptly stopped her.

"Unzip me and pull my cock out through the opening," he commanded in a raspy voice.

He was hard as stone for her already. Had been since she first appeared in his kitchen all fresh and pretty after being a fucking gorgeous mess for him the night before. It had been so hard not to shove the pancakes aside and eat her as a meal right there on his dining room table.

The corners of Ava's mouth tilted upward.

Damn little brat.

She knew how badly she affected him and found it amusing. Any other time, he would have used that smugness as an excuse for punishment, but right now, he relished it. It was a sign that she was forming a small measure of trust with him.

And he was starting to crave *that* as much as he craved fucking her.

Once she trusts me, protecting her will be easier. And when she hears the truth of her parents' death and falls apart, I'll be the one to put her back together.

The feel of her warm fingers unzipping his pants and gently grabbing his shaft brought his mind back into whip-sharp focus.

"Goddamn, your hands feel good," he breathed out with a whoosh of air. Staring down at the top of Ava's head as she focused on the task, Kingston felt a rush of tenderness. Dizzy with the unfamiliar emotion, he still managed to growl out commands. "Open your mouth, Ava. Wider. Keep your eyes on me. I'm going to stretch those lips until they are a custom fit around my cock."

Ava's eyes widened as he pushed into the recesses of her mouth. His girth stretched her lips apart, but his length had her choking on him.

"Easy, baby. Slow. Take me slow," he murmured, resisting the urge to thrust down her throat until he exploded. "Relax your throat muscles and let me in all the way. There. Goddamn, right there. *Fuck me...*"

Kingston's head fell back with the exquisite sensation of her tongue wrapping around him. The muscles of her throat clenched around his cock each time she swallowed without gagging. Closing his eyes, he savored the moment before focusing his attention on her. Her gaze was still on him as he had demanded, the deep green irises darkening to the color of the rarest emerald. Bracing one hand against the door to his office, he used the hand tangled in her hair to pull her down further on his cock.

Ava gagged, her fingers digging into the material of his trousers and gripping his thighs. But she did not stop him from surging down her throat nor did she break eye contact with him.

The sounds she made as she choked and gagged, the sight of tears leaking from the corners of her eyes, switched on something primal deep inside Kingston. He thrust forward again and again, using the grip of her hair as leverage.

"You like my cock down your throat, don't you, Ava? You like how fucking crazy you make me. Suck me harder, baby. Make me believe you love being used like this."

Ava responded by twirling her tongue around the head of his dick like she was sucking on a lollipop. Her hands tightened on his thighs, pulling him closer with a hum of pleasure.

"You'll swallow what I give you because that's what I want. You'll swallow my cum when I shoot down your throat and you'll thank me for it." Kingston pulled her off his cock, a wicked grin splitting his face when the action made a popping noise. "Open that beautiful mouth. Stick your tongue out for me, baby. Flatten it out and stay like that until I say you can move."

"Yes, sir," Ava gasped, taking a deep breath. She obeyed his command as Kingston took his cock within his hand, gripping it firmly. Twice he slapped it against her tongue before surging back into the warmth of her decadent mouth. Her eyes watered but she stayed on her knees, accepting how he used her for his own enjoyment.

"Just like that, Ava. Such a good fucking girl, sucking my cock like you've been starving for it. Letting me fuck that gorgeous mouth."

Kingston knew he shouldn't be so rough, but it was impossible not to take what he wanted after a long night of self-imposed denial. Gripping Ava's head in both hands, he began thrusting into her mouth and as far down her throat as he could go.

It seemed Ava instinctively knew what he needed. Obedience. Acceptance. Her throat worked to swallow him while at the same time fighting the impulse to gag. Her willingness to please him was one of the greatest pleasures he'd ever experienced. It engulfed him. Melted his icy soul and warmed his heart with such violence, it weakened his knees.

When her lips closed around him and she began sucking in earnest, Kingston abruptly exploded with a muffled groan. His cock pulsed with delight as he came so hard, he nearly passed out.

A rumble escaped his chest as he once again braced a hand on the door behind her, holding himself up. There was a sputtering sound as Ava swallowed, so full of him and his cum that some of the fluid leaked from the corners of her mouth. Even with the lingering innocence that came from giving her second blowjob ever, her eyes glittered with accomplishment, fierce and bright as she stared up at him from her knees. She was so obviously proud of herself that Kingston huffed out a surprised laugh.

He released the grip on her hair, allowing her to sink back onto her heels as his cock slipped free of her mouth. Swiping a hand across swollen, pink-stained lips, Ava gave him a tremulous smile as he tucked himself back into his trousers.

"Was-was it okay? Did I do it right?"

Kingston wrapped his hands around Ava's upper arms and hauled her to her feet. His mouth crashed down on hers. He kissed her until she whimpered and kissed him back, her sweet flavor mixed with his own as they devoured one another.

He finally retreated, his hands bracketing her tear-stained face so he could study her. "Ava, I swear you'll be the fucking death of me."

"But it was okay? I wasn't sure I did it like you like... the last time was such a blur. I hated you so much and it's all I could focus on." She let out a bitter laugh that hung between them like a wall of barbed wire. "I hated that the other men in the room knew what I was doing. I hated that you *forced* me to do it when I was so scared and confused. But this was different. I *wanted* to do it. It was *my* choice." She twisted her hands, her voice lowering with the enchanting shyness of a seductress finding her power. "I wanted you to forget any woman who has ever done that for you in the past. Because I want to be the only one in your memory."

"You are fucking perfection, Ava," Kingston said somberly, recognizing the uncertainty in her quiet statement. That same damn need for approval had made her the victim in the past was raising its head again. Only this time, he was the abuser.

Something twisted and shattered inside Kingston. Something that broke his heart free from the shards of ice encasing it.

Somehow, he would make damn sure Ava knew how

worthy she truly was. How precious and rare the gift of her submission was to a man like him. She was a treasure. She deserved to be coddled, punished, loved, and worshipped.

"Let's get you cleaned up." Wiping the corner of her mouth with his index finger, a devious smile promising future pleasure curved his lips. "We still have a day of exploring ahead of us, and I plan on returning this favor when you least expect it."

～

KINGSTON SENSED Ava's surprise when they stepped off the elevators onto the eleventh floor. A set of double doors emblazoned with his signature lion's head tattoo was etched into the frosted glass. *Winter Enterprises* was prominently displayed beneath the image.

Pushing through those doors brought them to a long, sleek receptionist desk with a central phone console buzzing and ringing with incoming calls. A wall of glass with a waterfall effect blocked off access to multiple office suites, all bustling with frenetic activity.

The woman standing behind the granite desk was one of Kingston's first employees. Hired on referral by Ava's dad, Linda Scott was a highly treasured Winter Enterprises asset. Quick with a smile and blazing efficiency, the middle-aged woman ruled over the office like a battlefield general.

"Good morning, Mister Winter," she trilled cheerfully.

"Good morning." Kingston smiled, one brow lifting in question to see her standing at the desk which usually had a receptionist manning it. "Everything alright?"

Linda waved a hand. "Fine and dandy. Just filling in while Michelle is on a bathroom break. Says that baby won't stop kicking her in the kidneys."

"How is she doing?" Kingston was aware that Ava watched the exchange with fervent curiosity.

"Oh, just fine. She's a real sweetheart and a hard, dedicated worker. I'm so glad Doctor Abbott sent her over. We're just delighted she's here." Linda glanced past Kingston, giving Ava a friendly smile. "Hello. You must be Miss Blue. Mister Winter mentioned you'd be stopping by with him for a visit." Coming around from behind the desk, she extended her hand toward Ava. "I'm Linda Scott, senior director here for the company's New York division."

"Please call me 'Ava.'" Ava shook Linda's hand. "It's very nice to meet you. Have you worked for Mister Winter for very long?"

"Let's see. A little more than five years now, I think." Linda laughed, her warm brown eyes twinkling. "Of course, this office is much nicer than the one I reported to that first day."

Kingston smiled. "Linda came highly recommended by your father, Ava. I'm glad I took his advice and hired her."

Ava's face lit up. "You knew my father?"

"Oh, yes, dear. I worked for him for a short time before moving back to the city. I never met a nicer man than your father. He's the reason I landed this job. It was a godsend, really. I've two parents in a senior care facility, and a son attending Cornell University. Without the generous salary Mister Winters pays me, I don't know how I would manage. You'll hear no complaints from any of our employees on that issue. There's always a steady stream of hopeful job applicants trying to land a position here."

"And I thought those potential employees were simply interested in my sparkling personality," Kingston teased.

"Well, I'm sure that's a factor as well." Linda flashed a grin at Ava. "We don't talk about our employer's good looks when he's around. We don't want him getting too full of himself."

Ava giggled. "It's probably too late to take such precautions. I suspect he already knows he has an unfair advantage over average men."

"Linda, we stopped by so I could give Ava a quick tour before heading into the city," Kingston said with a slight scowl now that the conversation shifted to talk of his appearance. Taking Ava by the elbow, he gave it a gentle squeeze while speaking to the other woman. "Give your parents my best. Michelle, too, if we don't see her on our way out. And keep me up to date on the baby's arrival. I'd like to send a gift when the time comes."

CHAPTER
TWENTY-FIVE

*S*hould you decide to fly
Just take my hand.

AVA FOLLOWED Kingston around the various offices, pausing at times to be introduced. What she found most surprising was the overwhelming number of women working for Winter Enterprises. They outnumbered the men two to one.

After about twenty minutes, he finally led her to his private office. A young lady not much older than Ava sat at a desk just outside it. She was very pretty, with dark brown hair and bright blue eyes. She smiled widely at Kingston and immediately stood up from her seat.

"Good morning, Mister Winter."

"Good morning, Jane. Do you have those buyer reports ready for me?" Kingston asked, keeping Ava's hand trapped in his.

Jane smiled brightly. "I sure do, sir. They are in a folder on your desk. I also took the liberty of sending a courier with a copy of the documents to your estate just in case you decided to fly home last night. They should be arriving right about now so you may also peruse them there at your leisure."

"That was very astute of you, Jane," Kingston murmured, and Ava felt a piercing stab of jealousy at the cool affection in his tone. Tugging her forward, he wrapped an arm around her waist in a display of ownership. Jane's smile faltered a little, her brow creasing.

"Jane, this is Ava Blue. Ava, this is my very efficient personal secretary, Jane Becker."

Jane extended her hand, her smile not nearly as vibrant as it was before. "Nice to meet you, Miss Blue."

Ava returned the pleasantries while Kingston rubbed his thumb over the curve of her waist, reminding her of the pleasures his hands could deliver. She couldn't help but wonder if Jane had enjoyed the same experience. The girl certainly appeared smitten, her blue eyes roving over Kingston's form when she knew he wasn't looking.

"Jane, see that I am not disturbed, please," Kingston commanded as he touched an index finger to a pad on the wall. There was the sound of an invisible lock tumbling into place followed by a low beep. He pushed the double wood doors open, stepping aside so Ava could precede him into the room.

"Of course, sir," Jane said cheerfully, but Ava recognized the sad jealousy behind her false gaiety.

The doors closed behind them with a soft snick. Kingston leaned back against them, watching Ava as she looked about the room, taking it all in.

The office was shaped like a triangle, with the wall facing Jane's desk paneled in oak that had been stained a dark acorn shade. Behind a wide chrome and glass desk were two walls of floor-to-ceiling windows, joined together in the corner by invisible seams. It gave the illusion of a floating nest perched high in the sky. Or maybe the bow of a ship, the sharp angles slicing through a sea of clouds.

"It's beautiful," Ava said softly.

"It is. I've never seen anything more gorgeous." Kingston's voice rumbled behind her, and when Ava glanced back at him, she realized he wasn't talking about his office nor the view from the windows. She was the only object in his sight at that moment, his gaze fixated on her.

He kept his casual position against the doors as Ava continued exploring. There were various decorative pieces on the built-in bookcases framing the double doors and expensive works of art hung on the walls. It was a masculine space, and she felt a little out of place. Like a bit of fluff that drifted in when no one was watching.

"You have so many women working here," she commented suddenly.

"Do I?" Kingston shrugged his shoulders. "I didn't realize."

"Are they all from Doctor Abbot's charitable foundation?"

"I leave the hiring to Linda, but it's common practice to hire from there when it's feasible."

"Helping women like that... some people might consider it noble."

"Don't get all weepy about it, Ava," he replied evenly. "It's only admirable on the surface. I'm still a bad guy with plenty of irons smoldering in illegal fires."

Ava's cheeks burned with the blunt admonition. Kingston didn't want acknowledgment for doing a good deed. Warning her away was a bristling act of self-preservation, and it made her heart ache a little.

"Your secretary... did you hire her because she came from Doctor Abbot's charitable endeavors?" Ava traced a finger over a lion's head bust sitting on the corner of his desk. Carved from a single chunk of alabaster, it appeared antique and very heavy.

"No. Jane is the niece of my favorite art dealer."

"She's very pretty." Ava glanced back at him over her shoulder, gauging his reaction. "She's also in love with you."

Kingston's eyes crinkled at the corners as he finally stalked toward her. Grabbing her hand, he pulled Ava around his desk and seated himself in the plush leather chair. He pinned her against the desk's edge as he slid her purse from her shoulder. It dropped onto the glass desk with an audible clank.

Inwardly, Ava winced, wondering if the hidden weapon would finally be revealed.

"So?" Kingston murmured absently, his gaze lingering on her lips.

Ava felt that heartbreaking tremble of envy once more. She tried sounding nonchalant but failed miserably. "It's probably very painful for her. Seeing you with another woman."

Kingston settled his hands on her hips. Lightly gripping her, he leaned back so he could peer up into her eyes. "Whatever Jane feels, it's not reciprocated, Ava. I don't fuck my employees in this sector of my business ventures."

"But the women working at your club…you've obviously slept with some of them."

"I have in the past, yes," he admitted slowly. "I'm a man of few morals and particular tastes. And no desire for attachments of the romantic nature. The women employed by LIST understand this." Moving his hands up, Kingston cupped Ava's breasts, molding them to the shape of his palms. His thumbs rubbed over her nipples, coaxing the twin points into diamond-like hardness. "What's this all about, Ava? Tell me the truth."

She shivered as he touched her with such expertise. Like a musician tuning his favorite instrument, he casually explored her body until she wanted to rip off her clothes and invite him to feast on her.

It was foolish, but witnessing the gentler side of Kingston, a man helping broken women start new lives, giving them jobs in his *almost* legal organization, splintered her heart open just a little more. Despite his protests to the contrary, he was not a complete monster.

"I don't like thinking of you with someone else," Ava said in a rush. Embarrassment flooded her. She should not have admitted that out loud, but it was the god-awful truth. She was becoming too territorial over this man, and that was dangerous.

Kingston laughed softly, his dark gaze holding hers. "No more than I can stand the thought of you with another man." He pinched her nipples until a whimper of need rose in Ava's throat. "I'll kill any man who touches you, Ava. Do you understand?"

"Yes."

"Do you agree that you are mine?" His beautifully cruel mouth lifted at the corners, revealing the pleasure he found in forcing her admission that she belonged to him.

"Yes," she whispered, drowning in her desire. "I'm yours, Kingston."

"And I'm yours, little lamb." His gaze flicked to the purse laying on his desk. A hard glint shimmered in the blue-black of his eyes. In a torturous descent, his hands left her breasts, skimming down to her thighs before tracing the inside of her legs.

His admission shocked her, but Ava couldn't think rationally when the pressure of his palms forced her legs further apart. Moving her hands to the desk behind her, she braced her palms flat on the glass. If he pushed her midsection, she'd have no choice but to sprawl back across the desk and over the folder containing... what was it Jane said?

Booking reports. Whatever those were. It didn't really matter. Those reports were in danger of becoming a scattered mess as the blood in her veins pounded in a wild dance. Hoping Kingston would touch her there at the apex of her thighs, she was also frozen with fear that he would discover the weapon in her purse.

I can explain it away. Say I'm an undiagnosed kleptomaniac. That I love stealing forks from various restaurants. It's a thrill and completely harmless. It's not like I would ever stab a man with it. Really, I wouldn't... not even a deranged kidnapper deserves that.

"Is there something you want to tell me before we leave my office?" Kingston purred, drawing circles over her pussy using only his thumbs. The sensations were muted because of the fabric covering her flesh, but Ava's heart still lodged in her throat. She suddenly wished she'd followed his "no jeans or pants ever" edict. She wanted his hands touching her everywhere.

Shaking her head, she resisted the urge to look down at her purse.

"Are you sure?" He pressed one thumb hard against her clit.

Ava let out a helpless groan. "I don't know what you're talking about."

Kingston stared at her for a long moment, faint disappointment crossing his rugged features before he transferred his hands from the inside of her thighs to her forearms. He tugged her upright, holding her steady when she swayed.

"I'll pull it from you eventually, Ava, using methods you never dreamed existed."

Ava shivered with the threat. "If I was guilty of something, that might actually frighten me."

His gaze was intent and almost contemplative. "Maybe

tonight I'll do just that. Maybe I'll take you down into LIST and show you the delights of the dungeon there." Raising her hand to his mouth, he kissed the tips of her fingertips, one by one. "Trust me and be rewarded, Ava. Or keep your secrets and be punished. As always, it is your choice."

TWENTY-SIX

D*ark designs fill the void until*
Your surrender coats my tongue.

KINGSTON KEPT Ava busy as they visited his favorite art gallery and the quaint little bookshop two blocks away from Winter Enterprises. Just as he'd dreamed, he cornered her in the back of the bookshop. Pressing her against the shelves, he kissed her until they were both breathless and her hands clutched at his shoulders.

If another customer had not entered the store, setting off the tinkling bell above the door, Kingston might have done something foolish. He might have unbuttoned her jeans and pushed his fingers into her tight cunt. He would have finger-fucked her until she cried out his name into the crook of his neck, her sweet essence smearing her thighs and his knuckles. It was a struggle, but he contained those urges and satisfied himself with deep, lush kisses.

With Jack always close behind them, Kingston and Ava strolled the city streets. Several times Kingston had the uneasy feeling someone was trailing their steps, but he never saw anything to validate his suspicion. Nor did he look very closely for evidence. Ava's enjoyment of the day was a distraction hard to ignore. Over the course of a few hours, she had relaxed her guard, slipping her hand into his, grinning as they shared a cinnamon roll and mugs of hot apple cider.

"It's past one o'clock, already, Ava. What would you like for lunch?" Kingston asked as they walked in the general direction of their next destination.

"I'm not hungry, to be honest, especially after that amazing cinnamon roll. And breakfast was so filling, I don't think I could eat of another bite." Her heated gaze met his, a blush staining her cheeks with the remembrance of what they'd done after breakfast in the penthouse hallway.

"We'll grab a bite later then. After your spa appointment."

The day was cool, but not so chilly that coats were needed. But when Ava shivered in the shadows of the tall buildings, Kingston whipped off his suit coat and draped it over her shoulders.

"Are you cold? I knew I should have insisted that you wear something thicker than that sweater."

"No, no. I'm fine." Ava's smile was faint. "It's just this spa thing. I admit I'm nervous. I've never done that before. You know, the waxing stuff."

"I can't say that it won't hurt. I've been told it does, anyway." Kingston gently squeezed her hand. "It will please me if you do what I ask, Ava."

"I'm not refusing. Just a little scared, I guess." She shook her hair back from her face when a gust of wind caught hold of the curls. She looked so beautiful in that moment with her hair blowing free and her cheeks glowing pink from the brisk wind.

"I'll stay with you and hold your hand during the worst of it."

"Can you do that?" Ava asked, surprised. "They'll let you come with me?"

With abrupt quickness, Kingston tugged her closer, one arm wrapping around her waist while keeping her hand captive against his chest, trapping it between their bodies. The kiss he gave her was deep and encompassing. Heat and longing tied up in the tangle of their tongues until they finally broke apart, their breath escaping into the cool air like miniature puffy clouds. Kingston brushed a wavy tendril of Ava's hair from her forehead, tucking it behind her ear.

"If you want me there, lamb, nothing will stop me."

BECAUSE THE WEATHER had turned cooler, Kingston decided against walking to the exclusive spa located further up on Fifth Avenue. He instructed Jack to contact the limo. A short time later, they were picked up and rode the remaining few blocks.

They entered through a door at the back of the building. A beautiful girl with straight red hair and startling green eyes greeted them with a wide smile.

"Good afternoon, Mister Winter. Miss Blue. My name is Chloe. If you'll come this way, I'll show you to the room where Mary will be taking care of you."

The interior of La Maison was elegantly decorated in shades of ivory and soothing pale blue. High ceilings were painted the same blue as the walls, embellished with intricately carved medallions and corner fretwork. The wood floors were cushioned by plush rugs with subtle terrace designs in shades of blue, ivory, and soft grey. It looked as though it had been plucked from the middle of Versailles and plopped into its space in New York City. Soft, classical music played as they were shown to a luxurious room.

"Once we get Miss Blue settled, you are welcome to wait in the private waiting room, Mister Winter. We'll let you know when we're done."

Ava shot Kingston a worried glance, her hand clutching his. Giving her a reassuring squeeze back, Kingston smiled at Chloe. "I will be staying with Miss Blue for her appointment."

"You needn't worry, Mister Winter," Chloe said with a patient nod. "We'll take excellent care of her."

"Of that, I have no doubt. But the lady is requesting that I stay. An inconvenience for the spa, I realize, but one which must be accommodated."

"As you wish, sir. Mary will not mind an observer to her artistry."

The room reserved for Ava was as soothing as the rest of the spa. Delicate sprays of flowering vines decorated the hand-painted wallpaper in muted shades of green and yellow. Crystal sconces emitted a soft glow, and the elevated table was thickly upholstered. Luxurious towels and a robe so soft it might have been a cloud sat ready for use. Two elegantly carved chairs occupied one corner, and Kingston eyed them both.

"They are very sturdy chairs, Mister Winter." Chloe smiled, understanding Kingston's unasked question. She turned to Ava, instructing her to remove her clothes and don the provided robe. "You can hop up on the table when you are ready, Miss Blue. Mary will be here shortly."

Ava waited until the door shut behind the girl before sinking into one of the chairs. She began removing her boots while Kingston grabbed the other chair and placed it in the opposite corner. Throwing himself onto it, he sat with his long, muscular legs sprawled out, using the chair's arm to set his elbow and prop his head within the palm of his hand. He watched intently as Ava self-consciously removed all articles of clothing. When she was finally gloriously nude before him, his hands curled into fists to keep from touching her.

"You are so damn beautiful, lamb," he breathed in reverence. "Like the goddess of springtime."

Ava blushed, her arms coming up to cross over her breasts.

Seeing her like this was a shocking reminder that the pretty, pale pink of her nipples was the same exact shade as the inside of her sweet pussy. Kingston fought his arousal, determined to be a gentleman at least until the waxing was over. But it was difficult when the woman he was obsessed with was just a few feet away. Gorgeous. Nude. Shy. And most importantly, obediently standing before him for as long as he wanted to look at her.

Dragging his heated gaze over her body one more time, Kingston growled, "Put your robe on now, Ava."

"Okay," she responded softly. Snatching the garment up from the table, she plunged her arms into the sleeves and quickly tied the belt around her narrow waist.

Which was precisely when the technician knocked on the door and entered the room.

"Hello, Miss Blue. I'm Mary and I'll be taking care of you today. My notes say this is your first time getting a wax of any sort?" Mary tilted her head down, studying Ava over the rim of her readers. She was an attractive older woman with dark brown eyes and a head full of darker brown curls pulled back in a low ponytail. Kingston knew immediately that Mary, with her wide friendly smile and comforting aura, put Ava at ease. The tension in her shoulders relaxed as Mary began preparing the necessary items.

"Yes. First time. And please, call me Ava." Ava giggled, and Kingston could only stare at his little prisoner, entranced by the sweet, lilting sound. "As close and as personal as we're about to be, I'm fine with being on a first-name basis."

Mary laughed in appreciation. "All right, Ava. That's a deal." Her attention swung to Kingston, a speculative gleam in her dark eyes. "I see you bought some moral support."

"Not only that, but financial as well," Ava quipped, her eyes sparkling with mischief as she studied his reaction. "Mister Winter is mostly here to hold my hand and whisper words of encouragement. If it hurts too much, I'm allowed to dig my fingers into his hand as hard as I like. And since I chew my nails, I'm also allowed to use teeth on him. He should feel some pain, too, since this was his idea."

"You will feel a bit of discomfort, but it is minimal. Our biggest concern is that you refrain from sex of any kind for a while. We recommend at least twenty-four hours, but for some people, it's okay to indulge before that." Mary helped Ava remove the robe and get up on the bed.

"Bet you didn't know that, did you?" Ava crowed, flashing Kingston a grin filled with smug victory.

What. The. Actual. Fuck.

Kingston was stunned by Ava's playful cheekiness. And so fucking turned on, he needed to cross his legs to conceal his bulging erection.

He listened as Mary patiently explained the procedure for the Brazilian wax, slightly gratified when apprehension slipped over Ava's suddenly pale features. When she glanced his way, he was the one with the smug smile. "Feel free to bite me when it gets to be too much."

Ava's eyes narrowed, although a reluctant smile lifted the corners of her mouth. "Oh, I will. I won't hold back, either. Not even a tiny bit."

"I hope not, little savage." He liked this version of Ava. The quick-wittedness she exhibited when sparring with him was a welcome change from the sadness she usually wore.

I'm the reason for a lot of that sadness.

Kingston ducked his head with that internal reminder.

Ava, to her credit, never made a peep while being waxed. Nor did she reach for his hand or even act like she needed support. If there was pain, she bore it well, and that had Kingston fantasizing about all the ways he could make her cry out for him.

The last area to be treated was her underarms, and Ava let out another giggle as Mary spread the heated wax there.

"Sorry," Ava said, training her eyes on the ceiling, her body shaking with laughter. "I've always been very ticklish there."

"Oh, I get it," Mary replied. "Touch me behind my knees and I might just drop-kick you."

Kingston's head tilted. How did he not know Ava was ticklish? He knew everything about her. Or, at least, he thought he did.

With a slight frown, he filed that bit of information away for future use.

"All right, sweetie. We're all done here." Mary snapped off the surgical gloves and helped Ava sit up. Handing her the robe, Mary quickly went over the aftercare instructions. "You should repeat the waxing in about three or four weeks. After that, the time between treatments will naturally become longer and longer. Now, take your time getting dressed and we'll get you set up for your next appointment."

"We'll need a few minutes. No more than a half-hour," Kingston murmured, coming to his feet. Opening his wallet, he pulled out a couple of crisp hundred-dollar bills and handed them to Mary. "For you and your discretion, Mary. And as thanks for taking such excellent care of my Ava today."

From the corner of his eye, Kingston saw Ava bite her

bottom lip at the exchange. Or maybe it was his choice of words that caused her discomfort.

My Ava.

Mary's eyebrows rose high, but after a second of consideration, she grinned and tucked the money into her pocket. "My pleasure, Mister Winter. Take your time. There's certainly no rush. It was so wonderful meeting you, Ava. The robe is complimentary so feel free to take it home with you. I hope I see you again at the next appointment. You can request me if you like."

"Thank you, Mary. Thank you for being so kind and patient with me," Ava murmured softly.

Once Mary exited the room and the door closed behind her, Kingston quietly locked it. When he turned back to Ava, he found her huddled in the robe, her cheeks flushed with charming embarrassment.

"Oh my God, Kingston. She must be thinking the very worst." Ava clutched the robe high against her neck with a nervous laugh. "It won't take me thirty minutes to dress. Maybe five at the most."

"Don't get off that table," he instructed calmly when Ava went to hop down.

She stilled, her eyes wide. "What?"

"Remove the robe and lie back down."

"But why?"

Ava wore such a look of adorable confusion that Kingston could not contain a dark chuckle. "Because I want to examine you. See how good of a job Mary did."

Ava clenched her teeth. "Don't you think you saw enough from your vantage point?"

"Some things require, ah, a hands-on inspection." His smile was warm, but his tone was firm. He expected obedience and he would get it. "Now, be a good girl and let me examine you."

"They'll know what we are doing in here. Or, at the very least, suspect what we are doing," she argued in vain. "They'll think this is some kind of devious kink we share."

"I own this spa, lamb, so I really don't care what they think."

The admission hung in the silence between them, and Kingston waited until Ava slumped with the revelation, relief flashing across her features. Like a lion stalking prey, he moved carefully toward her with a determined purpose.

"You do?" Ava's voice was trembly, full of unasked questions. Kingston knew her well enough to know she was silently wondering how many women had been brought here before her. Wondering how many times he sat in that same chair and watched this same procedure undertaken on a lover.

"I've never done this before, Ava," he assured her. "I would have requested Mary come to the penthouse, but I thought you would be more comfortable this first time in the professional setting of the spa." He stood so close now he could see her eyes were dilated, the green of her irises slowly swallowed by darkness. She was aroused, too, and he reveled in it. "My hope was you would find it less intimidating. Knowing other people were around... women like yourself having the exact same thing done in the other rooms... would make you feel safer."

"Oh," Ava squeaked, clearly affected by this unexpected thoughtfulness expended on her behalf. He could also see the wheels of her mind turning as she tried to determine if this was a trick of some sort or a truly sincere gesture.

"Oh, indeed." He grinned, reaching out to tuck a strand of her soft blonde hair behind her ear. "Now, lie down so I can see what belongs to me."

TWENTY-SEVEN

I'm unhinged
Just like you.
Unbalanced together.

HEARING the cool possessiveness in Kingston's voice, Ava quickly shrugged out of the robe, tossing it aside. Swinging her legs back onto the table, she took a deep breath and slowly lay prone.

Blood pounded in her veins. Hot. Heavy. Thick.

"You heard what Mary said." Ava forced herself to relax, but Kingston's nearness made it impossible. Between her thighs, a throbbing need arose. The intensity of it was maddening.

"What's that, lamb?"

"No sex," she blurted out. That directive was a terrible shame because it was all she could think about. Sex with this man. Sex that made her forget her name and cry out his. Sex that forever changed who she was.

"No sex," Kingston repeated in bemused agreement. He stood beside the table now, his gaze sweeping over her nude body. She tried not to move, tried not to react to the intense scrutiny, but the trembling in her body could not be concealed. Her nipples contracted into hard, little buds begging to be warmed in the heat of his mouth.

"Are you cold?" he asked softly.

"No," Ava quickly answered. "I-I just don't know what you intend to do. It scares me. And the fact I *almost* like being scared only scares me more."

"I'm not going to hurt you, Ava. At least not right now. Or even tonight." Kingston trailed his index finger over the top of her thigh in a teasing manner. "But I haven't forgotten you owe me one of your secrets."

"What do you think I'm hiding? You know everything about me. You've seen all of me that there is to see."

"We'll discuss that later. When you are ready for it. Right now, I want to look at you. Fuck, you have no idea how torturous it was to watch you being waxed without touching you here. I wanted to grab the stuff out of Mary's hand and do it myself. I would have, too, only that kind of wax is not my area of expertise. I might have hurt you without meaning to." His finger moved until he was finally tracing the mound of her pussy. "You're gorgeous like this. So plump and pink. Smooth. Silky." He stroked her with just that one finger until Ava's legs fell apart, exposing more of herself to his hot gaze. "I can't wait to run my tongue all over this pretty cunt. To taste every part of you."

Slipping between the swollen folds, he found her clit and gently brushed it with the pad of his middle finger.

Ava's breath hitched, a whimper of lust rising in her throat. Every fiber of her being screamed that he touch her there harder. Faster. She wanted more than just this light, feathery touch of his finger. She wanted him deep inside her, healing the emptiness of her soul and solidifying that sense of belonging she found only with him.

"Remember, lamb. No sex. I'm only touching you. Nothing more." Kingston's tone turned rough, his own lust evident in the husky words. His gaze fixated on the junction of her thighs where his hand moved so, so gently. "But oh, how I want to do more. So much more that it scares me. I want to fuck you until I collapse from the pleasure of being buried deep inside you. I want you screaming for me. Begging for me. I want you to need me as much as I need you. I'm fucking obsessed with you, Ava. You're all I can goddamn think about."

Despite the tenderness of her swollen flesh, Ava did not want him to stop. She wanted to come with his clever fingers plunging her into dark, magical oblivion. "I feel that way, too." The admission was a sob of frustration when his movements halted, the promise of sweet completion quickly fading away.

The deep blue depths of Kingston's eyes softened as he stared down at her. Ava realized with abrupt clarity this was how he often looked at her now. As though she might be the most precious thing in his brutal life.

It confused her, this strange, fragile affection which had sprouted between them practically overnight. There was desire, of course, the sexual attraction that was always present, but somehow there was this now as well. This exhilarating, confusing new bond.

Is it real? Or am I just desperately searching for a connection with my kidnapper as a way of justifying my own needs?

"I do need you, Kingston. I need *this*. You. Just you."

But he was already withdrawing from her. Ava fought off a wave of disappointment. He wasn't going to grant her the orgasm her body so desperately craved.

Was this a punishment for some unknown transgression? Or a gift she should be grateful for?

Kingston's smile was a cross between anguish and terrifying victory. It strangled Ava's heart. Filling her with fear that something awful was coming. Something she might not survive.

"Sweet little lamb. I've treated you so badly, and yet you cling to me as though I am your savior." His eyes grew shuttered, hiding secrets from her. Ava quickly gripped his wrist, trying to trap him in place so he was still connected to her. "I don't deserve your trust, but I want it anyway. I want all of you. Always." With a deep sigh, he pried her fingers free and removed his hand from between her legs. Helping her sit up, he draped the robe around her shoulders like a makeshift shawl. Then he tugged her off the cot and onto her feet, enfolding her into a tight embrace.

Crushed against his suitcoat, Ava melted into the spicy familiarity of his cologne and the warmth of his leanly muscled body.

"I won't let anyone hurt you, Ava." Kingston sounded oddly tortured, a far cry from his usual coldly cynical manner. "You know that, right? You are mine. I am the only one who will *ever* know the pleasure of seeing you cry. The only one who will experience the exquisite joy of watching you break into a million pieces." The kiss he pressed to her forehead was hot enough to brand the skin, but Ava desperately wished it was her lips he claimed. When he pulled away from her, she hated the distance between them. "Now, let's get you dressed so we can go home where I can take care of you."

~

THE LIMO WAITED in the alleyway as Kingston and Ava exited the spa through the same door they'd come in.

Jack came jogging up from the end of the alley that connected to the main thoroughfare. Approaching the backside of the vehicle, he removed his dark sunglasses which were now unnecessary in the dim shadows. Before the driver could get out, Jack reached for the rear door handle and abruptly stopped.

"Boss… take a look at this," Jack snapped in a hard voice, stepping aside so Kingston and Ava could see what had caught his attention. The bodyguard's hand came up and rested on the butt of a firearm holstered at his hip. Tearing her gaze away from Jack, Ava saw what looked like a yellow sticky note on the tinted window. Something was written on it in red. She read it before Kingston snatched it down.

Whatever her price, someone will always pay more.

"What the fuck," Kingston hissed, staring up the alleyway into the places where the shadows were much deeper and darker. "Jack, who's been in this alley other than you and the limo driver?"

Jack shook his head. "Other than a homeless guy? No one."

"Are you sure he was homeless?"

"Dressed in dirty clothes and pushing a shopping cart full of trash." Jack opened the car door as he spoke. "He came through about five minutes ago. Can't have gotten very far."

"What do you mean to do, Kingston?" Ava asked, chewing on a fingernail. "You aren't going after strangers now, are you? Over a scrap of paper? It's nothing."

"Get in the car, Ava," Kingston ordered in a tight voice. He clutched the note in his fist as though debating the benefits of ripping it to shreds. "My driver will take you to the penthouse. I'll meet you there soon."

"No, come with me, Kingston." Clutching his coat, Ava

pressed herself against him. "It's just a piece of paper. It doesn't mean anything. I mean, the wind... the wind could have blown it down the alley and it just happened to stick to the window. Or maybe the guy was crazy, and he put it there as a joke. He might not even have known what he was doing. It's just a coincidence."

"Coincidence, lamb?" Kingston's smile was grim. "There is no such thing." With a jerk of his chin, he curtly addressed Jack. "Give me a minute here. Go check the end of the alley. Send out word that I want this person for questioning."

Jack nodded, taking off toward the end of the alley just as a shot rang out. The sound echoed down the length of the alleyway accompanied by Ava's startled scream. There was the sharp ping of a bullet ricocheting off something metal and answering gunfire. That most likely came from Jack firing at the potential assassin. A split second later, there was another loud retort. The bullet ripped through the fabric of Kingston's suit, leaving a bloody tear in his outer bicep.

Ava screamed again when he shoved her into the limo. He quickly slid in behind her, blocking the open door with his body before slamming it shut.

"I want you to follow my orders, Ava," he bit out.

"Oh my God. Kingston! You're bleeding!" Ava said in a voice strangled by terror. She pressed an open palm against the wound to stem the copious bleeding while with her other hand, she snatched napkins from the limo's bar. But when she tried tending to him, Kingston gripped her hands.

"It's minor, Ava." He squeezed her hands until she gasped in pain. "Listen to me now. You'll be taken to my building by my security team. They will escort you inside through a private entrance. Only certain people are authorized to bypass the fingerprint security and access the penthouse. They are people

I trust, and now that includes you. The code to lock and unlock the doors is zero, nine, two, two."

Ava's stared at him, dazed. "You're bleeding."

"Ava!" Kingston barked. "That doesn't matter right now. Do you understand what I just told you? About the code? Repeat it back to me."

"Zero. Nine. Two. Two." Ava's gaze dropped to where he held her hands, their fingers now bloodstained. "I don't understand. The numbers. They are the same as my birthdate."

"That's always been the code, Ava. Just like you've always been mine." Kingston released her hands only to lift her chin using his index and middle finger. He stared intently into her eyes. "I told you there are no coincidences. Not in my world, anyway."

"Who just shot at us?" Someone wanted them dead. Someone had just tried assassinating them both.

"I don't know for certain." Kingston's jaw clenched. "Several times today, I felt we were being followed. It could have been paparazzi or something more sinister—I wasn't sure until this."

Ava shook her head. "Who would do this?"

"Someone attempting to steal what matters more to me than anything else in this world." He leaned forward, staring into her eyes. "I wanted to tell you this at the right time, but it can't be helped now. My hackers uncovered the evidence proving Carson murdered your parents. And Judd Vanderhoff, along with his father, helped him. They've all been blackmailed by Carson using the video of your assault. Your brother still intends to sell you to pay his many debts. And Ava, you would not survive the buyers he has lined up. Your broken body would be found much later, allowing him to eventually claim your inheritance."

Fear spread like icy spiderwebs through Ava's vein as she listened. Carson was responsible for her parents' deaths.

Carson.

Her greedy, murderous brother.

"But why kill me now?" Ava was numb. She couldn't make sense of the past few moments. The information Kingston revealed had the effect of a bomb landing on her.

"You aren't the one he wants dead. I'm pretty sure both of those bullets were meant for me. Once I'm out of the way, there is no obstacle to Carson carrying out his plan." Kingston pressed a hard, quick kiss to her mouth. "You must go now, Ava. My men will keep you safe until I return."

Ava's heart thumped hard and fast inside her chest as an awful suspicion reared its head. "You knew he killed my parents. You knew last night, and you didn't tell me."

"I don't have time to explain everything right now but I'm trying to take care of you. You must trust me. Can you do that? Can you trust me, Ava? To keep you safe?"

Ava could not answer his question. Not when it felt like the world was crumbling away beneath her. "When did you know?" The insinuation hung in the air, poisoning it. Did Kingston know when he made her fall apart for him in a crowded restaurant? Did he watch the video and decide to one-up her brother? Or had he simply used her with the belief she enjoyed everything those men did to her that awful, stormy night?

Nausea saturated her body when she realized Kingston likely watched the video. Maybe it turned him on to see her held down and forced to submit. After all, he freely admitted to doing such things and gaining pleasure from it. The things he did to her was proof of that.

Images flashed in her mind's eye like a slow-moving photo reel. Her chained to the dungeon wall, locked in that cell.

Anchored over Kingston's lap and spanked until she couldn't think straight. Crawling to him on her hands and knees. That chase through the woods and how he laughed at her struggles when he bound her hands with zip-ties.

And how could she forget the belt around her throat? The way he groaned with pleasure as she choked on his cock while his men listened and lusted.

Hot tears of shame stung Ava's eyes. Because while she hated her brother and his friends for what they'd done, she couldn't say the same about Kingston. She obeyed his twisted command and followed his rules because she needed it. Even if she despised the overwhelming desire to fall further into this man's grasp, she would let herself sink. She would believe him. Let him take care of her. Give him the power that somehow, irrationally, made her stronger.

"It wasn't until you fell asleep that I got the call from Paulie." Kingston's hand curved around Ava's jaw, smearing it with blood. "I can't say anything more right now. Just do what I tell you, Ava. For fuck's sake, we can argue over this and anything else you want later."

"Just a few minutes ago, you promised to take care of me. Do you remember saying that? Come with me now, Kingston. Take care of me." Her challenge was brash and heated despite the frozen bite of fear chilling her bones. She hoped she was making the right choice. "Come with me and let me take care of you."

Kingston's face softened. "I won't apologize for this, Ava, or even be sorry for disappointing you. Keeping you safe takes priority over what you want. Now, I'm going to go take care of business and you are going to the penthouse. End of discussion."

"But your wound. You need medical attention. We should

be headed for the hospital instead of hunting down whoever shot at us."

"I don't have time to blister your ass for ignoring my order," Kingston said, moving to exit the limo, even as Ava grabbed hold of the corner of his suit coat to prevent his leaving. "But later, you can be sure I will do just that."

TWENTY-EIGHT

Winter fires burn bright.
Icy hearts made of snow.
I stand in their puddles.

As the limo pulled away, Kingston's brow furrowed.

It was an uneasy feeling letting Ava out of his sight. But catching whoever left the mysterious note and took a shot at him would lead to the real culprit.

He spent the next minute or two firing off texts with instructions for her safety, finishing up as Jack came jogging back down the alley out of breath.

"Just got word Franco's team caught him at Madison and 68th. He was ditching the shopping cart and flagging a car down. Older Mercedes. Black. Tinted windows. It took off when Franco wrestled our subject to the ground, but we got a partial plate. Our man at the precinct is running it now." Jack's eyebrows rose high upon seeing the bloody gash in Kingston's upper arm. "Damn. You got winged?"

"Minor wound. What about the shooter? Same man or someone else?"

"I'm thinking a different guy. My guess would be the guy in the Mercedes. Franco says the one they grabbed was unarmed. No weapons were found in the vicinity, and I found nothing in the alley or on the street." Jack lit up a cigarette. "Got a car coming for us now. What's the plan?"

It was an unnecessary question, but Kingston still answered. "Meet up with Franco at The Block. We need to question the one we caught and cast a net for the one that got away."

"Miss Blue is unharmed?"

That uneasy feeling crept through Kingston again, but he was reminded of the immediate issue of gaining information. "She's okay and headed back to the penthouse. Blair's unit is shadowing the limo and will stand guard until I get back."

Jack nodded. Taking a drag on his cigarette, he squinted against the smoke and scuffed the concrete with his shoe.

"Spit it out." Kingston knew the man well enough to know when he had something on his mind.

"Just wondering if you should take Miss Blue back to The Den sooner rather than later. Probably safer there."

"Maybe. Maybe not." Kingston shrugged, taking a cigarette from the pack Jack held out to him. "Who's to say it isn't Oliver behind this? He knows how to push my buttons, and when it comes to Ava, he's made it very clear he wants her, too. Returning her to The Den could be just what he hopes I'll do."

"There's the car." Jack motioned toward the sleek, black Lexus gliding to a stop at the end of the alley. "And you're right about Oliver. Brother or not, he can't be trusted for shit."

Kingston blew out a swirl of smoke then stubbed the

cigarette out with his shoe. "I'm well aware of his lack of loyalty."

It took forty-five minutes or so to reach the strand of remote dockside warehouses known as The Block. It was a collection of spaces buildings serving many purposes. Storage for illegal imports. Meetings and negotiations. A place where interrogations sometimes turned murderous.

Back when Kingston's father lorded over this kingdom, it was a place where trafficked souls were housed before being sold off like prime livestock.

Turning onto the pothole-riddled street running parallel with the docks, hemmed in by both water and buildings, Kingston recalled the first time he'd come here with his father. The night he was instructed to murder a falsely accused man.

He had refused at first, sickened by his father's demands and frightened as hell. Because the man tied up in a chair waiting to be slaughtered was not the man sleeping with Rebecca, his stepmother.

That man was Kingston himself. And he carried the evidence of his father's rage because of that refusal.

Absently, he rubbed the scar integrated within the lion tattoo over his heart. He hated The Block. Hated what the buildings represented. Hated the smell of dead fish and stale water. The stench of diesel fuel and rotting garbage decimated the very suggestion of fresh air and sunshine.

Mostly, he hated the faint odor of blood and death that never quite faded away.

But today was one of those days when he didn't mind it so much. Today, someone would be taught a very short lesson on why one should never fuck with Kingston Winter and those under his protection.

Despite his misgivings over Oliver, Kingston suspected Carson was behind this incident based on one simple fact. The enemies he had in the criminal underworld would not have missed the shot. And that included Oliver. He would have never even heard him coming if his brother was the assassin.

Once the man they'd caught was questioned, Kingston planned on moving his focus inward. Smaller and smaller circles would enable him to reach and punish every person who hurt Ava in the past. Her brother. Judd Vanderhoff and by extension, his father. The twins who had held her down that night were first on the list. Word of their deaths would be coming through shortly.

They would all bleed. For Ava's sake as well as his own.

"You okay, King?" Jack asked with a raised brow.

"I'm fine," Kingston replied, a faint scowl twisting his lips. "Let's get this shit done so I can get back to Ava."

He'd already received notification Ava was safely secured within the tower-like penthouse, verified by the security camera system installed in the vestibule. As instructed, she keyed in the code to lock the doors and now waited for his return. Knowing she was currently guarded by one of his most trusted teams made breathing a little easier but not by much. He wouldn't be satisfied until he was physically with her.

Entering the cold and damp warehouse, Kingston saw four of his men standing around a single figure seated in a folding metal chair. The man was bound at his hands and feet with lengths of thick rope, a dirty gag clenched between his teeth.

He might have been homeless. He may have even been mentally ill. But one thing was certain. The guy was terrified. Or maybe he was just tweaking. Every now and then, he tried jerking his hands free, noisily rattling the chair legs on the concrete floor. In his late twenties with shaggy brown hair, dirty jeans, his face was marked with sores commonly seen with meth addiction. Eyes wide above the gag, he stared at

Kingston's men as they laughed and casually made jokes while ignoring their prisoner.

Franco and his crew grew silent as Kingston approached. His shoes clicked ominously on a concrete floor stained with so many different things it was hard to tell their origins.

"Has he talked?"

Franco stepped behind the man, resting large hands on the prisoner's shoulders and squeezing them hard. A grin creased his swarthy face. "Before we gagged him? Yes. Diarrhea of the mouth."

"Anything useful?" Kingston snapped his fingers, and Jack immediately handed him a fresh cigarette and his own personal lighter. It was a habit he'd given up only recently, and here he'd already smoked two in less than an hour.

"Debatable." Franco shrugged. "Says his name is Hopkins."

Kingston grabbed another chair, dragging it over to their hostage. Turning it around backward, he straddled the seat and rested his forearms on the chair's back. "I'm going to ask you some questions now, Hopkins. And each time you give me the wrong answer, my associate here will yank out one of your fingernails. If we make it through all ten, we'll move on to cutting off extremities." His voice lowered into a husky threat of violence. "I imagine those will be things you're probably very fond of. Fingers. Toes. Ears." He leaned forward, holding the man's gaze. "Your balls."

The man's eyes widened with fear. He jerked against the restraints with greater ferocity, a muffled exclamation of panic bubbling from behind the gag.

"First question. Are you the one who placed this note on the window of my limo in the alleyway behind La Maison?" Kingston uncrumpled the yellow sticky note and held it up.

Hopkins stubbornly shook his head.

Kingston made a *tsking* noise. "Wrong answer. I saw you on

the video surveillance. Same hoodie. Same hat. Same pants." He made a circular motion around his face with an index finger. "Same unfortunate, douchebag chin strap beard." Keeping his gaze steady on the man, Kingston addressed Franco. "Franco... you may begin."

"Sure thing, boss." Franco pulled a pair of pliers from his back pocket and without preamble, knelt behind Hopkins. A quick jerk and a thumbnail was yanked free. It was dropped into the man's lap.

A wail of muffled pain came from behind the gag.

"Want to amend your answer?" Kingston asked calmly.

When Hopkins did not respond, Kingston nodded at Franco. Another scream and a second fingernail landed beside the first.

"Let's try again, shall we?" Kingston asked as the prisoner's head slumped forward. A slight nod indicated Hopkins' willingness to cooperate.

A wave of Kingston's hand silently indicated that Franco could remove the man's gag.

"Did you fire a weapon at us?" Kingston asked in a soft, deadly voice.

"Fuck you guys," was the weak answer.

"Jog our friend's memory." Kingston leaned back as Franco stepped in front of their prisoner. His fist slammed into Hopkins' jaw so hard it nearly sent the metal chair toppling over.

Hopkins groaned loudly, spitting out a mouthful of blood. Most of it dribbled down his chin and onto his shirt.

"That wasn't me." Hopkins spit more blood out. "I just left the note, man. That's all, swear to God. You gotta believe me. I've never shot a gun at anyone before."

Kingston's head tilted, measuring the man's response. There was a ring of truth in his desperate denial, but there was no denying most people would say anything under circumstances like these.

"Who took the shot, scumbag?" Jack snarled.

"I don't know! All I know is it wasn't me, man. It wasn't me!" Hopkins shrieked when Franco grinned, holding up the bloody pliers and clacking the tool. "Please... please don't. I'm telling you the truth. I don't know anything about it."

Kingston held up a hand, indicating Franco should await further instructions. "What happened to the other guy? How did he get away?"

"The Mercedes. That asshole was supposed to wait for me, but he took off before I could jump into the car. I don't know where he was headed, but the plan was to let me out on a corner over Broadway. I don't know the guy... just the car and the pickup spot."

"Who hired you?" Kingston asked.

"I don't know his name."

"Franco—a third, if you please." Kingston's demeanor remained eerily calm, even while Hopkins screamed in pain. "We'll run out of fingernails eventually. Then we'll start on the fun stuff."

"I-I just got released on bail last week. Upstate in Bitter Springs. Someone from the judge's office called me. Asked if I wanted to make a few bucks. If I did what they said, Judge Vanderhoff would dismiss my drug charges. Said the job was risk-free." The words ran from Hopkins' mouth like a stream of vomit.

"Does this seem "risk-free" to you?" Kingston smiled. "You scared my girl. Do you know that? And I get very angry when someone other than myself frightens her."

"Dude, I took their money and did what they asked. That's all I know."

Jack stepped forward and punched the guy hard enough to

snap his head back. "Show some respect. That's 'Mister Winter' to you. You know who this is, don't you? Even a low-life criminal like yourself can't be that ignorant."

"Mister Winter?" Hopkins groaned, spitting out fresh blood. Dread and recognition drained his face of any color. "I'm fucking sorry. I didn't know. They didn't say whose limo it was. And it was just a piece of paper. Thought maybe it was a joke they were playing on you. Or some kind of frame job."

Kingston sat back. The urge to kill Hopkins was overwhelming; however, there was some value in keeping him alive. He could deliver a very personal message to both Judd and Carson.

"I'm going to let you go, Hopkins." Kingston watched the man heave in a deep breath of relief before continuing. "But you are going to deliver a message for me. If you fail, I'll find you and finish what we started here today. Only I won't stop until I've personally torn you into a thousand little pieces. Pieces so small no one will ever know what happened to you. Do you understand?"

Hopkins nodded his head with such frantic enthusiasm the chair rocked back and forth. "I'll do whatever you want, Mister Winter. Anything."

Kingston nodded his head, indicating Hopkins be set free from his bonds.

Once Franco untied the ropes, Jack jerked the man to his feet, whispering in his ear, "Lucky for you, the boss is feeling generous today. Otherwise, there'd be nothing left of you but a greasy stain on that concrete."

TWENTY-NINE

I howl for you
   Lost and alone.
   My soul searching for yours in the darkness.

AVA SHOOK out two ibuprofen capsules from the bottle and swallowed them down with a sip of water.

A quick check of the bedside clock revealed it was close to seven o'clock in the evening. Two hours had passed since Kingston shoved her into the back of the limo and had her delivered to the penthouse.

Outside the bedroom suite, she could hear the faint sounds of the men guarding her. They made small talk and while she strained to hear what they might be saying, the living room area was too far away.

The group of seven could have been in a mafia movie. All wore matching suits and ties with black sunglasses and nearly invisible earpieces. They'd barely spoke as she was escorted up the private elevator and hustled into the penthouse. In fact, she wasn't even sure they'd looked at her while closing ranks around her. They maintained a respectful distance as she keyed in the code and unlocked the doors with her fingers coated in Kingston's dried blood.

Following her inside, the guards lingered behind in the living room as Ava ran to the master bedroom and slammed it shut. She locked it with a little sob before hurrying into the attached bathroom. Grabbing a thick cloth, she had washed the blood away from her face and her hands before jumping in the shower and scrubbing until her skin was pink.

Now pacing the bedroom in agitation, Ava paused to stare down at the city from the enormous windows. It was dark outside. Hugging herself, she wondered how much longer Kingston would be gone. Was his wound being tended by someone who knew what they were doing?

A soft knock interrupted her thoughts, and Ava crossed the room to the bedroom door. Should she open it? Her hand hovered above the doorknob.

"Miss Blue, Doctor Abbott is here. Boss said it was alright if he came, but it's up to you if you want to see him. If you do, I'll key him in."

Ava let out a sigh of relief. Finally, a familiar face and someone she had no reason to fear. "Yes. Thank you. I'll be right out."

Neil was already seated on one of the leather couches, concern evident in his features when Ava entered the room. Only one of the seven security guards was close by. Acting as the team's commander, the man sat at the kitchen island, sprawled across a barstool. He had introduced himself earlier as Blair and he nodded at Ava now.

"Two guards are in the vestibule. The other four are located within the penthouse in strategic spots as well as the pool terrace."

"Thank you, ah, Mister Blair." Ava gave him a tremulous smile.

"You're welcome, Miss Blue." He remained where he was, his eyes watchful as Neil jumped up from the couch and hurried toward her.

"Ava, are you all right?" The doctor gave her a warm embrace before leading her to the couch.

"I'm fine." Ava picked up a sofa pillow and plucked at its hem, her brow creasing. "But I'm worried Kingston hasn't come back. He's been shot. Oh, he says he's okay but maybe it's more serious than he thought. Maybe he needs a doctor. He wouldn't listen to me..."

"I got the impression he would be finishing up his business soon."

Ava scoffed. "You mean hunting down an unsuspecting, most likely innocent, man who may or may not be homeless?"

Neil smiled. "From what I've gathered, the man isn't innocent. He was paid to leave that note as a warning. Those two bullets were meant to do a job."

"A warning from who?" Ava asked, cocking her head. "My brother?"

Neil glanced at Blair who still sat perched on the bar stool, watching them intently. "I can't say anymore, Ava. Kingston will explain it all."

Ava had the strangest feeling Blair did not trust the doctor. Or maybe the man was just naturally distrustful of everyone apart from Kingston himself. Shifting nervously on the couch, she wondered if Neil was aware of the guard's faint suspicion.

For the next few hours, Neil kept Ava's attention with stories of his charity work and the women he helped with

Kingston's financial assistance. She did not realize how late the hour had grown until her eyes drifted shut more than once.

"You're tired, Ava. You should go on to bed," Neil said gently.

"No, I'm okay," she insisted, rubbing her eyes while fighting back a yawn. "I want to be awake when he gets back."

"But you're exhausted. Maybe even a bit shellshocked."

"I'm fine, really." Stretching her arms over her head, she felt a bit more invigorated. "I'll make coffee. I'm sure the men would appreciate it."

"No need, Miss Blue," Blair said from his stance by the dining room windows. "Just got word the boss has arrived. He'll be up in about five minutes."

Ava did not examine too closely the relief that flooded her. The tension she did not even realize was stringing her insides so tight was instantly dispelled.

"See? I told you everything would be fine." Neil stood up from the couch, stepping over to the bar in one corner of the room. He poured two glasses of scotch and had them ready when Kingston walked through the penthouse's double doors.

Ava restrained herself from flying into Kingston's arms. He looked as tired as she felt, but the worry etching his forehead into little furrows eased when he spotted her on the couch. Was it her imagination that a spark of reluctant tenderness lit the blue-black depths of his eyes?

He no longer wore the suit coat from earlier that day, and the white dress shirt bore evidence of his wound. Dried blood saturated the fine cloth, and she could see through the material that a stark white bandage encircled his upper arm.

"Thanks, Neil." Kingston accepted the glass of scotch and then turned to Blair. "The threat has been neutralized for the moment; however, the team will remain on high alert until I say otherwise. You did an excellent job tonight keeping Miss Blue safe and secure. Thank you for that."

"Sure thing, boss. I'll keep two men posted in the vestibule and two in the lobby." Blair touched his forehead with a two-finger salute and glanced in Ava's direction. "Miss Blue, it was our pleasure."

"Thank you, Mister Blair," Ava replied, giving the man a tremulous smile. She immediately dropped her gaze and nibbled on a fingernail when she saw Kingston's jaw tighten. Possessiveness rolled off him in waves, but he did not comment on the exchange between his security team's leader and his captive.

Once the door shut behind Blair, Kingston took a sip of the scotch and directed his attention to Ava. "Why are you still up? It's nearly midnight."

"I wasn't tired," she fibbed, then ruined it by stifling a yawn. "Besides, Doctor Abbott was kind enough to stay up with me. We were both worried. How is your arm? Are you in pain?"

"I told you there was no need to worry. I'm glad Neil came to sit with you. I didn't want you to feel alone." Kingston smiled at the doctor who waved a hand in dismissal of Kingston's words.

"You know it was no problem, Kingston. If you need me to look at that arm, I can."

"Just a flesh wound. Nothing serious. Jack put a couple of stitches in it."

Neil sighed. "Hopefully, he has improved his sewing skills since the last time. It appears the incident has been resolved?"

"For the moment, yes," Kingston said in a dry tone. "We'll speak more on it tomorrow. Right now, I'd like to see Ava get settled for bed."

"Of course." Neil drained his glass of scotch. "I'll say good-night to you both."

Ava smiled at the older man. "Thank you again for staying with me."

Once Neil was gone, Kingston sighed heavily and rubbed the back of his neck before tossing back the alcohol remaining in his glass.

"So, you caught the man?" Ava asked in a soft voice.

Kingston nodded, setting the empty tumbler down on the bar. "We did. One of them, anyway. Whoever shot at us got away, but not for long. My men will track him down, no matter who he is or where he goes."

Ava twisted her hands in her lap. "And the man you caught … is he dead?"

Surprise was evident in Kingston's features before he answered gruffly, "No. He's alive. I showed mercy."

"That must have been difficult for you." Ava did not take her eyes off him, hoping to see some evidence of humanity within that steely blue gaze of his.

"It was necessary."

Kingston stalked toward the couch and sank down beside her. His head fell back against the plush leather cushion.

She didn't mean to, but somehow, Ava found herself curled up against him, her bare feet tucked underneath her body. Kingston's warmth and the sense of safety she experienced in his presence made her drowsy. She could drop all pretense and fear when he was around her. Lower her guard. Allow this man to watch over her.

When and how the previous feelings of dread and hate began merging into these new emotions was baffling.

"Why was it necessary?" she murmured, breathing in the faded aroma of his cologne. The tea and pine were accentuated by the sharpness of the scotch he'd swallowed. And the tangy iron scent of blood

"Because I used him to return the message. You are mine and I'm keeping you."

"But who is that message intended for?" She rested her head against his chest as his arm curved around her shoulder.

Kingston was silent for a long time before answering.

"Your brother. And I'm going to have to kill him." He sounded so weary. So... resolute and extremely deadly. "Along with every man who victimized you with his approval. He also murdered your parents, and it doesn't sit well with me to close my eyes to that. I want to avenge them for your sake. And perhaps a little of my own." Letting out a heavy sigh, he pressed a kiss to the top of Ava's head. "But this is a discussion for the bright light of day. Right now, I want to fall asleep with you wrapped around me. We'll deal with the ugly truth of things in the morning."

DESPITE BEING EXHAUSTED, Ava lay awake most of the night. Mulling over the information that had been heaped in her lap, she wondered how Kingston would make her brother pay for what he'd done.

His harsh words echoed in her head, reminding her of his brutality. Kingston meant to kill her brother. Or, at least, he would try. But it was also possible Kingston might not survive making an attempt on her brother's life. Especially when Carson was receiving help from those he'd blackmailed over the years.

How could her brother be responsible for the death of their parents? Had he truly murdered them? It didn't seem possible. The horror of it was almost too much to bear.

"What's going round that pretty head of yours, lamb?"

Kingston's warm, drowsy voice startled Ava. She thought he'd fallen asleep already, but her tossing and turning must have awakened him.

"Nothing," she murmured as she pressed against his side. "Just a little trouble falling asleep. And I'm worried about your injury. Are you sure it's okay?"

"You're a terrible liar." Kingston stifled a yawn while tightening his good arm around Ava's waist. "Should I add that infraction to your growing list of punishments? You must know I haven't forgotten a single one."

Ava squirmed a little at the mention of punishments. It was strange how something so dreaded could also elevate anticipation. This man was truly doing an excellent job of corrupting her. And where she'd once despised it, she now found herself almost eagerly drowning in his attention.

"I'm sorry for waking you, sir," she replied in a soft voice, hoping the show of obedience would soothe him back to sleep. "It's nothing."

Kingston let out a heavy sigh. "If it were nothing, you'd be asleep instead of thrashing about." He hesitated again before continuing in a gruff tone, "And I'd rather you say my name."

Ava tensed, surprised by the unexpected request. "I am following your rules."

"Well, don't. Not right now, anyway." His voice turned even lower and huskier than before. "Are you in pain from the waxing? Is that why you can't sleep?"

Clenching her legs together at the reminder, she answered truthfully, "No. It doesn't hurt at all."

"A nightmare?"

Ava shook her head. "I've not had one of those since—" she faltered then continued in a stronger voice. "Not since we began sharing a bed."

Kingston shifted their bodies until they lay on their sides facing one another. The bandage on his upper arm was startlingly white against his tanned skin. "Your parents, then."

Ava could not escape the scrutiny in his gaze, not even in the shadowy darkness of the room. He had her pinned, and she relented with a small, anguished cry. "Yes! And... Carson. I can't understand why he would do this... how he could..." Tears welled up in her eyes, tears she couldn't seem to contain. Although she tried stemming the tide, they seeped out, tracking down her cheeks in silent rivulets as the pain she'd held in check for so long escaped under this man's watchful regard. "They loved us both so much. Why? Why would he do something so horrible?"

Ava buried her face in her hands, horrified by her own sobs and this display of weakness, but it couldn't be helped. Some sort of emotional dam had burst, and everything inside her since the day of her mom and dad's deaths—maybe even from the night Carson sold her to his friends—was now crashing through.

She half-expected Kingston to roll away in disgust, but what he did instead shook her entire world.

He gathered her in his arms, those muscled limbs wrapping and encircling until Ava almost felt safe. Holding her tight as she wept, he whispered comforting words in her ears and against her temples, stroking her back with large, brutal hands that had once caused pain but now soothed her.

"Let it out, little lamb. It's okay to cry. I'm here to wipe away those tears for you." Kingston's voice was rough and smooth all at once, the timbre of it rumbling through her body and reaching every corner of her broken, tattered soul. "I told you before. Carson will pay for what he's done. He won't be able to hurt you ever again. I promise you that."

Ava clung tighter to him, moving her arms until they

looped around his neck. "I'm scared. Scared he will hurt you, too. Hurt you like he did today. He could kill you like he did my mom and dad. And I-I don't want that."

Kingston chuckled. "You can't kill the Devil. And for you, I will become Lucifer himself."

Large hands bracketed her face as Kingston stared into her eyes. He held her gaze for a long moment, searching and intense. When he apparently found what he was looking for, the corners of his lips curved upward in what could almost be called a smile.

"Damn you, Ava. I can't fight this. I can't ignore it. I damn sure don't understand it. But I need you like I need air to breathe. And it fucking pisses me off."

His mouth descended on hers in a flurry of unspoken words. Emotions which could not be named aloud battered the walls between them until every hurtful act was stripped away. Left behind was pure, unapologetic hunger. Need. Lust. A mutual desire to forget the world and everything awful in their lives.

Ava knew what Kingston silently vowed as he ravaged her mouth and kissed her tear-stained cheeks. She knew because her heart was screaming in return.

You are mine. I am yours. No one will destroy what we feel for each other. No one can steal what we give each other.

Kingston cared for her as much as Ava tragically cared for him.

And that was a dangerous thing. It left them both vulnerable and desperate to protect what had grown like a fragile, flowering vine in the midst of a desolate wilderness.

Kingston kissed her so wildly that Ava thought her heart might explode. She kissed him back with the same ferocity, wondering how her feelings for him had changed so completely.

Hatred and despair had morphed into something else... something *savage*. It could not be named out loud just yet, but Ava knew. Her heart knew.

Love.

She loved him, and even if he never said the word itself in return, Ava was positive Kingston felt the same.

CHAPTER
THIRTY

On broken glass we slept
Regrets slicing like a thousand knives.
My memories escaping in rivulets.

"Make love to me, Kingston."

He withdrew from pressing hot kisses to her neck and savoring the sweetness of her mouth and shook his head. "I'm trying to be strong here, Ava."

She frowned, obviously puzzled by his restraint when before he would have taken what he wanted without consent or invitation.

"Strong?" she repeated. "I don't understand."

"I don't want to hurt you. At least, not in that way."

A small smile curved her lips as she swiped the last of her tears from her cheeks. "You won't. If you are worried about the waxing, I assure you it feels fine. I feel fine. Other than aching for you in ways I still don't understand."

Her admission bought a surge of hot blood racing through

Kingston's veins. It pooled in his groin until he was hard as a fucking rock for her.

"Jesus, Ava," he growled. "Your emotions are all jacked up right now. The shooting, everything that comes with that, the note. It's all messing with your head." He smoothed a tendril of her hair back from her forehead. "I want to fuck you until you scream, but it's not a good idea right now."

"Why not? Are you hurt more than you let on?" Ava scooted closer; her brow furrowed with worry as she lightly touched the bandages wrapping the circumference of his bicep. "I knew it was worse than you said."

"It's not that." Kingston lay still, discomforted by her concern. It'd been a long time since someone bothered showing true concern for his wellbeing. He couldn't decide if he liked it or not.

Tilting her head, Ava kissed the hollow of his throat. One of her hands drifted to his chest, and with gentle fingertips, she traced the outline of the lion's head tattoo. "I want you, Kingston. I want you, and I don't care if it makes me seem weak or stupid."

Kingston immediately grasped her chin, holding her face with hard fingers. He glared at her, angry that she thought so little of herself. "Don't you ever say that again, Ava." His words came out harsher than he intended, but she needed to understand her value. To see herself as he saw her now. Someone who was strong enough to survive abuse and assault and still be the most tender-hearted person he'd ever known. "You are neither weak nor stupid. Despite everything that's been done to you, including the hell I've put you through, you are braver and stronger than anyone I've ever met. You are priceless. A goddamn queen I should be bowing to."

Ava regarded him solemnly. "Do you really believe that?"

Kingston huffed out a rueful laugh. "I can't explain it.

Because *this* has become something I never intended or expected. No matter how hard I fight against feeling any emotion for you, you somehow keep wiggling under my skin. The only thing I'm sure of is that I am a heartless, cruel bastard, and you deserve so much better than me. I'm the monster who stole you away from the world."

Ava gave a tiny, stubborn shake of her head. "You're wrong, Kingston. You are not heartless."

His mouth twisted in a wry grin. "That still leaves my cruel nature, Ava. And that's something that will never change. The way I'm wired when it comes to women... The depraved things I want to do to you... That part of me will *never* change."

"I don't want you to change." Ava gripped his wrist, pulling his hand from her chin and placing it on her throat. "I want you just as you are. Controlling. Possessive. Dominating me and keeping me safe. Don't you see, Kingston? You've said many times that I have always been yours. I understand what it means now, even if I fought it—and you—at first. But it's also true that you've always been mine as well."

Ava's words were an aphrodisiac, enticing Kingston's fingers to twitch until they were flexing around the slim column of her neck. He wondered if he was dreaming. Because what she was confessing was the stuff of fantasy.

"*Fuck*, Ava. Stop provoking me to take what I want when I'm trying so fucking hard to think of someone other than myself."

Ava arched into him, her firm breasts burning his skin through the thin nightgown she wore. "Stop thinking, Kingston. Take me like you want to. Take me because I need you. You told me once that I would beg for you, and I'm begging now. Make love to me. Prove that I mean *something* to you." She sighed with frustrated desire when he still did nothing more than tighten his hand around her throat. "I want to be a part of your life, and this is the only way I can accomplish that."

Kingston stared at her, baffled that this girl did not recognize the depths of his need. The absolute fucking *obsession* he suffered for her. His admission tumbled out before he could rethink the words and their implication. "Somehow, you've become *my* life, Ava. Even if I don't deserve you."

"Show me," Ava whispered desperately. "Punish me. Fuck me. I'm giving you everything." She dug her fingers into his hand where it wrapped around her throat, leaning into his grip with fever-bright eyes. "Everything, Kingston."

"We're supposed to wait twenty-four hours before having sex, remember?" Kingston's tone wavered, and Ava leaned on his shaky resistance.

"I know my body better than they do," was her tart reply. "And so do you. You know every curve and line. Every hollow. Every need and desire and the taste of my skin. You *know* me, Kingston."

Kingston groaned at her words. "If I do what you're asking, I'll end up hurting you."

"Isn't that what you've always wanted? To hurt me?" Ava taunted, pressing her mouth to his tattoo. She kissed it softly, running her tongue over the white line scar making up the lion's fang before nipping him with sharp, devilish teeth that made his cock roar to life. "You may have broken me, just like you said you would." Her head rose and she stared him in the eye. "But I think I can break you, too."

Kingston's control melted away like ice during a spring thaw. "So, the bad girl wants to play, does she?"

His hand abruptly tightened around her throat. Ava gasped as her airway was constricted. Still, she nodded in consent, her green eyes dark with desire and a spark of foolish challenge Kingston could not resist.

Rolling onto his back, he dragged her along with him using only the grip around her throat. The pillows propped his upper body up against the headboard. Ava awkwardly sprawled across his midsection, scrambling until she ended up straddling him. His cock tented his sleeping pants, thick and hard as an iron pole, as it nestled against the plump cheeks of her delectable ass.

"Pull my pants down."

The order was guttural, his patience snapping in two as her eyes darkened even more with excitement. How lucky was he that his girl liked it just as rough as he did?

"How?" Ava responded in a strangled voice.

Kingston's eyes crinkled at the corners. His fingers flexed and tightened again. "I don't give a fuck *how* you do it. Just do it."

Her lips parted as she drew a quick breath. Kingston could see her mind furiously working out how she could accomplish the task with his hand wrapped around her throat, keeping her hostage.

Bracing one hand on his chest, Ava reached behind her and slipped her fingers into the waistband of his pants. Somehow, by contorting her body, she succeeded in pushing the garment down far enough that his cock finally sprang free from confinement.

"See how clever you are when you want something badly enough?" Kingston crooned. Using his free hand, ignoring the sharp pain in his injured arm, he reached beneath the nightgown she wore and slid his palm over the bare flesh of her ass. Higher and higher, his fingers traveled until he could hook them in the thin, delicate strap of her G-string. One quick motion and the fabric ripped in two.

Ava inhaled, her hands now clenched into fists and

pressing into his wide chest. She was caught between the grip he maintained around her neck and his aching cock.

"Take this off before I rip it to shreds and use the pieces to gag and bind you." His eyes drifted over her body still concealed by the dark green nightgown she had thrown on. "I want to see you. All of you."

He let go of her throat so she could do as he demanded. Throwing the garment aside, Ava straddled him, naked and shaking with invisible tremors racing through her body. Her bare breasts rose and fell with quick pants for air, no doubt anticipating when his hand would control her air supply. Staring down at him, she waited for his next order.

Kingston moved his legs, jostling her as he worked his pants down until they bunched in a heap beneath the covers at the end of the bed. Now, they were both gloriously naked, other than the bandaging around Kingston's bicep.

Ava's gaze flickered to the white gauze and medical tape, concern flaring in the depths of her eyes.

Kingston slid a hand up her side to the curved underside of her breast, molding his hand around it. Just as she began relaxing from the gentleness of his touch, he lightly pinched one of her pink nipples, eliciting a shocked gasp. Pulling her down, he ran his tongue over each nipple in turn, sucking on the sweet buds and biting the tips until Ava moaned.

"Eyes on me, baby. I already told you not to worry about my injury. Look away from me again and I'll fuck that pretty mouth of yours instead of your cunt."

Ava whimpered in response, her gaze immediately locking with his. Where her silky, bare pussy brushed his stomach, Kingston felt the heat and dampness of her core. She was wet. Fucking drenched. Her response to his domination was intoxicating as hell.

"Do you still want me to make love to you, Ava?"

She began to nod, but remembering his instructions from before, she choked out, "Yes, sir. Please."

"Do you agree that your pussy is mine to use however I want? That this gorgeous body of yours is mine and I can play with you in any manner I choose?" He stroked her breasts, loving their soft fullness before pinching one nipple a little harder.

"Yes!" she quickly agreed as he lifted his hips until his cock pressed more firmly against her ass.

"Good girl."

The praise sent a wave of goosebumps skittering across Ava's body. Groaning, she rocked back against Kingston's dick, her hips rolling in eager anticipation for the moment he would fill her.

His hand rose to encircle her throat again, holding her still so he could stare at her. "I've said this before, lamb, but you are absolute perfection. Since your gorgeous body belongs to me, you will do whatever I say. Tell me you will do anything I tell you to do."

"Yes. Anything, Kingston."

Kingston slid his free hand down the center of Ava's body, marveling over the silkiness of her skin. In the dimness of the room, illuminated only by the bed's platform lights, he could see how wide her eyes were, how they sparkled with need and lust. Her features were practically glowing as she waited for his instructions.

His finger traced the softness of her pussy, gently touching the outer lips which were so smooth and bare that the glistening of her arousal was evident. He spread her flesh, exposing her even more as he gave his first order.

"Take hold of the headboard and pull yourself up until you are straddling my face. I want to taste you. I want to eat this perfect," his finger pressed against her bared clit, "pink," he pressed harder until she moaned, "pussy."

"Kingston?" Her voice was shaky and unsure, but her legs tensed in preparation for following his orders. "Are you sure?"

Kingston's actions stilled. He steadfastly held her gaze. "I won't hurt you, Ava. Not with this." Releasing her throat, he stroked the softness of her cheek.

Ava leaned into the palm of his hand, her eyes closing before nodding in agreement.

"Good. Now, move your sweet little ass into position like I told you."

She quickly shifted into action, gripping two of the many tall spindles that made up the headboard. Kingston slid down the pillows so that he wasn't as upright as before.

But once she was in position, her thighs bracketing his head, she hesitated again.

"Um... I don't know what to do now. I've never..." she said in such a sweetly innocent voice that Kingston was instantly crazed with the need to corrupt her.

"Lower yourself onto my face, baby. And don't you fucking move away until you come. I want you flooding my mouth."

"H-how long will it take?" Embarrassment colored her words, and Kingston knew her eyes were squeezed tightly shut just from the timbre of her voice.

"For you to come? Not long at all. For me to have my fill? An eternity." He chuckled, sliding his hands up to cup the firm globes of her ass and support her weight. Since she wasn't moving fast enough for his liking, Kingston gave her bottom a swat so hard she jolted forward from the contact.

"Oh!" Her fingers tightened on the headboard spindles.

"Oh, indeed. Now, do as I say." He helped her surrender by squeezing her ass cheeks and jerking her down.

The instant her pussy met his mouth, Ava let out an anguished cry while Kingston groaned in delight.

She was so soft. So sweet. Like fucking cotton candy melting on his tongue. He lapped at the smooth skin then ate at her folds, tugging gently at them with his teeth before circling her clit with his tongue. Ava let out a helpless whimper, her body moving with the motion of Kingston's mouth as he devoured her.

"Oh, God," she cried when he speared her opening with his tongue, using the point of it to lash her swollen clit. Her legs shook almost violently, her breathing hard and shallow. Kingston doubled his efforts, relentlessly holding her in place for his rapacious mouth until Ava abruptly stiffened.

Pressing his tongue flat against her clit, he felt the fluttering pulse of her heartbeat as the orgasm tore through her body.

"*Kingston, Kingston, Kingston,*" Ava chanted, riding the pleasure out as her essence flooded his mouth.

When she slumped forward, her legs slack and her breathing slowing to deep breaths, Kingston smoothed his palms over her ass and nuzzled deeper into her pussy. He licked her again in encouragement.

"Oh, no. No, no, no, no," she implored beneath her breath. Her body tensed, rushing toward a second climax before the first had even subsided.

Oh, yes, little lamb. Fuck yes.

Giving her no reprieve, Kingston quickly drove her to the peak of another orgasm. Her muffled screams of pleasure were a beautiful symphony to his ears when she plummeted into the abyss.

Releasing her death grip on the headboard, Ava slid down Kingston's body, fluid as a swath of expensive silk. For a long moment, she simply lay flat atop him, shaking in the aftermath, her breaths eventually slowing until they were almost normal. And he allowed it. Allowed it because, for some fucked up reason, he liked how good it made him feel. Liked that she trusted him enough to show vulnerability in such an endearing way.

Kingston smoothed a hand down her bare back. "Did I hurt you?"

Ava sighed heavily, burying her face in the crook of his neck and shoulder. "Of course not." She pressed a soft kiss there, and Kingston knew she was smiling when she continued, "That's the one thing I *wasn't* worried about. What you just did... what I felt... it was amazing. You are amazing. Thank you, Kingston."

"No need to thank me, Ava. I'll gladly give you as many orgasms as you can stand. I'll give you anything you want in this world. Ask and it's yours."

She raised her head, peering into his eyes as though she could see straight down into the depths of whatever remained of his black soul. Minuscule droplets of sweat beaded her upper lip, and Kingston slowly licked them off. What was she thinking as she stared at him so intently?

He slid a hand to the nape of her neck where the tracker rested beneath her silky skin. It was reassuring to feel the tiny, almost indiscernible bump there. It was smaller than a grain of rice and unless he pointed it out, she would never even know of its existence.

But he knew. And it fucking drove him crazy with lust. Knowing his lamb was under his thumb at all times, even when she wasn't with him.

"Will you give me my freedom, Kingston?" she finally murmured, eyes glittering with emotions held in check for too long. "Will you give me that and the opportunity to punish my brother for what he has done?"

CHAPTER

THIRTY-ONE

*T*he darkness takes.
    Gives.
    Hides.
Reveals.

AVA STEADFASTLY HELD Kingston's gaze while simultaneously holding her breath.

Surely, he wouldn't deny her this. She deserved the chance to see Carson's face when she told him she knew everything. She would confront him and be unafraid when she did it. She would tell him she knew he had betrayed their family. Their parents who loved and supported him.

And herself. His own sister. How cruelly he had deceived her.

"Kingston?" she whispered, silently begging him to support her in this quest for the truth and retribution. "Answer me."

"Yes."

Ava slumped in relief. "You aren't lying? You will set me free?"

Kingston's smile was crooked as he stroked the curve of her cheek with his fingertip. "I won't ever lie to you, lamb. I might omit the truth, or delay it, but I'll never lie to you. You will have your freedom once all threats to your life have been eliminated."

Ava's jaw clenched. "You know that's not what I meant. I'm asking to be set free. Completely free. Not in little increments or bits and pieces."

"Have you forgotten the contract you signed?"

She shook her head. "I've not forgotten. I know what I signed, but you could tear that up into a million shreds if you wanted to. You could forgive the debt and allow me to go wherever and whenever I please without your chains wrapped around one of my ankles. I want to make Carson pay for what he's done. And for that to happen, you must release me. Please, Kingston. You must understand how important this is to me."

"I know, baby. And I wish I could let you go. I'd love nothing more than to sit back and watch you do whatever your little savage heart desires when it comes to your brother, but it's too dangerous. There are too many others involved in this. Too many men with evil intent and nothing to lose now that video evidence of your assault has been destroyed. I suspect my own brother to be included with that group, but that remains to be seen."

"The video... it's gone?" Ava could not believe it. That slice of her life, immortalized in digital context, had hung heavy over her head for so many years. She'd lived in constant fear of it being released. Exploited. Sensationalized. For the moment, she forgot her unspoken plan of revenge against Carson and instead absorbed the news that her brother no longer had evidence of that night in his arsenal of weapons. Relief overwhelmed her. Tears pricked her eyes, hot and insistent as gratitude wiggled into her heart.

Kingston did this for her.

"From Carson's data files, yes. I have the only file now, and no one will ever see it again."

"You watched it?"

Kingston softly replied, "I did."

"Oh my God." With a moan of disgust, Ava tried rolling off him, but Kingston's palm pressed her lower back, keeping her in place and pinned against him.

"Stay where you are, Ava," he growled. "And listen to me. Yes. I watched the damn file. And do you know what will happen now? I will destroy every man involved in its creation that night. For you, lamb. Because you are mine. You've always been mine. And no one touches or harms what is mine." His hand came up and lightly encircled her throat. "There will be no further discussion of this subject. I'll handle it. And I'll let you go after it's all over if that's what you still want." Kissing her lightly on the mouth, he ordered, "Sit up and straddle me like you did before."

Ava tilted her chin. "You can't stop me from wanting to do this on my own, Kingston. Carson is my brother and I want to make him pay."

"You're right. I can't stop you. But I can make you forget for a little while."

"How will you do that?" Ava muttered. "By chaining me up? Beating me into submission?"

"Oh, baby." Kingston's fingers tightened around her throat, and despite her best intention to stay unaffected, Ava could not contain the small whimper that escaped her. "I will restrain you, put you in cuffs, and probably tie you up with pretty silk ropes one day, but I would *never* beat you."

It wasn't fair he could so easily incite her lust with just

those simple words. Her body reacted as though she'd not enjoyed two climaxes only moments ago. She was instantly ready for him, primed for his possession and willing to do whatever he wanted. This weakness was a curse, one from which she would never recover.

"If you care anything about me, if you have any feelings for me at all, Kingston, you will let me go so I can do this on my own."

Kingston's smile was darkly tortured. "It is because I care that I cannot do that. Don't you understand, Ava? If something happens to you, it happens to me. You get hurt, I hurt. You are in pain, I suffer, too. If you should die, then I am dead as well. And I will never rest until I avenge you."

Ava stared at him in amazement, her treacherous heart thumping madly at his unexpected confession. "Do you really mean that, Kingston? Am I finally more to you than a debt to be paid?"

"You've always been more, Ava. You've always been everything." His fingers tightened again, dark blue eyes glittering like stars in the night sky. "Now, sit up," he directed in that silky smooth, dangerous voice that always sent shivers through her. "Slide your soft, tight pussy down on me. Fuck yourself on my cock while I watch you come undone."

"N-no," she stuttered, trying to pull away from him. He sounded like a man intent on keeping her prisoner forever, and while she wanted him with every overly stimulated, desperate cell of her body, she wanted so much more than a lifetime chained to his side as some sort of helpless, pretty pet.

"That's not what I want to hear from you, lamb." His voice was sad but resolute as he shoved her upward until she straddled him as he desired, her legs on either side of his hips. "It does no good to tell me 'no'. Because neither one of us can deny what we both want. Nor can we deny what we share between us. *This.* My desire for you and yours for me. This mutual obsession. This fixation. This all-consuming *need.* I can hardly admit it, even to myself, but the truth is, I'm begging you, Ava. Begging. Do you understand? Because I want you that much. I want all of you. You asked me to make love to you but I have my own request, lamb. I want you to make love to *me.* You set the pace. You decide how much or how little. I'll give you all the control but not until you sink that sweet pussy onto my cock. Your chance to play at domination begins then."

Ava's body melted against him. The very idea she could control of Kingston Vaughn Winter was irresistible. But if she stood any chance of personally making her brother pay for his treachery, she must remain strong in the face of this unexpected temptation. Convincing Kingston to grant her wish required clear thinking and cunning strategy.

All of which flew out the window with his hand encircling her throat and his thick cock nudging her backside.

"What do you say, Ava? Do we have a deal? Either way, I'm fucking you, but I'd like it noted you were given a choice in the matter."

"It's not a choice." Bracing her hands on his midsection, she rolled her hips back against his hot flesh until it again nestled in the crack of her ass. Just feeling the heat and size of him there was enough to make her feral. "It's an ultimatum."

"True." Keeping one hand around her neck, he gripped her hip with the other. "And I'm waiting to see what you do about it."

"Take your hand off my throat," she demanded breathlessly. "So I can think clearly."

Kingston chuckled, apparently amused by her bossiness. "Nice try, baby, but it stays. I may be giving you control for a while, but this is just a reminder of who owns you."

"You don't *own* me," she breathed while lifting her hips and gliding down in one smooth motion onto his cock. She was so wet, so ready, there was just a momentary pinch of pain as her body accommodated his. She sucked in a breath of agonized pleasure.

"Ah, hell, Ava. Maybe it's you who owns me." Kingston's satisfied grunt was accompanied by his hips jerking upward, burying his cock further inside her than Ava ever thought possible. He seated himself to the hilt and waited as her flesh stretched and clamped tight around him.

Ava saw stars. Her hands clenched, squeezing the muscles that defined his broad chest. He felt so much larger in this position. Bigger. Harder. Longer, somehow. He filled her right up to the fine line of pain and ecstasy. Her newly waxed pussy spasmodically quivered in discomfort, but Ava ignored it, focusing on the exquisite pleasure instead.

"Am I hurting you?" Kingston groaned, holding still so Ava could adjust. "Because you are damn near killing me. Your cunt is so goddamn tight, it's strangling me."

"I'm okay. Honest. Give me a second. It's almost too much, but I don't want you to stop," Ava whispered. "I think I like the little bite of pain. Reminds me I'm alive. And that right here is where I want to be. Where I'm meant to be."

"You're hardwired to take that pain just as I'm hardwired to give it, Ava." Kingston remained motionless as Ava lifted and sank down on him again. "Once you accept that this is who you really are, things become much less complicated. This... this is who *we* are. Who we have always been."

"Yes," Ava moaned.

He rubbed his thumb down her carotid artery but did not lessen the tightness of his grip around her throat. "I'm trying to be patient. Trying to remember I gave you control, but, baby, if you don't start moving, I'm gonna go wild and fuck you to within an inch of your life."

Ava sputtered a giggle. "You're not a monster after all. You're really just a caveman at heart."

Kingston pinned her with that blue-black stare of his. "I don't have a heart, little lamb. Remember that."

Ava turned somber, rolling her hips just enough to make them both inhale a sharp breath. "I guess I'll have to help you grow one."

The lust in Kingston's eyes flared brighter along with the tiny, unmistakable light of something else. Something Ava recognized because she'd seen it in herself, but not until years after her parents died and she found the courage to move on with her dreams. It was the spark that led her to a Savannah hotel elevator and ended in a dungeon cell, face to face with this man.

Hope.

Hope that everything would be okay. Hope that life would right itself. Hope that one day, love would barge in and take over. Hope that she would find happiness, even after death and loss and unbelievable heartache.

Somehow, without even trying, she'd become Kingston's glimmer of hope. He looked at her as though she could grant him freedom from the burdens of his life. She gave him hope of something better. Something brighter. Something they could share together.

A future.

"I have a confession," Ava murmured as she rose and sank down again with excruciating slowness.

"Whatever it is, I don't care right now." Kingston's hand squeezed her hip hard enough to leave bruises. "Just keep fucking me like this. You're doing so well, baby. Taking all of me with hardly a whimper."

"I want to confess anyway." She threw her head back until the length of her hair brushed the tops of his muscled thighs.

Kingston laughed under his breath. "If you are still able to talk, I'm doing a terrible job of fucking you."

"This is serious," Ava protested, still rocking back and forth. "I stole something from your restaurant. It's crazy, I know. And it sounds so ridiculous when I say it aloud. I took a fork. Not even a knife, but a stupid fork. In my defense, I thought it wouldn't be easily missed."

"Why did you do it?"

"I thought I could use it as a weapon. To protect myself." Ava leaned forward, brushing his lips with the tease of a kiss. "God, I don't know. It was an absurd thing to do."

"It was stupid." Kingston agreed, pulling her down with the grip of her throat and holding her so her lips hovered over his. "And your confession is wasted because I already knew." He captured her mouth in a hot, bruising kiss that seemed endless.

Ava kissed him back although dread sent tingles of foreboding down her spine. *He knows what I did and never said a word? Has he been waiting for my confession? Or for the moment I tried using it against him?*

With a shudder, she nipped his bottom lip as he'd done to her so many times and quickly sat up, wondering what he might do to her now. Admitting she'd thought of using a weapon, even if it wasn't specifically against him, was very foolish.

Kingston grinned up at her, the tiny spot of blood that welled up from the injury demanding she lick it from his lip. "Did that make you feel any better, lamb?"

"No," she admitted softly. "But I had to tell you. Because I did lie when you asked if I had something to tell you. Do you remember? When we were in your office? I'm sorry." She kissed him again, the metallic taste of blood mingling with the wintergreen flavor of his mouth. "I should be punished for lying."

Kingston's hand tightened around her throat until Ava's breathing hitched with almost sadistic delight. "And you will be. When I'm in control instead of the other way around." His grin deepened, recognizing her reckless need for his punishments. "Now, fuck me like your life depends on it. Make me come before I lose my patience with this game I started. Make love to me, Ava, as if you really do love me."

But I do love you. I love you even if it is dangerous. And foolish.

Ava did not dare say that aloud, but with her body, she told him everything. And as their movements became more frantic, their mouths clashing and fighting for dominance, Kingston's hand tightened until she feared passing out from lack of oxygen. Hot, scalding tears leaked from the corners of her eyes, splattering on his hand, but she did not push him away nor did she fight his grip. There was no need to struggle. She was where she should be. Under his control and protected in the most depraved way.

"Give me everything, Ava." His whisper was dark and beguiling. "Your breath. Your tears. Your body. Everything. I won't accept anything less than all of you, heart and soul. Because you finally realize what I've known for a long time. Every inch of you belongs to me."

Ava's body greedily sucked at his as she rocked back and forth until the sensations pooled together, bursting through her veins like a flooded dam. The waves pulled her under until nothing existed of her former self.

This must be what addiction felt like. This drug-like hunger and its heavenly high. It was something she needed now. Like air to breathe. Or water to live. There was no going back to a mundane existence after experiencing the depths of such craving.

Kingston grunted as Ava's body convulsed around his, her pussy milking his cock. The next instant, he exploded inside her, bathing her womb with hot cum as he thrust harder inside her, his own cry harsh and guttural.

"Mine, Ava." His breath feathered her cheek as she collapsed over him in an exhausted, satisfied, boneless heap. "You're mine."

THIRTY-TWO

*B*etrayals cut the deepest
When they come from those you loved.

"WE GOT THE SHOOTER," Jack said over the phone. "Tracked him down in Bitter Springs. He's at The Den now, waiting for you."

Kingston scrubbed a hand over his face. Relief wasn't all he felt at that moment. Rage battled for a place in his emotions, but he retained control by the barest of margins.

"Does Oliver know?"

"Yeah. He insisted we chain the guy up in the dungeon until you arrive. Says he has no idea who he is, but he'll keep him primed for you. I think he'll be calling you soon."

Shit. He didn't want his brother having any part of this, especially when it wasn't clear if he was in on the plot to abduct Ava. "What about Carson? Anything to report?"

"Holed up in his house with a couple of officers standing guard. Detective Redding was seen leaving the house about an hour ago. Guess they got the news Jeff and Brad Turner were both found dead this morning."

"No one knows my hackers found and erased the video evidence. If they did, Carson would most likely already be dead. And that would be a shame." Kingston glanced down the hallway toward the master bedroom where Ava was sleeping. "I intend to give his sister the opportunity to get some answers. I want eyes on Carson until I say otherwise. If he makes a move, I want to know immediately."

"Sure thing, boss. When do you want to head back?" Jack asked.

"Today. As soon as Ava is ready. And Jack? Tell Paulie to keep an eye on Oliver." Kingston ended the call, wondering if this was the day Oliver finally snatched the power he wanted by eliminating his only brother.

He was sipping a second cup of coffee, debating what he would do if Oliver was greedy enough to attempt murder when he heard the bedroom door click open. A few seconds later, Ava glided in from the hallway, making her way toward the kitchen. She wore a silk robe over her nightgown, her hair a disheveled mass of curls and her feet bare.

Kingston drank her in. Earlier that morning, she'd been fast asleep, curled against his side. A mournful cry had escaped her, and she thrashed a bit until he smoothed a hand over her hair. Worried she was slipping into one of her nightmares, he was on the verge of shaking her awake. But she settled down with a sigh, nuzzling into his shoulder as his grip tightened around her waist. He had held her like that for hours before slipping from the bed to answer Jack's phone call.

Drawing up short at the sight of him standing on the other side of the island, Ava's toes curled against the cold marble floor. Her pale features were tense, anticipating what his mood might be in the bright light of day.

"Good morning, lamb," Kingston said, warmly.

Ava visibly relaxed, her kiss-bruised lips curving into a smile. Her eyes darted over his naked chest and the low-slung sleeping pants he wore. "Good morning."

"What would you like for breakfast?"

She padded into the kitchen until she stood before him. Tilting her chin upward, she regarded him in silence as Kingston took her hands in his and kissed them. She let out a shaky laugh that died when her gaze landed on the fresh bandaging wrapped around his bicep.

"Is your arm alright?" she asked softly. "Did I hurt you before...?" Her words trailed off in embarrassment, cheeks turning pink under his perusal.

Kingston's eyebrow arched. "You didn't hurt me, Ava. Enchanted me, yes. Captivated me, yes. Made me crazy with wanting you, also a yes. But you didn't hurt me. If anything, I'm afraid I might have hurt you. I was too rough."

"Oh, but you weren't," Ava exhaled in relief. "I'm fine. A little sore maybe, but it's nothing. Really. I'm hardly made of glass, you know."

Kingston wrapped his arms around her waist, concealing the slight wince from the movement. He didn't want her to know it was a bit stiff with pain. It would ease as the day went on. "We'll discuss later just how breakable you really are, lamb. But for now, I'll make you breakfast."

"Just coffee will be okay. Maybe yogurt, if you have it?"

Kingston frowned. "You missed dinner last night in all the excitement. I'll not have you collapsing later from hunger, so you will eat something more substantial." He pecked a kiss on the tip of her nose before reluctantly letting her go. "Sit down at the island there while I scramble up some eggs."

Ava nodded obediently, moving to the other side of the island. Sliding onto one of the bar stools, she watched as he poured her a coffee, preparing it the way she liked it; two creams and two sugars. When he placed the cup in front of her, she took a sip of the doctored brew and sighed in appreciation.

While Kingston prepared the eggs and heated a skillet, Ava drank her coffee.

"Are your guards still here?" she asked, breaking the silence that fell between them while he cooked.

Pulling two plates down from the cabinet, Kingston shook his head. "I released them this morning, although Jack will be here later. One of my other security details caught the man who shot at us yesterday."

"That's good to hear. So, he's in jail now?"

Kingston smiled at Ava's innocence. "No." After spooning the scrambled eggs onto their plates, he turned to retrieve the toast once it popped up.

"But you said they caught him. Do we need to go pick him out of a line-up or something?" Her brow knitted with confusion. "I mean, even if we didn't actually see who was shooting at us."

"I don't use the police for things like that, Ava." Kingston gave her a meaningful stare, setting the plate of eggs and toast down in front of her. "Law enforcement is an unnecessary nuisance in my world."

Ava picked up her fork, waiting until Kingston sat beside her before taking a bite. "What happened to him? Where is he?"

"He's waiting for me at The Den."

Her relief was evident as she chewed her eggs and swallowed. With wide eyes, she said, "I guess you'll get information on who hired him to do such an awful thing. If it wasn't Carson pulling those strings, I'll be shocked. You'll turn this man over to the police, right? I mean, once you have what you need?"

One of his contacts within the police chief's office provided the guy's information based on the partial license plate, but that was the extent of the law's involvement in this matter. And it was safe to say no one would come looking for him when he went missing.

"No, Ava." Kingston took a sip of coffee, his tone nonchalant. If Ava knew the horrors waiting for the man who had endangered her life, it would only frighten her. "With this new development, we'll be heading home today. The jet is waiting on standby for us."

When Ava's fork clattered on her plate, it was a reminder of the makeshift weapon she'd stolen. He knew it was still inside the purse she'd left lying on the dresser in the walk-in closet.

He still needed to punish her for that little transgression, as insignificant as it was. Along with a host of other things he'd been keeping tabs on. When the time came that he could administer the appropriate correction, his little lamb wouldn't be able to sit properly for at least a week.

"You intend to hurt this man?" Ava's question was soft.

"He isn't a good guy, Ava, so erase any thought that he doesn't deserve what's coming." Kingston abruptly stood, gathering their plates and cups and loading them into the dishwasher. "This one would just as soon slit your throat and rape you while you lay dying for all your concern about his miserable life. Placing you in danger by shooting at me means he'll pay dearly for his mistake."

Ava nodded, but Kingston could see she was still disturbed by what might happen to the man.

What will happen, you mean. I am going to rip him from limb to limb for his role in this. He's earned every minute of pain I will inflict before I move on to the next man.

"Go get your shower and get ready to leave," he ordered brusquely, not liking the unease glinting in her eyes. "I've got some phone calls to make."

Ava slid down from the barstool, wrapping the robe tight around herself. "We could stay in the city for a few more days. You don't need to rush back to The Den just to torture someone."

"Don't you understand what is happening, lamb?" Kingston bit out in frustration. "Your enemies, who are now *my* enemies, will be looking for any chink in the armor. Yesterday's events put everything on a fast track, and there's no stopping what will happen now. Men will die. Your brother... will die."

Ava's chin tilted in that stubborn way he both adored and dreaded. She was about to make things very complicated for them both.

"I don't want to be there while you torture and kill men just below my feet. I can't, Kingston. Please don't ask that of me." Her gaze turned pleading, and damn if he didn't feel himself softening. "If you won't stay here with me, then let me stay behind without you. Just until your... business... is finished. Have your guards watch my every move if you must, but don't force me to be present while you commit murder."

"Damnit, Ava. It must be done."

"I know. And I understand your reasoning. Just don't make me a part of it. As I was with Malcolm." A delicate shudder shook her body at the memory of that horror, but her gaze remained steadfast and locked on his. "You can punish me for my disobedience when you come back."

"I could punish you now and still force you to come with me. All it would take is a set of handcuffs and a gag." Kingston scowled. His fists clenched into tight balls to keep from grabbing her and giving her a damn good shake. There were a million reasons to justify not letting her out of his sight, but he suspected she would argue each one until his head spun.

"That's true. You could do that. But would you?" Her head

tilted as she watched his internal struggle between pleasing her or bending her to his will.

Was she even aware her eyes were filled with tears, tugging at the heart he swore no longer existed? This tiny slip of a girl was making a liar out of him. Because the hole where his heart once lay was now thumping with confused worry and something else which had become foreign over the years since Rebecca's death.

Fear for someone else.

And the thought of Ava in danger was more terrifying than anything Kingston had endured in his lifetime.

"Ava, you'll be safest with me." Kingston sighed, raking a hand through his hair.

"Of course, I would be. But I'm also safe here. Like Rapunzel in the tower." She was so pragmatic as she argued the merits of remaining in the city. "How could anyone get to me up here? It'd be like trying to break into the National Treasury with all the security measures you have in place. No one is getting in here unless you want them in here."

Kingston growled, frustrated by the truth of her words.

"For some goddamn reason, I find I cannot deny you anything anymore. All right, Ava. You win this time. Enjoy your little victory for now. I won't take you with me, but you can be damn sure you'll pay a price for this show of rebellion. At the rate you're going, you'll be tied up and at my mercy for weeks."

Ava nodded solemnly. "I understand, sir."

"It does no good to try and placate me now with a belated show of respect. I want you to listen carefully, Ava." Cupping her elbow, he pulled her so close she flattened against his body as if a hurricane was blowing her into him. "You will not leave this penthouse, and no one comes in other than the guards. The kitchen is stocked, but the restaurant can deliver whatever else you might like. The guards will bring in whatever you order. But no one else comes in, do you understand? No one. Not even Neil, although I imagine he will ask to check on you. It's too dangerous, and right now, I can't afford to trust anyone."

"I understand the rules of my captivity have not changed." Ava's voice was husky, her eyes tracking his features as if memorizing them. She stared at his mouth like she wanted very badly to kiss him. "You once told me I could not explore The Den without you, Jack, or Paulie by my side. What has changed? Are your men suddenly more trustworthy than before? Or is it because there's no chance that I'll make a run for it? The only way I could escape is to jump off the side of this building."

"Don't test me right now, Ava," Kingston grumbled. "I'm a hair's breadth away from popping you with tranquilizers and dragging your unconscious body onto that jet with me. You'd sleep through the torture session I have planned for our dungeon guest. By the end of the day, you'd forget he ever existed. And then, I would take *you* down to the cells and show you what it means to fully submit."

Ava's teeth sunk into her bottom lip with such force it left an indentation. The emerald green depths of her eyes darkened with apprehension. "Please don't do that, Kingston. Don't drug me. I swear I'll do as you say until you come back."

Gripping her face in the palm of his hand, Kingston squeezed in warning. Her cheeks sunk in with the pressure of his hand, hollowing her face.

"I wouldn't want to be you if you disobey me, lamb." The corner of his mouth twitched. "Don't disappoint me unless you want to find out what happens when you do."

THIRTY-THREE

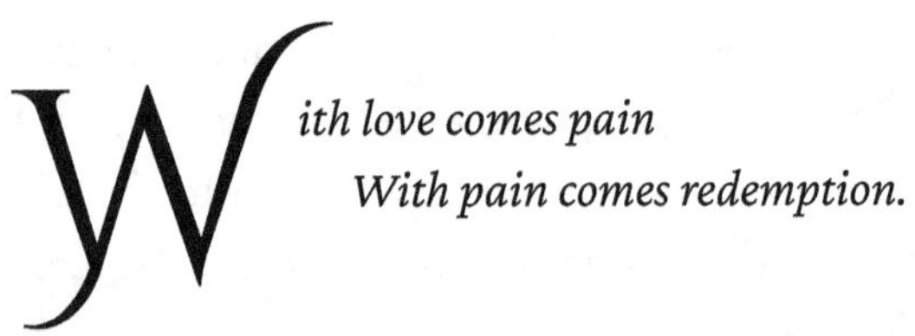

With love comes pain
With pain comes redemption.

AVA PACED the living room until she heard the low roar of running water in the master bathroom.

She'd already had a shower and now wore black leggings and an oversized white angora sweater that was soft as a cloud. Knee-high black boots completed her outfit, the low heels clicking softly on the marble floor.

Peeking around the edge of the door, she quickly scanned the bedroom. It was empty, confirming that Kingston was in the shower. He wouldn't be able to stop her.

But still, fear paralyzed her. What she was about to do was extremely foolish. Even more idiotic than stealing a fork. She was stealing from Kingston himself. When he discovered what she'd done, which was inevitable, Ava feared she might not survive his wrath.

"Ava, get a grip on yourself. If you want this badly enough, you will do what you must."

The muttered advice she gave herself was not very helpful.

Kingston's gold money clip, simple and elegantly masculine, sat on the large island in the middle of the custom-appointed walk-in closet and dressing room. The clip drew her attention, although more specifically, her interest lay in the money it contained.

Folded into the clip was more than three thousand dollars. The dark brown and cream tones of the granite gleamed in the light of the modern chandelier overhead, the rich, walnut cabinetry and mirrored elements reflecting Ava's worried features as she stared at the money.

While getting dressed earlier, Ava explored as much as she had dared. Inside one of the drawers of the gentleman's bureau, she found an obscene amount of cash. It proved how disgustingly wealthy Kingston Winter truly was, and while she'd never really cared about wealth, she was grateful that he possessed it in abundance.

She was stealing from the man who had held her captive for nearly two months. The same man who now held her heart in his brutal hands.

Because this was the only way to get back to Bitter Springs.

Bitter Springs and her deceitful, murdering brother.

Taking a deep breath, Ava opened the money clip and peeled off two one-hundred-dollar bills. Before she could rethink her actions, she quietly slid open the bureau drawer she'd discovered earlier. From the stacks of money, she counted out another twelve hundred dollars. It should be enough to convince a taxi to take the three-hour trip north to

Bitter Springs. At least, she hoped it would. She'd never needed to go so far in a cab before.

After folding the money into a square as small as she could make it, Ava shoved the wad deep into the inner pocket of one of the handful of coats Kingston had purchased for her. She also removed the fork from the designer handbag and placed it in the coat's outer pocket.

Carefully leaving everything exactly as it was before, Ava crept from the closet, half closing its doors. Returning to the living room, she sank onto the sofa, waiting anxiously for the moment Kingston joined her. Folding her hands in her lap, she planned out the next step of her escape plan.

When it came to the rooftop pool, a staff elevator existed along with a fire escape. The exits were armed with the same fingerprint and code security system, although the fire escape door lacked anything preventing its full use. A safety measure, although why someone like Kingston would bother following the rules in any capacity was surprising.

She could leave through the fire escape, exit onto one of the lower floors, take the public elevator, and walk out of the building as though she was simply one of its many employees. Once out on the street, she would hail a taxi and somehow convince the cabbie to take her all the way to Bitter Springs.

It's an amazing plan. It will work.

Kingston's shoes were a sharp staccato on the shiny floor, shaking Ava from her thoughts. She sat up straighter, nibbling a fingernail before abruptly lowering her hand to her lap.

He sat in the low-slung chair across from her, his eyes dark and unreadable. With his long legs stretched out before him and his forearms laying atop the armrests, he looked like a sullen king upset over a missing slave. It was intoxicating, the way he watched her. As though he wobbled between worshipping the ground she walked on and throttling her unconscious.

"Have you changed your mind, lamb?"

"No," she replied with a small shake of her head. "I haven't."

"I thought as much. I still think I should drug, hogtie, and take you with me."

"Have you much experience with hogtying?" She smiled, making a somewhat pathetic attempt at finding levity in the situation.

Kingston's lips barely curved. "You'd be surprised just how proficient I am with ropes."

Ava said nothing as he continued watching her. She wondered when he planned on leaving her. Surely, he was eager to return to The Den and begin his afternoon agenda of torture and murder.

"Come here, Ava."

She did not even consider disobeying, too eager to have his hands on her at least once more before he left her. Rising from the couch, she approached the chair and stopped at his feet.

With a smirk, Kingston spread his legs wide and crooked his finger at her. Provocative and triggering, that simple gesture made her body flush with longing. She thought how that same finger of his, used in the same motion, could so easily make her come.

"Come closer," he murmured.

Ava moved between his knees, standing motionless until he encircled one of her wrists and tugged forward so she bumped his crotch.

His other hand rested lightly on her hip. The power implied by the flexing of his fingers made Ava dry-mouthed with both desire and trepidation. Did he know the treachery she had planned and was subtly warning her to rethink it?

"Straddle my lap."

"Kingston," she protested, even though she didn't mean it at all.

"Do as I say," he replied, gazing up at her as she remained standing. His eyelashes were so long and thick they gave him a boyishly innocent air. "Please," he added with a wicked smile that told Ava he wasn't really asking so much as coercing her to do what he wanted.

With an innate gracefulness, she swung a leg over one of his and then the other as she settled atop his lap. Her core now rested over his groin. Evidence of his growing arousal pressed against the material covering her pussy. His hand moved to cup her backside, her ass filling his palms as he held her snugly in place.

"That's much better." His eyes were heavy, and Ava was transfixed by his masculine, brutal beauty. She licked her lips, and his molten gaze immediately fastened on her mouth.

"Don't go," she asked in a whisper.

"Don't stay." A muscle ticked in his jaw.

Ava leaned forward, pressing a soft kiss to the corner of his firm lips. "You know the reason why I must."

Kingston's tone was reflective. "I think I'll bring you a gift when I come back and collect you."

Ava shuddered. "Please do not bring me a man's head... or the heart you ripped from his chest."

Kingston tilted his head back, chuckling in obvious surprise. "What a bloodthirsty savage you've become, Miss Blue. But that's not the kind of gift I have planned. I was thinking more along the lines of a collar and a little leash. Something I can buckle around your neck so I can control you better."

"A collar?" Ava repeated, hating how everything inside her tightened at the very thought of Kingston shackling her in such a manner. How could she possibly want something so demeaning and twisted? Why did the thought of this man owning and keeping her forever make her heart thump faster and her thighs clench helplessly?

"Yes. A collar. A leather one, maybe. Black, with a pretty, shiny lock to which only I hold the key. And a chain link leash you can't break free of." He squeezed her ass cheeks, grinding her lower body against his erection. "I know you are wet, Ava. Fucking soaked for me. I can feel the heat of you through our clothes. Goddamn, the way you respond when I tell you what I'm gonna do to you makes me so fucking crazy. You don't know how much I hate leaving you like this, so wet and needy for my cock, but I have no choice." Kingston searched her eyes, an odd note of melancholy seeping into his arousal-roughened voice. His hands inexplicably grew gentle, even as he shoved two fingers into her mouth, slowly plunging them in and out in a pseudo blowjob until she closed her lips around them with a frustrated sob of lust.

"Remember, I've promised to take care of you." Kingston yanked his fingers free, his palm closing around her jaw and holding her immobile. He gazed into her eyes while she stared back, terrified and aroused to the point of insanity by this man's calm, murderous rage. "And I will. Trust me, Ava. I will. Even if that means I must kill every last motherfucker that ever hurt you."

CHAPTER

THIRTY-FOUR

*B*etter to torture
   Than to be tortured.

KINGSTON HAD BEEN GONE NEARLY an hour before Ava decided it was time.

The same team that previously watched over her reported for duty shortly before Kingston departed. Their leader, Blair, wasn't nearly as friendly this morning, however. Ava wondered if something had been said to change his demeanor. Mindful of Kingston's possessiveness, she decided he must have threatened the guard. The man would hardly make eye contact with her.

"I want to sit outside by the pool for a while if that's okay," she told Blair while heating the kettle for tea. "Read my book in the sunshine."

"It's allowable," Blair agreed after a quick perusal of the terrace. He snapped a finger at one of the other men, obviously intent on having her accompanied, but Ava shook her head.

"I'd like some privacy." She held her breath. "I'm not used to being watched so closely by strange men."

Blair slowly nodded his head, apparently swayed by her quiet request. "He'll stand just inside the door so he can see you through the window."

It wasn't ideal, but Ava couldn't argue his decision. It would appear too suspicious if she resisted the security guard's small concession by demanding complete privacy.

Once outside, Ava huddled on one of the covered lounges, shielded from the brisk wind of the autumn day. A cup of hot tea sat at her elbow on the low table, and in her lap was one of the books Kingston purchased for her at the quaint bookshop. The man assigned to watch over her stuck his head outside once during the first thirty minutes she was on the terrace. Ava suspected that when she came in and refreshed her tea, the same timeline would be followed, possibly giving her a half-hour window to escape.

The second time Ava ventured into the penthouse, she put the next part of her plan into motion.

"It's gotten colder outside," she explained to Blair where he stood in the living room. She placed her teacup on the countertop next to the stove where an assortment of tea was arranged for selection. "I need to grab a coat. Maybe even a blanket."

The man merely shrugged a shoulder at her nervous explanation. Ava casually made her way down the corridor to the master bedroom, hoping he attributed her behavior to unease with the current situation.

Once inside the master closet, she pulled out the camel-hued peacoat where the money was stashed. Ava threw it on, then quickly scraped her hair into a messy bun.

Now, she looked like any other woman on the streets below them. Casually dressed for the slight chill and prepared for the damage the blustery winds could wreak on a hairstyle. Bland, blonde, and boring. Nothing about her would attract unwanted attention. The nondescript clothing would make it easy to slip away.

Right under the watchful eye of the guards assigned to protect her.

She grabbed a thick lap blanket made of luxurious faux fur before heading back to the kitchen. After preparing a fresh cup of tea, she lifted it as if toasting the security detail watching her so silently and slipped back out onto the terrace. Her heart thudded in anticipation. She couldn't be sure of the exact time-frame, but it was likely Kingston was probably just now boarding the private jet at the small airfield outside the city. And once he was in the air, he would not be able to do anything about her escape when Blair notified him.

Before plopping back onto the lounge chair, she made a great show of adjusting it so it would appear she wanted the sun's rays shining on her. It was part of the plan, blocking the guard's view while also making him think she still lay under its domed canopy.

The wall closest to the lounge chair was in the shadows of the building itself, with a hidden sharp corner Ava planned on ducking around. Once on the other side of that corner, she could run unnoticed to the fire escape door and the terrace elevator.

Carefully, Ava arranged the blanket so it seemed to be covering her legs and feet. For nearly ten minutes, she simply lay there, the wad of stolen money burning like a bonfire inside her coat pocket.

Her stomach flip-flopped as she thought of the moment Kingston discovered her treachery. How his jaw would clench.

The way his eyes would darken with both disappointment and rage. Not only was her plan dangerous, but the consequences for stealing while thumbing her nose at his protection was practically suicidal.

I'll repay every penny. That is, if he doesn't kill me first.

~

THIRTEEN MINUTES LATER, Ava was staring out the back window of a taxi as it wove through traffic. With her heart in her throat, she watched the entrance to the building, praying that Kingston's men would not come pouring out like commandos, ready to drag her back inside.

But there was no one.

Her escape was incredibly easy, considering the extraordinary security measures Kingston had in place.

Once she emerged from the fire stairs onto one of the lower floors, there was no one waiting at the bank of public elevators. On the ride down, however, the lift became more crowded which allowed her to blend in with the mix of professionals working for Winter Enterprises. She garnered a few curious glances, but not a single person on the elevator or in the huge, elegant lobby bothered looking closer. Even the friendly concierge who welcomed Kingston and herself just two nights before did not glance at her twice as she attached herself to a small group of women exiting the building while discussing their lunch plans.

"Should take about three and a half hours to reach Bitter Springs, miss," the taxi driver said as Ava turned her attention back to where they were headed. "Traffic's pretty heavy for a Tuesday."

He was an older man with a scruffy beard and kind eyes. A plain, gold wedding band gleamed on his ring finger. Earlier, when Ava explained where she needed to go, he had tilted his head at the desperation in her voice.

"Do you want to go to the police station? I can take you there... no problem," he had offered. "If someone is bothering you, that is."

"No, no. It's just very important I get to Bitter Springs as quickly as possible. If you'll help me, I can pay more than the mileage rate."

"Well, sure, miss. It's no problem. I'll enjoy the drive, to be honest. Something out of the ordinary. Just gotta notify dispatch." He clicked on the car's communication system. "Donovan, here. Got a long-distance fare to Bitter Springs."

After getting the all-clear, Donovan had eased the car into traffic while Ava nearly collapsed in relief.

It didn't take very long to leave the bustling city streets behind and reach the interstate heading toward her parents' home. The scenery flew by, the day bright and sunny compared to the darkness inside Ava. Thinking of the moment she would confront Carson was making her nauseous, but it did not shake her resolve.

She wished she had a gun instead of the paltry weapons she'd gathered.

Earlier, while making her tea, she had taken a steak knife from an extra set in the cutlery drawer. She'd slipped it into the pocket of the coat where it now clinked alongside the fork from CRUSH.

All I need now is a spoon and butter knife, and I'll have a complete set.

She nearly laughed out loud at her train of thought.

"Everything all right, miss?" Donovan's dark gaze met hers in the review mirror.

"Yes, thank you," Ava murmured. "Just thinking about how my arrival will surprise some people."

"Been a long time since you've been back?"

"Yes and no. I've lived in Bitter Springs my whole life until recently, but it's been years since I've been *home*." She fingered the knife in the coat pocket, thinking she might be revealing too much. Smarter to keep silent about some things, especially when murder was potentially involved. "It's complicated."

Donovan sighed in agreement. "It always is."

Time passed quickly as the car hurtled north on the interstate and turned off at the Bitter Springs exit. It appeared they would beat the timeframe Donovan had predicted.

Kingston must know she had escaped by now. Would he respond by taking out his frustrations on the man imprisoned in his dungeon? Or would he hold on to that rage and unleash it on her when he recaptured her?

Pulling up to the open gate outside of her parents' home, Ava was shocked to see a police car blocking the overgrown driveway. Two men leaned against the hood of the vehicle, their gazes trained on the cab. They did not come forward to inquire who she was or why she was there, which Ava found odd. There appeared to be no obvious reason for their presence other than guarding the house she'd once called home.

"Thank you for helping me, Donovan." Ava pulled cash from her coat pocket, counting out a generous tip along with the required fare.

"Like I said, nice day for a drive. Do you want me to wait? Just in case you decide against staying?" Donovan's concerned gaze migrated toward the two officers. One climbed into the patrol car, picking up the receiver for the two-way radio. He spoke into it, but at this distance the conversation was unintelligible.

"No, it will be fine." Ava handed over the money. Including the extra tip, it was nearly half of her funds.

"Whoa. This is too much, miss. Way too much," Donovan

exclaimed. He attempted to give her back some of the money, but Ava waved it away as she slid out of the car.

"Please, I want you to have that. Drive safe back to the city and thank you for being so kind."

Donovan tipped his hat, and she watched the taxi pull away before straightening her shoulders. She began the walk up the driveway's steep incline toward the police car.

"What can we do for you, ma'am?" One of the officers sauntered toward her, a hand on his holster. His fingers tapped the butt of the pistol jutting up from the leather.

"This is my parent's house." Ava swallowed hard at the threatening gesture, but it did not deter her. "I'm here to see my brother, Carson Blue," she added in a stronger voice.

"Can't let you go up to the house without checking ID first."

The other officer came closer, head tilting as he studied her. "Let her through, Fitzgerald. She's the one they've been looking for."

CHAPTER

THIRTY-FIVE

My rage will carry me.
Love will save me
But vengeance will heal me.

KINGSTON WIPED blood from his hands with a towel. Sweat dripped from his brow as he considered the prisoner hanging from long chains in the center of the cell. The man wouldn't survive much longer if the damage already administered was any indication.

This particular cell was a cold, dark, dank room nestled in the furthest corner of The Den's underground dungeon system. It bore no resemblance to the aesthetically pleasing and luxurious cells Kingston used for satisfying wicked fantasies and scenarios. This cell might have been transported from a medieval castle and plopped into place beneath The Den. The few nods to modern conveniences were electricity—very useful for those shock therapy sessions— running water that was always icy cold, and a sophisticated drainage system that allowed blood and other fluids to be washed away with the simple use of a hose.

"I told you what you wanted to know," the man groaned, spitting out a mouthful of blood. He still swayed back and forth from a vicious blow to his stomach just seconds before.

"I appreciate your cooperation, Pickett." Grabbing a fresh towel, Kingston blotted the sweat on his forehead. He grinned at the man. "But I'm convinced you have more to tell me. Although, if I'm being honest, I might just keep going for the sheer pleasure of it now."

Pickett's head dropped until his chin rested on his own chest. "Fuck."

Kingston approached the man, grabbing a hunk of his hair and lifting his head. Peering into Pickett's swollen eyes, he quietly said, "Do you have any idea how terrified she was? Or was that part of the plan? To scare her into running so someone could snatch her up."

"I don't know."

"Oh, I don't believe that's true. I think the truth is rattling around in your mouth, trying to get out." Kingston tilted his head. "Maybe there are too many teeth in there. Maybe that's what is keeping all this information bottled up. Let's see if I can fix that."

Pickett's moan was one of pure fright. Jerking at the chains encircling both wrists, he writhed desperately, toes barely scraping the concrete floor. "Please... I don't know anything else. I don't know about anything except what I already told you. The guy who left the note on the limo got pinched at the pickup location and I bailed on him."

"Did Carson know you were such a lousy shot when he hired you to kill me?" Kingston released the handful of Pickett's hair. Stepping toward a rolling cart that looked as though it belonged in a mechanic's garage, he perused the items displayed on the top rack. Picking up a hefty pair of pliers, he tested the tool's weight. "These should do the trick."

"Wait." Pickett's body flailed as though he could escape the inevitable. The chains kept him elevated off the floor, placing all of his weight on his outstretched arms and restricting his movement. He could do little more than buck his body until it swayed like a clock's pendulum. "Wait. Please!"

"I haven't the time nor the patience to wait. You see, you are a job I must finish before I can move onto eliminating the next lowlife. Got a few to get through before I can consider my girl safe. So, forgive me if I'm in a hurry." Kingston smirked, advancing with the pliers. "Jack? Hold his head still, will you?"

A muffled scream filled the cell, ending in a gurgling sound as Kingston opened the pliers and let the bloody tooth drop to the floor. "Now, let's get you evened up. Can't let you hang there with an uneven number of molars, can we?"

Another scream and a second tooth joined the first.

Pickett wrenched back and forth in a futile effort to escape the excruciating pain, choking on his own blood as details poured out. "Carson... gave me the details for the job. And...and Judge Vanderhorn fronted the money. His son got me an untraceable gun and a car. There's another guy, too. The one who first contacted me."

"What's his name?" Kingston held his breath. If Pickett named Oliver as that man.... there was no telling how much blood would be shed.

He would rip his half-brother into a thousand little pieces and show no mercy.

Pickett was taking too long to answer. Swinging the pliers in an arcing motion, Kingston smashed one of the man's kneecaps, eliciting a new howl of agony.

"FUCK! DA's office," Pickett mumbled as his scream died away. "Attorney in the DA's office. Corning-something or another. Oh, fuck. I can't think straight, man." His head dropped back, eyes rolling until only the whites showed. "It hurts too much," he said weakly just before he blacked out.

"Wake him up."

"Sure thing, boss." Jack snatched up a bucket of ice-cold water, tossing it over the unconscious man. Pickett gasped, sputtering as the shock revived him back to painful awareness.

Pickett's confession was surprising. Kingston wondered if he heard the man right. Apparently, Oliver wasn't behind the plot to shoot him, although there was no discounting his association in the scheme to take Ava from him just yet.

Drake Cornerstone. Was it possible the bland, unassuming lawyer Ava briefly dated was involved? The same man Kingston had FaceTimed while fucking his little prisoner just for the thrill of rubbing the conquest in the other man's face?

"Are you sure it's Cornerstone?" Kingston tapped Pickett's uninjured kneecap with the head of the pliers.

"Yeah... guy's name is Blake or maybe it's Drake. Just can't... remember... right now." Pickett wasn't moving as vigorously as before. No doubt, he was bleeding internally in addition to the blood dripping from the myriad of wounds decorating his body. "The judge... he promised the DA's office would get me out a jam if I got caught." He huffed out a pained laugh between cracked, bloodied lips. "And if you died, I could fuck the girl a couple of times as a bonus before they sold her off. There was something else about inheritance money but it's all a little fuzzy right now."

"See, now you've made me angry, Pickett. The very *thought* of you breathing the same air as her is enraging. As for you fucking her...if you weren't already a dead man hanging, I'd cut off your balls and shove them down your throat." Kingston laughed as Pickett bucked with renewed vigor. "And Judge Vanderhorn is dead, my friend. Shot himself a little more than an hour ago." Kingston picked up the Glock, double-checking the attached silencer and racking the slide.

Unfortunately, he was not responsible for judge's death. The man took the easy way out rather than waiting for Kingston to collect him. No matter. It freed up extra time to eliminate the other players in this nest of deceit and greed.

Pickett's eyes closed in defeat. "Knew I shouldn't have gotten mixed up in this fucking mess."

"I agree," Kingston said softly. Shoving the Glock's muzzle against Pickett's temple, he extended his arm, stepped back and pulled the trigger.

KINGSTON ENTERED the main portion of the house with Jack trailing behind him.

Although it defied reason, Kingston needed a shower before moving on to his next target. It made no sense to clean up after killing a man before moving onto the next, but he always found it necessary.

Drake Cornerstone. I'm coming for you next.

Paulie met him just outside the door to the dungeon. His expression was grim. "Bad news, King."

"Oh?" Kingston accepted his cell phone from the man. "What is it now?"

"She's escaped."

Kingston's brow raised high. "What the fuck are you talking about?"

Paulie scraped his jaw with his hand. "Blair says she's gone. She was out on the pool terrace. Drinking hot tea. Reading a book. And now, she's just gone."

"That's not possible."

"They've searched the penthouse, the building, the restaurant, and the alleyways around the building. They even searched LIST. She's gone. They checked surveillance cameras, and somehow, she managed to make her way down to the ninth floor. Hopped on the public elevator and rode it all the way down to the lobby." Paulie's laugh was one of reluctant admiration. "She waltzed right out the front door, and no one lifted a finger to stop her."

"Fuck!" Kingston slammed his fist into the wall, leaving a splintered dent in the thick plaster. "When?"

"Almost four hours ago," Paulie responded, watching as Kingston swiped the new blood staining his knuckles onto his pants.

"Why wasn't I told sooner, goddammit?" Kingston stalked down the corridor, headed for his office. He wanted to see it for himself, this daring escape his little lamb concocted while fluttering her lashes as she flat-out lied to him.

"You remember the rules. No interruptions when work is underway in the dungeon. No matter how important it might be." Jack's laugh was sharp. "You put the damn things in place yourself."

Kingston swore under his breath. That was true. He wanted no interruptions when he was down in the cells. It did not matter if he had a woman chained to the wall, waiting to be pleasured, or a man hanging from the ceiling, battered and bloody and begging for a bullet. No one disturbed him once that thick dungeon door closed behind him. There was no cell phone service that deep underground anyway, at least not in the torture chambers.

Once in his office, Kingston flipped on his laptop and pulled up the security camera recording from earlier that day at the Winter Enterprises building. He clicked on the feed for the rooftop terrace, focusing in on his errant little lamb.

There was the pool terrace, the covered chaise Ava was

lying on. He saw her hand reaching for the teacup and replacing it on the table beside the chair. Her legs were covered with a dark grey fur blanket. A few minutes later, she placed a book on top of the blanket somewhere in the vicinity of where her hip would be.

It was one of many he purchased for her at the bookstore near the penthouse. A first edition copy of *Tess of the d'Urbervilles.*

She'd been so excited about that book. Her eyes glowed with pleasure and reluctant affection when he paid for it then handed it over so she could thumb its pages.

Shaking aside the recollection, Kingston focused on the chaise and how the blanket was bunched up. It was difficult to tell whether Ava was under the material or not. He continued watching the camera feedback, focusing on every detail.

Then he saw it.

A shadow, on the wall closest to the chaise lounge. A sharp corner hid the elevator and the fire escape stairs from the camera feed, but that fleeting shadow told Kingston what he needed.

Ava had made a covert dash for that door. She'd used the fire escape stairs, knowing the use of the service elevator would alert someone to its use. Even armed with the code he gave her, there would still be a recording of the elevator doors opening and closing, and the camera would have picked her up inside the lift.

Switching feeds, Kingston pulled up the camera for the public elevator. There was footage of Ava entering the ninth floor lift just like Paulie said. When it reached the lobby, he clicked on that camera and watched his little lamb walk right out the front door of his highly secured building without a backward glance. The camel-colored peacoat was a smart choice. She blended right in with others wearing similar items.

Even her luxurious blonde curls had been pulled up into a nondescript bun.

If he wasn't so infuriated by her cunning and daring escape, Kingston would have felt a bit of pride in her resourcefulness. Admiration even.

But where had she gone from there? She had no money. No identification. Not even a cell phone. Where did she think she could go? And how would she get there?

"Tell us what to do, boss," Jack said, swearing beneath his breath. "Where do we start looking for her?"

Kingston contemplated that. Pulling his money clip from his pocket, he quickly counted out the bills. It was two hundred dollars short. Not enough to get very far, but enough to get her out of the immediate vicinity of the penthouse.

"Where's Oliver?" he asked softly.

"Left about an hour ago. Didn't say where he was going. We also received word from the man watching Carson's house. Says a woman arrived by taxi a short time ago, and the cops watching the house let her through. Might have been one of his usual prostitutes, but maybe not." Paulie's worried tone echoed what everyone was thinking.

Clicking out of the building's security system, Kingston pulled up the app for the tracker implanted in Ava's neck. Within seconds, it revealed her location.

1212 Morning Brooke Lane. Bitter Springs.

Kingston got up from his desk, his heart pounding with both rage and fear. *Oh, Ava. You foolish, foolish girl. When I get my hands on you, you won't be able to step outside with a chain around your ankle and a leash around your neck.*

"She's gone home."

THIRTY-SIX

E*vil awaits to be crushed.*
Fear to be conquered.
Love to be protected.

AVA WALKED past the officers as she continued up the driveway toward the house. She heard the chatter of their police radios, but like before, she could not make out what was being said.

She was near the front door when she heard the police cruiser start up. Looking back over her shoulder, she watched the car slowly ease out of the driveway and onto the road. Through the bare trees shielding the house from the neighbors, she saw the car accelerate, then it was gone.

It was odd they were there to begin with, and even stranger they left so abruptly. Slipping her hand in her coat pocket, Ava fingered the steak knife's handle. It was just as well they were gone. Especially since she planned on hurting her brother very badly.

Standing on the soaring open porch of the home she'd

grown up in, Ava chewed her bottom lip as a sob bubbled in her throat. The place looked horrible, the paint on the front door and porch columns peeling off in ragged strips. Overgrown honeysuckle vines had taken over both the columns and shutters bracketing the wide windows. The overhead chandelier was covered in cobwebs with several of the lightbulbs missing. Dead leaves lay scattered across the porch's floor. The overall look of the house was one of neglect and decay.

Hot tears stung Ava's eyes. Coming home and seeing the state of disrepair of the once beautiful house was devastating. It shattered her heart into a million pieces.

Finding the front door unlocked was not surprising. After her parents died, Carson treated their home like a flophouse. People came and went at all hours, day and night. Drug users. Dealers. Prostitutes. Hangers-on with nowhere else to go. Even high school kids looking for a place to party and crash sometimes took over the house. Local law enforcement always looked the other way, and Ava contributed that to the men her brother had bribed over the years.

Carson didn't care that he had ruined their home. He didn't care that it was now ugly and broken down. His only concern was how much money and drugs and alcohol he could get his hands on—no matter the hurt it caused others.

It wasn't difficult for Ava to piece everything together as she hesitated in the doorway. Every act of disrespect, every argument, every incident of cruelty committed by her brother came into sharp focus. The things he'd done to her. The things he allowed others to do. It was all so clear now. Carson despised Mom and Dad, but most of all, he hated her for reasons she couldn't begin to understand.

Her brother was the true monster.

He had murdered their parents. And he wanted Ava to

disappear forever, but only if there was money to be made from his crimes.

Ava squared her shoulders, brushing the tears from her cheeks. Keeping one hand in her coat pocket, she gripped the steak knife and slowly pushed open the door.

The foyer was eerily silent. Empty beer cans and broken bottles littered the space. Graffiti of all colors marred the once gleaming oak-paneled walls while cobwebs floated in the corners. The furniture was missing, as was the huge, gilded mirror which once hung over an antique Sheraton buffet. Seeing the deterioration, Ava faltered, suddenly unsure of her ability to make her brother pay for the destruction of their family.

She took a deep breath, standing straighter.

She was no longer a victim. She was stronger because of everything she endured. Carson's abuse. Assault. Abduction. Loss. Betrayal.

None of that mattered anymore. She was Ava Bella Blue. And she would make her brother pay for everything he had done to hurt her and others. Payment for his sins would begin now.

"Carson!" Her voice echoed through the empty foyer, so loud and fierce it hurt her own ears. When there was no answer, she shouted for him again. It was a battle cry that rang through the silence and bounced off the walls.

A shuffling noise came from down the hall. Ava tensed as the footsteps came closer, and when Carson entered the foyer, hands shoved into the pockets of dirty blue jeans, his blond hair a messy mop, she was shocked by his appearance.

Red-rimmed eyes narrowed when he scowled at her. He was either drunk or high. Most likely both.

"Well, look who has come to visit. My sweet little sister." His words slurred. "You taking a break from fucking my friend?" His laugh was raspy. Cruel. "I can't imagine you've worked off very much of my debt, but I bet you've given it all during your suck and fuck sessions."

Ava's fingers tightened around the knife, listening to the filth he spouted until she had enough. "You killed Mom and Dad."

"Kingston tell you that?" Carson's gaze raked Ava's body, a grin twisting his pale, bloated face. "He's a bad guy, sis. A kidnapper. A deviant. I hear he even sells women and little kids into sex slavery. Probably shouldn't believe anything he says."

"There's evidence, Carson. You and Judd Vanderhorn. His dad. I want to know how you did it." Ava sidled away as Carson advanced on her. They circled each other like wary animals. "Why you did it."

"Do you think I'm stupid?" Carson snarled. "I'm not telling you shit, not that it matters if I did. You won't be around much longer. The little fucking princess of Bitter Springs. Mom and Dad's golden child. Soon, you'll be nothing but a piece of meat for men to use however they want. For as long as they want."

"I won't let you hurt me anymore, Carson." Ava's eyes narrowed. "I'm not that frightened, scared girl you abused and sold to your friends. You will pay for that and for what you did to Mom and Dad. And Kingston, too."

Carson advanced on her slowly, his laugh a raspy cackle. "What I did to Kingston? Oh, you're talking about the hit I put on him. Lot of good that did. The stupid motherfucker we hired missed his target. But that's okay. When I find him, I'll carve him up myself for screwing up the job."

Ava shook her head. "You won't find him. Kingston beat you to it. He has him, and if the man isn't already dead, he soon will be. Kingston is one step ahead of you, Carson. Always one step ahead."

"Well, guess that explains why Jeff and Brad are both

dead," Carson sneered. "Drug overdose and suicide by hanging, my ass. Their bodies were found yesterday, but I've got serious doubts when it comes to the official cause of death. I mean, everyone knows Kingston Winter is a killer. And so clever when covering up his tracks."

Shock vibrated through Ava. "They are dead?" *How did Kingston manage it? Was there anyone or anywhere the man couldn't reach?*

"Yeah, Ava. Dead. As dead as you will be when your new owner tires of you."

Carson lunged at her with a speed Ava did not believe possible, considering his condition. Gripping her by the arms, he shoved her against the wall with such force it knocked the breath from her. She lost her grip on the knife as she struggled with him.

For all his drug-induced wiriness and pale features, Carson retained some remnants of his high school and college football days. He was still so strong, so overpowering. Within seconds, both of his hands circled her neck. When he squeezed, his eyes glittered with hate and excitement.

"I don't want to kill you, little sis. Just need to get a little more cooperation from you until everyone gets here. We've got a going away party planned for you. Something a little whore like you will enjoy. Bet you've got some tricks you learned after all these weeks fucking Kingston. He always was a kinky bastard."

Pinpoints of light flashed behind Ava's eyelids. She opened her mouth to scream, but nothing came out. Carson was strangling her to the point of unconsciousness. Once again, she would be at his mercy. A repeat of that awful night at Judd Vanderhorn's house, only a million times worse, loomed before her. If she let this happen, if she didn't fight back with every fiber of her being, the true nightmare would begin.

Instead of grabbing the hands wrapped so tight around her throat and trying to force them away, Ava blindly thrust a hand into the coat's pocket. The knife's serrated edge sliced two of her own fingers but she did not react to the pain. Her survival, her life, was at stake. It was all that mattered.

And Kingston. He matters most of all. God, please don't let me die before I have a chance to tell him I love him. That I've always loved him...

Somehow, Ava withdrew the knife from her pocket. Gripping the handle as tight as her oxygen-deprived brain allowed, she wedged it between their bodies. Carson did not react, his fascinated gaze riveted on her face as she struggled to breathe.

Ava stabbed wildly at his midsection.

Carson was so high that at first, the attack did not register. He stared into Ava's eyes, watching as her lips surely began turning blue. A satisfied grin curved his mouth before agony invaded his drug-dulled nerves. His gaze dropped to where the knife protruded from beneath his ribcage. One hand released its grip around her neck and touched the blade's gleaming handle.

Ava took a deep coughing breath, sucking in air. Her throat burned as if liquid fire was being poured down it. She swayed, the wall behind her a brace that kept her from collapsing.

"You little bitch. You stabbed me. You fucking *stabbed* me!" Carson wheezed. Grabbing the knife, he jerked it free and threw it across the room. It clattered to the ground while he pressed his palm to the wound, blood quickly seeping through his fingers. "Oh, you're gonna pay for this, Ava. Me and the boys, we're gonna leave you in pieces."

His hands came, ready to wrap around her throat again, but Ava anticipated the attack. Jamming her knee into his groin, they both fell to the floor with Carson landing on top. He crushed her body as Ava held tight to the piece of silverware she had stolen. With an anguished cry, she reached around her brother as if embracing him.

The fork plunged beneath Carson's left shoulder blade. She pushed it in as far as the tines would go.

He howled, rolling off her while desperately reaching for the fork's silver handle. But it was no use. The only way it was coming out was if someone did it for him.

Ava scrambled to her hands and knees, coughing as darkness threatened to overtake her.

Get up! Get the knife. Kill him before he gets his hands on me again. I won't get a second chance.

Through bloodshot eyes, Ava frantically looked around the room, locating the weapon where it had skittered across the scarred and dirty wood floors. Adrenaline fueled her as she crawled toward it. The knife was just inches away from her bloody fingers when a pair of arms wrapped around her waist.

She was hauled upward until her feet dangled off the floor and spun around until she could see Carson getting to his feet.

He was still grabbing at the fork embedded in his shoulder, spewing curses with such vehemence that spittle flew from his lips. It was almost comical, watching him go round and round in circles. Ava couldn't tear her eyes away from the spectacle of it until Drake Cornerstone rushed in from the hallway.

He stopped Carson's futile spinning and jerked the fork free. Tossing it aside, the prosecutor grimaced at the blood now staining his hands before his gaze snagged Ava's. He grinned as the arms wrapped around her body kept her imprisoned. Arms that she now scratched and clawed while the man she once dated simply watched. Why wasn't he helping her?

"Drake?" She cried in a rough voice. "Please...help me!"

"Gotcha, little Ava," Judd Vanderhorn whispered in her ear. "Nowhere for you to go now." His arms tightened with cruel pressure until it felt as though one of her ribs cracked. Ava sucked in a scream as pain rocketed through her body. The room swam in blackness. Through watery lashes, she saw Carson stumbling toward her. Reaching her, he slapped her so hard she bit her own tongue. Blood filled her mouth.

"Are you ready to finish what we started that night so long ago?" Judd asked with a laugh, licking the tears streaming down Ava's cheeks as she slipped away from the horror of her imprisonment. "I know I am. And I can't fucking wait."

THIRTY-SEVEN

F rom where I stood
I saw the Devil.
And his beauty was terrible.

AVA SLOWLY SWAM UP from the depths of a black, swirling sea.

Her throat hurt so bad it was difficult to swallow. When she did, the metallic taste in her mouth was a reminder that she'd bitten her tongue. Attempting a deep breath resulted in dizzying pain, her ribs throbbing as though she'd been kicked several times. And her shoulders, oh God, they ached like nothing she'd ever experienced before.

Ava glanced around the room as her vision cleared. Most of the furniture was missing, the artwork long gone, and the bar no longer held a dizzying array of liquor, but she knew where she was. It was their family den, and she was currently hanging from a rope swung over one of the ceiling's exposed wood beams. The opposite end of the rope was tied off around the end of the bar, creating a makeshift pulley system to raise or lower her body.

Dropping her head back, Ava looked up at the ceiling. Her arms stretched far over her head as though reaching for the beam she was tethered to. Rope looped several times around her hands, and with the knee-high boots now missing, her bare feet skimmed the floor. The overcoat she'd worn was gone, but the rest of her clothing was still thankfully intact. During the struggle with Carson, her hair had come loose from the messy bun. It now hung around her face in a tangle of waves now, the strands sticking to tears that had dried on her cheeks.

Her brother sat on the sofa in front of her, his upper torso bare and a patch of white bandaging blending with the paleness of his skin. He glared at her, the hatred in his eyes so vicious that Ava hurriedly looked away, trembling with fear.

"She's awake," he announced, taking a long swig from the bottle of whiskey balanced between his legs. "About damn time."

Judd stepped into Ava's line of sight. He looked mostly the same. Harder around the eyes. Puffier in the face. Still handsome though, despite the air of dissoluteness. His dark brown hair was tousled, as though he'd run his fingers through it numerous times. The gleam in his eyes was terrifying. The spoiled, beloved son of the most prominent, well respected criminal judge in the state looked... unhinged.

She shrank away, her mind whirling with thoughts on how she might escape this nightmare.

"Hello, Ava," he murmured. "Now that you're awake, we can start the party."

"You don't have to do this. You don't have to be like Carson." Ava breathed through her nose in an attempt to stem a wave of nausea. The pain in her ribs pulsed along every nerve ending in her body. "You can let me go."

"Let you go?" He laughed softly, mocking her suggestion. "After all the trouble you've caused? You won't get out of this so easily, Ava."

"You murdered my parents. I know you helped Carson," she choked out in desperation. "I know you were in it together."

Judd glanced at Carson, his eyes narrowed with annoyance. "Who told her?"

Her brother shrugged, answering with one word that explained everything. "Kingston."

"Guess it doesn't really fucking matter now. Do you know why that is, Ava? Because murder is really hard to prove. Especially in this town." Judd gripped her chin, holding it tight so she couldn't jerk her face away. "Getting rid of your mom and dad was so easy. When we ran them off the road, they didn't even try their brakes. Just smashed over that embankment and into those trees until it looked like the fucking demolition derby shit you see on YouTube."

He abruptly let her go, grabbing the bottle of whiskey from Carson and taking a swig. "I had no choice but to help Carson. You know that, right? He has the video of what we did to you that night. It would ruin me. My dad. My family's reputation."

"There is no more video," Ava said softly, closing her eyes in pain as the truth of her parent's death washed over her. "Carson has nothing else to use as blackmail, Judd, once Kingston found it. It's been destroyed."

Carson's laugh ended in a racking cough and a groan of pain. "Even if that's true, it doesn't matter now. We're all in this so goddamn deep. But there's the money we can make from selling you. Not to mention the inheritance. Your portion comes to me, remember?"

"You could have killed your brother, Ava," Judd *tsked* in mock disappointment when Carson coughed so violently that blood dribbled out of his mouth. "What on earth were you thinking? Stabbing him like that?"

"I wish I could do it again. I would slit his throat if given another chance. He deserves it for what he's done," Ava responded defiantly, her lips curling into a snarl of hatred. "You deserve it, too. You and your father." She glanced around the room, looking for the other player in this betrayal but unable to see him. "And you, Drake."

"Right here, baby," Drake crooned, moving behind her. He brushed her hair off the nape of her neck and pressed a kiss to the skin there. Ava twisted her body to avoid his mouth, but it was useless.

"Yeah, my dear old Dad couldn't make it today," Judd said, standing in front of Ava and grabbing a hunk of her hair. He wound it tight around his hand like it was a leash. "Shot himself this morning in his study. One quick bullet to the temple and bye-bye, daddy."

Ava blinked in confusion. Judge Vanderhorn was dead? His son did not look devastated by the news. Instead, he appeared extremely pleased by this unexpected development.

Is Kingston to thank for that? Did he kill Judd's father as well as Jeff and Brad?

"We're waiting for one more person to get here so we can start the party. We've only got so much time before Winter shows up to collect you for your new owner," Drake said, rubbing his hand down her back until he cupped the curve of her ass. "Gotta have our fun while we can."

Ava jerked against her restraints. A low moan of despair vibrated inside her chest, robbing her of breath.

No. No. No. It can't be true. Kingston would not be so cruel. He wouldn't betray me like that. Or go to such lengths to break me. He wouldn't sell me... not after everything we shared. Not after his promise to protect me.

A sob of despair welled up from the depths of Ava's soul. She was being broken in two by Kingston Winter, and he wasn't even here in person to witness the death of her love.

"Oh my God," Carson hissed in cruel amusement. "Are you really that fucking stupid, sis? Drake is talking about Oliver. He's found a buyer for you. One who will make sure you eventually disappear from everyone's memory."

"Carson's getting a sweet incentive out of it," Judd piped in. "Three years from now when you are declared dead, he'll get the bonus of your inheritance payout. And we'll each get a cut from that as well."

"You and I both know there won't be any money left," Ava said in a wobbly voice. Kingston wasn't the one sending her to her death. She was almost glad for the ropes around her wrists because they kept her from collapsing with relief. "You'll have to face Oliver at that point, and I promise you, you won't be alive for long if you don't have his money. He's just as ruthless as Kingston."

"I'll deal with that problem when it gets here," Carson snarled, rising from the couch but slumping back when his knees gave out. "Goddamn it, Judd. Get on with it so I can listen to this bitch's screams instead of just her mouth running."

"Thought we were waiting for Aaron, but I'm good with getting things started," Drake murmured, squeezing her rear end even harder than before. "This little cock tease strung me along for months, always making me think I was gonna get in her pants. But then she ran off to Savannah and was stupid enough to get herself abducted. Kingston Winter sure enjoyed fucking you, Ava. Based on what I saw that day you called me, I'd say you enjoyed it, too. I'm gonna love pounding this pussy just like he did. Maybe I'll even return the favor and let him watch me do it. Rub it in his face like he did mine."

Ava vaguely remembered making that phone call to Drake. It was the day Kingston took her virginity before bending her over the bathroom vanity counter. The two men had spoken, she knew that much. But had there been more to their conversation? More she didn't know about while she floated in a pleasure-induced haze?

"Had I known he was going to Facetime it, I would have recorded our conversation," Drake said, slapping her ass so hard she twirled away from him, spinning on the end of the rope like a ballerina set free on stage. She screamed as the movement wrenched her arms until it felt they were coming out of their sockets. Her ribs expanded and contracted with a pain so intense the agony degenerated into a bubbling cry.

Judd caught Ava by the wrists, stopping her spiral. Grabbing her face with his free hand, he squeezed her cheeks until her lips smooshed together in an exaggerated pout. "Let's get you out of these clothes, okay?" The distance sound of a car door slamming had him tilting his head. "Aaron's finally here. Time to line everyone up for a turn at sweet little cunt."

Ava closed her eyes, trying so hard to contain her sobs. She wouldn't let these monsters watch as she fell apart with terror. Had Kingston learned of her escape by now? Would he even care? She wondered if he would bother looking for her. Because by the time he learned of her escape, if he wanted to save her, it would be too late.

She wished she'd obeyed Kingston and stayed in his penthouse. Waited for his return. She should have given herself to him completely so he could decide her fate. It might have been far more merciful than what these men had planned for her.

"Careful now, little slut. Wouldn't want to cut you too

badly." Judd pulled a huge switchblade from his back pocket. He began slicing off her clothes as Drake held her immobile.

"You can cut her if you want," Carson remarked sullenly from the couch. "See how she likes it."

Detective Aaron Redding stepped into the den, removing his suit coat as he approached. His mouth curved into an ugly smile. "Thought my guys were nuts when they said Ava Blue was here at the house. Said she waltzed up to the front door like she owned the place." Removing his badge and the holster containing the department-issued gun, he set them on the bar. "Has anyone had her yet?"

Ava whimpered, terrified by the unspoken threat. The knife had already cut through her shirt, ripping it into ribbons that cascaded to the floor like confetti streamers. They intended on raping her. One after another while she spun in helpless circles.

Her mind threatened to shut down with the horror of it. If she could just close her eyes and drift away... drift away and never come back.

Judd slapped her across the face, splitting her bottom lip open.

"Uh-uh, Ava. Stay with us now. The fun is just beginning, and we want you awake for this party. You see, we've been waiting a long time for this. Some of us longer than others." Brushing his lips over hers, he whispered conspiratorially, "I get the feeling that even your brother, for all that he hates you, will want a piece of you." His fingers cruelly twisted the nipple of one breast, grinning when she cried out in pain. "Here are those pretty tits I've been dreaming about."

"Get the rest of her damn clothes off her. I'm going first," Drake demanded like a petulant child while undoing the button of his pants and ripping the zipper down.

"No fucking way. I'm first, you fucking prick," Judd

growled, slicing through her bra until her breasts fell free from the material. "You'll get your turn after me. Then Aaron. And Carson at the end if he wants. Hey, Carson. You wanna fuck your sister when we're done with her? Bet you won't be able to resist when you see how she screams for it. She'll be moaning like the whore she is by the end of this first round."

Ava's pants were stripped from her body, her underwear sliced at with short, jerking motions of the knife until she was completely naked.

"Fuck me," Aaron breathed, pulling his clothes off. His erection jutted out from between his legs like an ugly tool. "She's perfect."

"And you're pathetic. All of you," Ava sneered. "Is this the only way you can get a woman? By raping her?"

"Carson, turn on some lights so we can see every gorgeous inch of our little hellcat here." Judd trailed the knife down her throat, through the valley between her breasts, and on down until the blade's sharp point rested above her mound. "Would you look at this, guys? Our little whore went and got her pussy waxed. It's so shiny and smooth. So fucking pretty. Did you do that just for us, slut?" Cupping her sex, Judd shoved two fingers inside her as he brushed his mouth over hers. "I told you I'd get my chance with you, Ava. Do you remember?"

Ava didn't think. She reacted. Biting Judd's lip, she hung on like a bulldog until Drake punched her in the ribs on the side that was uninjured. She wailed in pain, but watched with satisfaction as Judd cursed and swiped at the blood on his torn flesh.

"Not very smart, Ava," Drake muttered, wrapping his arm around her waist. "Not very smart at all." Running his hand over her ass, he struck it over and over until she cried out for him to stop.

Judd spat out a wad of blood and saliva, tossing the knife

aside as he jerked his chin at Aaron. "Lower her down a little," he ordered. "Fuck this going one at time bullshit. We'll all get a piece of her right now. I want this to be so painful, she *begs* us to take turns. I'll take her pussy. Drake, you get her ass. Aaron, you fuck her throat. Carson? I don't give a shit what the fuck you do. Maybe jerk off for now."

Ava stifled a scream of true terror. They were going to rape her all at the same time, without a care for the damage such an act would cause. She would be ripped to pieces by their savagery, and no one would stop them.

"To hell with that," Carson said, standing up from the sofa with a hand over his bandaged injury. "She's *my* sister, and I'm going first. When I'm finished, you guys can do whatever you want until Oliver shows up." Leaning down to look Ava in the eyes now that she stood firmly on the floor, he grinned. "Get her on the floor and hold her down. I want her pussy before I use her other holes."

"You started without me? How fucking rude."

Everyone's attention swung to the den's entrance, and almost simultaneously came the muffled sound of a gun firing.

*C*lose your eyes.
  Fly away
  Until death turns his back on you.

AARON SANK TO THE FLOOR, landing on his knees in slow motion. An almost comical expression of surprise spread across the detective's features as a wave of scarlet bloomed on his chest. He toppled face-first without uttering a single sound.

"What the fuck?" Carson screeched. "What the everlasting fuck!"

Oliver gestured at the three remaining men, the gun waving in the air. "Back the fuck away from her unless you want to join him."

"What are you doing, Oliver? If you wanted her first, all you had to do was say so. I mean, goddamn. You didn't have to shoot the guy," Judd scowled, stepping away from Ava as instructed.

Ava trembled with both fear and relief. Because while she'd

just been possibly saved from a brutal gang rape, her dubious savior was just as psychotic as the men holding her hostage.

"You weren't supposed to touch her." Oliver's impassive, ice-blue gaze raked over Ava's nude body, narrowing on the blood dripping from her mouth before flicking back to the three men. "I made that perfectly clear."

"The buyer won't care if she's roughed up a little," Drake grumbled. Glancing at Aaron's lifeless body, his hands clenched into fists. "I've been waiting to fuck this little bitch for over a year. If you think I'm giving up that chance now, you're crazy. I'm going to fuck her until she bleeds for me like she did for your brother."

Oliver calmly picked up Aaron's forgotten weapon, unsnapped the holster, pulled the gun out, and shot a bullet into the middle of Drake's chest.

The sound was deafening. Ava was so stunned she could not react at all. Smoke from the gun's discharge swirled over her head as she suddenly snapped back to awareness. Her scream echoed on the heels of the gunshot as she covered her face with her bound hands, blocking out the image of Drake's face and the ugly shock now frozen on his features.

"What are you doing, Oliver?" Carson shakily demanded. He was ten shades paler now than just a second ago. Blood seeped through the bandage across his midriff, and he staggered a bit as he retreated. "What the fuck are you doing?"

"What does it look like?" Oliver replied, wiping Aaron's gun down with his coat sleeve. Bending down, he placed the gun in Aaron's hand, making sure the detective's finger rested on the trigger. "Creating a trail of evidence." Standing back up, he gestured at Judd. "Untie her. Now."

Judd quickly unraveled the rope from around Ava's wrists. "I don't know what your new plan is, but it's smart. Fewer people to split the money with." He nodded at Carson, who, without being told, had sunk down on the couch. "Might even lose one more. Carson here isn't looking so good."

"What happened to him?" Oliver's head tilted as he regarded the two remaining men.

"I stabbed him." Now that she was free of the rope, Ava covered her breasts with her hands. *Why is Oliver here? Where is Kingston?*

A sudden, horrible thought occurred to her. Maybe Oliver had killed him first.

"Fucking bitch stabbed me with a goddamn fork, too," Carson said weakly.

Oliver shot Ava a glance filled with admiration. "Well, well. I knew you had it in you, darling. That tiny streak of savagery." Picking up her discarded coat from behind the sofa, he tossed it at her. "Put it on."

Moving slowly because of the cracked rib, Ava slid her arms into the coat's sleeves. She buttoned it up all the way, grateful it was long enough to cover her ass. Shivering, she stood in the middle of the room, waiting for Oliver's next command.

He busily emptied his gun of bullets, putting them in his pocket then wiping the stock clean of prints. Before placing the weapon in Drake's hands, Oliver pulled a second gun from the waistband of his trousers and leveled it in Judd and Carson's direction.

Judd wiped his torn bottom lip. "What happens now?"

"Now? Now we wait for King's arrival. He's running a bit later than me, but he'll be here soon enough." Oliver shrugged his shoulders. "How he knew she was here, I have no idea. Maybe he really is the Devil that everyone says he is."

"What the fuck are you talking about?" Judd nervously shuffled his feet. "Man, don't joke around like that. No way he's coming here. He'll know what you did. That you're in on this, too."

"Oh, I never joke about Kingston. And I assure you, he *is* coming. While I do admit my part in the initial plot to abduct Ava, this derailment is all yours to claim. I knew the four of you would go off the rails at some point, and my involvement would place me in a unique position to either help my brother or help myself. You see, he and I don't have a very good relationship. In other words, he doesn't trust me at all—not that I blame him—and I usually don't trust him." Oliver's gaze narrowed on Carson. "But you contracted a hit on Kingston, and that is unacceptable. Because if anyone is going to kill my brother, it's going to be me. Not some half-assed, cut-rate assassin with piss-poor aim." Reaching his free hand into his pocket, Oliver withdrew a handful of zip-ties. Ava flinched when he waved the gun in her direction. "Ava, take these and secure their hands. Make sure they're good and tight."

Ava faltered, the pain from her ribs making her head swim. Oliver didn't miss it.

"Ava? Just a few more minutes and this will be over." His voice was strangely soothing, the glint of understanding sympathy in his blue eyes completely out of character. "Now, do as I say, darling."

She nodded, taking the restraints and stepping behind Judd. His body shifted as though preparing to grab her.

"Make one move and I'll rob my brother of the pleasure and kill you on the spot." Oliver stared at Judd, his voice detached as he instructed the man. "Put your hands behind your back. You too, Carson. Stand up so she can restrain you."

Once the two men were secure, Oliver directed them to sit on the floor.

"I still don't understand what the fuck is going on," Judd grumbled, glaring at Ava as though she'd captured the pair of them on her own. "What about the buyer you lined up? What about the fortune we're supposed to get for her?"

"Yeah. The money," Carson muttered weakly. Pushing the bandage on his stomach with the tips of his fingers, he let out a pained groan as more blood seeped through. "That's what I wanna know about."

"How is it that both of you are so damned stupid? There is no buyer. Never was. And there was no way in hell I was going to actually sell her. I mean, let's face facts here. Kingston will definitely gut the two of you like little pigs for what you've done. But can you imagine what he would do to me if I betrayed him like that?" Oliver smiled, his bright blue eyes twinkling with psychotic merriment. "Bad enough that I'll pay a hefty price for my role in all of this at the beginning. I'm hoping Kingston understands and shows me some brotherly mercy. After all, I just saved the woman he loves more than anything else in the world." He waved the gun at Ava, motioning her closer. "Come here, darling. You look like you're about to pass out."

Ava didn't even consider disobeying. She shuffled to him, her breath coming in soft pants now, her skin clammy and cold. Maybe she was in shock? She wasn't sure. She couldn't even make sense of what Oliver was saying. Did he just say Kingston loved her? Her brow furrowed as she digested that. Trying to determine if it was real or just another one of Oliver's tricks. Because trusting Oliver was a mistake. He was a snake. A bad man.

Sinking down onto the couch, Oliver pulled Ava with him, tucking her under his arm in an unexpected gesture of protectiveness. Ava did not trust him, but she had no choice but to slump against him. The leather of the sofa was cold on the backs of her thighs, and she shivered.

"He'll be here soon, darling. Then he'll take care of you."

"Why are you doing this? You hate Kingston. You want him dead," Ava whispered, her eyes drooping heavily. "You wanted to hurt him by hurting me. I don't understand any of this."

Oliver chuckled. "Hate is a strong word, Ava. Let's just say the relationship I have with Kingston is complicated. I've disliked him for so long… it's hard putting that aside all at once. But he's changed since you came in his life. And maybe I want to try changing, too."

"He loves you, you know." Ava sighed, fighting to keep from slipping under the dark waves crashing around her. "No matter what, Kingston loves you. And he loved your mother. Tried to protect her in his own way from your father. I hope you understand that one day."

Oliver's voice sounded like it was coming from far away. "I do understand, Ava. It's why I'm doing this for him."

Ava felt the air shift. Something tangible that maybe only she could discern. A sense of electricity-charged atmosphere and the faint scent of Earl Grey tea and snow-dusted pines. Maybe she was hallucinating.

Or maybe the Devil had come for her like he did in her nightmares.

Kingston is here. I know he is. I smell his cologne. I feel him… He's here. He came for me after all.

Ava struggled to sit up but fell back weakly against Oliver's side. She was quickly slipping into a shadowy abyss, but she couldn't go without seeing Kingston's face. Without explaining what happened and that Oliver saved her rather than delivering her to certain death. Her eyes fluttered shut.

She heard banging noises. Shouts. The thick sound of someone being punched and cries of pain. In the midst of that was a storm of deadly calm. It was the eye of a hurricane. And Kingston was its center.

"What do you *think* you've done for me, brother? Because I'm having a hard time seeing the *sacrifice* of your actions right now." Kingston's soft and deadly voice filled the room. It roared in direct from the depths of Hell, carried along on lightning bolts. "And get your fucking hands off her before I rip your goddamn arms off your body."

"About time you got here," Oliver grumbled. "Oh, and you're welcome. I already took down a couple of the fuckers but left these two alive just for you. I know you'll enjoy making them pay for their role in all of this. Hopefully, you'll remember that when you start thinking about how you'll punish me."

Ava forced her eyes open. A swarm of dark-clothed men were jerking Carson and Judd to their feet. After quickly tying gags over their mouths, the men snatched black hoods over their heads and shoved them hard up against the wall. One of them—Carson, maybe—screamed in pain.

Ava closed her eyes and opened them again to see Kingston bearing down on her.

He wore all black. Black suit. Black overcoat. Black gloves. Even his eyes were black, no longer that gorgeous shade of velvet blue she loved so much. He appeared so sinister that for a moment, Ava wondered if he really was the Devil who had come to take their souls and torment them forever.

She'd never been so glad to see someone in all her life.

"Kingston. You found me." Tears filled her eyes, flowing down to burn the cuts on her lips, bathing the bruises on her cheeks where she'd been struck. She couldn't catch her breath, but somehow, that had nothing to do with a cracked rib and everything to do with her heart.

With him. The man she loved.

Kingston's crooked smile made her soul sing with joy as he scooped her up and away from Oliver.

Crushing her against his chest for a long moment, he just held her, his breath ragged in her ears. Cupping Ava's face in the palm of a black leather-gloved hand, he softly reminded her of his obsession, even as her eyesight finally dimmed and ebony skies swallowed her whole.

"I told you before, lamb. You are mine. No matter where you go or how far, I will always find you. I will always come for you. Do you understand? *Always.*"

CHAPTER
THIRTY-NINE

Love isn't a weakness.
Or a myth.
Or a curse.
Or a torment.
Love heals all.

Five days had passed since Ava's rescue.

She slept most of that time, coming awake for sips of water and the pain medication Neil prescribed. Sometimes, Kingston made her sit up and take deep breaths, gently explaining how it would keep her lungs clear of the fluid build-up so common with fractured ribs.

He never left her side. On the second night, when trauma and pain sent her careening into a night terror, he was there. Holding her during the worst of it. Soothing her back into a deep sleep when the nightmares sputtered out along with her heart-wrenching screams.

Apart from the moment when he learned she was her

brother's prisoner, Kingston had never felt more helpless in his life. Knowing how close he'd come to losing her to the cruelty of others broke him.

He lay beside her now in their bed, entwining locks of her hair 'round and 'round his finger. Watching her sleep, he counted the rise and fall of her chest and the rapid twitching of her eyelids as she dreamed of things he hoped she would never remember upon waking. He kissed the tip of her nose and stroked her soft cheeks. Several times he applied a healing salve to the cut on her bottom lip and wanted to rip apart the man who had struck her.

During the darkest hours of the night, he whispered how much he loved her. That when she recovered, he would give her anything her heart desired. He promised to protect her always. Vowed she would never have any reason to feel unsafe ever again. He said these things in preparation for saying them for the day she was better and fully recovered. He said them as a prelude to begging her forgiveness.

He had no idea how he would live without her, but he was determined to give her a choice. Be his forever. Or be set free.

The possibility Ava would choose the latter was something Kingston had prepared for. He did not deserve her, and she should have the chance to live her life the way she wanted.

That meant letting her go. No matter how devastating it would be.

Kingston's eyes drifted shut as exhaustion seeped into his bones. The lack of sleep over the last few nights was catching up to him now. With a heavy sigh, he sank deeper into the pillows, curling his body around hers in a protective gesture. If she stirred or cried out in her sleep, he would be right there to comfort her. He concentrated on her steady breathing, matching it with his own as darkness overtook him.

It was much later when he woke to find Ava staring at him, those enchanting green eyes of hers wide and serious.

"Hi," she whispered.

"Hi," he whispered back.

"I thought I would never see you again," she said softly after a few minutes of silence. "But you found me. Somehow, you found me."

"You are the other half of my soul, Ava. Did you think I wouldn't want it back?"

"Oh, Kingston." Ava's chin quivered, tears filling her eyes. "How could I be so stupid, thinking I could handle Carson on my own? I wanted him to pay for what he did but all I did was make a mess of everything and place myself and you in danger."

"But you did make him pay," Kingston assured her, cupping her jaw in the palm of his hand. "He's dead, Ava. He died that same night and his body was taken back to the house so he could be found with the others. It looks like a drug deal gone bad, which is an outcome no one would find particularly surprising."

"But there were two policemen who saw me at the house. They knew me. They can place me at the scene. They'll arrest me and—"

Kingston shushed her before her panic could spin out of control. "I've taken care of that, Ava. They were just as dirty as Aaron Redding, and you don't need to worry about them, trust me. They'll never say a word about what they saw. I made damn sure of it." He deliberately left out the details of the officers' deaths in a fiery crash just on the outskirts of Bitter Springs. "Carson's death will be investigated based on what I allow."

"Did you... Did you do it?" Ava sounded both hopeful and scared of the answer in regard to her brother's fate. And while

Kingston wished he could say differently, he was not the cause of Carson's demise.

"No, lamb. He bled out internally. God, I wanted to string him up by his balls. Hear his screams for mercy while I made him suffer for hurting you, but it wasn't meant to be. I'm furious he cheated me of the chance to kill him myself."

Horror flashed across Ava's delicate features. "Then I did it. It was me. I actually killed him." Her voice caught on a sob. "My own brother."

"In self-defense, Ava. It was either you or him," Kingston said fiercely, tipping her chin to meet his gaze. "He signed your death warrant and would have profited from it. He deserved to die like he did. Slowly and in excruciating pain. I watched him take his last breath and reminded him who took his life and why. After all he took from you, what he did to your parents, it was only right that you got your vengeance. *You* made him pay the price for his actions, and I'm so proud of you for the strength it took to do that."

Ava's eyes watered, tears spilling over and wetting her cheeks. Kingston swiped at the moisture with his thumbs. "Don't waste your tears on him, lamb. He's not worth it. He never was."

She cried anyway, despite his admonishment, and Kingston understood why. He said nothing more, simply held her while she wept until she finally took a shuddering breath and wiped her face free of tears.

"I'm okay now," she whispered, a spark of survival glimmering in her eyes. "And—and you're right, Kingston. I'm glad he's dead."

Kingston's stomach clenched with pain-filled rage. Every time he saw evidence of the nightmare she had endured, murder danced in his heart.

Earlier this morning, while holding Ava's body against his

own in the bathtub and washing her hair, it was the sight of the bruises left behind when Carson strangled her. Right now, it was the raw, chapped skin of her wrists. Injuries that were caused by those monsters stringing her up like a freshly killed deer waiting to be butchered.

He wished each man was still alive so he could gut them himself. He'd drape their intestines around their necks like Christmas tinsel and set them on fire. Unfortunately, there was only one man was still barely breathing. Kingston had special plans for him.

"Is Oliver okay?" Ava's voice hitched. "You didn't hurt him, did you? He stopped them from raping me. I watched him kill the detective. And Drake, too."

"He's alive although I wish he'd left the slaughter of those two motherfuckers to me. I would have handled things much differently. It would not have been a quick death for either one."

Ava's eyes watered again. "He was helping you. And me. He knew he couldn't control all of them once they learned he was no longer with them. They would have torn us both apart. Are you angry with him?"

"I'm not sure how I feel about Oliver at the moment, to be honest," Kingston said gruffly. "His motives are still a bit murky, although I cannot deny his involvement kept things from being so much worse. I don't know why he changed his mind about hurting you... and hurting me, but he did. I've never understood him and probably never will. He is going away for a while. Of his own choice. Says he must work some things out for himself before we can try having a real relationship as brothers." His hands clenched as he thought of how close he'd come to losing Ava. And Oliver. He'd been prepared and more than willing to put a bullet between his brother's eyes. "I'll probably never fully trust him, but if it wasn't for him, I would have failed you, Ava. I wouldn't have reached you in time."

Kingston propped his back against the headboard and carefully pulled her beside him. "I should have never left you behind." He raked a hand through his hair, torment twisting his features. "I knew it was a mistake the minute I got into the penthouse's elevator.

"I should have trusted you to give me what I thought I wanted when it came to Carson," Ava confessed.

"You had every right to do what you did, Ava, although I'll likely take a riding crop to your backside at some point for disobeying me. You were so clever in planning your escape that I can't help but feel irrationally proud." Kingston let out a dry laugh, brushing her hair back from her forehead. "My heart is still shattered from seeing you at Carson's. Bloody and bruised but still breathing. Still fighting. Still alive. Had it not been four on one, I think you would have taken them all down, one by one."

"Does this mean you've grown one? A heart, that is?" Ava asked with a small smile. "You warned me before it did not exist."

"Oh, it exists. The problem is I lost possession of it a long time ago. It hasn't been mine since the day I saw you standing in your mother's kitchen. You've owned it since then, and for as long as you want it, it's yours. All of it. All of me. Everything I have is yours, Ava. Everything."

"Oh, Kingston." Ava's voice trembled.

His hand slid into the waves of her blonde hair as they stared into each other's eyes. "I adore you, Ava. You and your savage little heart. I love the way you kiss me. How you hold my hand. How you let me take care of you, not because you need it but because *I* do. But all of that will never be enough to keep you here. I'm setting you free. You can go anywhere in the world. Do anything you desire. Be anyone you want to be. There are no debts to be paid. No obligations or responsibilities. No contract. I may have threatened you with it, but I ripped that damn thing up the day after you signed it anyway. For the rest of my life, I will make sure you are safe and taken care of."

"I don't understand." Ava's eyes widened with panic. "Where would I go without you?"

Kingston exhaled a shuddering breath. "I'm letting you go, lamb. I have to. Don't you see? After hurting..." He choked on the word, hot tears stinging his eyes as he continued in a gruff voice, "After hurting you so many times that I've lost count, I can only say how sorry I am. I'm so fucking sorry, Ava. I hate myself for what I am... a monster. A beast who took something pure and innocent just so I could make her as filthy as me. But no matter how hard I tried to ruin you, I failed. You are so bright, so beautiful, Ava, so fucking *good* it hurts my eyes just to look at you. You deserve so much, and I have nothing to offer you that isn't drenched in blood and pain."

Ava laid a hand along the side of his cheek. Kingston could not resist the urge to nestle into the warmth of her palm. Her touch soothed him. Calmed him. It felt as though a thousand lions were tearing his heart to pieces when he realized this was the last time they would share such an intimate moment.

"How did you find me, Kingston? How did you know to go to my parent's house?"

Kingston clenched his jaw so tight he was in danger of cracking a tooth. "I'm confessing my sins, Ava, but I'm not ready to admit all of them out loud."

Ava's eyes narrowed the tiniest bit. "I know Oliver did not tell you. He specifically said he did not know how you knew I was there."

A guilty flush crept up Kingston's neck. He had nothing to

be sorry for. Everything he'd done was for her safety. Not because he was a psycho who craved control over one savage, headstrong girl.

"Tell me," Ava demanded. "Did you have cameras there? What?"

"I implanted a tracker in you," he blurted out.

"Wait." She stared at Kingston in shock. "You did what?"

"A GPS tracker. In the back of your neck. Oliver didn't know about it. No one did."

She immediately ran a hand over her neck, fingers searching for proof. When she found the tiny bump, her eyes widened in outrage. "You did that and never told me? You did it without my consent?"

"Yeah. I did. The first night you were under my roof. Birth control and a tracker. Common tools in the average kidnapper's toolkit," Kingston snapped.

Ava stared at him for a long moment, then for no reason that Kingston could see, a wide smile curved her lips. It melted into a giggle before she erupted into full-blown laughter. She held her sides to keep her ribs from hurting too badly. The more she laughed, the more confused Kingston became.

"I don't understand what you find so amusing. I've violated you in the worst possible ways, Ava. Do you have any idea the things I plan on doing with you if you stay with me? I want to tattoo my fucking name across your chest, so you know you belong to me every time you look in the mirror. I'll loop a chain around that pretty little neck of yours and lead you around, so everyone knows you are mine. And you won't be able to stop me from fucking you so hard you pass out from the pleasure. Don't you understand? That tracker was just one example of my obsession. Damnit, this is nothing to laugh about!"

"Oh my God," Ava gasped, biting her hand to keep from laughing harder. "I seriously thought you had otherworldly powers. That maybe you really *were* the Devil himself with the ability to find me anywhere, anytime."

She sobered, biting her bottom lip when she saw his fierce scowl was not easing away, and he really was not amused. "While I'm not happy about it, and I'm hurt that you never *told* me, I can't really be that angry. It led you to me when I needed you. And because I understand you, I understand *why* you did it." Ava placed both hands on his cheeks, resting her forehead against his. "You'll have plenty of time to make it up to me, though. A lifetime. Because I'm not going anywhere, Kingston. I am yours. There's nowhere in this world or the next where that fact changes. Even your flaws and all the red flags that make me question my own sanity aren't enough to make me leave you. I *won't* leave you."

"You've not even seen the tip of the iceberg, Ava. I *am* the Devil when it comes to you. A fucking beast. I'm unhinged with the need to protect you. For God's sake, there's a man in the dungeon I've restrained from carving up for one reason only. I've been waiting until you've recovered so when I rip his heart out by the roots, I can give it to you on a silver platter. That's how fucking insane I am when it comes to you."

"As long as your murderous qualities are focused only on bad guys, I'm okay with that," Ava replied calmly.

"You have no idea how savage I am." Kingston's jaw clenched tight. Couldn't she understand what he was trying to say? He would never be good enough for an angel like her.

"I know you'll never hurt me, Kingston." Ava's eyes sparkled with determination. For a long moment, they simply stared at one another, neither willing to back down until Kington's willpower deflated.

"Come with me," he growled in defeat. "I want to show you something."

He helped her rise from the bed, leading her to the locked

door inside the room. Kingston knew she'd tried opening it that first morning she woke up in his room. Her fingerprints were all over the lock and the keypad. But now he would show Ava the secrets it contained.

When the door swung open, Kingston stepped aside so she could enter ahead of him. The glow of nearly two hundred different monitors reflected on Ava's features as she took it all in.

There were screens running various financial tickers. Stock market news and updates for the United States and countries around the world. The lobby of LIST and the entrance to the restaurant lit up four of the monitors. But most of the screens displayed images Ava surely recognized from her time spent as his prisoner. It was the camera feed for the entire estate. All the rooms. The grounds. The stables. The woods.

And the cell in the dungeon where he had first imprisoned her.

"No one is allowed inside this room other than me. But you have every right to be here, Ava. This is the pulse of The Den."

Ava's gaze darted around the numerous screens before finding the monitor showing Judd's cell. He was hanging from the ceiling, metal chains wrapped around his body in an intricate pattern. "He's still alive."

Kingston came up behind her, wrapping his arms lightly around her waist and steadying her when she began to tremble. "He is. Barely. I have certain contacts I can hand him over to. He would never be free again, and the rest of his life would be nothing but degradation and pain. Or I can end it here. The final decision is yours, Ava. But only if you want it."

If Judd's appearance shocked Ava, she did not show it. The man was covered in blood, various cuts and bruises adorning his naked body. His penis hung flaccid between his legs, and a long slash on the top of his left thigh dripped blood onto the dungeon floor. Whenever he screamed or moaned, no intelligible sound emerged. As he'd promised himself once before, Kingston had cut out Judd's tongue.

When Ava finally looked away from the screen, her eyes were shiny with tears.

Kingston fought down the instant disappointment. Any further opportunity of ensuring Judd Vanderhorn suffered excruciating agony was now over. He would carry out Ava's wishes even if it meant abandoning his own.

"Whatever future they planned for me should never happen to anyone. Show him mercy, Kingston, although he doesn't deserve it. Give him a quick death. Not for his sake, but for mine."

"It will be done, lamb."

She threw herself into his arms with such force that Kingston worried she might re-injure herself. He felt her tears dripping onto his bare chest. Kissing the top of her head, he vowed he'd always stand between her and the merest hint of danger.

"You'll do this for me?" she asked, her voice breaking with a sob.

"I will do anything you ask of me, Ava."

Ava didn't say anything else. She simply pulled his head down and pressed her lips to his.

FORTY

Make me beg for more.
I am yours.
To crush.
To conquer.
To protect.
To keep.
To love.

AVA COULD NOT SIT STILL.

She fidgeted. Squirmed. Downed a whole glass of champagne and asked for another as the limo sped toward the Winter Enterprises building.

Five weeks had passed since the incident, and Ava was completely healed from her injuries. Even Neil was surprised by her swift recovery, although he often teased that love was known to work wonders. It was a rationalization he used whenever Kingston demanded Ava's activities remain limited so her body could recover faster.

"Ava, if you don't calm down, I'll have to take you over my knee," Kingston drawled, sipping his scotch.

"Boooo," she shot back with a smile belying her disapproval of his current sternness. "And don't threaten me with a good time."

"Sassy little thing tonight, aren't you?" Dressed in an impeccable tux, Kingston was the epitome of handsome wickedness. His eyes glowed blue-black in the limo's dim lighting.

"You like me sassy, remember?" Ava countered, flopping back against the leather seat, giving him an appreciative stare. "Have I told you how devastatingly hot you are in a tuxedo?"

"Have I told you how fucking delicious you are in this dress?" Kingston countered, pressing a kiss to her bare shoulder. Hooking his fingers in the pearl choker around her neck, he tugged her closer until Ava was plastered against his side. "I can hardly keep my hands off you."

"Why are you even trying?" Her words were breathless, something she couldn't help whenever Kingston gazed at her the way he did now. Like she was a treat to be devoured. She traced the small, half-moon scar on his cheek with the tip of her fingernail. It was the one she'd given him that first day in his office after he abducted her.

"Behave yourself, lamb. Don't worry. I plan to feast on you all night if that's what you truly want."

"You know I do. You've not touched me in weeks. I'm going crazy." Ava sighed, dropping her head back against the seat. "It's my first time at LIST. How can you expect me not to be excited?"

After pestering Kingston for days, insisting she was healed enough to resume sexual activity, he finally agreed. To celebrate her recovery, and as a reward for good behavior during her tedious confinement, Kingston planned a weekend in the city. It would begin with a night of dissolute activities at LIST.

In preparation for the occasion, Mary from *La Maison* personally came to The Den and repeated the waxing process she'd done before. And like that first time, Kingston sat through the process, his heated gaze roaming over Ava's nude body and a smile curving his lips.

"I'm afraid I've thoroughly corrupted you. Not many women look forward to being chained, gagged, spanked, and fucked." An amused smile twisted Kingston's firm lips.

"I'm sure that depends on whether you are the one doing all of the above," Ava said cheerfully. "In that case, countless women would line up outside our door waiting for you to get busy."

Kingston trailed a finger down her cheek in a softly caressing motion. "There's only one woman in this world I want for such activities. Only one woman I want in my bed. Sharing my life. Holding my hand."

"Who is this lucky woman?" Ava teased, wrinkling her nose at him.

"You just earned yourself another five strikes. Do you prefer my hand or the paddle?" Kingston grinned indulgently as Ava squirmed again, intensely aware of her lack of underwear. Her nipples were hard as diamonds beneath the strapless black cocktail dress, and she couldn't help but lick her lips when she stared up into Kingston's hungry eyes.

"The crop, sir. Did you know I'm not wearing panties right now?"

"Ah, someone has been doing their homework," he growled. "And I am very aware you have nothing on beneath that dress, Ava. I would expect you to obey that simple command."

"You told me to go through the list of things I might like."

Ava sulked when he gave no indication of taking advantage of her confession. "I did my research whenever I wasn't working on the charity Christmas Ball. Neil has been so grateful for my help. I think he's envious of my organization skills."

"You would remind me of that particular list when I'm trying so hard to resist you."

Ava pressed her lips together. "You don't have to, you know."

"Ah, but I must," Kingston retorted. "At least until you've chosen a safe word."

"Do I have to? Because I don't want one. I want you to do anything you want tonight. In fact, I demand it. I'm going crazy wanting you, Kingston. It's very cruel to deny me for so long. I thought you were obsessed with me?" She was egging him on. Ratcheting his lust until it burned like an out-of-control inferno. It was only fair that it matched the fire inside of her.

"I am obsessed with you, lamb." His husky voice was molten honey pouring over her soul. It calmed Ava, even as it enflamed her desire. She ached for this man to just spread her legs and take her to the edge of oblivion. Kingston continued, "Sorry, Ava. But if you don't select one, I will not touch you. I can't promise my control without it."

"I don't want you to have control." Ava pouted. "I want you wild. Feral. And I don't want to think about a thing."

"If I fuck you like you need to be fucked, you won't be able to think at all."

"Fine," she huffed in exasperation. "My safe word is 'more.'"

"Good God, I've created a monster." Kingston chuckled. "That won't do, lamb. Choose another or we'll go straight up to the penthouse, put on pajamas, and spend the night watching Christmas movies."

Ava laughed, slapping his arm playfully. "Oh! You wouldn't dare!"

"Try me," he said, leaning back with arms propped behind his head. "I think I'll have some popcorn while we watch the movie. Maybe even hot chocolate..."

"Okay! Okay!" She peppered his face and neck with kisses. "You win, beast. And there...that's my safe word, okay? Beast."

Kingston pulled her in for a real kiss, his mouth slamming down on hers and reminding Ava just how dominant he could be. "It's perfect."

THERE WAS SO much to look at.

Ava drank it all in. Every decadent swath of fabric. Every crystal that dripped from the sconces and the multiple chandeliers. The lighting was softly romantic, the music both sensual and potent. Heavy wood furniture with finely carved accents and black velvet fabrics sat scattered around the cavernous space. People perched upon them, laughing and sipping cocktails.

A gleaming, hardwood bar took up the length of one wall with bartenders of both sexes clad in crisp tuxedos and red bow ties mixing drinks. Waitresses carried trays while balanced on black heels and wearing slim-fitting, black sheath dresses. Slender ribbons of red encircled their necks. Everything was classy, beautiful, and so sexy that it was understandable why people fought for membership invitations.

There was a variety of men and women inside the club. Some had partners along with them, submissives in various stages of undress. A few wore collars with leashes attached. Some even wore masks but all members were recognized by one detail. A diamond-encrusted gold pin in the shape of a crown worn over the heart, or if one's clothes were missing, a bracelet of the same design encircled the wrist.

Kingston clasped Ava's hand and guided her down a long hallway. On either side were open doors, and each portal revealed rooms where different activities were underway. Some had Ava's mouth dropping in shock.

"Another night, Ava, and I'll indulge your every curiosity about what takes place in those rooms," Kingston said in a murmur when she lagged behind him. "But right now, I want you all to myself, and I've no patience for simply watching things when I'm going crazy for you." Stopping abruptly, he pulled her tight against his lean form. "Do you trust me, Ava?"

She smiled softly at his silly question. "With my life. You know that."

From his pocket, Kingston withdrew a length of pearls with diamonds nestled between each creamy orb. There was a clip at one end, and Ava realized it was a leash. A leash that matched the design of the choker she wore. Earlier, when he placed the jewelry around her neck, she wondered about the necklace's diamond-encrusted loop in the shape of a crown at its center. Now she knew.

He attached the leash to the collar and dragged her even closer, his eyes dark as blue-black velvet. "Later, I'm going to wrap this leash around your throat while I'm deep inside you, Ava. I want you to imagine it's my hands holding you so tight, giving and taking your breath. You will come so many times tonight, you will lose count. But after each climax, you will thank me. You will say 'thank you, sir,' and beg me for more." He kissed the end of her nose. "Do you understand, my savage lamb?"

"Yes. I understand, sir," Ava replied breathlessly, her knees wobbling with unbearable anticipation.

"Good girl. Now, come along. I have several surprises for you in the room that's been prepared for us."

The room into which Kingston led Ava was as scrumptiously illuminated as the rest of the club. Certain areas sat in pools of soft light while the rest of the room remained mysteriously dim. A bed with tall posts and spindles for a headboard was in the center of one wall. A large black structure in the form of an X occupied a corner, and in the other, a padded bench with a variety of buckles and leather belts dangling from it. In the center of the room, bathed in a circle of white light, was a reclining chair that looked like something found in a barber shop. This one, however, had straps to restrain a person. A rolling metal cart was beside the chair, the top level containing an instrument resembling a gun and what looked like small pots of some sort of paint.

Ava came to an abrupt halt. "What is this, Kingston?"

"First part of the surprise." Kingston laughed, tugging on the leash until she had no choice but to follow him. "Remember, you said you trusted me."

"Yes, but..." she stuttered.

"I'm giving you a tattoo, Ava. So, there is no doubt that you belong to me. The decision you must make is where you want it placed. Down the center of your back, running along your spine, or across your ribs." His eyes glittered with possessiveness. "Or maybe on the inside of your thigh?"

"You can do that?" Ava slumped in relief when he just nodded. She did not expect details on where he'd picked up the knowledge for that particular skill. There were so many things she still had yet to learn about this man. "You frightened me, Kingston. But I suspect that was on purpose, wasn't it?"

That sadistic streak she adored, the one that would always run through Kingston's soul, peeked out behind his smile. "Maybe a little. Make your choice. Oh, and Ava? I will be strapping you down for this. Can't have you moving around if the pain becomes too intense."

A half-hour later, Kingston worked on finishing it up while Ava wished he would let her see the progress.

"No peeking just yet," he said of the words inked down her left flank and over her ribs. Three words that meant everything to them both were now branded into her skin. Ava shivered, knowing this was a permanent link to the man who had placed them there.

Crush.

Conquer.

Protect.

While cleaning the blood welling up between the letters, Kingston trailed his fingers over her unmarred skin. He had touched various places on her body during the procedure, threatening to mark her in those areas. He aroused her to such a fever pitch, the buzzing sting of the tattoo pen nearly sent her tumbling into an orgasm.

Setting the instrument down on the cart, Kingston ran his hand down the middle of her back then smoothed his palm over the curve of her buttocks. "Do you want to come for me, lamb?"

Because she was on her stomach and strapped to the chair in a reclining position, Ava could not move a muscle. She clenched her teeth as he experimentally brushed a forefinger between her legs and teased her opening.

"If it pleases you, sir," she panted in delight.

"Everything about you pleases me, Ava, so it's only fair you come first. With my oath freshly inked on your skin and your sweet pussy weeping for me to fill it."

God, the filthy things that come out of this man's mouth should be outlawed.

"Yes. Please," she choked out.

"Good girl," he whispered in her ear while giving her what she desperately needed.

Once she had thanked him for the first of many orgasms, her body weak within the chair's binding, Kingston placed protective tape over the tattoo and unbuckled the straps holding her down.

She was wobbly as she slipped off the table, her knees shaking, but he quickly steadied her with an arm around her waist.

"Are you alright? Was it too much?"

Ava looped her arms around his neck. Other than the choker, the leash and the three words etched into her skin, she was naked.

"It was perfect. Perfect." She smiled, swaying into him.

"Are you ready for your next surprise?" Kingston asked while undoing his cufflinks and placing the diamond and gold studs on the metal cart. Unbuttoning his shirt, he drew it and the bowtie off along with his undershirt, tossing them aside.

Ava sighed, entranced by Kingston's broad chest and all the finely sculpted muscles that defined its expanse. Her gaze traveled his body with ill-concealed lust, admiring the lion's head tattoo emblazoned across his skin. She wanted one just like it embedded into her skin. She'd even let Kingston choose its location, although thinking of the tender areas where he might place it was a little frightening.

He was so exquisitely put together. Like a magnificent Greek sculpture. Caressing his chest, she trailed her fingers over the ridges of his abdomen. It was a few moments before she realized something was different. There was one word tattooed within the lion's open snarl, caught between the fangs, cradled there as if protected from the world.

Lamb.

Ava's gaze raised to his. "Oh, Kingston."

"That's where you belong, Ava," he swore fiercely. "Where you've always been. Burned across my heart and in my soul."

Ava had never felt so adored as she did in that moment. Happiness and a sense of belonging curled around her. "Make love to me, Kingston," she insisted. "Now."

"You don't want to play, Ava? Because I still do." His grin was wicked as his hands smoothed over her full breasts. He tweaked both of her nipples with a twist of his fingers, reminding Ava of the bejewled clamps she had come across while doing research. "You wanted me to control everything tonight and I will. But I can't go another second without your taste in my mouth. My cock deep inside you. Get on the bed, now. Hands and knees, Ava, ass toward me, your back arched."

She quickly did as he ordered, listening as Kingston took his time in removing his clothes. When she wiggled impatiently, a resounding slap of her ass had her squealing in shock.

"I owe you several of those, but we've all weekend to get them in, my impatient little brat," Kingston chuckled, moving up behind her on the bed. He positioned himself and pushed his cock inside her with agonizing slowness, groaning as her flesh closed around him. Slapping her ass again, he demanded in a silky rough voice, "Open up for me, Ava. Let me inside you."

Ava trembled with the onslaught of sensations. The pleasure took her breath away as Kingston sunk so deep inside her that he bottomed out.

"Fuck, you feel good," Kingston muttered beneath his breath. He gripped her hips, gently sliding in and out, mindful that it had been weeks since they'd made love and she needed to be accustomed with his size again. "You're so goddamn tight. I don't want to hurt you..."

Ava did not want gentle. She did not want handling as though he wore kid gloves and she was a fragile treasure. She wanted hard. Fast. Raw and almost depraved. She wanted Kingston as he was. It was that simple. And maybe this was all she could hope for when it came to a future with this man, but it was enough for her.

"Fuck me, Kingston," she demanded with a frustrated moan. "Do everything you promised. I need it. I need *you*."

Kingston laughed softly. "Whatever you want, little lamb. You know I'll do anything for you." Looping the pearl leash once around her neck, he pulled it just tight enough to create an exquisite tension, then whispered in a dark voice, "Do you remember your safe word? Good girl. Now, start counting how many times I make you see the stars."

EPILOGUE

S*ay yes.*
    Always say yes.
    Say you're mine
Always mine.
Say you love me
Always love me.

MUCH LATER THAT NIGHT, exhausted and satisfied but unable to fall asleep, Kingston and Ava lay on the couch in the penthouse living room. A movie on the television played softly in the background. It was something about Christmas in a small town, with a billionaire inadvertently falling in love with the disillusioned owner of the bed and breakfast where he hid from his many responsibilities.

"More hot chocolate?" Kingston asked as Ava snuggled beneath the blanket covering their bodies.

"Mmm. No. I think I'm hot chocolate-d out." She smiled up at him before turning her attention back to the movie. "It's not even Thanksgiving, and all the Christmas movies are playing," Ava said, sounding vaguely disappointed by that fact.

"I know. It's crazy."

"What's crazy is you putting up a Christmas tree. But what a wonderful surprise to see when we came in tonight." Running her hand through his hair, she ruffled it before giving him a kiss on the cheek.

"You know, this is the first time I've ever put up a tree because I wanted one," Kingston admitted. "There was never a reason before. I think I like it. It looks nice in here. Happier. Warmer." He wondered what Oliver would think of such sentimentality. The subject of his half-brother was one that he and Ava had avoided since the incident but Kingston knew one day they would have no choice.

Not today, however. Not right now. No, this moment was all about Ava and how much he adored her.

Ava smiled softly. "We should put a tree up in every room, I think. Even at The Den."

"My men will think I've lost my mind, but if my queen wants Christmas trees everywhere, then that's what she shall have." Carefully avoiding Ava's fresh tattoo, he tickled under her arms, eliciting shrieks of delight. "And anything else she desires."

She giggled, grabbing his hands so he could not continue the delightful torment. "A king to kiss me whenever I want. That's all I need, honest."

"In that case, you are really going to enjoy Christmas. I plan on shamelessly spoiling you." Kingston promised softly. "I'm going to hide presents all over the place and watch you search for them. Each time you find one, I'll give you a kiss."

Ava pulled the blanket up closer to her chin and burrowed closer to the furnace-like heat of Kingston's body. "I can't think of any better gift than that."

"I'll start by hiding presents around here."

"But it's not Christmas yet," Ava pointed out.

"That won't stop me. You know how stubborn I can be when I want something."

Ava laughed. "Yes, that's one thing I'm very much aware of. But still, it's not Christmas. No presents until then, and I mean it. You've given me too much already."

"Well, what should I do with this one?" From the pocket of his sleeping pants, Kingston withdrew a square, powder-blue box wrapped with a black velvet ribbon.

With a sharp intake of breath, Ava scrambled up onto her knees and faced him. The blanket slipped away from her shoulders. "*What* is that?" She looked stunned. Hopeful. Worried.

"Something for you. Did you think that's all there was to the surprises? What we did tonight at LIST? And your tattoo?" Kingston tipped Ava's chin up. "There's so much more I want to give you, Ava."

"I don't expect…" Ava protested with sudden fierceness.

"Nobody makes me do anything I don't want to do. You know that. Now, open this before we get into further arguments about when Christmas should officially begin."

"Christmas begins the Friday after Thanksgiving, of course. Only psychos celebrate before that," she responded absently while taking the blue box from his hand. With a deep breath, she pulled on the ribbon decorating the box and popped it open.

The three-carat diamond engagement ring twinkled, catching the lights of the Christmas tree and sparkling like a new star in the sky. Ava stared at it, apparently so shocked she couldn't say anything.

Kingston held his breath. What would she say?

God, please don't let her say no.

Sliding off the couch, he went down onto one knee, bowing before this woman who made all the colors of his world bright and vibrant. This woman he could not live without.

"Ava Bella Blue, I don't understand how it happened, or even when it happened, but I am madly in love with you. I can't imagine living my life without you in it. If you agree that the rest of our lives should be spent together, then say yes. Because I promise to love you for the rest of my life. I promise to keep you safe. I'll be a shoulder you can cry on and a shelter from all that is ugly in the world. I promise to support you in whatever you decide to do, and I will be a man you can always trust. I promise to make you pancakes and watch cheesy movies with you whenever you want. I promise I will hold you tight and chase your nightmares away. Most importantly, I promise that I'll kiss you every day." Kingston took a deep breath, aware that his voice was cracking with both nerves and emotions. "I'll never be a good man, but for you, little lamb, I will try to be whatever you want me to be until the day I take my last breath. I'm asking you to be my wife. My lover. My friend. My family. Will you save me from a miserable life without hope and love and marry me?"

Ava burst into tears, throwing her arms around his neck and squeezing until she practically strangled him. "How can I say no to such a beautiful proposal?"

Kingston let out an exhale of relief. At least she'd not slapped him across the face and rejected him outright.

"There's much more to this proposal, Ava. The truth of who I am and the beast you turn me into with just your smile." He laughed darkly, his voice lowering into a husky whisper. "I promise to spank you when it's needed and even when it's not. I will fulfill all your fantasies, even the ones you don't know about yet. I'll fuck you until you can't walk and be the reason you need a safe word. I promise to give you as many orgasms as you want and surpass that limit because it's what *I* want and what you need. I will be your monster. Your beast. Your villain. Your protector. And if you decide to burn this world down, I'll help you spread the flames and kill any bastard who gets in your way. I promise all this to you, Ava, but first, you have to say yes."

"Of course, I'm saying yes!" Ava laughed, kissing Kingston with sweet fierceness. "You made sure of that with the second part of the proposal. I love you, Kingston. So much so that I cannot put everything I feel for you into words. You saved me when I was lost, and my home is wherever you are. Good and bad, wicked or sweet, you are my life. My world. My heart. My everything."

Kingston removed the ring from the box and slid the sparkling jewelry onto her finger. "I wasn't sure you would say yes so, I didn't get the marriage license. But I'd marry you this very moment if we had one. Then, you would truly be mine in every sense of the word."

"I *am* yours," Ava said softly as he kissed her fingers. "I don't need a ring or a piece of paper to tell me what my heart already knows."

Kingston's brow furrowed with intensity, his eyes tracing the outline of Ava's plump lips. "This evening was intense, but I'm obsessed with your taste. Your kisses. Everything about you entrances me. I'm a selfish beast, Ava, and I want to make love to you again."

She giggled mischievously, fumbling with the hem of his shirt and trying to pull it over his head. "What are we waiting for?"

Sweeping her up into his arms, Kingston stomped down the hall toward their bedroom while she squealed with delight and peppered his face with a thousand tiny kisses.

Laying Ava gently down on the bed, he cradled her face in

his hands and claimed her lips with tender roughness. "I'm the luckiest man in the universe, and I don't deserve you. You are not the sacrifice I once called you but the altar at which I will kneel and worship for the rest of my life. There's not a soul alive who loves you more than I do, little lamb. You are my always."

"And you're mine, Kingston," Ava whispered, tears of happiness streaming down her cheeks as she lifted her face to meet his kiss. "Forever."

THE END

I HOPE you enjoyed A Heart So Savage and thank you for reading! I had so much fun plunging into the world of dark romance, and I promise I'll be writing more morally grey heroes and feisty heroines in the future. If you enjoyed this not-so-pitch-black world I've created, I'd love to hear from you! You can follow me everywhere on social media and through my newsletter.

A huge hug of gratitude goes out to my readers, ARC team, followers, and Honeybees from the Facebook group. Your support means everything. Thank you to the wonderful author community who have embraced and cheered me on over the years. Hugs and kisses for Cheryl Maddox, the best PA that ever PA'd, lol. I honestly don't know what I would do without that woman! All the mad respect and admiration for Dakota Willink and her skill in designing such stunning graphics and covers for my books. Kisses for my sweet editor, Kendra Gaither, for her everlasting patience when I push deadlines. And my undying gratitude for Cin Medley, Michelle Windsor and Linda

Kehn for being amazing beta readers and dear friends. You guys are all rockstars.

The Savage Duet
A King So Savage Book 1
https://geni.us/AKingSoSavage
A Heart So Savage Book 2
https://geni.us/AHeartSoSavage

The Taming Series
Taming Ivy
https://geni.us/TamingIvy
The Untamed Duke
https://geni.us/TheUntamedDuke
Untaming Lady Violet
https://geni.us/UntamingLadyViolet

Wicked Rogues Romance
My Darling Rogue
https://geni.us/MyDarlingRogue

The Seven Seconds Series
The Bloodfeather Promise
https://geni.us/BloodfeatherPromise
Seven Promises
https://geni.us/SevenPromises

Standalone Christmas Historical Romance Novella
A Scandal Before Christmas
https://geni.us/AScandalBeforeChristmas

Standalone Office Romance Novella
Whiskey Darling

https://geni.us/WhiskeyDarling

VISIT APRIL'S WEBSITE
www.aprilmoranbooks.com

SIGN UP FOR NEWSLETTER AND UPDATES
http://bit.ly/AprilMoran_BookUpdates
April Moran Book Updates

STALK APRIL EVERYWHERE
https://www.facebook.com/AuthorAprilMoran
https://www.facebook.com/groups/aprilshoneybees/
https://www.bookbub.com/profile/april-moran
https://www.instagram.com/aprilmoranbooks
https://www.goodreads.com/Author-AprilMoran
https://www.pinterest.com/aprilmoranbooks
https://www.tiktok.com/authoraprilmoran

www.ingramcontent.com/pod-product-compliance
Lightning Source LLC
Chambersburg PA
CBHW070559300726
48975CB00006B/1638